The Hermeporta
Beyond the Gates of Hermes

Hogarth Brown

Copyright © 2017 Hogarth Brown
All rights reserved.

ISBN: 9781521801093

DEDICATION

I dedicate this book to all the great minds that have contributed to the progress of human thought, and have thus shaped all our lives: past, present, and future.

The Canonical Hours

- **Matins** (approximately midnight); also called **Vigils** or **Nocturns** or the Night Office
- **Lauds** or Dawn Prayer (at Dawn, or 3 a.m.)
- **Prime** or Early Morning Prayer (First Hour = approximately 6 a.m.)
- **Terce** or Mid-Morning Prayer (Third Hour = approximately 9 a.m.)
- **Sext** or Midday Prayer (Sixth Hour = approximately 12 noon)
- **None** or Mid-Afternoon Prayer (Ninth Hour = approximately 3 p.m.)
- **Vespers** or Evening Prayer ("at the lighting of the lamps", generally at 6 p.m.)
- **Compline** or Night Prayer (before retiring, generally at 9 p.m.)

CONTENTS

	Acknowledgments	i
	Prologue	Pg 1
1	The Promise	Pg 7
2	The Dwelling Place	Pg 16
3	The Sacrifice	Pg 31
4	Space	Pg 49
5	Transformation	Pg 53
6	The Strangers	Pg 72
7	A Self Remembered	Pg 83
8	The Dance	Pg 97
9	The Fugitives	Pg 117
10	The Convent of San Matteo	Pg 126
11	The Bedchamber	Pg 135
12	Bedlam and the Blue Madonna	Pg 142
13	After a Deep Sleep	Pg 156
14	The Witch's Ball	Pg 180
15	A Return to Rome	Pg 199
16	A Steep Learning Curve	Pg 219
17	Hekate's Message	Pg 240
18	Love's Revenge	Pg 256

ACKNOWLEDGMENTS

I just wanted to thank all those that have supported me in this epic effort that is novel writing: one of the most sinew straining and exhausting of Man's intellectual efforts, yet one of the most rewarding. To write a book is like birthing a child and forging a sword at the same time. The Novel: at once a baby that needs constant nurture and attention, lest it starve and perish from neglect, and at once a sword that must be forged, and hammered till rid of dross, so that it can shine and be strong enough to defend the author from the blows of battle. I wish my child the strength to bare its sword, and to withstand the ravages of time.

For **Mother:**
An inspiration

THE HERMEPORTA BEYOND THE GATES OF HERMES

Prologue

Time is like a web of golden thread, and life is like the dew that clings to it - in the light a necklace of diamonds, in the dark a veil of tears.

Muckross House, Killarney, Ireland late summer 1967

'You can't catch me' shouted Neave, as her brother chased after her through the long grass. The pair stirred the meadow with the zig-zags of their chase - scattering dandelion seeds into the September sunshine. The twelve-year-old ran skipped and shrieked between attempts by her brother to keep up with her. Winston dropped his book, as he chased his little sister, and ran back to rescue it from the meadow flowers as butterflies dashed out of his way.

'You never put down that book', shouted Neave, thumbing her nose. Her freckles and dark hair caught the light.

'It's Ovid - a very important book' yelled back the fourteen-year-old,

'Well, I don't care because I'm going to be important one day' said Neave, before she blew a loud raspberry at her older brother, and stuck her middle finger up in the air.

Winston took in a breath,

'You're naughty. Where did you learn that? I'm going to tell mother when we get back to the teahouse.' Neave shook her head, stuck out her jaw, and taunted Winston again by stroking her chin as if she had a long beard. The girl then cried out with excited pleasure when Winston gave chase again.

Neave ran, outpacing Winston, towards the trees of an enclosed bank on Killarney Lake. Winston chased her as long as he could before he stopped. He held his ribs and tried to catch his breath in the hot sunshine.

Neave pranced about and laughed at her brother's fatigue; as the pair were watched from the dappled shade of the undergrowth and trees.

'C'mon, don't stop. I want to see the waterlilies' Neave protested, before Winston, panting, sat himself down, knees up, in the long grass. He flapped his arm through the air to wave her off before he opened his book and started to read. Neave put her hands on her hips and scowled. She glared at her brother as she saw him relaxing: waggling his tanned legs, feet in sandals, one leg crossed over the other. 'You're boring' said Neave, after she crunched back through the grass to stand over Winston.

'I don't care' said Winston, 'because I'm going to be someone important one day too.' Neave crossed her arms, and she narrowed her blue eyes as she looked down at her older brother. Winston ignored her.

'All you do is read that book' she protested, but Winston continued to leaf through the pages. Neave spun herself, in her summer dress dotted with flowers, to get his attention - she failed. Neave then stamped her foot, 'stop *ignoring* me', she said. Winston turned away from her and then noticed a spider in the grass next to him spinning its web, the silvery strands of its silk glinted in the light. He watched the spider do its work and mused on what he would say next to his sister.

'The ancient Greeks knew almost everything about everything' sighed Winston, observing the spider pull silk from itself as it began to add a spoke to its web. Winston took in a deep breath of the scented meadow air and stretched out his arm to the sky as if addressing a crowd of people. Neave recognised the gesture and huffed - anticipating what was coming as her older brother readied himself: 'imagine having all the greatest minds of all time in one place debating against the greatest Greeks - which side do you think would win?' Neave looked up to the sky, blowing air out of her nostrils, before she rooted around in the grass, and plucked a flower from its stem and sniffed it. 'They have lots of wise stories' Winston continued, while Neave played with the flower, 'that's why the Romans copied them you know? Don't you think so Nymph?' said the teenager. Neave let out a sigh,

'Stop calling me nymph' she said,

'But they're beautiful creatures' said Winston. Neave smirked, blushed, and then started playing with her hair. Winston smiled to himself: whenever he wanted to sooth Neave's short temper, he would pay her a compliment. Neave then puffed out her chest.

'When I grow up I want to be like Anne Foley and win The Rose of Tralee competition - she's got dark hair just like me' said Neave, standing up, before moving with grace and accepting an imaginary sash over her head like the one she had seen the winner receive on television. Winston rolled his eyes before he turned the page of his book,

'You're not that pretty' he said. Neave gasped.

'I *am* pretty, you liar, Nana told me so, she said I could be a ROSE, she said I could win the competition one day... and Nana never tells lies.' Neave chewed her lip, as her eyes began to sting with tears. Winston shrugged before he ignored his sister again. Neave clenched her fists, as Winston hummed and continued to turn the pages of Ovid's Metamorphoses. She stood still for a while before she spoke: 'I think you're just like Narcissus' said Neave, remembering the old myth Winston often told her, 'you stare all day at your books, but you're only looking for yourself' she declared, before she stepped forward to kick the book out of Winston's hands. Winston gasped,

'You're a spoilt brat' he hissed, and turned to stare at his sister. Neave covered her mouth. Winston snatched up the spider next to him and tossed it at her. The startled spider landed on Neave's neck and tickled her flesh as it tried to escape. Neave screamed, trying to brush the spider off herself. She detested spiders, 'Arachne's chasing you' Winston laughed, as Neave flapped at herself. Winston then went to fetch his book from the grass, as Neave rid herself of the spider.

'You're wicked - I'll show you' she shouted back, 'I can become a real nymph, I can bring the stories to life - I bet then you would listen to me' said Neave, before she stomped off towards the bank of trees that faced the lake. Winston saw her walking away drawing closer to the shadows, before glancing up towards Muckross house, in the distance, where he knew his mother and grandmother would be enjoying coffee, gossip, and a slice of cake in the teahouse. When he found his book, he heard his sister singing, as she often did, in her high sweet voice contenting herself. Neave passed through the trees and undergrowth singing before she emerged and saw the expanse of blooming waterlilies that stretched out in front of her. She observed the frogs that leapt from one lily pad to another, smiled, and acted as if she was a magical princess within in her enclave. Neave looked at the water of the wider lake, dark and vast, and then at the water closest to her,

'It's not too deep' she muttered to herself, as she slipped off her dress and unplaited her dark hair. Neave continued to sing as she stepped into the cold water, and enjoyed the freshness touch her pale skin - a relief from the hot September sunshine - her toes tangling with lily roots, as she felt fish brush past her legs.

Neave, oblivious, lost in reverie, walked down to her waist into the water before she picked a lily and placed it in her hair. She stood, amongst the blooming flowers and the dragonflies, arms raised, singing her favourite traditional songs that her Grandmother had taught her, bright and clear, across the water at the top of her voice - a twig fell and broke on the ground behind her. Winston listened to the distant sound of his sister's voice - they were alone this far from the main house - and mused that he would have told Neave that she was talented if she were not so headstrong. With a loud splash, Neave's song ended. Winston blinked for a few moments before he sat up.

'Neave, are you OK?' said Winston, putting down his book. No answer came. Winston stood up, 'Neave... can you hear me?' He stood and listened - silence, except for the rustled sound of crickets singing in the grass. Winston's walk then turned into a sprint as he bolted towards the trees. 'Neave!' Winston shouted - his heart racing by the time he reached the undergrowth. He scanned his surroundings, trying to remember where she had entered, but worried he had the wrong place. Winston called his sister's name several times again, his voice cracking, but no response came. Panic flashed through Winston's body; he ran through the undergrowth, his face scratched by branches.

'Neave' he yelled again, seeing a flash of silver in the shadows ahead. He dashed forward once more before he saw something lying on the ground. He drew closer and saw where Neave's flowered dress lay on the soil, next to her shoes. He could not see his sister anywhere. Winston looked at the waterlilies that swayed, as if stirred, in the water. He stood paralysed. Winston wanted to dive in, but a feeling from the water frightened him. Winston turned this way and that, and ran further along up the bank, till his lungs burned, but to no avail. He could not see her. Winston shook all over. 'Where are you?' Winston croaked, before he threw up his

hands to the side of his head, and howled in anguish till his voice echoed off the hills overlooking the lake.

Winston never saw his little sister again.

Chapter 1

The Promise

The Kings Road, London, Summer 1975

Gerald gave a ragged wave to the barman, after drinking yet another 'Rusty Nail', before he shuffled out of the Chelsea Potter pub, and staggered into the evening dusk that had gathered on the Kings Road. The sun had baked London all day, and the heat oozed back up from the pavements to envelop the fifty-four-year-old in an embrace that chafed at him like a woolly scarf. Street pigeons flew up to the roof-tops to stuff themselves into their dung streaked crevices, in contrast to the chic promenade below, and the birds, in their habits, had taken on much of the characteristics of London: grubby, crowded, and in need of a good wash. Gerald loosened another button on his pale blue shirt that grew damp at the pits,

'Damn this heat' he muttered to himself, and fussed with the grey coat slung over his arm, and tugged at the waist of his blue corduroy trousers, ignoring the sweat between his thighs, before he rolled up his sleeves, chastised himself under his breath, and shambled south along the Kings Road. Gerald looked at other walkers as he made his way along, and shook his head as fellow pedestrians walked past in hot pants - if they were female - skimpy shorts - for many of the males - and flares for much more: an item of clothing Gerald could not understand. 'Why must people walk around as if they're dressed for the beach?' he grumbled to himself, and attempted to move past the Chelsea Old Town Hall but tripped and fell on the dusty steps of the Victorian building, after he stumbled into a man walking with his girlfriend from the opposite direction.

'Are you alright?' said the woman as her boyfriend, with some effort, tugged Gerald up from the steps.

'I'm fine' Gerald bit back and ignored the frown upon his helper's foreign face. He waved the couple off, their comments a muffled distraction at the back of his mind.

'Could you smell him?' The accented man said to his girlfriend, and she nodded. The couple paused to watch Gerald's ramshackle advance down the Kings Road.

'He must have been drinking for hours?' she said before she pulled her lover along to continue their night together. The street lamps above began to give off a gaudy amber light, although the sky still clung in places to the sunset that had abandoned the humid air - air that carried a whiff of swollen bin liners that had bloated in the sun. Gerald swooned, lurching back, as a red double-decker bus swerved to avoid him as he drifted into the road.

'Watch where you're going' shouted the bus conductor, swinging from his pole on the number 19 bus, as Gerald lumbered back to the pavement. The conductor shook his head as the middle-aged man gave him a one-fingered salute, and carried on his meandering procession. Professor Gerald Sloane, an educated man, had done well at Cambridge and liked his status as a lecturer on Greek Antiquity, and often enjoyed popping into the antique shops to tell the owners that a prized vase of theirs was a fake, or congratulating them, in turn, upon acquiring a great find. Many of the shop owners along the Kings Road were old friends, and they had seen the worry creep, in ever deeper furrows, across his broad and angular face. *'He's not quite himself'* they would mutter to others when he left their premises and made his way to the pubs.

The traffic hummed along, punctuated by the rattling ding-ding-splutter of double-decker buses: full of some passengers that sprung to the pavements at their leisure. Whenever the buses paused, the fashionable leapt above dark plumes of exhaust fumes - they: so keen, lithe, and shiny to arrive, plat formed heeled, upon the newest thrill. Those left behind, the grey and beige of London, looked on and wondered aloud from where they got their spending money. Gerald spied some Union Jack's, with two black letters in the far corners, in a few of the terrace windows above the shops, although the flags were smaller than in other parts of the city, he raised a brow and wiped at his clammy skin. He walked past the colourful shop fronts, some too garish for his taste, but smiled at the vintage charity shops that sold clothes from the 'flapper's' era. Gerald closed his eyes for a moment to recall his mother and father, embraced, enjoying the heights of their age. Gerald's expression curdled, after he opened his eyes, as he walked along when he observed alien creatures that had gathered outside the Kings Road Theatre.

'They ought to shut the place down' he mumbled as he wobbled past excited fans of the Rocky Horror Show, dressed as they were in outlandish colours and striking makeup, resembling, to him, a gaggle of Macaws blown into London by a strange and foreign wind. 'Sweet Jesus' Gerald exclaimed further on, before he swiped his hand across his sweating brow, 'what's this place coming too?' He shook his head with an incredulous gesture in the direction of a fashion boutique with the word 'SEX' written in huge pink PVC covered letters hung above the shop door.

Gerald zig-zagged to navigate the traffic of Ford Escorts, Austin 1800's, and Opel Mantas. He ignored the jarring honks from the elderly driver of a goggle-eyed Triumph Herald, forced to swerve on its clapped-out axles and burp a cloud of soot from its exhaust. Once across the junction, Gerald advanced to the pink framed shop windows to peer inside. He looked at an event taking place within as he scrutinised a collection of odd looking people assembled inside. They listened to music, from a record player, that seemed to screech at him: the words sounded profane, but Gerald found what he heard unintelligible. He saw a woman among the group wearing a scrap of tartan tossed over her shoulder, clad with black PVC, her glossy body stocking cut out, here and there, to expose her pale flesh. With her lips painted dark, her hair orange and erect, she sipped red wine from a mug and passed among her acolytes, and clothes, which were as strange as herself.

'She looks like she's been electrocuted' Gerald said aloud as he leered on. Camera bulbs flashed, which further illuminated the figures within. One guest noticed the Professor and beckoned to him, but the man shook his head and waved the invitation off, as more of the clan accumulated outside. 'The world's gone crazy: all they talk about now is a revolution and Vivienne Westwood, but who remembers Vivien Leigh? That's what I call beauty.' Gerald let go a gust of breath.

He shook his head in dismay, and the memory of the actress seemed to strike at the man, and he paused to rest his outstretched arm against a wall as he turned into Limerston Street. His lips quivered, and his robust features collapsed into grief. His shoulders, still sturdy, wobbled as his chest heaved and it took all his command not to howl out with anguish. Gerald clamped his hand over his mouth and shut his eyes to staunch the flow of tears, which stung his eyes before they fell over his wrist. Children that had been out playing all day, yelling and skipping home as the night drew in, flew about the streets like sparrows, but tumbled into silence before they passed him: so shocked were they to see a man crying. One boy stood and stared at Gerald before he reached into his pocket to toss him his handkerchief, but then his friends yanked him away from the man as if he were the angel of death.

Gerald nodded his thanks to the boy, a street sprite, who had paused to observe him again from a safer distance with his companions, and he returned the adult's gesture with his own before he ran off with his friends for home. Gerald wiped at his nose and face with the fabric and thought how the boy's mother might scold him for losing his hanky. Gerald then thought of his son for a while.

'Pull yourself together, old boy. He'll be here soon' he whispered to himself, blew his nose, threw his shoulders back, and stood up as straight as he could manage to advance up the street. One thoughtful resident had flung one of their windows wide open to share their house-party and music with the rest of the road, at high volume, and the sound of ABBA's hit S.O.S rang in Gerald's ears, which he covered before he walked into the entrance of St Stephen's Hospital.

Winston strolled into the hospital ward of St Stephen's, which reeked of bleach but still could not stifle the smell of sickness that slunk through the muggy air. Some windows were open, but they offered no relief for it seemed the wind - drugged to stillness by the humid summer - had given up. The Hospital baked and it seemed to him that the bricks of the hospital building were as keen to throw off their heat as the cracked paving slabs outside. Winston passed flush faced nurses in their starched pink and white uniforms, who longed to toss off their elaborate white hats that crowned their encircled heads like the sales of ships.

Winston advanced, tall and slim - a strawberry blond - in his full flares, his height further accentuated with heels, and his wide collared shirt open to the third button with his sleeves rolled up to the elbows. He spied his father, slumped somewhat, sat on a bench and propped up by the walls. Gerald, sensing his son's advance turned his way, and Winston paused, his guts tugging when he saw the redness of his father's eyes. His father managed a languid smile when he saw him, and he tried to ignore the waft of alcohol that curled out of his father's breath when he crouched down to embrace the man. Gerald squeezed at his son's shoulders, as Winston sat down.

'Why must you always look as if you've just come from a club?' his father chided, before prodding at Winston's body and clothes, 'skin tight' he tutted, 'and can't you do something with that hair? You look homeless' said Gerald, flouncing his hand through his son's long locks. But Gerald did not have the energy to add to his reprimand, as Winston fixed himself, and yielded into a smile when he recognised his physique in the youth - recalling when he had been his son's age. 'You have my shoulders; remember I gave you those.' Gerald sighed. 'Oh, I envy you, boy. Not a drop of sweat on you, but look at this heap' he said, before pointing to himself and his sweat patches that had expanded into arcs beneath his arms, 'you seem to glide through Iceland while we suffer here in India.' Winston smiled somewhat,

'The Empire's over now, Daddy.'

'Not for *everyone*' added Gerald, with a raised finger. Winston rolled his eyes, but he did not turn away when his father's gaze settled upon him and contemplated. 'You got my call then?' Gerald said, after some time, and his son nodded. Gerald gave out a protracted cough. 'She's in there' he whispered and bit down on his lip to stop himself crying.

'Are you coming in?' said Winston, before he stood. His father shook his head,

'I can't' he answered and stared down at the polished floors. Winston stroked his Dad's face and Gerald, clinging to the caress as his breath chopped at itself, held onto his son's hand that so reminded him of another's. Gerald then let his son go before he entered the ward to find his mother.

In a quiet voice, a nurse ushered Winston in the direction of where his mother lay, behind a curtain. Winston drew the curtain back and, for all his coolness, he could not stifle a gasp when he saw her. He struggled to recognise the woman on the bed as his mother, for her often-complemented figure, the pride of his father's and then envy of her friends, had shrunken to tissue paper about her bones. Nails, once glossy and bright, had become lined, chaffed and brittle. Winston approached his mother's bed as if a withered changeling were in her place. The sheets were rolled almost halfway down the bed to give the woman some relief from the heat, but she lay there as if sweat were beyond her. Winston hesitated but approached again when he saw her breathe. One side of her nightie had fallen open, and he observed the raw scar, and dents, that ran from under her armpit and across one-half of a barren chest stripped of the flesh that had once suckled him. Winston approached as if his mother were a car bonnet deformed by a crash.

He drew up a chair to sit next to the phantom that masqueraded as his mother, and lifted her tepid arm and hand - always dainty - but since wasted to the lightness of a bird's wing. He puzzled at the arms that had once cradled him, and, although always a slender woman, he seemed appalled to witness how much of her power she had lost. His Mother awoke at his touch, her eyes creeping open. Her head turned with an effort to look at her son.

'You made it' she whispered, the soft Irish lilt still sung somewhat in her voice if much diminished. 'My boy, my boy' she said turning her head more to look at him and leaving a clump of straw like hair upon her pillow. Winston grimaced. His mother's hair, once so vigorous, that once smelled of sweet peas, and French lavender had shone like copper silk in the wind when she would whirl him up into her arms, and rub her freckled nose upon his forehead.

He looked at the half corpse speaking to him as the memory burst into his mind, and a tear rolled off his cheek to plop on the floor. 'There, there' Mora cooed, 'don't cry my boy, it'll be over soon', but her words only made her son shake, as he tried to steady himself by holding her hand. 'Don't be sad my boy' she said, with some of the former warmth of her voice returning to comfort him, 'I'm happy now because I'm looking at one of the best things that ever happened to me in my life…'

Winston's face shook, an involuntary mass of twitching, and he kissed his mother's hand but shrank back when it seemed that the grip of death was already upon her. 'The first was meeting your father' Mora continued, and managed a rasping chuckle that made her cough, and Winston held on until she recovered. She smiled, 'can you imagine my luck? A girl from Killarney, bagging herself an aristocrat - my mother did a cartwheel'. Winston smiled, and wiped away another tear in silence, and admired his mother's spirit that still clung to her protesting body.

His father often told him how his family had lost almost all its wealth after the crash of '29'; they had to abandon the country piles and sell up, but there had been enough put aside for Gerald to marry - and set up home with Mora. 'Your grandfather was dead against us, at first' Mora said, Winston nodded with recognition, as her eyes retraced the past, 'he wanted your father to marry money, a wealthy debutante, but your Pa preferred me - after all his running about.' Winston's mother seemed amused. '"Stiff as kippers"' said Mora, imitating her husband's voice with the thrust of her hand. '"Marble Girls" that's what he called them, but I guess it all worked out in the end.' Winston gave an anguished frown.

'Mother, you must rest. *Please*, let's not talk about the past again. Save your energy' said Winston, his voice choked. Mora shook her balding head and tried to wave her hand,

'*Argh*, no point, they said I left it too late, my boy. "A lump like an apple," the Dr told me, fancy that. I said "you should have made me a pie of it to go with my other breast" - but I don't think he saw the joke in it.' Winston grimaced, but shook his head, sighed, smiled, and wiped more tears from his face.

'Would you like some water?' said the nurse to Mora, who had been hanging back to watch, but she refused the young woman, and said she had all she needed beside her.

'I could have done without the chemo' she announced, 'if I'd known it was pointless I'd not have bothered. Look at me, laying here like a Barn Owl's chick, not worth the bother, not worth the bother...' Her voice, still weak, nonetheless managed some of its spirited defiance. 'Is he out there?' said Mora, and Winston nodded. Mora read her son's expression, and pouted her dry lips, 'don't blame him' she said, 'I don't - *look* at me. I told him once that I thought he loved my hair more than I did. When it started to fall out, he wept over it. I've never seen him like that; I didn't mention it again.' Mora yawned for some time, her every breath an effort, 'I don't blame him, or the others.' Mora looked off into the distance before she turned back. 'They took some of my *ribs* you know?' She announced as if burgled. 'No one knows what to say to you when you get like this' she said, gesturing to herself as if she were a scrap-heap.

With that Mora coughed hard, and the force shook her fragile body to the extent that Winston wanted to cradle his mother in his arms, as she had done when he had been a baby, and protect her from the cancer that gnawed, pitiless, at her body. Mora's coughing stopped, and so it seemed had her breathing, and Winston bolted upright to shout for the nurse, but his mother opened her eyes again, though with more effort than before.

'Not long now, my boy. Not long now' she said considering his face. 'I've only one regret in my whole life...' she said, but Winston shook his head and interrupted,

'No you mustn't, I know what you're going to say, mother, please.'

'Your sister... There, I said it, it's true' she added. Winston sat down, before he lost control of his lips, as they quaked and trembled. Memories of Neave, her face the image of her mother's, rushed back into his mind along with the guilt to have been free from thoughts of her, for the first time in years, when so in the depths of his studies. 'We couldn't find her' she continued, 'and I didn't protect her - I failed.'

Winston shook his head with violence, but his mother gazed beyond the walls in memory of her daughter. With effort Mora crossed herself, 'God only knows where she is - what happened to her?' Mora looked back and pointed to her stitches, 'that's why I got this you know?' She said, tapping at the red scars of her mastectomy. Winston shook his head again, but she nodded: 'it's true, my darling, it's true'. Winston's nose ran, and he had to brush it against his shirt sleeve to dry it. 'Listen to me, my bright boy' his mother said, increasing her intensity, 'soon you'll have your certificate from Oxford, and know that you've taught me more about the heavens than any old nun could do for a Catholic girl in Ireland... Find her for me' she said, fixing him with her gaze, 'and seek out if you can, what's the point of all of this?' Her eyes looked around the hospital as if to question the purpose of life itself. The nurse, once close, left off to keep her distance. Winston nodded,

'I will. I *promise*'. The youth trembled all over.

'My boy' she smiled, 'my bright boy...' said Mora, with half closed eyes before she raised her emaciated hand to wipe away the tears on her son's face, and died. For a moment, Winston held his mother's hand in place, sat rigid as if welded to his chair, as he looked into the once dazzling hazel-green eyes that grew dry and cold, and at the last of her beauty that escaped her withered body and flew off in peace. Mora's frame seemed to flatten into the bed, as her ribcage ceased to rise. Winston let go, unable to speak, and the hand of a corpse fell from his face: she had gone. His mother had left him, and a young man who almost never cried as a boy, could not stop crying for six weeks.

The following weekend he collected his first in Physics from Oxford, without pleasure, and dedicated his degree to his mother: she had passed at 44 years old.

Chapter 2

The Dwelling Place

Turkey, August 1992

Iona flapped her colourful silk scarf above her head to wave goodbye to the Blue Mosque, and the Hagia Sophia, as the ship cut through the waters of the Bosphorus to embark upon the Marmara Sea. A tall man grabbed her from behind,
'Come here' he said, squeezing her before the woman gave out a girlish squeal, which turned some heads on the boat.
'You're a beast, Winston' came her reply, before she smacked the large tanned hands that had encircled her waist, and slipped beneath her dungarees. 'H'hey, naughty boy, not here' she said, in her Bostonian lilt, before she leant her head back against his shoulder and yanked his hands away from their wanderings.
Iona turned to Winston with a frown, obscured by her sandy blond hair that blew into her eyes, and wrinkled her nose before her faced opened with a smile that was pure Hollywood. She giggled and planted a kiss on the attractive face in front of hers, and gazed deep into the grey eyes that studied her. Iona stretched up to throw her arms around Winston's neck, and he lifted her to himself and clasped his hands to her buttocks: she wriggled and squealed again as the ship rocked from side to side. Some people on the vessel shook their heads and whispered; others smiled, but a squat woman wearing a head scarf prodded her chubby grandson towards some benches further along the deck. The boy then resisted, his neck craned, as she pulled him away from the couple.
'Now, remember what I told you about my friend?' said Iona, as she and Winston crossed the deck to lean over the balustrade of the boat, and look at the rushing blue water. A smile died on Winston's face.
'He's a creep' he said. Iona frowned.

'Don't say that, he's a great guy really' Winston pulled a face, 'no, honestly he is' she protested while fussing at his collar, 'he just never got over us breaking up after college.' Winston's shoulder's tensed as air hissed between his teeth,

'Harvard was a while ago now, Iona: he needs to grow a pair.'

Iona tutted and stroked strands of hair from her face.

'Don't be like that, honey. We're archaeologists: we like to *hold* onto things' she said, before clenching at his muscular bicep.

'I think five years is long enough, don't you?' Snapped Winston, shrugging her off, and shaking his head, before running a hand through his gold-red hair. Iona stared down at the deck, before she pondered the tall Thirty-nine-year-old, as he looked out to sea. She thought that for a man on the cusp of forty he still looked as if he were in his late twenties. Iona remembered her shock at learning his age on their first date.

Although the morning sun glowed overhead Iona's bare legs recoiled from the breeze that blew colder as the boat went further out to sea, and, like a kitten, she padded forward to seek shelter from the wind next to Winston's honed physique. His face looked stiff, but she nuzzled at his shoulder as he turned to look down, and he threw his arm around her before he planted a kiss on her head. Iona's hair still smelled fresh from the shampoo she had used in Istanbul. 'This was supposed to be *our* trip' said Winston, rubbing at Iona's slim shoulders to revive her from the chill.

'It still is' she said, 'when we get to Phocaea we'll rent a car, drive down to see Duggie, at Kyme, and then we'll drive back and enjoy the coast as planned.' Winston clapped a free hand to his forehead,

'Of all the places, Douglas has to put himself there?'

'Kyme is part of his research' she said, toying with Winston's collar, 'and he's leading a great team there: I wrote part of my thesis on Kyme, remember? If I can finish maybe...'

'But there's nothing there...' Winston interrupted, 'it's just a scrape in the ground, just a bunch of old blocks and bushes' he huffed, 'gosh, even the locations he chooses are boring.'

'Don't say that' said Iona biting her lip.

'Oh c'mon, the place is a shit-hole' replied Winston. Iona's face fell,

'We can't all be "great" Professors' she said. Iona then untangled herself from his arm, paced across the deck, and turned to rush downstairs. Winston slapped his thigh, cursed, and then gripped at the balustrade. He turned to the sea and then turned back again to look towards the stairs that Iona had taken down below deck.

The chubby boy watched him from where he sat next to his grandmother, licking at his ice-cream, as he saw Winston shake his hand again through his hair, sigh, and slope towards the stairs.

■ ■ ■

After disembarking the ship, the couple walked about Phocaea, the lovely seaside town, with its boats, red-faced Germans, and white houses topped with terracotta roofs. Iona tied her coloured scarf about her head to protect it from the fierce sunshine. The couple rented a Renault car from a moustached man, which seemed to be the newest of the haggard bangers that Phocaea had to offer, dumped their luggage in the boot, and drove it back to the shore. The pair enjoyed a meal - at a waterfront restaurant - of rice, and red mullet, just pulled from the sea, grilled with garlic and lemons. Winston smacked his lips and sucked and picked at his teeth, with the aid of a cocktail stick, before the pair washed their food down with a local wine so good that Winston had to have another glass. He breathed in, with satisfaction, to swill the liquid in his mouth, and enjoyed its crisp flavour as it mingled with the salty air.

'Don't drink too much' said Iona, 'you're driving remember.' Winston put the glass down.

'Well, if I'm going to be bored I may as well be drunk' said Winston with a smile, but he slowed at the second glass, while Iona rubbed her bare foot along his calf, up to his thigh, and then massaged her toes into his groin under the table.

'Be a good boy now' she said with a devilish smirk and a raised brow, 'I've still not forgiven you' she added, pressing her foot forward and enjoying the feel as Winston's flesh responded. The waiter arrived to top up the water, and exchanged glances with the couple, as Iona slipped her foot back into its former position.

'Let's get the bill' Winston coughed, with some colour in his cheeks. Iona pouted. He called the waiter back to pay for the meal but took his time before he stood up to leave the table as Iona sashayed to the car.

The couple rolled down their windows upon entering the Renault, which had already become too warm in the early afternoon sunshine. Iona dug out her road map as Winston started the engine which spluttered and heaved as the car drove up the bank, and gave out all sorts of rattles and groans as Winston cranked through the gears when upon the main road. The azure waters of the Aegean glittered below the elevation of the coastal pass. Winston relished a sense of freedom as the rental car improved on flat roads at greater speeds. Iona ignored the coastline and pushed strands of her hair behind her ears as she consulted her map before she wound her window higher to reduce the wind that disturbed her reading.

'If we just follow the coast,' she said, 'then we can reach Duggie's site in about a couple of hours.' Iona looked across to Winston, who kept his eyes on the road or glanced at the sea. 'I wonder how he and his team are getting on with their work?' She added, 'He wrote me to say that they're excavating a temple mound devoted to Athena.' Iona tried to make eye contact with Winston. 'Look she said' fishing a Polaroid photo from her bag, 'you can see the base of the temple mound.'

Winston ignored the picture of a burly Douglas, surrounded by an admiring team, squat next to an unearthed boulder, wearing shorts and an open-necked t-shirt that erupted with his chest hair. Winston gritted his teeth, said nothing, and then fiddled with the radio until he found a station that played traditional Turkish music. A sonorous female voice floated over the plink-a-plink of plucked strings and rhythmic taps of tambourines, and goblet drums, to fill the car with sound. Iona reached forward and turned down the volume.

'You don't want to visit Kyme, do you?' said Iona, as the car sped along,

'There are better places to visit... Look, I'm not against it, but why do we have to go there *today?* We have a week here.'

'Duggie will be returning to the states soon, and I promised him I'd visit the next time I was in Turkey.' Winston waved his hand through the air at the comment, 'he's been here for almost two years', she said, but Winston tapped his fingers on the steering wheel, 'we shared research, remember?' she added, her face strained. 'I've always wanted you to meet him: he's a fascinating guy.' Winston rolled his eyes.

'Yeah, right' he said. Iona crossed her arms.

'We can't always talk about physics, you know. Sometimes I want to talk about what I'm interested in'. Winston glanced at Iona and huffed.

'FINE, let's get this over with' he said,

'Don't be like this' said Iona, rubbing her forehead. But Winston reached over for the map, which he had to tug from her grasp before he slowed the car to consult it.

'Look, we can cut across here and save time so that you have more of it to wave a final goodbye to "Duggie."' Iona ran her tongue across her teeth and shook her head.

'I think we should stick to the coast' she said, 'the roads are bad in the hills, and the mountain roads are worse.' But Winston ignored her, glanced again at the map, and turned the car up the nearest dirt road that had presented itself. Iona rubbed at her forehead while the sinews raised around her jaw. The car bumped along as it climbed, the road less smooth than the motorway, and clouds of dust rose from the track as the vehicle advanced higher. Iona switched off the radio, rummaged in her bag as the car jostled along, and pulled out a tape before prodding it into the car's cassette player. Soon the sounds of Mariah Carey's 'Emotions' rang out from the car.

'Not her again' Winston growled,

'If you're going to take this "shortcut" then I get to listen to Mariah.'

The car creaked and heaved as the arid dirt road climbed into the hills and some of the tall peaks that lay beyond. The car gave another grumble as Winston changed gear, and he flinched when Iona added to the engine noise by attempting to sing along with the virtuoso pop star at the top of her voice. Like most people, she failed in her attempts imitate the diva but did not care, and screeched like a hawk in pain as the vocalist climbed to notes higher than the mountain tops that dotted the distance. Winston stopped the tape.

'My ears will bleed if you carry on' he said, pressing the eject button, tossing the tape to Iona, and unzipping his side pouch to retrieve a cassette tape of his own.

'But she's talented' Iona protested, as the car bounced along the road that worsened as they progressed,

'Yes she is, but you're not' said Winston before he shoved his tape into the player. He ignored Iona's incredulous expression and cranked the volume up as the mellow sound of Bob Marley's Buffalo Soldier filled the car. Iona clenched her small hands into fists.

'Why must we always do what you want to do?' Iona shouted, 'we always talk about what you want to talk about? You never listen to me or think about what I want' Iona bellowed, as the car shuddered along the dirt track and the sun beat down upon the car from overhead. The sound of pebbles and rocks hitting the chassis punctuated the shouts and music. A vein rose in Winston's neck.

'Well, I'd be more inclined to listen to you if you didn't keep prattling on about "Duggie" and his shitty dig. My dad wouldn't even bother to glance at where he's scratching around.' Iona's face had turned a dark red.

'Well he's *dead*, so I don't care what he thinks!' Winston's eyes widened to saucers at the remark, and Iona's then implored with an apology as Winston glared at her.

'You, bitc...' Winston exclaimed, but could not finish, when the car hit a pothole and a pop-crack sound wrenched through the music, and the car lurched off the dirt road. Iona screamed, and Winston struggled to control the vehicle that glanced off a large rock with the scraping sound of torn metal and wrestled with the steering wheel as if it were a bear trying to claw at his face. The car swung, rotating in a cloud of dust, almost flipping over as a tire hit a boulder and lurched upward. Pebbles cracked and clattered at the windscreen, and hailed in through Winston's half open window before his foot found the breaks and shoved forward. With more bumps and screams the car ground to a halt. The couple sat, shell-shocked, for a moment in silence, glad to be alive, as the smell and acrid taste of dust filled their mouths. Winston coughed.

'My God, you're bleeding' said Iona, undoing her seat belt, and reaching forward toward a cut above Winston's eye. He unclipped his seat belt to check himself in the rear-view mirror.

'I'll be alright' he said as he looked at the streak of blood down his face that had begun to mingle with the dust that dulled his hair. Iona's lip began to tremble, and her eyes moistened.

'I'm sorry' she said, 'I didn't mean to say...' her voice trailed off into tears. Winston closed his eyes for a moment and thought of his father,

'It doesn't matter now. It doesn't change anything'. Winston shoved several times at his car door, but it did not budge. 'We'll have to come out your side' he said, Iona nodded and wiped at her tears before the pair crept out into the appalling heat of the landscape they found themselves within. Iona held her face with her hands and shook her head. The couple checked each other for breaks, found none, but identified what were to become severe bruises. The car looked awful. The left tire had been burst by the pothole and hung like a rubber flag from the disjointed wheel. A tearing scrape ran the length of the car which revealed the metal beneath the green paint and punctured the door on the rear passenger side. The pair traced their eyes over the winding skid marks that told the story of how the car came into its state.

Overcome, Iona wept again, and Winston held her to himself till she stopped - although his arms and legs shook all over. 'We have to get out of this heat' he said, 'we'll roast to death out here.'

'But, shouldn't we walk back?' she said as if gripped by panic.

'We've just had a car crash, Iona' said Winston, 'I think we should find shelter and sit down', Iona nodded again and coughed. 'It's too hot to walk back now. Do you have any water?'

'Yes,' Iona said, 'I've got a small bottle in my bag.' Winston stretched and clutched at his back, and then rubbed his neck. Iona then fussed over him. She took a tissue from her purse and mopped at the drying blood on his face.

'Look' said Winston pointing to a collection of massive rocks in the near distance, 'we can take shelter over there.' Iona glanced towards where Winston looked and agreed before she reached into the car, which still played Bob Marley - the upbeat music in such contrast to the devastated vehicle - pressed stop, switched off the engine and took out the keys.

The pair limped, somewhat, to the tall rocks and the steep sides of a craggy hill that stood almost like a mountain. Reaching their destination took longer than expected, and the pair sipped from the small bottle of water to prevent swooning in the oppressive heat. The land around them looked desolate, save for a few tired bushes to punctuate the harsh sandy Anatolian landscape. The baked environment ironed the pair's earlier memory of the sea.

Winston's eyes stung as he looked up into the sun. The black shadows of vultures circling above were the only things to disturb the cloudless sky, a sky that would have been a blessing in a wetter country, but with its relentless blue glare, it took on a menace: a numb implacable anger that did not care if they lived or died. The pair passed the leathery carcass of a goat with rib-bones picked clean, that protruded through its hide and bleached in the glare.

'We have to get out of this heat' said Iona, losing her balance for a moment, and feeling the prickle of sunburn upon her brow, cheekbones and nose.

'We're almost there' panted Winston. To their surprise and relief, the rocks they reached had obscured the entrance to a small cave. 'We can climb this' he said, eyeing up an awkward slope of stone like a leopard, before pouncing upward as the beast would into a tree, 'it's not too high' he added from his new vantage point. Iona looked upward, cringed, but gave a pensive nod, and raised her hands above her head to allow herself to be whisked up onto the rocks with a lunge and pull from Winston. He lifted her like a toddler. Her sandals lost their grip on the skittish surface, and Iona slipped several times before she grazed her knee. Winston patted her down, and the pair were glad to enter the modest opening of the cave and get instant relief from the heat.

'Let's stay here a while' said Winston, as his voice echoed in the chamber, 'when the sun sets we can try to walk back.' His voice echoed again, 'wow, this place is much deeper than I thought' he said, testing the sound with repeated calls that reverberated back to him from the grey-brown darkness within. Iona plonked herself down upon a smooth boulder that made a convenient seat and watched Winston pace around the cave with pensive curiosity while testing the echo of his voice. 'There's a lot of room in here' he said, 'can't you hear how much space there is?' Iona shrugged, flicking her hand at Winston, her face stinging, and rummaged through her bag in search of face cream: lost in her thoughts. 'I'm going to walk further in' he said.

'OK' Iona called back with detachment, 'I'm going to sit here a while.' She fussed at herself and frowned into a pocket mirror as Winston walked deeper into the cave.

The coolness of the vaulted cavern provided relief, and Winston took in deep breaths of the damp musky air that soothed his throat, 'there must be water in here?' He muttered as he progressed forward. The light grew dimmer as he walked. The cave began to dip and broaden as Winston advanced and he noticed a bat, disturbed from slumber, which flew deeper into the cave. The ample space darkened as the depth increased, but Winston could still see the bright sunshine of the cave mouth some distance away. His progress stopped when what seemed like a dirt wall blocked the oval shaped cave. 'This is odd' Winston thought aloud, before he called back to Iona at volume, '*Hey*, I think you should come and see this' Winston said feeling on the wall, that came away in clumps of dirt as he groped it.

'Huh?' came Iona's distant voice,

'There's a wall back here?' he said, 'look, I've found some bricks' added Winston as he pulled more dirt away to expose some neat mud bricks behind their soiled covering.

'What?' said Iona, 'in a cave?'

'Yes, and I think I can see a hole at the top where the bat flew in' he called back.

'Wait, I'm coming' said Iona, 'I should probably see this.' But Winston did not hold on a moment and began to claw at the wall with a frenzy. He put his face next to the bricks and felt cold air caress his skin as it seeped through from the other side.

'This wall is not a thick one' Winston spoke aloud and tapped his knuckle upon the barrier. A hollow sound came back. The scuttle of Iona's footsteps grew closer,

'Wait for me' she called as she skidded along. In a moment, she stood next to him, with a shiny pink face.

'Why is there a wall in here?' said Winston, pacing the space with his hands on his hips - animated and pensive.

'I've no idea' replied Iona, 'but there are some lantern sticks' she said gesturing to some objects in the far reaches. 'But this wall looks ancient' she added, her neck crooked and eyes agape, 'but I'll need to inspect this carefully', and she walked towards the wall to caress it. But Winston's breath became shallow, and his pulse raced.

'Stand back' he said, and Iona just got out of the way in time when he gave the wall a mighty kick which blasted a hole in it. Iona exclaimed with shock.

'I'm an archaeologist' she protested, 'this is not how we're supposed to do things' she added shaking her head,

'Well I'm a particle physicist, and we like to bash things together' replied Winston, as a rush of cold air surrounded them and an unpleasant odour filled their nostrils. Iona snorted her disgust but wasted no time to step forward to peer into the breach.

'Oh, my, GOD' she exclaimed looking back, 'there's something in there.' Iona needed no further encouragement, as the pair clawed at the pliable bricks and in a short time they had created a hole large enough for them both to get through. 'Do you have a torch?' she said breathless, and Winston dug into his side pouch to draw out a pocket flashlight, 'Geek' she said with a smirk, before she snatched the torch from his grasp, clicked it on, and thrust herself into the dark space. 'Holy SHIT' Iona exclaimed, which disturbed some of the bats that clung to the roof of the cave, and the pair both coughed as the full stench of their dung choked the air. Iona shook all over, Winston's jaw dropped open, and the few hairs on his body stood on end while chills ran up and down him as the pair tried to make sense of the object they saw.

'What is it?' Winston demanded as Iona did her best to illuminate a stepped plinth on which rested a vast marble bowl, sat upon a taloned pedestal encircled by carved serpents rendered in exquisite detail. Iona did not answer and just shook her head in disbelief. 'Hold the torch still' said Winston as the flashlight wobbled over the object's surface. She couldn't do it, and shrieked, almost dropping the torch, when light wandered onto a shrivelled human corpse near the object on the floor: the mangled person looked like they had died in agony. Winston held her hand steady and moved the light around. He shuddered too, and Iona tried to stifle another scream that seeped out between her fingers, as Winston cast the light over more tortured corpses that littered the space. Winston counted fifteen at a glance. 'They must have been sacrificed here?' he said, and Iona nodded somewhat mortified.

'I've never seen anything like it' she added, taking back control of the torch and casting the light about with more confidence as if to prove she was no longer afraid. The cave seemed to lead further on toward the back, the sound of water trickled in the distance, but the pair ignored the deeper reaches to focus their minds on the enormous object in front of them. Together the pair cast the torch light over the sculpted stone and walked closer trying to ignore the corpses. The carved serpents around the bowl were crafted so well from their marble that they looked almost life-like, and gave the impression of movement as the light moved across their etched scales.

They both ascended the steps chiselled into the plinth and stepped closer to the object. Their breath became ragged. Iona, compelled, reached out to touch the marble, but an instinct within Winston snatched forward to draw her hand back. Resisting, she turned to him with surprise, but then intuited his feeling and held off. Iona instead began to walk around the oddity to inspect it.

'The carving is exquisite' she said, 'consistent with some of the best sculpture of the classical period.' Iona scrutinised the object, 'whoever crafted this had great skill and probably had many assistants to produce a work of this scale' she said, eyeballing the details, her voice filled with awe: as if she were presenting a documentary on cable TV.

'How old is it?' said Winston, Iona furrowed her brow in concentration.

'Looking at the style I'd guess 400-200 B.C. This has to be from the Hellenic period, but I've never seen anything like this before, this is unheard of, and this...' Iona said pointing to a cast metal ring that encircled the whole vessel, adorned with animal and human figures protruding from it at intervals above her brow, 'I've no idea what this is yet.'

'It's the zodiac' said Winston, deadpan, his height giving him a better view. Iona's mouth fell open to let out a torrent of surprise mixed with expletives,

'Of course, it is, I see it now' she said, once recovered, and shook her head in disbelief, 'this could be Zoroastrian? But the carving looks Greek, not Persian - some joint effort perhaps? Oh, my God, this is huge, *HUGE*' she emphasised, fidgeting, shaking her head and clutching at her mouth as the enormity of their discovery dawned on her, 'this rewrites history' she said, 'I think this object - sculpture - is unknown.'

'I see the basin is filled with something too' said Winston, looking on mesmerised as if speaking in a dream, 'look' he said, lifting Iona up so she could see the vast breadth of the bowl. More exclamations followed as Iona wriggled in his grasp,

'Mercury' she said her voice trembling, 'it's filled to the brim with liquid mercury.' She gazed at the dish, caked in places with accumulated bat droppings, but the lustrous shine of Quicksilver lay unmistakable. Winston put her down. Iona almost ran around the object, got half way, and gasped again. 'The serpents have been carved with open jaws' she said, 'look they have bronze teeth.'

Winston drifted to her side as if in a daze, as she pointed at the teeth that had turned a green-brown with time.

'I think they must have held something in their grasp'

he said, 'a tooth is missing.'

'You're right' said Iona, with a cocked brow, and at that moment began to cast the torchlight around the floor. Something glinted. 'What's that?' she said thinking aloud and flew down from the plinth, like a Robin, and rushed to the object that reflected the light, ignoring the mangled bodies that littered her path. 'It's pure quartz crystal' she shouted back, 'but it's cleaved in half' she added in wonder, 'the tooth's stuck on this edge.' She then probed the shadows with light in search of another reflection, something else flashed, 'and there's the other PIECE' she exclaimed, scrambling in the dark, and united the two circular halves of the broken crystal above her head, before brandishing the gem like a trophy.

Winston felt a pulse of energy pass through him, upon the joining of the halves, and he thought he saw the carvings twitch, but he found it hard to tell as the torch light jerked around on Iona's wrist, which caused distorting shadows. Iona jumped about with the flashlight dropping down her arm, unable to contain the excitement that built within her like a tidal wave. Winston stood still as if made of lead.

'My father mentioned this: and I didn't believe him' he said under his breath, but his lips were out of sync with his words as his mind flew beyond the cave to reach into the past. Iona almost skipped back to the plinth and climbed the steps with pace to reach his side. Her eyes had gained a wild expression; her pupils dilated, her cheeks flushed.

'Look, look, *look*' she said, like a little girl, as she held the thick quartz in her hands, and tried to give Winston one-half. But she could no longer separate the crystal, 'oh?' she said with cocked brows and a grin that seemed wider than her face, 'it's stuck back together.'

Winston shivered but stood, rigid, and he heard Iona's breath become a pant as he felt her warm breath drift up to his neck. Iona's iris' became gaping holes of black banded with a thin strip of colour. Winston bit his lip as he looked at her. 'Let's see if it still fits?' said Iona with shrill glee. Winston stood magnetised to the spot, only able to move his eyes at that point and glanced at the heads of the snakes. He noticed that their carved eyes had opened to reveal large garnets of blood red that gave off a glow. Fear bolted through him. Iona, seeing his hesitation, then barged past him, where his feet stood as if rooted, and began to reach the crystal up to the jaws of the snakes that seemed to widen to receive it.

'STOP' screeched Winston at the top of his voice, and it took all his strength and reach, his movements like treacle, to swipe at the crystal in Iona's outstretched hands. It slipped from her grasp, and she clutched several times at the air as it fell, but it split again upon the plinth corner, and the halves came to rest upon the ground. At that moment, Winston felt freed, and Iona's mania ended. They both stood still.

'What... was... that?' said Iona, confused and shocked at herself.

'I don't think we can tell anyone about this' said Winston, who had broken into a sweat upon his brow, and a patch grew on his chest, 'not even Douglas' He shivered. Winston noticed the carved serpent's eyes had closed once more. Iona shook her hair and blinked as if she had received a blow to the head.

'But this, this is a find of a lifetime' she said, 'this discovery could rewrite, let alone add new chapters to history' she said incredulous, 'I want the world to know about this. Winston, this could become my PhD.'

'You can't write about this' Winston said, striking his finger through the air, 'do you remember what happened just now?' Iona shook her head before she replied,

'Something odd I think, I remember running over there, but I'm not sure how I got back here.'

'Did you see anything else?' said Winston,

'Not that I remember, why are you acting weird?'

'Look around you' said Winston, and Iona gazed about, 'there are bodies everywhere. Look how withered they are: they look like they've been chewed up and spat out. Doesn't that strike you as odd?' Iona's face scrunched like a ball of paper,

'Don't lecture me; this is not your area. You don't have the *expertise.*'

'Don't be blinded, Iona, this is bigger than you or me.'

'And you don't think I know that?' She said peering at Winston as if he were an imbecile, 'I see exactly what's going on here: you don't want me to progress. You don't want me to tell Douglas because you're jealous, and you don't want me to tell the *world* because you don't wish me to become better than yourself.'

'That's not true' he said,

'Yes, it is. It's written on your face' she declared swiping her hands downward, before thrusting them in Winston's direction.

'Listen to me' he said, 'my father mentioned something like this, but I didn't believe him.' Iona shook her head and guffawed.

'Your father...' she pointed but then hesitated to rephrase her tone and gestures. 'Your father - with all due respect - was an exceptional scholar, and, I admit, I enjoyed his lectures at Harvard. No one would dispute a great deal of his knowledge, but we both know, near the end, a lot of what he said was discredited...' Iona's voice trailed off, her face still vexed as she glared at Winston. Some of the bats stirred high overhead as they sensed the reducing hours till sunset.

'I think this thing, and what happened just now, proves some of what my father talked about before he died.'

'That's *impossible*' said Iona, with a flap, 'what he talked about was ludicrous, ludicrous: he got laughed out of Cambridge' she scoffed, unable to contain her frustration.

'I know: and he drank himself to death over it' said Winston, his eyes trembling. Iona chewed at her lip and sighed as her shoulders slumped.

'This is not fair, Winston. You can't do this. This find could make my career, and you can't keep mentioning your father just to end an argument.'

'I don't want to stop anything' he urged, 'I think we should work on this together, just the two of us. Write your PhD about this area, but if this is what I think it is' said Winston with a threatening gesture to the unusual object, 'then we both know that we can't tell anyone about it.'

Iona's lip trembled, and she rubbed her hands over her forehead before her eyes welled up. Iona then chewed on her fingernails.

'I don't want to do this' she said, shaking her head again 'I don't want to listen to this.' But Winston reached forward to grip her arm and pull her into his embrace. He held her fast and squeezed her to him.

'You read all my father's published work, and saw the rest that didn't make it' said Winston rocking Iona in his arms.

She wriggled, but he gripped her neck, and Iona tried to twist away somewhat before he kissed her, thrusting is tongue between her teeth, and massaged her body to try and make her yield. Iona tried to push him off, but he held her face in his hands and looked deep into her, 'let go of me' she said gritting her teeth. But Winston did not listen.

'I don't think now, standing here, that my father was crazy' he said, his voice unsteady, his face gripped with revelation. A tear rolled from Iona's eye, as Winston held her in place, and stood like a man having a spiritual vision, 'what if his theories were valid Iona?' he declared with almost evangelical conviction, his hands encircling her neck, 'what if my father was right? What if everything he said was true?'

Chapter 3

The Sacrifice

The Island of Maui, Hawaii April 2004

Illawara smiled to herself with satisfaction, her transformation complete, and fussed here and there at her seventeenth-century ball gown of midnight blue damask. She turned herself in front of her mirror, this way and that, to be sure the split at the front of her dress revealed her blue-gold embellished Petty coats, which ballooned forward over her wide French farthingale - an item which had taken her so long to find, on-line, and then improve. The nineteen-year-old ruffled and clinked as she moved forward: every inch of her dressed from head to toe like a late Renaissance woman of the highest standing.

Illawara then walked over to her Hi-fi stereo as a small hummingbird darted about, here and there overhead, and reflected the fading afternoon light off feathers that flashed like emeralds. Illawara then plugged her headphone jack into her iPod, selected an album, and burst into a movement as a song boomed out from the speakers, and filled the expansive living space with the brassy exuberant sounds of the year's smash hit. Illawara spun with glee, a passionate dancer since a small girl, and flung herself about the room with abandon.

'I love Beyonce' Illawara exclaimed, as she jangled like a jewel box, with faux pearls strung about her neck and through her dark hair, as she combined her best ballet moves with the bump and grind of an MTV dancer. As the music rang out, the bird tried to communicate over the trumpeting beat, but she carried on dancing. Lost in joy, Illawara raised her arms, encased in slashed puffed sleeves peeping with gold silk, into an arched port de bras above her head and high-wired ruff. Holding the pose, she leant back, as if blown by the wind, before she beat her arms like swan's wings. Giggling Illawara spun forward - her arms a wheel - and then leapt into the air, kicking her legs into splits, and tossing her head back mid-flight as if expecting to be caught by Rudolf Nureyev.

She landed with ease, and grace, upon her platform chopines: the pale blue fabric of the shoes embellished with glass gems and her embroidery. Illawara then shook her shoulders to the beat. The bird tried to communicate again, over the clamour, and called out:

'Illy, Illy, what will we take for Galileo?' But the young woman ignored his calls, and then imitated her favourite recording artist, as if it were she in her music videos, and sashayed forward throwing her hips from side to side like a supermodel upon a catwalk. Illawara stomped ahead, deaf to the bird's calling, with each step striking upon the beat while she imagined flashing cameras blazing at her sides. Illawara arrived at the other end of the room and threw up her hand to pose before she stopped to lick her thumb and graze it down into her corseted bust with as much sass as she could muster. As if facing a gallery of paparazzi Illawara, with her free hand, then clutched her trim waist above her hips and threw a smouldering look over her shoulder as if she were a megastar herself. Illawara's faux pearls jangled about before coming to rest, holding her pose with a pouted expression, before she erupted into laughter, her smile just as pearly as her necklaces, and giggled at herself for her abandon. She strutted forward to her Hi-fi and turned the music down.

'Yes, Hermes' she said, with a waft of her hand, to the hummingbird that still buzzed around.

'You weren't listening to me' the bird complained, 'you always lose yourself in music, and stop listening when I'm trying to talk to you' he added.

'I can't help it' she said, 'when I hear a good tune I just have to dance.'

The emerald coloured bird flew down, from where he hovered, to his perch - one of several dotted about the place - and came to rest on a table strewn with framed photographs. Many were of a younger Illawara, among others, standing next to a tall and distinguished man.

'They won't be playing this sort of music in 1611' chirped Hermes, rolling his little eyes,

'I know that' Illawara huffed, 'I'm not an idiot - but they'll have drums or tambourines: there will still be a beat...' The hummingbird stuck his long beak into the air as if to give her the brush off,

'I prefer Bowie anyway' said Hermes, and started to inspect his feathers. Illawara walked over to the table where the bird perched, Hermes ignored her while grooming, and she picked up a silver-framed picture of her younger self, gazing up at the well-dressed man standing next to her. She caressed the handsome features of the man through the glass,

'I miss him' she said before she kissed the image and put the frame down with care.

'Do you think he'll be there?' said Hermes, done with his grooming,

'Of course, he will' came the tart reply, which could not quite mask the doubt in her voice.

Illawara looked at pictures of herself with her father in Italy, an adventure for her twelfth birthday, the Leaning Tower of Pisa behind them, before she looked at more of the pair in Rome, Padua, and Florence. Illawara observed herself, the girl - her smile ecstatic and eyes filled with pride - as if she were a stranger that had lived some other life. She then sighed before she took up another photograph: one showing the same man upon a Maui beach embracing a woman with sandy blond hair. He does not smile, but his grey eyes burn with passion, the woman smiles enough for them both, but her eyes express an effort to pose and do not match her stilted grin.

'I miss her too. I still wonder what she's doing now?' said Illawara, stroking the hair of the woman's image,

'Forget her' said Hermes, 'you know she'll never get back to you.'

'Yes, but...' Illawara slumped somewhat and hesitated before she put the picture down and then turned away from all the other photographs of Iona and Winston: the successful Professor of Physics and Astronomy. Some pictures showed Winston surrounded by colleagues, or winning prizes: usually with Iona, in the background, or off to the side, smiling with empty eyes. Illawara had not seen her or the Professor for seven years. Illawara walked about in her costume, like an actress upon the wrong set before the start of filming: so at odds she stood with her environment of white leather furniture, shelves stuffed with books on philosophy, physics, and the classics.

Rothko and Van Gogh paintings adorned the high walls and shared space with framed drawings by Leonardo da Vinci and Michelangelo, and medieval maps of Europe with the land and sea populated with serpents and monsters writhing from their water coloured depths. Hubble space maps of nebula and constellations of stars also covered the walls, and large photos of the ongoing construction of CERN's Hadron Collider - her father present among the engineers - hung next to those of telescopes atop barren hills, and pictures of students at the Maui University. The most recent photo, a Polaroid, of her father stood amongst his research colleagues at the Haleakala Observatory: a moment, captured on impulse, which had become an image of significance in Illawara's life. It was the last picture she had of him before he left.

Illawara navigated the Professor's inherited collection of Greek and Roman busts upon plinths - a bronze mask or sculpture placed here and there across the expanse. Illawara's skirts rustled as she walked among exotic potted plants of ripening pineapples, aloe Vera, rare herbs, and an array of orchids that Hermes could sip from at his leisure. Illawara, in haste, inspected some Petri dishes, rested upon a shelf, which contained unusual growths. She squinted at the samples and curled her lip before she added some liquid to them from a syringe nearby. Illawara then adjusted the temperature control on the wall: her secluded home an odd combination of a greenhouse, laboratory, living room, study, and art gallery.

As the evening approached, some of the orchids began to release their heady perfume into the living room, which never failed to make Illawara feel nostalgic. She sighed, whimsical, breathing in the orchid scents that weighed upon the air, as the setting sun coloured the white walls to coral pink via the massive skylight that lay above in the vaulted ceilings.

'Dad always loved the smell of these flowers' said Illawara with her arm swept towards the potted orchids dotted about, 'do you think he still remembers them?' Illawara paused. 'Do you think he still remembers me?' Illawara turned to glance at the bird, but Hermes said nothing. Illawara stood still for a while, glaring at Hermes before she realised she was clenching her teeth.

'You said we need to hurry' said the bird glancing back. She muttered under her breath in reply, flicking her hand through the air, before turning away from her friend to retrieve a large, but simple, brown leather bag that closed with a drawstring. Illawara used the strap on the bag to sling it across her shoulders. The bag contrasted with Illawara's grand appearance but would not look out of place in earlier times. She then glided over to a large television, attached to the wall, which bore a frozen image of a doll-like woman standing in a field in Italy. The woman wore Edwardian clothing.

Illawara spun a miniature orrery that sat upon the coffee table and glanced down at how all the planets raced through their orbits above Ovid's Metamorphoses - the book that changed her life. The book lay open, for years, at the story of Jason and Medea. Illawara brushed fluff off the pages and traced her finger over Ovid's words. The chapter lay still wedged with a piece of paper, ragged and handled, that bore the code breaker that unlocked all her father's research secrets - years ago.

Her eyes glazed over, lost in pictures of him for a moment, before she bent down to pick up the DVD remote control from the coffee table, turned up the volume, and pressed play. Illawara watched Lucy Honeychurch step, with coy apprehension, into a poppy-strewn field before being taken into a forceful embrace and kissed by George Emerson who stood there. The serene voice of Kiri Te Kanawa exalted the scene and swept out of the TV to engulf Illawara with romantic longing. Honeychurch was led away, by her chaperone, and Illawara pressed rewind to watch the scene from A Room With a View - yet again.

'She's so beautiful' breathed Illawara, as she gazed at the young actress and guessed her to be the same age as herself. Hermes flew to Illawara's shoulder as the singing began over and the scene replayed.

'You always watch this bit' said Hermes, 'almost every day now, over and over. I'm bored of it' he said. Illawara frowned.

'I'll guess you'll never know love?' She replied, took off her leather bag and started to put some of the other items on the coffee table into it. The bird sat rigid upon her puffed shoulder for a while: stung into silence.

'Is that everything we're bringing for Galileo?' he asked after a while, but with less enthusiasm than before.

'Yes,' she said, 'I've packed a few rolls of cartridge paper, I think he'll like that, some sealing wax and quality ink. Oh, and I've packed some excellent Koh-i-Noor pencils, a sharpener, and rubber to give him for his drawings.'

'So you've not brought much then' said Hermes, deadpan,

'No, not really' she said, staring back.

In of themselves the objects were ordinary items, but the pair debated in length about bringing pencils. In the year 1611, that they were about to visit, paper remained expensive but the artisan pencil did not exist.

'I still think the pencils are a risk; Illy' Hermes, said. Illawara flicked her hand through the air,

'It's worth it - we have to impress him. No point in going all that way and getting ignored. We need to be near him, make an impression - then maybe Dad will see us and...' Illawara's voice trailed off. Illawara turned away to glance again at the pictures of her father: Hermes shook his head when she looked away. Illawara had chosen her gifts with much thought and they pondered the chance that items brought from the future could arouse suspicion - or even dangerous accusations of witchcraft. But Illawara got her way. Illawara checked the time, *'shit*, I have to hurry' she said. Hermes tutted aloud at her language

'Did you remember to pack the Mystify, the Forked Tongue and the Transformation Tincture?' Hermes added, running through his mental list as if Illawara had just returned from the shopping Mall. She rummaged through the satchel and pulled a face.

'I've got the Mystify and Forked Tongue, but I forgot the Tincture. Oh, and I've just remembered I need to bring some fruit juice for you.'

Hermes rolled his little hummingbird eyes and tutted to himself, while Illawara hurried back to her bedroom, her skirts billowing out behind, to grab the small glass phial of the tincture: which, with his other elixirs, represented years of hidden research by the Professor. She scrambled, in the fading light, through the feminine furnishings of her room, past her four-poster bed, and walls adorned with colourful posters of music stars: Beyonce and Destiny's Child, Justin Timberlake, Rihanna, Grace Jones, Kate Bush and David Bowie among many others. Illawara drew inspiration from the stars she loved.

Illawara hopscotched over her illustrated designs of Bowiesque clothes, mixed in with Elizabethan and Baroque styles, which lay strewn everywhere upon the carpeted floor, along with swatches of fabric samples and pages torn from fashion magazines. Her designs, samples and pages all intermingled upon the floor with random buttons and fixings that had escaped her haberdashery chest. Illawara's mannequin wobbled, as she rushed past, adorned with her newly finished prom dress of star spangled bodice and long purple skirts. Illawara paused mid-flight to be sure the dress would not topple over:

'I'll get Dad to take me to the prom in this' Illawara whispered to herself as she looked at her creation before she moved on.

A collection of fantastical potted orchids, a personal project of hers, ranging from the gorgeous to the macabre, sat glowing in a sheltered spot - the wall laced with twisted shadows created by their light. Some of the flowers turned as she rushed past. Illawara struggled to locate the bottle upon her dressing table amongst all her makeup and perfumes. She then pressed a switch to her side, and light bulbs blazed around the rectangle of a mirror. Some of her orchids tried to shield themselves; others seemed thirsty for the extra light. 'Sorry, girls', she said to the plants, absent minded, before she located the tincture, 'remember I won't be gone for long.' Illawara took up the phial of Transformation Tincture and shook the small glass bottle. The liquid inside then glowed with a blue-green fire: spinning like a dust devil within the glass. Illawara smiled and switched off the mirror lights, while the bottle illuminated her fingers as she hurried back to the living room.

On her way, she snatched up a small glass bottle of fruit juice from the fridge, its doors covered with gaudy magnets - souvenirs - of iconic buildings from around Italy: Rome, Florence, Padua and Venice were all represented. Illawara had outgrown the fridge magnets, but could not bear to toss away the mementoes. She scurried ahead and then stopped to tear off a ripening pineapple, with a snapping twist, from one of the potted plants and stuffed it into her swag before she carried on.

'Is everything ready?' said Hermes fluttering above as she rushed about. Illawara's head twitched with irritation.

'Not quite yet' she replied, 'but I'll need to hurry up.'

Illawara rushed to the far back of the property and slid back a tall, weighty door, which took her some effort to push aside. This part of her house she shied away from, but necessity compelled her to prepare for the journey they were about to make. The door slid back to reveal a large extension, which had been gouged and cut out of the volcanic rock of the hillside on which the house rested. A picture of Maui University campus lay mounted to the wall inside. Illawara stopped, chewed her fingernail, and thought for a moment of some of her friends and fellow Students. The Prom would be in two weeks. One glimpse of her father delivering her to the Prom could end years of speculation about his whereabouts: a burden she longed to throw off. Apart from the extensive education received from her father, Illawara had since amused herself and out-witted her tutors - which only added to the mystique that surrounded her on campus: the rich-odd-cool-geek-girl too smart for her own good.

Illawara entered deeper into the vaulted passageway, the air chill upon her skin, and passed the impermeable polished walls of volcanic rock that curved around to the left. On the way, she closed the reinforced door to her father's laboratory, filled with classified documents and rare equipment - some of which Illawara had added to herself - and closed the door with a thud and twisted the handle till the sounds of bolts locking into position echoed along the chamber. Illawara hurried her way to a side room topped with a modest skylight that allowed the late glow of sunset to come down into the space like a column.

Part of the room stood divided by a screen of red velvet that reached from floor to ceiling. Illawara scurried, knowing herself to be running out of time, and laid her bag opposite the curtain, and tried to ignore the quiet hiss that crept through from the other side. She shuddered and hurried back to the main house, her skirts floating out wide as if she were Cinderella fleeing the ball at midnight. She saw Hermes flitting from side to side, flicking his head, looking from corner to corner of the main house, 'are you sure you want to do this?' the bird said. Illawara paused.

'Do I have any choice?' she answered, stopping, before she reached into a cabinet drawer and took out a small aerosol, and then a Taser gun. Hermes buzzed around her, fluttering here and there, as he watched her and spoke:

'Once you do this our lives will change forever, Illy.'

'I understand that' she said, her face focused, 'but I need to know what's happened to him, where he is... why he left the way he did'

Illawara's voice wobbled, 'I'm not a child anymore, Hermes - I deserve answers.'

Hermes seemed pensive in his flight and whirled back and forth. 'But you know already what he's done' said Hermes, 'you've read all his research: is there anything left to know? We've talked about this for ages.' Illawara's mouth tightened to a crease as her eyes narrowed.

'You know why I have to do this, Hermes' said Illawara, her face a picture of determination before she checked to be sure the Taser still had a full charge. Satisfied, Illawara hid the weapon in her side pouch attached to her ornate girdle made of costume jewellery. With her weapon concealed Illawara maintained the illusion of having just stepped out of the early seventeenth century. But Hermes buzzed about with agitation,

'This is a big step, Illy, no going back' he said,

'Hush already, you'll make me more nervous' Illawara then looked at her hands - they were shaking, 'you know I have to do this' said Illawara scowling. Her palms became sweaty; she waved them through the air to dry them, 'no more *doubts*, I'm tired of doubts' she said, 'I'm sick of not knowing what may be happening to him' Illawara looked up to the hovering bird, 'don't you even want to know why Dad left us here, Hermes?' The Bird tried to reply but could not as if sharing his thoughts were beyond him. Illawara clenched her fists, 'Dad could have taken me with him, I'm smart enough - smarter than my tutors - why didn't he let me go with him?' Hermes swallowed.

'You were twelve, Illy, isn't it obvious?' said Hermes. Illawara's blue eyes then welled up, she coughed, took a deep breath, and waited for the sensation to pass. Illawara then fussed at herself and neatened anything she felt to be out of place on her dress until she calmed down. Illawara coughed before she spoke again.

'If he thought I was old enough to help him when Iona left' she continued, 'then I was old enough to be taken with him. We were a *team*. He didn't have to shut me out and hide everything from me. I could have been trusted' she said with frustration. Illawara turned to point at Hermes, her chin set. 'But I'm older now. I'll get him back here, he'll tell me everything, and then we can do things properly.'

'And do what exactly?' Sneered the bird, 'you want to chase him through time just so that you can drag him back here to take you to the Prom Ball? That's what you want isn't it?' Illawara's eyes grew wide before she jabbed her finger towards Hermes where he hovered in the air,

'I don't know how long I can keep this place – you know that – and people are asking too many questions. The lease runs out in *two months.*'

'Why can we just get an extension?' said Hermes. Illawara rolled her eyes as she crossed her arms.

'How many times do I have to tell you? If Dad doesn't sign the papers in person the university won't extend the lease' she huffed, 'I've wasted so much time already'

'Don't beat yourself up, Illy, you only got the letter a few weeks ago'

'Duurh?' said Illawara, flicking her fingers off her temples, 'and I've told you what it's like for me at college. He's still my Dad, and I'm tired of all the lies and gossip about him. You don't have to hear what they whisper about me on Campus.'

'Calm down' warned Hermes,

'And *you* she added, flapping her arms, 'don't you want anything?' she said raising her voice, with a tense brow. Hermes faltered.

'You know what I want, Illy. But you've made the price for it very high.' Illawara put her hands on her hips before she then gestured again at the hovering bird,

'So I suppose you want to stay as you are forever then?' She declared. Hermes fell silent, descended to land on a perch, and then shook his beak. 'Well, that settles it' Illawara added, folding her arms again, and ending an argument that they had wrangled with for years.

'You could free me; you could free me now... you could have freed me years ago' Whispered Hermes. Illawara's face clouded.

'Then you wouldn't come with me, would you?' She said with a stare. Hermes knew well enough the conditions for his release but still felt the urge to needle his friend.

'One day maybe you'll know what it's like to feel trapped. And... and' Hermes seemed to be grasping for thoughts, '...the Professor may have left you, Illy' he added, keen to have the last word, 'but he didn't leave you poor.' Illawara dismissed the comment with a huff before she checked her appearance again in a mirror, 'but if he doesn't come back we'll be *homeless*' she said, before tweaking at herself again. She took a deep breath to egg herself on. Hermes observed how her olive skin had honeyed into glossiness in the Pacific sunshine. She then glanced back to her reflection to check her white teeth and checked the time on her 24-hour clock before she called up to Hermes. 'It's 18:26. Now fly back and keep quiet before that creep gets here' she said, her face becoming tense again.

She heard the front door close toward the front of the house, her eyes flashed, '*shit* - that's him' she whispered back to Hermes, and waved the hummingbird off towards granite volt area. Illawara's breath quickened, and her pulse increased as she heard the heaviness of steps, hesitating at times as if to search, before again moving forward. Illawara spied the balding head of a medium build man move between the artefacts and plant pots of the living room area, as he progressed with slowness taking in his surroundings. Illawara's eyes squinted as she looked the man that often followed her home, sometimes via truck sometimes on foot, and she felt herself shiver with disgust to see him creeping about her living room, taking in her space: her independent dwelling for so many years.

He spotted her, his shifting eyes at once fixed upon her, gawking, she dressed so different from the shorts and t-shirts she usually wore. He puzzled, digesting what he saw, but then prowled forward with a smirk. Illawara took several steps back, 'so you've made it then', she said. Her voice, although cold, assured him that he had the right girl. The man whistled,

'This is quite some place you got here' he uttered casting his gaze about the place. He made the sound again, the noise that made Illawara's skin crawl. She walked back; he walked forward. Hermes watched from his vantage point unseen upon a perch high above, knowing that, in his current form, he would be unable to help Illawara. His own heart trembled. Illawara kept moving backwards with her hands behind her back, not taking her eyes off the shabby man for a moment. 'Don't keep walkin' away, honey, I'm not gonna hurt you' he said, with a leering smile, but started to unbuckle his belt that held up his khaki shorts under his pot belly. Illawara gnashed her teeth but maintained her concentration, although all she could hear was the blood that pumped through her ears.

He whistled again, 'that's quite some get up that you're wearin'' he said, eyeing her over, 'you some kind'a *royal* or somethin'?'

'More royal than you'll ever be' Illawara snarled back,

'Whoohoo, sassy gal' said the man that wore a faded Hawaiian shirt, pockmarked with food stains, hanging somewhat over his shorts that contained a robust pair of tanned legs.

Illawara sized him up, her first chance to study the man in detail as she walked backwards, he looked quite strong, a Texan day labourer or part-time trucker perhaps is all she could assume from his accent and appearance. His swollen nose with burst capillaries and veined ruddy cheeks suggested a thirst for alcohol: she understood that she would have to be careful - even while walking away from the man she could smell him. A waft drifted to her off the man: a smell of drink, body odour and dry cologne. The reflections of Illawara and the man passed across a mirror three meters high and four meters wide, cut through with her ballet barre: Illawara dressed in all her pomp stepping backwards, the Trucker, pink, sweaty, and unkempt, stepping ever forward. He tossed his belt to the floor with a clatter.

The man made a sudden lunge ahead, but Illawara, lithe and agile after many years of swimming and dance, maintained her distance from the aggressor with ease, even while moving backwards. Hermes almost screeched with fear at the pounce, although if he did, he knew the stranger would not comprehend him: Illawara being the only one to understand. Bird cries and a pecking beak would not be enough to spare Illawara from the man if he got hold of her. 'So you like to play dress up, huh?' he said with another leering grin, admiring Illawara's outstanding efforts as if they were for his benefit. He puckered his lips as if titillated. 'I like a kinky woman... but I've never seen a gal wearing this' he added with a broad gesture in her direction. 'Why don't you run along and put'on those tight little shorts you usually wear: shame not to see that purty li'll booty you got goin on there' he added with another lunge and groped forward as they then passed into the Vault area at the rear of the house. Illawara jangled but avoided him again. 'I hope this is leading to your bedroom - you li'll prick tease' the man shouted as they passed along the corridor before Illawara glanced back to see if she were close enough to the curtain,

'Almost there' she thought. The man dashed forward, the moment she looked away, and grabbed Illawara's corseted waist. She almost screamed when she felt his hot reeking breath, as he tried to smother her lips with his mouth. His slobbering jaws grazed off her neck and chin, being no George Emerson, and Illawara answered his assault with pepper spray in the man's face. He howled like a dog and struck out, but Illawara, fast and nimble, ducked the uncoordinated blow, but the man lunged forward again. Illawara sidestepped him using her superior balance and stuck out her Chopin clad foot to trip up the man: no match for the block of satin covered wood. He crashed downward to the floor, and almost disturbed the thick velvet curtain that hung, somewhat dim, in the failing sunshine. A loud hiss emerged from behind the veil. Illawara leapt forward after the man fell, and unleashed another dose of pepper spray into the red face of the man that howled even more and thrashed around.

'You bitch!' he screamed, 'just you wait, you li'll prick teasing whore' he hollered again and tried to get up to make a lunge for Illawara's legs. Illawara leapt back, whipped the Taser from her pouch, her hands trembling, forced herself to be still, took aim, with a point of light, as the man tried to thrash his way upwards, and discharged the firing pins into the man's struggling torso. He recoiled in pain, but before he could tear the bolts from his flesh, Illawara pulled the trigger again to unleash the full voltage into the man's body. He screamed, wrenching the air with his howls, and convulsed where he lay, unable to stop his body moving as the voltage ripped through him.

The hairs left on his bald-cap head stood on end like sheaves of wheat: 'that's the last time you ever touch me again!' Illawara screeched, her face angular with vulpine contempt, as she remembered the ugly groping she had to escape from only weeks before.

As she relived her fear, she pulled the trigger again to electrocute her foe, who jerked and writhed about on the stone floor. *'I'm sorry'* the man wailed, 'stop - I beg you' he implored as Illawara yanked back the velvet curtain to reveal the Hermeporta: the antiquity whole again and intact from its resting place in Turkey. It was too late for mercy. The man froze, paralysed by a force greater than himself, as the marble serpents about the pool of liquid mercury softened and uncoiled into life. Illawara stepped back and watched with morbid fascination as the eyes of the snakes opened, revealing the red glow of their garnet eyes in the fading light.

The man, rigid with fear opened his mouth to scream, but nothing came out, as his body slid across the floor towards the Hermeporta as if magnetised. The electrocuting cables tugged out of his flesh, while Illawara gripped the Taser gun before the man flew up into the air above the Hermeporta and hung there suspended. With an invisible force, the serpents began to bend and break his body. Illawara, wide-eyed, cried out when she saw and heard the man's legs and ribs snapping, she dropped the Taser gun as his piercing shrieks split the air. She wrenched back the curtain to obscure her view, covered her ears, and ran back into the main house where she half slid back the heavy door to muffle the man's agonised cries. Illawara then sprinted to the stereo and fumbled to turn on the device, dropping the remote several times, before turning up the volume to let music smother the last screams of the dying man.

Illawara shook from head to foot, her heart a locomotive, her lungs bellows, and she gulped several breaths to try and calm herself down. But Illawara burst into tears, overwhelmed - revenge, guilt, and relief combined. After a while, Hermes flew down from his perch and nuzzled at Illawara's neck. 'Turn off the music. It's over now' he said, returning to her elaborate sleeved shoulder and using his little eyes to peer up at her. Illawara, hands shaking, switched off the stereo. Silence dominated the space. 'You did what you had to do, Illy, it's done now' said Hermes. Illawara dried her eyes with her fingers and nodded before she sobbed again.

'Oh, God, what have I done?' she said, gazing into space. She shook her head several times, trying to rid herself of what she saw. 'I hope... I hope it's worth it' she coughed. Illawara then shook her head again, 'but he was a horrible man. *Wasn't he?*' she added, Hermes nodded, '*yes, horrible.*' She stood up. Illawara walked forward, wobbling with dizziness, to take up a tissue from the coffee table and blow her nose. Her chest heaved again but, with an effort, she forced herself to try to be calm. She tapped herself several times on the face – as if to revive herself - before she walked back to straighten herself out in the mirror. She adjusted her wire ruff and smoothed her glossy hair with trembling hands.

Illawara tried to forget the man that had menaced her, and many other girls on campus.

With her breath still shaking she took a long hard look at herself – her mind far beyond her reflection. Her eyes looked pink but fierce, gleaming with a flash of brilliance and power she had not seen before. 'I guess this is how Dad felt' she muttered as Hermes buzzed above.

She had crossed a threshold: part of her had changed forever.

Illawara tore her eyes away from her reflection and the new revelations that emerged within her. But she had looked at herself with more self-respect, no longer a victim, and somewhat awed by what she, and the Hermeporta, could do. 'We have to get out of here' she said, pushing thoughts of her victim to the back of her mind, and focusing again on the uncertain journey that lay ahead. Illawara walked across to a small hinged door on the wall. Her shaky hands turned the dial this way and that, inputting the correct code, before pressing forward with a click to open the mini volt. A jewel dazzled upon a black cushion, and Illawara felt a tremble of excitement within her - even then - when she lifted out the brilliant cut diamond choker upon a black leather thong. The diamond sparkled and seemed illuminated within with a fire of its own. The gem refracted light in rainbows over Illawara's arm: the only real jewel she owned. She closed her eyes to picture her father and a corner of her mouth smiled. Illawara secured the diamond upon her forehead by tying the thong in place: crowning herself as the mistress of her own destiny. Illawara coughed, but checked herself one last time by straightening her pearls, drying her eyes, and regaining her composure.

'It's time to go' she said. She gazed about her living room as if to take photographs of it with her mind, and accepted that she would miss her plants, her music and her new iPod. 'I'll be back soon' she called out into the space as if her plants would cry out in protest when she left. Her botanical experiments would be fine: they were fed and watered with automatic pumps and timers. Illawara slid back the heavy door of the passageway to return to the Hermeporta. She walked forward with trepidation in the silence.

The Trucker had to be dead. Seeing her leather bag where it lay she picked it up and slung it over one shoulder to avoid bending her high wired ruff. She looked at the Taser on the floor and kicked it aside not wanting to touch the weapon again. Hermes fluttered above, careful to keep himself the correct side of the hanging velvet that obscured the antiquity, as Illawara began to make her preparations. She reached down into a small ancient box made of fossilised oak, set close to the velvet screen, and began to remove its precious contents.

The first item being a silver incense burner with a silver chain, and then the incense itself contained within a tied parchment: the faded ribbon frayed at the edges. Next came a small rusk of charcoal combined with saltpetre: this she ignited with a small gas lighter, and cursed aloud after scorching herself when the saltpetre spat. The rusk crackled to into life as she dropped it into the burner. Last, of all, she pulled from the box a candle made of a greasy yellow wax enriched with rare oils that gave off a numbing vapour when burned. Illawara stared off into the distance, but once the charcoal had turned a grey-white, it proved ready for the incense. Using her fingers, Illawara placed a small clump of the sticky substance into the burner, where it began to smoke. The sweet, and musky scented cloud filled the air and defined the last beams of light that could still reach the skylight as the evening took hold.

Like a priest, Illawara waved the burner by its silver chain above her head till the air became dense with the soporific smoke and choked the area around the Hermeporta. Illawara hesitated as she moved towards the velvet curtain, breathed deep, and slid the fabric back to reveal the antiquity - it glistened. The serpents gave out a low hiss. Illawara grimaced when she saw the mangled and withered body of her attacker. 'Oh, my... God' she whispered through clenched jaws before she covered her mouth. She looked at his remains curled up and dry on the floor, seeming like a digested pellet wretched from the crop of an owl. He looked like he had been dead for twenty years: reduced to a waste product, a dismal end to a dissolute life. Hermes buzzed overhead, wanting to comment, but remained silent. He had seen bodies such as this before.

Illawara pitied the desiccated corpse, but thought of what could have happened to her should he have won. She clamped her eyes shut, shook her head, concentrated on her purpose, and carried on with her preparations for the dangerous Hermeporta. The opiates within the candle had done much to pacify the serpents. Illawara felt light headed, the smoke dulling the raw edge of her emotions.

She took great care to avoid her image being reflected within the mercury pool of the Hermeporta. She reached up, standing on a stool, with an arm extended to place the yellow candle into a mirrored fixture, which protruded from the wall behind the antiquity. After reaching down to a flowerpot of Anemones nearby, she tore off two of the blood red flowers.

With a nod Illawara checked that Hermes had made ready, before, slow and deliberate, she began to ascend the marble steps leading to the brim of the Hermeporta. The hissing of the alabaster serpents grew louder, as her reflection passed into the pool of quicksilver. Her body flinched, when she felt the slow squeeze of the serpent's invisible grip, as they increased their focus upon her. Illawara stood numb and stiff clinging to her breath, as their hard stone bodies softened yet more into life. Their marble scales shimmering in the ebbing light. Like two hefty pneumatic screws, the alabaster snakes began to uncoil themselves. The serpent's garnet eyes lit up to throw a ghoulish red glow into the foggy area, as they increased their height by arching their bodies upwards.

Their hissing grew louder, as the quartz crystal fixed within their jaws drew level with the mirrored candle. The light intensified, as the candles glow became refracted and scattered by the stone, which caused trembling strings of honeyed light to strobe about the area. Illawara fought to maintain her breathing, and in a solemn manner she tore the petals from the Anemones, before projecting her words:

'Blood to spare blood' she then tossed them into the pool where the petal's dark red hues were bled of colour. The symbolic offering satisfied the serpents, and their hissing became less ferocious. The petals along with Illawara's reflection then vanished, and she no longer felt the serpent's icy grip so strong upon her. She, then able to breathe with more ease, focused her mind on her destination. Using all her concentration the diamond on her brow began to glow and take on life, shining like a star on her forehead, as its light mingled with that of the snakes and the candle.

Illawara raised her arms and, like the birth of a new Tornado, the different colours of light began to blend, merge, and then swirl together at ever-greater speeds, becoming an orb like matrix that engulfed Illawara and the Hermeporta. 'Now's the time, Hermes' she declared in full voice, as the hissing of the serpents rose again with increasing volume. Hermes darted into action flying as fast as he could around Illawara, and with such pace, he blurred into a wavering band of streaked green light. Illawara's body began to rise from the steps and to hover directly above the Quicksilver pool. The hissing of the snakes became deafening. Illawara used all her focus to project an image from her mind, via the diamond, onto the surface of the pool, where a silvery leaning tower could be seen upon its trembling surface. She raised her voice to a high soprano, and held the note for as long as she could before screaming:

'To Pisa!' over the loud din boomed out by the writhing serpents.

In an instant, an almost blinding flash emerged from below temporarily filling the Volt, and illuminating the domed glass nearby above like a lighthouse obscured by fog in the dying sunset. Illawara and Hermes crashed into the image upon the Mercury's surface, which parted itself to let them through, and devoured them whole with a bang as they broke the sound barrier: their bodies shattering into light before vanishing into the antiquity.

Tentacles of electricity lashed out from all sides of the Hermeporta's egg like amethyst at its base, as the vessel shuddered. The bronze claws of the Hermeporta's foot struggled to keep hold of the gem and its pedestal. The force of the sonic boom extinguished the candle in its fixture and blew the Trucker's corpse aside like tumbleweed. The sound and force rippled the fog of the volt as it ebbed into darkness. With the sun gone, slow and languid the serpents coiled back to their former positions as the troubled air relaxed to a steady calm. The vipers yielded their bodies once again to stone and gave out a long, deep, satisfied hiss. The dying embers of their garnet eyes just visible through the smoke.

Chapter 4

Space

The limitless void

Illawara observed, after the initial blast and acceleration upon entering the Hermeporta, that her environment seemed to stretch and slow down. While travelling close to the speed of light, and in the last glimpses of her home, she saw solid objects contort and pull into glowing strings of colour, only to be erased by glaring white. Illawara clasped Hermes close to her chest as they emerged into the blackness of the void within an orb both weightless and suspended: two beings alone in space enveloped by stillness and conquered by silence.

Illawara then saw more stars than she could ever have imagined, and the full enormity of space in every direction. Illawara screamed her lungs empty as a look of terror gripped her face. Hermes shrank into her. 'I feel like a grain of sand' she wailed, 'oh, my GOD. This is too much, too much', Illawara shrieked again, flailing at the air in their bubble, while Hermes' heart pounded.

'Calm down' he said, as Illawara then tried to shrink and pull herself away from what she saw all around her, 'please quiet down, or you'll make it worse.'

'What if we die like this?' she exclaimed, looking from side to side, as the orb moved forward, 'what if we float on like this forever until we're dead?' Illawara's eyes grew wild. Hermes would have to calm Illawara down, but was unable, bound as he was, to share his own experiences of the Hermeporta. Illawara covered her face with her sleeve and then peeped through the fingers of her free hand: unable to turn her face away from the spectacle. Her shining eyes then became glassy and transfixed.

'Let me go' Hermes said, and struggled against her grip, Illawara shook her head and clung tighter, 'you're crushing me - *please*' he gasped. Illawara trembled and held onto him like a comfort blanket as he wriggled, before pecking her hand as hard as he could. With a cry, she released him. Hermes floated from her grasp, 'you were choking me' he coughed before he encircled Illawara and buzzed around the space - tracing the circumference of the orb with his flight. 'Stop panicking; we're safe in here, nothing can get us' he said, unable to stop moving. Hermes stopped flying but his movements showed their confinement. 'Catch me please' said Hermes still in orbit. Illawara nodded, and caught him, before she stretched her arms and legs out wide, and felt a cool resistance against her palms and pressure at her feet. Illawara then closed her eyes and did her best to control her ragged breathing. The layers of Illawara's dress lifted like petals from her bodice as she tried to calm herself down. After a while, she opened her eyes again.

'Look' said Hermes. Illawara turned to look behind her and saw the Earth. She gasped and clamped her hand to her chest.

'Oh... isn't it beautiful? Look at it' Illawara reached out her hands towards the planet, 'I've seen so many pictures before, but never like this. Up here it looks a jewel, a blue, green, and white jewel.'

Illawara then pointed to the continents and oceans she could see, a storm forming in the Indian Ocean and the aurora borealis in the Northern Hemisphere - she then stared at the Earth in silence, mesmerised. Hermes floated from her grip to cling onto Illawara's shoulder when he could see that she had relaxed.

'You could have killed me... I didn't think you would let go' he said.

'I'm sorry' she said, 'I wasn't prepared for this. What happens now?'

Hermes tried to reply before he felt a crushing weight move through him, stifling any details he could have mustered into a response. 'Let's just wait, something will happen' he said with great effort. Illawara recognised his behaviour, nodded, but did not question him further. As the idle pair floated, they began to feel a gentle tug of gravitation upon them: the two became magnetised toward the next stage of their journey, by a vessel not yet visible ahead. 'Something's happening' she said, and Illawara tensed again, but tried to stay calm. She marvelled at the astonishing clarity of space around her.

Every phenomenon of the night sky had sharpened and intensified. Without an atmosphere to obscure them the stars shone without twinkling, and the Milky Way erupted into a chorus of colour: embroidered with stars like a Persian carpet. Silence dominated, but Illawara felt a choir of awe rise within her, as they gravitated at ever-greater speed toward a translucent tunnel that was about to envelop them. 'This is incredible' she said, her voice shaking, 'whatever happens, I'll never forget this, we've become astronauts Hermes - we've seen the stars up close. How many down there on Earth could ever say that?' Illawara said as their speed increased, but Hermes, as if paralysed within, could only twitch in acknowledgement - unable to divulge what he had witnessed and learned long ago. Up ahead, like spun sugar, the faint threads of a tubular matrix could be seen, gentle and rotating in space, reaching back in an arc toward the Earth's orbit. Illawara's eyes widened, 'what's this?' she said, peering at the strands that drew closer.

Hermes sat rigid perched on Illawara's shoulder.

Once inside the tube's delicate structure, the universe began to blur around them. The narrow tunnel in space held them close and squeezed the pair as they began to accelerate onward. Colours once distinct and perfect then merged, and fanned outwards as their speed intensified. 'Whooohoooo, oh my, God' Illawara cried again, stretching out her hands to the sides of the orb, 'this is incredible: like riding a rollercoaster. I love it; I love it, love it.'

Hermes hurried to Illawara's neck to bury himself there while trembling and sick with nerves, as the colours of a distant nebula merged with an intense blue in the birthing of a new star. Both phenomena appeared to blur together to create a shimmering purple haze, which stretched by in silence like the silk ribbons of a flying kite. Hermes turned his head away to ignore the yellow stars that crisscrossed one another in a lattice of honeycombed light, as he and Illawara raced along the time tube created by the Hermeporta.

'Hermes' said Illawara, 'you've become mute. Don't you want to look at all of this?'

'No, I feel ill' he said,

'But it's beautiful, look at me, I'm not scared anymore' smiled Illawara, who then reached forward with her fist and clenched back the other to her bust, to take on a pose of Superman flying. Hermes shook his head before he turned his face away from the space that rushed past him. Illawara then focused on their destination, as the pair raced back towards Earth when Illawara then noticed the cloud and vegetation patterns on Earth had changed. Within that realm, they inhabited, the known physics of the universe made a loose fit. So close to the speed of light travelling backwards or forwards within time became much the same thing, the only difference being the intentions of its travellers.

    The pair could have inhabited the time tube for an instant or an eternity, but once inside only imagination bettered the speed of light, as Illawara continued to focus her mind on the location of Pisa. The diamond fastened at her brow began to send out a beam of pale blue light, just ahead, that guided the pair to the destination that awaited them. The orb began to glow white as they approached Earth, and Illawara shielded her face and closed her eyes to surrender to her fate.

Chapter 5

Transformation

Pisa, Italy, Saturday October 1st 1611

The sun in Tuscany on the October evening of the year 1611, had taken on a rich yellow-orange like a burnished egg yolk, and cast a golden veil of light across the hills that surrounded Pisa, as it sank into the western horizon. The Autumn sun still held its strength in the daytime, but not enough to keep away the mists that began to form at sunset, as the cooling earth yielded a haze that undulated from the bases of the hills. The darkness of the night would soon arrive.

Within the sky, the last of that year's swifts and swallows darted around above, and cut the air, with their wings and calls, in swooping arcs preparing to abandon the land and the weakening ties of summer. They fed fast, gorging themselves on insects before the biting winds of winter would crash against the hillsides. The Campo dei Miracoli stood, glorious, but on that October evening, the vision that greeted the eyes of the living could have raised the dead, such was the beauty of the enclosed space. The precarious Leaning Tower of Pisa stood crowned with gold, as the sun almost dipped below the horizon, while the tower's white stone enhanced the light's brilliance. The tower's stance contrasted with the vertical walls of the Duomo nearby. The imposing building holding itself up so well it appeared to pull against gravity, and seemed to barely touch the grass that clothed the ground on which it rested.

Next to the Duomo stood the vaulted walls of the Camposanto cemetery: restful and unsuspecting. Its rectangular construction, overlooking a grassy enclosure, seemed an edifice of rigid calm, but within the spaces were adorned in a sensuous display: the walkways populated with soft-limbed statues that heralded the great achievements of their dead patrons, or draped in languorous poses over their cold tombstones. The whole scene within further enhanced by soaring Gothic windows, with glass held in place by carved stone so delicate it seemed as if woven by spiders. To the far side of the Camposanto, across from a footpath that intersected the grass and roses, a vast barren vessel of carved marble began to fill from its base with liquid mercury. Beneath the timbers of the soaring wooden ceilings, the surface of the liquid rose within the vessel, at first calm, before stirring to move and glow with light and twist into a spiral: a wormhole in space opened at the bottom of the twister. Emerging with a howl and a flash Hermes and Illawara's orb flew out of the vortex to burst on the stone floors of the vaulted cemetery.

Illawara stumbled forward, clutching Hermes as she staggered into a recess; together they waited to gather their breath and strength - as their bodies yielded to gravity. Their chests heaved. It was a while before either one spoke. In time Illawara broke the silence after first pondering the shadows that stretched and deepened, as twilight began to descend upon the Campo dei Miracoli.

'That is the weirdest thing that's ever happened to me' said Illawara, propping herself against a pillar quite breathless. Hermes wriggled again from Illawara's grasp to alleviate the tightness he felt in his chest, a feeling he thought he had forgotten. The little bird glanced about, from Illawara's shoulder, with agitation at his new surroundings. 'That was a wild ride. I'm shaking' Illawara said, her voice becoming husky, as her lungs adjusted to the humid air. She shook her head as she stared about her. Illawara took in a deep breath before laughing, 'but it all seems the same. Like the first time we were here' she said, looking around some more. Illawara then ran her fingernail down the pillar she rested on, to collect the dust, before she stuck it in her mouth. She sampled the flavour like a wine. 'It tastes the same and smells the same, almost. But now everything is richer, fresher.'

'Buildings don't change in Italy unless there are bombs, sackings or Earthquakes - you know that' said Hermes, eyeing the space with suspicion, 'the rock probably tastes the way it always did.'

'Maybe, but I wonder what will be different here in this time?'

'Well, you've read enough about it' said Hermes, before casting his eyes about the space again. Illawara stroked another pillar and saw herself on her holiday visits as a girl with Professor Sloane, and with Hermes smuggled into her hand luggage.

'How are you feeling?' She asked again. Still recovering Hermes looked around himself as if expecting an ambush.

'I'm a bit better, thanks, except I'm half deaf from all your noise, crushing and screeching.' Illawara pulled a face.

'Sorry about that' She coughed, 'I was scared, at first, and then the excitement just took over. I still can't quite believe we're back here in this way. It's surreal.' Illawara then adjusted her ruffled skirts before she brushed them back down to neatness.

'It is surreal, but let's hope we come out of this alive', said Hermes. Illawara frowned,

'That's a bit drastic, please don't doom monger. Let's be *positive*. Besides, I can't see how much danger we would be in anyway. No one knows us, we've no enemies, and we've brought all that we need, let's not worry.' The little bird gave a look of dissatisfaction,

'Yes,' he said, 'but that's a problem: no one knows us, no one knows we're here. If we get in trouble no one can rescue us' he said while inspecting the rafters for hidden enemies. 'Think about the thieves and criminals, Illy, waterborne diseases, Malaria and Bubonic Plague. Let alone what else could await us here?' he added.

'There's no plague outbreak now, I checked, and I've taken every jab I could before getting here - you know that. This trip won't take long. We'll find Dad and bring him back, and that will be the end of it.' Hermes looked sceptical. Illawara crossed her arms. 'If you're going to be like this I don't know why you bothered coming. I should've left you at home to find my Dad by myself.' Hermes hopped several times on Illawara's shoulder.

'That's not fair' he declared, 'you've given me no choice, and besides, you wouldn't last ten minutes without me.' Illawara pouted.

'Maybe not' she said, knitting her eyebrows, 'but if you're going to be like this, I'll be tempted to try.'

The statement jolted the bird: Illawara delivering her threat with enough conviction for Hermes to believe it. The pair stood motionless a while longer before Illawara walked forward to search the floor with her eyes. Hermes began to fidget. 'Illy how can we be sure that Professor Sloane will be at the party?'

'We can't' she said, as she scanned the floor. The little bird paused.

'You'll have to do better than that' he said, but Illawara gave a dumb shrug. 'Illy, this is a huge risk being here, and it would help me if you were surer of things.'

'I can't be a hundred percent sure Hermes; you knew that before we started all this.' Hermes stomped on Illawara's shoulder. 'OK, calm down' she said, 'I know it's seven years since I've seen Dad, but I'm sure I'll still recognise him when I see him?'

'I'm worried' he said. Illawara flapped her arms.

'But every clue he left me points to this time now, and the Duke's party.' The little bird began to look ill.

'God's, please help us' sighed Hermes, 'this is a reckless gamble Illy, at home you seemed SO sure.' Illawara rubbed her brow.

'Oh, keep your feathers on: this was always going to be risky, but we've made it this far. If I'd shared my doubts, and not twisted your arm, you'd never have come. Why must you peck everything to pieces?' Hermes hopped and flicked his tail several times before buzzing into the air to hover in front of Illawara.

'I'm not pecking everything to pieces. I'm realistic. I came here to be freed. But now I'm stuck here, lost with you in old Italy, all to try and sneak into a party, attended by all and what-not. But where no one knows us, and with all the risk that entails.' Hermes then whizzed in frantic circles around Illawara's head, 'what if something goes wrong and one of us dies? What if we've got the wrong *year*?'

'You're panicking, we're not going to die, I'm a hundred percent on the date, and no one knew you back home anyway' said Illawara, flicking her wrist at the bird, 'how's this any different? I'm the only one that can hear and understand you - anyone that's met you just assumes you're my pet.' Hermes hovered for a moment before he flew from side to side in the air,

'True, but not the point' he argued, 'because now you say you can't even be sure the Professor will be there.'

'You sound like an old woman' said Illawara, swiping her hand through the air. Hermes flashed green in the twilight.

'If you ask me I think you've acted like a reckless fool' exclaimed Hermes. Illawara's cheeks started to burn.

'You know what it took for us to get here' she said pointing at Hermes, 'and what I did to make it happen - but you still came, and I'm not asking you anything, but I know for sure when someone's acting like a coward.' The little bird seemed to shrivel with the insult, and Illawara noticed his eyes glaze over before he flew down to a tombstone and turned his head away from her. Hermes tried hard not to let his body shake. Illawara looked at him and gnawed at her lip before she put her hands on her head.

'You should never call me that' said Hermes, 'my coming here took more courage than you could ever know, and more than I can ever tell you' he whispered. Illawara swallowed – her tan turning pink. A silence fell between them while contemplating their new reality. With an extended sigh, Illawara spoke first:

'Look, Hermes, I'm sorry, I shouldn't have said that. I know this is a bit... "up in the air", but I'll find Dad, bring him back, and it will be over - *simple*' she said. Illawara walked over to where Hermes sat, her skirts brushing the ground. 'But think' she continued, 'this could also be fun. Just imagine when we get to the banquet and all the things that'll be there. Think of the food, the drink, the music, and the *people*' Illawara swayed herself from side to side as if moving to music, 'we're tasting history, Hermes, literally tasting HISTORY. We'll know how things really were and are first hand. We'll get to see Galileo's demonstrations of science - live, Maffeo Barberini, and the Medici up close: the real people at Duke Cosimo's party. Who else from our time can ever say that?' said Illawara with her arms outstretched, before cupping her hand to her ear, 'no one' she added, 'is that not worth the effort alone? A chance to experience the impossible.' Illawara flung her arms wide, turned, and beamed a smile, 'hello brave new world.'

Hermes shook his head, 'you've watched too many costume dramas. History can be ugly' he said. Illawara's shoulders slumped, before she sighed, and then resumed her search of the courtyard, scanning the ground and peering behind tombs. 'What are you doing?' said Hermes,

'I'm looking for clues' came the reply, 'Dad lead me here, I know him, he would have left me something...' Illawara continued to search the ground and alcoves nearby, her dress rustling as she went. She searched the area for some time. 'Aha! I *knew* it.' She cried after peering behind a stone pillar, crouching down, and yanking up something small from the stone base. A look of triumph flashed over Illawara's face as she held out the small circular object in her palm. 'Look at this' she said.

'It's a coin' said Hermes, after flying to her wrist in a blur, 'that doesn't mean anything.'

'Yes it does, look closer' the bird peered into her palm, 'it was minted in 1997 - the year we first visited Italy. Dad is HERE Hermes, and he's left this coin to prove it.' Seeing the date on the coin Hermes abandoned his protests.

'OK, you win. But don't get too carried away' said Hermes flicking his crest and puffing out his feathers, 'let's keep calm and stay out of harm's way. Don't say anything radical or risqué.'

'I know my own mind' said Illawara, tossing the coin in her palm.

'Yes, but you forget that I've seen what you're like when entertaining at home - when you start to drink and dance - you forget yourself, and get carried away.' The teenager raised a brow.

'Whatever' said Illawara, rolling her eyes, before tossing the coin the Professor had left behind into her side pouch. 'I know how to conduct myself' she added. Hermes raised his long beak into the air and fixed her with a knowing look. Illawara shrugged off his insinuation.

'That reminds me' chirped Hermes, 'do we still have everything we need and the Mystify? If things go wrong, we may need it - to correct errors.' In a flash of panic, Illawara clutched at herself for her satchel and became reassured when it was still there. Hermes resisted the urge to shake his head, pretending not to notice, and continued with what he was saying: 'I want to see the bottle.'

'Oh for HEAVEN'S SAKE, I packed it earlier, don't you trust me?' she said, before plonking her satchel on a sarcophagus and rummaging through her bag. Illawara pulled out the Pineapple to aid her search.

'Why have you brought that?' Hermes said, his beak dropping open.

'Wait... *wait*' said Illawara raising her finger, 'listen to my logic' she composed herself, 'it's here to impress or bribe people' she added. Hermes raised his crest. 'Look, if all else fails, and we can't get into the party, with this Pineapple we can convince others that we're nobles - people of high standing - being able to afford such things from "The New World" it will prevent awkward questions' she enthused. 'It's like a Pineapple-key, and all barriers shall fall away from us in awe.' She added with a stage like gesture.

'You're crazy' said Hermes, 'it's just a fruit, they litter the ground back home.' Illawara rolled her eyes.

'But only the richest can afford them HERE, Dodo, trust me they'll become very excited: how many people would have seen, let alone tasted such fruit in person? The smell alone will intoxicate them.' Illawara then wafted the pineapple in the air so that Hermes could sniff the fruit's pungent aroma - its sweet juice so familiar to him. 'I'll say it's a present for Cosimo Medici, and I'll insist we give him the present ourselves' Hermes pondered her with a quizzical look, as if his life were in the hands of prank salesman, while she rattled through the satchel. 'Aha, it's here, and all the other stuff. Happy now?' Illawara dangled a tasselled perfume bottle in the air, containing a glowing pink liquid. Hermes looked relieved.

'Good, we can spray a bit around if one of us messes up. Could be dangerous if people remember what we said if we forget ourselves.' Hermes let his sentence linger in the air, as Illawara picked Hermes up to put him down next to her and nodded her agreement.

'Too right' she said, 'without Dad's stuff we'd be screwed.' Hermes tutted again at Illawara's language.

'He didn't do it all on his own' scoffed Hermes, 'you helped him too - give yourself some credit' he said calling up from the floor,

'I didn't do everything, Hermes, he did most of the work – and then hid the rest from me' she breathed, 'but without this stuff, I'd be more worried.' Illawara slipped into silence as she looked off into the distance beyond the walls of the Camposanto.

Illawara had regained a deeper understanding of Professor Sloane's chemical research in previous years after decoding his notes. She recalled years as a small girl helping him take cuttings and samples of medicinal plants, and cataloguing their characteristics and active compounds: he praising her inquisitive contributions. Iona would end a telephone conversation and go quiet whenever they entered the room. She did not know what that meant then: she was too young. Illawara found some of the newer data contained within his coded research almost incomprehensible.

She discovered strange alchemical charts and allusions documenting plants and ingredients that she had not heard of before - but which fascinated her. She learned for certain, however, that the Professor had perfected every recipe for alteration that he could find: from the ancient to the classical world. To perfect his new disciplines, he had read everything relevant up to the 20th century including Tribal Lore. The Professor either bought or crafted all the kit he needed for his laboratory: blending his gift for maths and physics with his newer skills of chemistry and botany. He had raided every Botanical library or museum archive that granted him access, and few sources lay untouched in his search for knowledge. Illawara found his scope breath taking.

Turkey yielded some of his richest finds. His notes were littered with Anatolian references and indicated that he had managed to improve upon original recipes in most cases - increasing their potency, and documenting his discoveries – and changed objects and living things from one thing into another.

Illawara read from the dated entries that many of the herbs, medicinal barks, resins, alloys and animal ingredients had taken him years to collect - often harvested, on forays, when she had been away at school. Iona his unwilling accomplice. Illawara had noticed with increasing concern as she progressed through the Professor's research, that he had come close to and then crossed the line between the rational sciences and the esoteric. His notes as she read on became ever more strange and disoriented.

Images once delicately drawn with pencil and ink, then evolved into nightmares scrawled with paint and then with blood, as his experiments progressed from Alchemy into Witchcraft.

Iona had told her, when he left for longer periods, that he had been away on business or visiting other Professors or Universities. In time, she had learned the truth. Illawara still gazed off into the distance as she pondered the things she had learned. 'Have you ever thought of making some of the potions yourself, Illy?' Hermes asked. Illawara frowned, before putting the Mystify back into the satchel.

'At times, maybe' she shrugged, 'I could release the research and claim Molecular Bionics for myself - if I wanted - I know enough' Illawara gave out a long breath, 'but I couldn't do that. *NO*, I want us all to go back, I'll have Prom, he'll sign the papers, and then I'll release my research with Dad's. I've so much to show him. I've made so much progress.' She smiled somewhat at the idea. 'We'd win the Nobel Prize with just ten percent of it' she mused, 'honestly, *we would*" she added as if Hermes did not believe her. She chewed at her fingernail, 'but the price, Hermes, the price.' Illawara smoothed her hair - her diamond glittering at her brow. 'I guess that a lot of people and other things must have died to make all of this stuff, and everything else he created...' Illawara reflected.

'Shall we go back home then?' said Hermes.

'Of course not' snorted Illawara, 'life goes on: since when has politeness long prevented progress?' She shook her head, and breathed in the cooling air of Pisa, 'no, it's over now. He did what he did, and I've done what I've done, and nothing can change that.' Illawara cleared her throat, but took in another deep breath before she stood tall. 'Which reminds me' she said creeping into a smile as she looked at Hermes, 'I need to be a good friend and honour my bargain. It's time we got you changed' she said, 'besides if I'm caught talking to a bird, I'll burn as a witch.' Illawara laughed, at once full of cheer.

Hermes hesitated, looking concerned, before hopping and fidgeting about on the ground. He had anticipated this moment for years with excitement and quiet dread - 'C'mon dear don't dawdle' said Illawara, sounding like a Cockney governess, 'let's see wha' ya look like under *aawl* them fe'vers' she added as if she were a street character from Oliver Twist. Hermes shuffled around.

'Well... Where should I stand?' he said before Illawara snapped out of character.

'I'll put you over there on the floor; looks like this stone won't crack from the heat of the changes.' Hermes bulged his eyes but gave a small nod in resignation as Illawara scooped him up to put him down again with care in front of her, after stepping to a wider expanse of stone flooring. Hermes did his best to stir courage within himself.

'I've spent so many years like this, Illy' Hermes paced on the spot, 'I'm not even sure if I can remember what I looked like?' Hermes looked down at himself, 'to become human again - what if I don't like it? What if I don't like myself?' Hermes added before jumping up to hover above the ground in rapid circles, as Illawara checked the slab of stone again for cracks. Illawara took the fruit juice out of her satchel and offered some of it to Hermes to give him energy, before finishing the rest herself. Illawara clapped her hands together, 'well, there's only one way to find out. You've said for years that this is what you wanted. Now stop flapping and rest on that stone.' She said. Hermes obeyed her but did not stop talking.

'I'll be able to eat and chew again' he said with excitement, 'and use my hands to eat solid food, break my own bread - pick my nose even' Illawara giggled.

'I'm curious to see what you look like - I'll still love you, but I'll be disappointed if you're ugly...' She said. Hermes beak dropped open. His feathers stood on end.

'I doubt that...' He guffawed. Illawara raised her finger,

'A quick question, I hope you don't mind, but I've always wanted to ask you: how did it feel the first time you were changed? Why and when did it happen?' Hermes froze and seemed to gasp for air.

'I, I...' He tried his best to speak, but he couldn't get the words out, as a flash of painful cramp darted through his stomach, he tried to conceal it, but Illawara winced in sensing his pain. In a rush, she crouched next to him.

'Hush... it's ok Hermes, its ok, I shouldn't have asked: that was selfish of me. I know you can't tell me yet what happened to you.' she bent down and stroked the crest on his head. 'But one day I'll learn of it, I promise.' Hermes nodded. Her words encouraged him.

'Ok, let's get this over with' said Hermes, able to speak again. Illawara clapped her hands again with glee, before reaching down to rummage in her bag for the little glowing bottle of Transformation Tincture. She gave the phial a shake to enliven its formula, which coiled and twisted like a blue storm behind the glass.

'Are you concentrating Hermes?' He nodded, 'try and remember yourself as you were before.'

'Yes, yes, I'm concentrating, Illy. Let's hurry up it's getting cold around here.' He said, calling up from the rapidly cooling floors. With great care, Illawara began to unscrew the lid off the tincture. A wisp of gas escaped from the phial as the seal opened, and curls of cold blue fire began to ripple around the edge of the bottle, as Illawara began to expose its dropper. Crouching to aim above Hermes, Illawara pressed on the rubber of the dropper to allow three fire-like drips to fall on Hermes' head and body. Hermes flinched. 'Keep still' Illawara cautioned, as the drops spread across him, until his entire body became encased in the gentle lapping of blue flames. When done so Illawara stood back with a grand gesture before she uttered the words she had practiced:

> 'What has passed shall come again,
> What is forgotten shall be remembered.
> Unjust be the form this body maintains,
> So be this curse dismembered.'

With a rush, the blue flames leapt up, and Illawara stood back as Hermes began to crackle like a firework. His short legs began to lengthen at speed: his petite wings began to stretch out into arms, and his primary feathers became fingers, while his long beak shortened into a fine nose. From the little bird emerged healthy bones, and new flesh could be seen manifesting through the shimmer of the blue flames. The curve of a neck, the arch of a spine, sculpting and forming as his sinews reshaped and knitted together, and ran in rivulets across the emerging body, as his ribcage, acting like a loom, gathered the loose threads of his flesh.

Eventually, any remaining feathers were pulled within and absorbed by a rich brown human skin. Hermes' little crest of feathers, so familiar to her, unfurled and spread across his scalp to become a thick mass of dark curly hair, as before Illawara's eyes Hermes transformed back into a handsome youth. After the last of the flames had subsided, Hermes clutched at himself with embarrassment, trying to protect his modesty at finding himself naked in front of Illawara. She stood open mouthed at the manifestation before her - vapour lifted from Hermes' skin as he shivered in the chilling air.

'OH, MY, GOD' she exclaimed, 'so this is what you *look* like. Not what I imagined at all' she said, as Hermes glanced down at himself like a stranger. 'My goodness' said Illawara gawking as she walked around her friend, 'you're a *real* person...' She then corrected herself 'I mean, I've always known... it's just I couldn't imagine you like...' Hermes clutched at himself to try and avoid her gaze. 'Let me look at you' she said in half shock, and half giggle, her hand over her mouth. Hermes stood un-amused.

'I will not. Are you trying to flirt with me?' Illawara almost screamed with surprise, stifling the sound by cupping her mouth with her other hand.

'Your voice is SO different... I'm going to have to get used to it.' Wide-eyed, Illawara shook her head in disbelief, 'well, you're definitely *not* ugly.' Hermes clutched at his nakedness

'Stop staring at me. You're acting like that Trucker. You should be ashamed of yourself with your gawping.' Illawara frowned and crossed her arms.

'Oh c'mon – how could you say that? That's cruel, *please*' Illawara scowled, ogling, before giving out a wobbly whistle with he hands braced on her hips, 'seems like the bird has become a cat' She purred before sweeping away, 'besides, can you blame me for staring? I've had no idea of what you looked like before' she said before tossing her side pouch behind her, 'you can cover your modesty with that.'

'You've nothing else?' said Hermes, 'this not funny, Illy, I'm standing naked here'

'I know' Illawara said still turned away, 'have you covered yourself yet?' Hermes snatched up the side pouch from the floor and held it to his groin.

'Yes, but do I have any clothes? Did you bring anything?' he said, almost tumbling to the floor from dizziness and exposing yet more of himself.

'I didn't pack any' said Illawara turning around, half shielding her eyes.

'*What?* No clothes? You're joking?' Illawara shook her head.

'I don't remember you asking for those'

'Oh, that's just typical of you.' Hermes raised his voice, 'do you expect me to go to the Medici's party naked? You're totally irresponsible' he huffed, 'we've travelled here through hundreds of years in time, and you can remember to bring a pineapple but not trousers or UNDERPANTS.'

'There are no trousers or underpants here in these times - even you should know that. But you may not need to wear very much after all?' she declared.

'Why not?' asked Hermes,

'Because I'm thinking of taking you as my Moorish manservant.' Hermes stood incredulous as his jaw dropped open, 'all the rage right now' she added with a casual air. Hermes scowled.

'Illy, *really?* Sometimes you're too much, just too much. You go too far with things. I'm not going to be paraded like some seventeenth century, Tarzan. If you're going down that route, you're on your own.'

'Oh Stop your whining' she said with a swipe through the air, 'you said I was acting like that *Trucker* – or whatever he was: seems like you've lost your sense of humour along with your feathers' she said, but with Hermes' evident anger Illawara could see that she had taken her joke far enough. 'It will be fine once I've figured out the best way to dress you.' Illawara scanned the courtyard with her eyes, 'but don't fret the tincture will sort it... Besides, can't a girl enjoy herself?'

'*NO*' said Hermes as he knitted his brows in disapproval.

'You're not my type anyway' she added with a throwaway air. Hermes seemed unconvinced. But while Hermes observed Illawara peep around the enclosure he began to reflect and soften in his private opinion. She had made a huge sacrifice for them to be there. Hermes' humanity would return to him in fits and starts. Illawara then saw something before she clicked her fingers, like a magician, and then rubbed her hands together before she declared with bravado: 'OK, it's time to go shopping.'

'She's crazy' Hermes whispered to himself.

'Hermes, my friend, watch and learn, watch and learn...' added Illawara, as if in the character of a travelling showman. Helpless, Hermes shook his head with woe and tried to ignore the chill that crept across his buttocks. With nonchalant leisure, Illawara strode into the green enclosure, at the middle of the cemetery, where some wild roses were climbing their way up one of the side walls of the Camposanto. She plucked one of the yellow-pink flowers, a sprig of leaves and three of its thorns. She then half skipped back to place them in a small pile on the scorched stone that Hermes had vacated to shelter in an alcove. Illawara used the tincture again, allowing three drops to consume the flower and its parts before uttering:

'For what is leaf be woven grained,

For what is flower be fabric tamed,
And from its pollen, our money gained.
In rosy thorn - thy find thy scabbard,
In rosy boots - thy stride maintained.'

In an instant, the flames rose again as the tincture got to work on the rose and its parts. The petals of the flower began to stretch and then billow out, and to turn themselves into a wide sleeved silken shirt: yellow on the body, and then graduating to a blush on the cuffs and collars.

The leaves, and then the veins of the plant began to break off here and there, and to twist themselves into elegant brocade that entwined at the cuffs and collar, before stitching and fixing in the present centuries' style. The yellow pollen and stamens at the centre of the flower, swelled like seeds, to burst open into coins of Tuscan Scudo. The remaining leaves twisted and wove themselves into differing items: a fine green coat, followed by a cape, a hat, a waistcoat, stockings, and breeches, all with similar trimmings to the shirt. A pair of the thorns became two fine red boots, the third a handsome dagger and scabbard.

With the work completed Illawara shook the items out in the fading light and the garments gave off a heady scent of wild rose, which filled the air before passing. She took up the dagger, and with a grand gesture unsheathed it from its scabbard - the high-pitched sound the metal gave out seem to shatter from the walls in tiny pieces. Glowing red reflections shone up and down the steel in the twilight as she inspected it. Illawara found a drying stem to drop upon the blade and posed satisfied when it fell sliced in half. Hermes looked on agog.

'I take back what I said - wow, when did you learn to do all this?' he added, but she gave a wry smile and remained silent. 'I'm impressed'. Illawara nodded and tried not to look too smug.

'I know my plants, remember... it took lots of patience and practice, but they can teach you their secrets - if you take care of them.'

Contented with her work she turned away from Hermes and smiled to herself: 'try on your things' she said before returning the blade to its scabbard. Illawara turned away before Hermes dashed from the alcove to snatch up the clothes and try on his new attire.

They fitted him perfectly. Once changed, and without a mirror to check himself, he allowed Illawara to make any required adjustments before subjecting himself to opinion. Standing back in his fine boots with his arms outstretched he asked:

'How do I look?' Illawara paused and tried to be objective in assessing him.

'You look like a handsome nobleman, and one fit to grace any Medici gathering.' Hermes grinned, the first she had ever seen of his, his smile as natural as the Moon. Illawara rubbed her eyebrow, 'I hope I've not overdone it with the clothes? You're very... colourful' She said tilting her head, 'I think we'll get tongues wagging. I'd say we're just ahead of the times, which isn't a bad thing I suppose.' Hermes could not help but respond to her praise. She watched his shoulders arch back, and his chin rise. With her main tasks achieved, Illawara removed the diamond from her brow to adjust the gem's strapping and attached it to her neck to wear the jewel as a spectacular choker. As if looking at a mirror, she adjusted her hair, making sure her dark silky locks lay untangled upon her high-embroidered collar. Cupping her hands, she then tweaked her bodice under her bust to pull herself up, and with a swish, she then straightened her skirts. Illawara didn't need to ask Hermes how she looked - she shone.

Confident that things were correct and everything in place, the pair chatted, reviewing, complementing and renewing their friendship in its changing nature - before remembering to take a dose of the Forked Tongue potion that Illawara had also packed in the bag. They took it in turns to place a few drops of the tincture on their tongues, and then swirl the liquid in their mouths. Their faces contorted to start with in taking the liquid, as the bitterness of the Forked Tongue tasted almost unbearable. They both shook their heads in a fit of discomfort at the flavour.

But with time the mixture began to sweeten like honey as menthol vapour began to infuse their faces, and escape from their noses and ears. As the powerful concoction began to take effect, their confidence increased as their pallets arched and relaxed. The pair both gained a lucid sense of knowledge; knowing they could understand and answer Italian with clarity, and seemed to leech their knowledge from the very stones that surrounded them - stones that had absorbed conversations over so many years.

With the unpleasant sensations over, Illawara and Hermes then readied themselves. With hasty practice the pair began to test each other: setting forward wild riddles, playing 'I Spy' and singing bits of David Bowie songs to each other in Italian. They cackled with glee, as the Italian language bounced out of them like bubbles of Prosecco. Satisfied they were fluent, the proud pair, with Hermes holding Illawara's arm for balance, swaggered to the other side of the garden to make a discreet exit from the Camposanto. Few people were around as they strolled past the leaning tower of Pisa, and left the hallowed square via one of its side entrances. For a while at least, Hermes forgot his prior concerns and revelled in being human again - free, in part, from the curse that had bound him.

In the deepening dusk, they both walked down Via Santa Maria, past some of the inns, taverns and Trattorias in search of a meal: Hermes grumbled that he had not eaten solid food in years, and Illawara also felt hungry. The locals of Pisa busied themselves either closing their stalls and shops or lighting candles inside to get their businesses ready for evening trade. The pair walked the streets – with Illawara supporting Hermes - while collections of small golden flames began to flicker behind the street windows: illuminating their path and flattering their grandeur.

Carriages, Carts, and wheelbarrows abounded, as the evening progressed, while local people mingled about the streets surrounding the Campo dei Miracoli. In the hubbub of activity, the pair spoke quietly to one another as they took in the look of the people of the times, and the people themselves looked back and muttered. Some looked on with discreet curiosity, others with necks craned in surprise at seeing such fine and well-dressed people walking around. Most onlookers took the pair for a wealthy foreign merchant with his splendid wife. Others just took them for a pair of attention seekers wandering through town: strange as they were.

After a short time, the pair found a Trattoria they liked. So Illawara and Hermes sat down and ordered some of the region's good local wine, to celebrate, and a mediocre pizza: it arrived without cheese. Illawara pulled a face. Hermes struggled to sit still, almost overwhelmed by old and new feelings that responded to the stimuli around him. Hermes wiggled his fingers in anticipation. In defiance of convention, Illawara ordered an egg of mozzarella cheese, before tearing it up and scattering it over the hot bread and topping, and had it baked again till the cheese melted. Some people on other tables nearby gossiped and took Illawara for a madwoman as the pair tucked into their new pizza. Another guest, however, impressed by Illawara's tastes and finery quietly ordered herself some of the said cheese and had her pizza done the same.

Hermes didn't care about the glances. He just marvelled in the sensation of eating solid food again - almost forgetting how to chew - he could not remember the last time he had eaten in that way. Illawara cut Hermes' pizza for him – he not knowing yet how to handle utensils. Illawara forgave her friend's table manners, while she looked at Hermes as he grappled with his pizza as if it were a live octopus. He slurped, chewed and mewed at the sensations of eating – like a baby trying solids for the first time.

'How can anyone have a pizza without cheese?' Illawara bristled, between lady-like mouthfuls, 'it's such a classic combination' she said before reaching for the salt,

'Keep your voice down and just be grateful Illy' Hermes whispered, between munches, before wiping sauce from his chin, 'you said yourself that things would be different here, we're not in America now – we're not in Pizza Hut.' Illawara shrugged,

'I know, but I forgot about the cheese' she tittered, as a man ambled by, declaring his goods to help sell his trinkets. She shook her head. 'But look' she whispered, 'it's already a tourist trap around here.'

'I think the food is *delicious*' said Hermes. Illawara paused her chewing to eyeball her friend, before her expression softened.

'And what would you know? You've only *seen* me eat pizza' said Illawara, reflecting on Hermes words with nonchalance, 'before today all you ate was juice and sugar syrup. Your pallet is starved. I bet if I'd sprinkled salt on a cow pat you'd think it'll taste good.'

Hermes chuckled and then threw his head back and laughed, which further liberated his voice from the squeak of its previous form. His voice continued to broaden and mellow out. The other diners looked on as the pair chatted, joked, bickered and speculated, lost in their quipping, as they, in innocence, provided others with entertainment and contemplation. No one had seen such a couple of characters, like them, in town for some time.

■ ■ ■

The meal they started ended somewhat scoffed and hurried, realising the time as they sampled their desert, as it would take the best part of a day for them to reach Florence by carriage. Over the evening, and many glasses of wine, the pair had discussed an overnight stay at a tavern along the way, as Illawara, with discretion, consulted a photocopy of an old map. Illawara was only part satisfied with the meal, but she joined Hermes in praise of the vintage. Hermes who was accustomed to drinking nectar for so many years complained the wine burned his throat, like fire, but did not refuse his refills. The contents of almost two bottles of wine found a home in their stomachs. The pair paid up, with Illawara's manufactured coins, and left, light headed, before attempting to flag down a carriage. After a few frustrated attempts to flag carriages down - which all seemed to be full or unwilling to stop - much bickering ensued between the pair at the roadside, as Illawara struggled to remember the proper custom to go about such things.

'Sweet Lord, this is a nightmare!' Illawara declared with a flap of her arms and wobbling on her feet, 'we're never going to get to Florence at this rate. We'll have to walk for it.'

'Have you lost your mind?' said Hermes, trying to concentrate on keeping his balance on Illawara's arm, 'I'm just getting used to walking again' Hermes hickuped, 'you said Florence is over forty miles away from here. What state do you think we'll be in by the time we get there?' He belched, 'not fit for a Medici party I know that much.' Hermes then began to cackle to himself quite amused at his observation. Illawara formulated her response as the full effects of the wine took hold of her upon exposure to the freshening air.

'It doesn't matter what state we arrive in; I could make us some brand-new clothes with the tincture, silly.'

'Where?' said Hermes leaning into Illawara, as if half his blood were red wine, 'would you be turning leaves into piles of clothes at the roadside? We'd both be burning on stakes in the town square before you could say Shish Kebab - you, you...' Hermes then laughed again, tottering, as he groped for words, and began to enjoy the effect the wine had upon him - allowing him to feel like a youth once more.

'HA' said Illawara, gulping at the air and holding her sides as the sound of a carriage approached. But before she could formulate a reply the speeding Carriage, being pulled along by four horses, had scattered a collection of geese pecking at the ground as their owner walked them home from the market. The old man set forth a spirited torrent of imaginative abuse at the surprise, while his geese shrieked as they dispersed, only to quiet himself when he saw the imposing wealth of his disturber.

The coach then clattered to a juddering halt next to the pair where they stood. The elegant four-seated carriage with large 'U' springs looked attractive in its dusty yellow livery. The horse's shiny bridles jangled like cow bells in the early night, out chiming the honks of the agitated geese in the distance. The coach driver sat illuminated by the orange light of the coach-lamps after bringing the vehicle to a standstill to obey a prompt from the passenger inside. The window glass of the carriage opened, and a gloved hand beckoned them to come closer. Illawara and Hermes forgot their bickering but then muttered to each other in Italian for some time, exchanging gestures with one another, and whispering, before they moved with care in the direction of the alighted carriage. Upon getting closer to the vehicle, a refined voice called to them from inside,

'Do you speak English?' said the voice. The perplexed pair made eyes at each other before they nodded. 'Where are you going?'

'To the Uffizi' Illawara inflected in an Italian accent - with her native English then becoming somewhat awkward in her mouth.

'Good, I thought so - that's where I'm also going', came the jovial reply.

Illawara and Hermes, quite drunk, whispered to each other again, eyeing the carriage before they looked at the gathering darkness around them. After more glances around and muttering they shrugged at each other, and then resigned themselves with upturned hands. The inhabitant of the carriage bid his footman stationed at the back of the vehicle, to welcome his new guests into the coach. The footman looked immaculate dressed in his pale blue uniform as he skipped down to open the carriage door, and unfolded velvet-padded steps, concealed within, that matched the coach's soft blue interiors. The pair, both a somewhat unsteady on their feet, were granted access. First Illawara and then Hermes teetered in assisted with confidence by the footman into their seats, as orders were then given to continue to Florence. The pair, still marvelling at their good fortune, had realised that they would be in the company of two distinguished guests: as the carriage made its way through the night like a pale-yellow moth.

Chapter 6

The Strangers

The Road to Florence

Within the carriage, Illawara and Hermes discovered that they would be sharing their journey with not one, but two people; both were men and seemed to be in their late twenties. Sitting opposite Illawara, and to the right, sat the man that gave the command to stop the carriage. His apparent youth struck in contrast to the plush, and mellow tone of the voice that had greeted them. He wore a small powdered wig that complemented his face well, but his nose, protruding with a hump and ending with a curve, dominated his face and gave the impression of being held up in the air. Illawara noted that his taste could not be faulted, and admired his tailored clothes that hugged his physique.

'Allow me to introduce my Valet, Antonio' he said, in English, gesturing to the man that sat next to him with a waft of his hand. 'I'm Edward de Vere...' he added, and then went on to announce himself as an English aristocrat: The Seventeenth Earl of Oxford. The Earl spoke with as little fuss as if announcing teatime. Illawara arched her back and tried not to look impressed as if she expected the man's announcement. Casual and breezy, with the turn of his wrist he informed Illawara and Hermes, after they introduced themselves, that he had decided to take himself on a Grand Tour of Italy. Illawara then saw coats of arms, stately homes, and moonlit rides on horseback next to the Earl in her mind's eye: but drew a blank on references to Earls of Oxford. She struggled to keep her face vacant as her eyes and mind searched him for clues.

The Valet Antonio, also well dressed, held himself back, chin lifted, with his hands cupped in his lap: unable to avoid the yawning legs akimbo of the Earl, who's knee batted his as the coach moved along. His head lay uncovered, which showed how his blond hair entwined with itself - reflecting the lamplight. Illawara - quite drunk - resisted an unexpected urge to stand up and ruffle his golden locks.

But if the Valet's body remained stiff, then all life lived in his eyes. Like two blue thunderbolts, Antonio's look had fixed the pair as they entered, assessing them: inspecting Hermes and Illawara as if the pair lay sandwiched between sheets of glass. It seemed to him the couple looked almost too grand. Illawara and Hermes also sat with their hands in their laps and tried to avoid the Valet's gaze. But the Earl, in his way, sensing tension, did his best to put his new guests at ease in his company. Illawara avoided Antonio and focused her attentions on the Earl when he addressed her:

'So, fine Lady...' the Earl said in English again, then paused, before changing into heavily accented Italian, 'if I may address you as Lady?' Illawara nodded that he may. Hermes almost smirked with wry surprise at the new Illawara emerging. He looked out of the window to keep his face straight. 'What business takes you to Florence and the Uffizi?' The Earl enquired continuing in Italian.

'Well, I assumed you had guessed my business already?' she said. The Earl acknowledged the remark, despite her not answering his question.

'Well, seeing a pair so finely dressed on the first of October, one could assume that you're both to be guests of the Medici?' he added, 'there is no other gathering of such merit in Florence, and I doubt you're both going there for cock fights and dancing bears' Illawara lifted her nose, and stretched out her neck before responding,

'You assume correctly, as we are indeed to be guests of the Medici' she paused to glance at Hermes, eyes unfocused, her diamond choker catching the light, 'we have a friend of ours who is part of the Medici court' she added. Illawara put out her hand to steady herself. Hermes shifted in his seat and glanced at Antonio, who continued to scrutinise the pair. The Earl nodded before pausing. The insincerity of the statement seemed to register with more with Antonio, however, whose eyes flashed in the candlelight.

'Is that so?' the Earl continued 'I also have some friends there, who are very close to the Duke.' Hermes swallowed, and clenched his fingers, anticipating the Earl asking who their friend was, and if the fictitious person had any relationship with his contacts. 'So what is the name of your friend at court?' the Earl asked in innocence. A bead of sweat began to form on Hermes' forehead. He waited for Illawara to reply as adrenalin rippled through his body. Illawara, misty eyed, smiled at the Earl.

'He's called Rodrigo Salvatore. He tutored us in English while we grew up in Torino - so now we are fluent in both languages.' Hermes looked as if all breathable air had emptied from the carriage, but Illawara, although tipsy, carried on to deliver her improvisations like an actress. Antonio interjected in a light tenor that cracked his exterior:

'So... a *Spaniard* tutored you in English? How curious.' Illawara didn't flinch, and answered Antonio in his native tongue,

'Yes, it is, but only his father was Spanish – a carpenter - his mother was Italian, and from Torino. Like me, he grew up there. He travelled across Europe frequently, and also spoke French and German.' The Earl looked impressed. Hermes then pulled down the door window to let in more air: whistling the breeze into his nostrils as Illawara's yarn spun forth. Antonio's eyes narrowed as he listened to Illawara, his gaze then flicking to Hermes while he formulated a response. Hermes beat him to it.

'So have you both travelled all this way for an audience with the Duke of Tuscany?' interjected Hermes in English, somewhat revived, but still fuzzy headed.

'Well yes, I'd say that's obvious' answered the Earl looking unsure for a split second, 'Haven't you?' Hermes and Illawara hesitated, and the Valet's eyes narrowed again.

'Yes of course. We seek an audience with The Duke, as you wish to, but also with our friend and tutor - there's much we want to ask him' said Illawara, trying to stay upright.

'I see, good, good' said the Earl rocking with the movement of the carriage. 'I've heard Duke's an excellent fellow, and the finest amongst men - so I'm told - and as for your tutor I look forward to meeting him.' Illawara hesitated, and Hermes sensed that she wished to say more. Illawara wrung her hands for a moment in her lap, before glancing at Hermes.

'But we also seek words with a very eminent professor', she added, unable to hold back. Hermes twitched in his seat. The Earl leant forward to listen to her. Illawara's neck grew hot.

'So you seek an audience with Galileo?' said the Earl, before raising a gloved hand to the side of his mouth, 'it's rumoured that the great man is to be guest of honour at the gathering tomorrow' the Earl added in a stage whisper.

'Oh yes, we'd love to meet him too' she said,

'So there's *another* professor you know attending? You seem to have remarkable *connections*' said Antonio. Illawara hesitated and forced a smile,

'Oh, it's nothing really, just someone that once tutored us...' Illawara then trailed off. The Earl and Antonio seemed intrigued, as Hermes made eyes at Illawara for her frankness. A smile crept across the Earl's face.

'So you were also tutored by a professor you say? What an education you've both had - I'm impressed, and what a curious pair you both are.' The Earl rubbed his chin.

'So you were both raised together in Torino, and seek not only your former language tutor but *two* professors at the gathering?' The Valet said. Antonio peered at them both like a falcon: noting the clear differences between the pair. Hermes seemed to read the Valet's mind.

'We were not quite raised together, but we're cousins. I lived nearby.' Hermes interrupted to try to add plausibility to Illawara's statement. Illawara gave Hermes a side look.

'Only cousins? I thought you were brother and sister' the Valet chortled, 'my, my, it's quite something to be in the presence of two such curious, educated, well connected, individuals - you'll both be a triumph at court I'm sure' Antonio mewed, with some irony, as the pair fidgeted like children. The Earl and Antonio then exchanged glances with one another. The Earl could have spared them discomfort by changing his line of questioning but saw the sport as too good, so he decided to continue.

'So this professor that you seek' he said sliding into a smile, 'what are his powers of thought? And is he more eminent than the great learned Galileo? Can he describe the heavens and the motion of the stars?' The Earl accompanied his remark with an extravagant gesture to the ceiling of the carriage, as Hermes and

Illawara looked perplexed at such questioning: both caught short and unprepared.

The pair sank back into the cushioned chair of the carriage, like freshly laid dung steaming in the frosty air. Neither Illawara or Hermes could sit still, as they fielded questions directed at them by their hosts more numerous than flies. The pair struggled, as both were sucked dry of inspiration; their sobering minds chilling to crusts as the questioning continued. The pair glanced out their windows as if seeking escape, the moonlit Tuscan countryside rolling by, as the carriage rattled toward its destination. Illawara tried to assess their speed and pondered how harmed she would be if she leapt from the carriage before she composed herself.

After a long pause, she chose to gamble with some truth. 'Well, it could be argued that our professor is excellent indeed' she replied to the Earl, who would not stop pestering her with enquiries about her father. 'He doesn't yet have the fame that the great Galileo enjoys, but he's no less significant in his way - someday, with help from his friends' said Illawara turning to Hermes, 'he'll be one of the most famous men in history.'

'He sounds like a fascinating man' added the Earl; eager to hear more, 'is he also Italian?'

'No, he's an Englishman like yourself. He went to Oxford' Illawara declared, throwing caution out the window instead of herself. Hermes held his breath.

'So you must have really learned English from him then?' said Antonio. But the Earl raised his hand.

'A man from my country no less' the Earl hesitated, 'as one would imagine, I went to Oxford too. What's his name pray tell?' Illawara had reasoned the Earl could never have met the Professor at Oxford, with another side glance, it seemed like Hermes had reached the same conclusion.

'He's called Professor Winston Sloane.' Just saying his name seemed to cast a spell upon both men, and, at last, it seemed the Earl had drawn a blank. He sat still for a moment to ponder. Illawara and Hermes held their breath.

'Never heard of him' the Earl said, 'must have been before my time?' The fraudulent pair both smiled,

'Yes, I suppose it was?' said Illawara, as her shoulders relaxed. No one spoke for a while in the carriage, and its passengers were rocked like babes in a cradle, as the clip-clop of hooves beat out a muddy lullaby on the road to Florence. But the Valet, eyeing Illawara for some time, broke the soothing silence.

'That's quite a gem you have. Is it diamond or glass?' Illawara frowned,

'It's a DIAMOND' she shot back, 'do I look like the type that would go around wearing Glass?' She hissed. Illawara had forgotten she was even wearing the stone; it felt such a part of her. Both men raised their brows at her reply. Illawara mellowed herself, 'it's a *precious* gift to me' she confessed after lowering her voice - surprised by her own ferocity, 'it reminds me of someone' she continued, 'someone important to me.' Illawara rubbed at the stone on her neck that dazzled in the lamp light.

'Is that so?' said the Valet 'who gave it to you? You're a very young woman to be accustomed to such things?'

'What are you implying?' said Illawara, it had never occurred to her that things could be any different. Antonio slid a look to the Earl but said nothing. 'My father gave it to me before he left... not that it's any of your business' she continued, 'and yes, I'm accustomed to it, and I deserve to wear it, is that such a bad thing?' She retorted. Antonio whistled.

'Spoken like a Queen' Antonio said in an extended tone, crossing his legs. Illawara narrowed her eyes, and it seemed the carriage began to darken. The Earl shifted in his seat, and Hermes sat rapt as the air prickled among them. Illawara spoke through clenched teeth, her temper roused, the smell of drink curling from her jaws 'and I *also* call the stone Aphrodite after the Goddess, it's the only name that fits.' The Diamond crackled at the air with its fire as if responding to Illawara's spirit. Antonio folded his arms and held her gaze.

The Earl manufactured a smile: 'and yet she is not as beautiful as her owner' he interjected. A rush of colour leapt to Illawara's face in response to the complement, arching her back as if his words had tickled her spine. Hermes didn't know where to look as the Earl continued, 'I think you'll cause quite a stir at Cosimo's party. Were he not so in love, as I'm reliably informed, I'd be certain you'd turn his head.' Illawara retrieved a lace fan from a concealed pocket in her dress, and unfurled its ivory arms with a snapping flick to cool herself, acting like a Duchess in a period drama. The men noted the effect the complement had had on her, and the Earl smiled to himself. Hermes and Antonio noted her haughty composure.

The complements softened the air in the carriage, and Illawara seemed to surge with confidence. The Earl then changed the subject. Amongst themselves the group spoke in passing the hours, bouncing the conversation between them. Even Antonio began to warm to the pair as Illawara and Hermes as if sharing one mind, relaxing, made up fanciful stories to beguile their hosts. The Earl and his Valet seemed to care less and less if the stories they heard were true or not. The double act started to enjoy themselves - sensing the danger had passed - taking pleasure in their sport, as the tall tales they coined became ever more entertaining.

■ ■ ■

The night sprinted ahead, and amongst themselves, the foursome agreed to find tavern lodgings in San Miniato, as suggested by Antonio who doubled as a tour guide. Hermes and Illawara complied. Everyone arrived at the recommended tavern late in the night. The coach passengers had become weary after the journey, with a change of horses midway, on the long road to the Florentine capital. The carriage taxied into the coach house - plain but neat - so that the animals could be fed and stabled for the night. Antonio made the room reservations.

Illawara and Hermes were to share a double room with two single beds, with the excuse given that as a relative Hermes made a suitable guardian for the single woman. The fiction did little to appease the un-approving eye of the pot-bellied tavern keeper, as he jangled the door keys in his porky hands. He had heard such stories before - none of them true. The Earl and Antonio requested the same type of room, but without objection from the sweating portly man.

A foreign noble on Grand Tour with his guide raised fewer eyebrows than in previous years, and the extra revenue from the new lucrative trade gained a ready welcome. The corpulent innkeeper made a gesture in the direction of the rooms, while his puffy eyes moved with nimble speed over Illawara. She cringed inside and pretended not to notice the ravenous look from the sweating man. The innkeeper then gave Hermes a run over with his shifty eyes: the Moorish occupation of Spain and Sicily still soured in the collective consciousness of the people. But Hermes' European fashion and smooth Italian had confused the man; assuming Hermes to be a wealthy, and swarthy, southerner - ready to enjoy his pretty whore.

After the Earl's luggage had got carried into his booked room, the Earl and Antonio hung back to exchange words with the innkeeper in hushed tones, as Illawara and Hermes were encouraged to move upstairs. Illawara kept her leather bag with her, and Hermes only carried what he wore. Antonio, in whispers, negotiated an exchange before he handed some extra money to the innkeeper.

Hermes and Illawara were then shown to their room by a stout Slavic maid, with rosy cheeks and fair hair, who bustled about with impatience as she lit candles in their bedroom, and fluffed the pillows. Having done her work in haste, she gave a demure curtsy, with eyes downcast, till the domes of her bust swaddled her chin: moving backwards the maid left the room and closed the door. The maid then cocked her head to check the hallway, all clear, before she tiptoed like a hen to follow the Earl and Antonio. No need to chaperone them, as Antonio knew the way. The maid once outside their door had it opened to her after she gave it a girlish tap. The door then closed behind her with a click of the lock.

After the maid had left Hermes and Illawara, both gave out a sigh before flopping onto their creaky beds and chattering away in their new mother tongue.

'What a day Hermes, what a DAY. I can't quite believe we're doing this' Illawara buzzed,

'Me neither - and to be like this' he replied, pointing to himself with pride before he turned his hands and arms in the candle light.

'I feel like I'm in some play at the theatre, except that I don't know my lines' said Illawara, 'but here we can make everything up, no one knows us, we can be whatever we want to be', Illawara chuckled.

'I agree' said Hermes, 'but for me, it feels so new just being myself - getting to know ME again.' But Illawara was not listening to him, she clasped her hands together and wriggled with pleasure.

'You know, I'd be sitting there talking, and then I'd realise where I was, and either want to scream or burst out laughing' she gushed. In truth, she had hidden her pangs of fear to maintain the illusion they were both creating. Hermes watched Illawara's animated gestures, she missing what he had said, and chose instead to join her in revelry.

'What was that stuff you made up about Rodrigo Salvatore? Him being our tutor and us coming from Torino' he said, Illawara gasped and clutched her hand to her chest,

'I know' she crowed, as if full of shame for herself.

'I've never heard you come out with such things before.'

'I don't know where it came from' said Illawara, throwing her head back, 'I just ad-libbed ... the moment just took me, and I went with it.'

Hermes then prodded his bed like a bird inspecting a strange nest, as he contemplated how he would sleep without perching. He scratched and pulled at the bedsheets as if arranging twigs. Illawara lay still to observe him.

'Are you getting ready to lay an egg?' she said, as Hermes fussed with the bed linen. A look of embarrassment then crossed his face when he realised what he was doing. He paused to look at the bed with most of its linen scrunched up.

'I can't remember the last time I slept laying down' said Hermes, under his breath, before he perked up to change the subject. 'You're quite the actress. Where did you get that fan from?'

'*eBay*' declared Illawara, with triumph. Hermes smiled before he fluffed at his pillow and plucked out one of the feathers that had begun to poke out of the fabric. He eyed the feather in silence, turning it in his fingers, and lifted the pillow to feel its weight. He shook his head. But Illawara continued to laugh as she relived her dramatic behaviour. Illawara then speculated on the fortune she could make back home by bringing items back to the future and selling her goods Online or to museums. She kicked her feet in the air as she thought of the potential.

Standing on the bed with his arms outstretched sideways as if to balance, Hermes turned to crouch and ease himself back onto his pillow, and then under the covers. Illawara chatted away, coming up with ever grander schemes for what she believed she could sell when they returned home, but Hermes' mind lay elsewhere. 'Where do you think he's from?'

'Who?' said Illawara, jolted enough to pause her speculations.

'Antonio the Valet, he's quite mysterious, isn't he? Did you notice he said almost nothing about himself for the whole journey?'

'I guess he didn't' said Illawara before she closed her eyes and saw Antonio's golden hair, 'but I tried to avoid looking at him' she waggled her hand, 'he's a bit sharp for me. I forgot to ask what part of Italy he's from.' Hermes gazed up at the ceiling, as he lay still,

'Those eyes, piercing...' said Hermes trailing off. One of Illawara's eyebrows lurched upward.

'Are you ok?' she said,

'Yes, I'm fine, Illy' Hermes coughed, 'it's just strange to have myself and my body back: I've realised there's so much I've forgotten.' Illawara glanced over to where Hermes lay, and he looked as if he inhabited another world. Seeming to float back to himself Hermes continued, though his voice sounded unsteady: 'Illy, I just want to thank you....'

'It's alright... it's been a long, long time hasn't it?' She said, reading his expression, as Hermes failed to wipe away a tear before it caught the candlelight, and tumbled down his face. He nodded in silence, 'I know you can't tell me how things ended up this way' she said in lowered voice, 'but don't worry, I don't have to know. It doesn't matter.'

'But you do Illy. It does matter' Hermes protested, clenching his hand into a fist, 'I wish I could tell you everything every day. You see...' But Hermes let out a pained groan before he could finish, as he felt a grinding nausea roll through him like a millstone, that squashed his insides, and crushed him into his bed.

'Oh, Hermes are you ok?' asked Illawara when she saw the youth curl into himself like a foetus. Her heart knotted with anguish. Hermes rolled from side to side clutching his stomach. 'Please, Hermes stop trying to tell me, it's too painful for you. When we find Dad, I'm sure he'll know a way to break the fix that you're under?' Hermes shook his head as he clutched at his ribs, struggling for breath, and used his face to bury his face into his pillow. He then coughed before he snorted the contents of his runny nose into himself. Illawara observed Hermes with concern: he seeming to her no more than a frightened boy, with the weight of an old life upon his shoulders. She then breached the gap between their beds to embrace Hermes: acting like an older sister trying to comfort him from nightmares.

For some time Illawara soothed him and stroked his forehead, playing with his curly hair that coiled like springs of woollen velvet, until his pain had passed. After a while Illawara decided that they had better get some sleep: so both undressed to their underclothes, and hoped there were no bed bugs before they wished each other goodnight and blew out their candles.

■ ■ ■

Antonio had chosen their tavern well. The sheets were clean, and the beds were soft. Illawara and Hermes, the exhausted pair, became engulfed by sleep as soon as their heads reached their pillows: both lay deaf to the rhythmic creaking of a bed in a room down the hallway.

Chapter 7

A Self Remembered

San Mianato, morning, Sunday October 2nd 1611

Hermes awoke as if reborn from the deepest sleep he had known in years. He looked again at himself with surprise to see his own brown limbs, instead of a tiny body covered with feathers. After rubbing his face, he turned to look at Illawara's bed and found it empty. He pawed and scratched at himself, feeling an urge to preen, before standing up to draw back the shutters, stretch his arms wide, and then look out of the window. The sky had become bright, although streaked with grey clouds that could threaten a shower later in the day. He saw a few leaves blow past in their autumnal colours, reminding him of the changing seasons - in Hawaii he had lived a life that belonged to summer.

Hermes surveyed the neat houses and shops of San Minato: with their terracotta tile roofs, and pastel painted walls before he locked eyes with a housewife across the cobbled street as she stood on her balcony. The forceful woman had begun to beat the dust from her hearthrug with a thick stick. She paused her work to take him in as his skin caught the light. Her gaze gripped him, unwavering, smirking as she arched her body toward his direction, and then continued to beat the dust from the colourful fabric.

A bolt ran through his body, and Hermes looked down at himself and saw that he only wore his stockings, so, with a snap, he looked away and slapped the shutters closed. He shook himself and paused to let his heart stop racing. Next, to his dresser, he found a pail of water, a bar of soap, a cloth, and a washing bowl. He then understood that every day from then on he would have to wash: not preen himself. Cleaning his body with his cloth took some time to remember and master, becoming familiar again with his physique – and the soap, like a fish, slipped his grip many times - but he freshened up and then dressed before making his way downstairs to find Illawara.

The dining area of the tavern already heaved with the bustle of hungry people ready to satisfy their appetites. The maids in their brown wool dresses and white aprons busied themselves by topping up the jugs of water or adding autumn's fresh bounty of fruit to the wooden bowls on the tables. Hermes could decipher from the range of languages spoken, that most guests at the inn were an international crowd. He suspected from some of the fineries on display that more than a few could also be guests at the Grand Duke's party. Two Flemish men, with dark brimmed hats, seemed to be negotiating a deal over some plant bulbs. A German couple, glowing like newlyweds, chatted with one another by a window. They chuckled as they watched a group of nuns, arm in arm huddled like ducks, as they crossed the cobbled street in haste trying to avoid the horses and carts of merchants that clattered about the town.

Hermes found Illawara sharing a breakfast table with the Earl and Antonio. Together they ate some of the local cold meats and salamis with fresh bread - still warm from the community oven. In the centre of their small table sat a large omelette in an earthenware bowl, still hot, while wisps of steam lifted from its surface. The omelette, made in the Tuscan style, lay scattered with shavings of black truffle from the woods on the hills, slicked with vivid green olive oil, and garnished with snowflakes of sea salt. The smell of the food made Hermes' mouth water. Hunger gripped him. He tried not to think of how many eggs had been used to make the meal, and yielded to a desire to eat that verged on the cannibalistic for him.

'So he awakes. Our bronze prince.' Antonio's voice rang out in greeting, as the Valet spied Hermes looking lost from the corner of his eye. Hermes flinched at the greeting and stood rooted to the spot, before attempting a move forward. Antonio had watched the hesitant approach before he got up to embrace Hermes, but the youth stood like a new-born foal and blushed, while Illawara and the Earl cooed over their breakfast.

'Come and sit down' said the Earl, observing the streak of pink that had rushed up Hermes neck, before pulling out a chair. Hermes obeyed, as the maid, who he recognised from last night, brought him a plate and a fork. She clucked and fussed about the table like a yard hen, removing crumbs and topping up the water, while a rosy flush in her own bust grew deeper as she exchanged glances with the Earl. Illawara pretended not to notice, but could not help the twitch of her eyebrow, as she made a start on the omelette.

'You must be starving?' She said to Hermes, 'we've not eaten since we were in Pisa.' After serving Hermes, Illawara began to pile food on her plate.

'Yes, I think I am' said Hermes, in an absent-minded way. The Slavic maid brought another wooden board bedecked with meats as the Earl smiled at her and nodded his satisfaction. Hermes began to sample his food and enjoyed the pungent saltiness of the salami as it raked over his taste buds before he chewed on his bread that he had dunked in vinegar and olive oil.

That day everything seemed different to him: colours looked brighter and more lucid. The clamour of the guests eating and chatting danced in his ears, and the odour of food and people mingled with the rings of church bells outside. Illawara seemed especially fresh and alive, glittering in her attire, as she chatted away to the Earl, and Antonio looked a different man entirely. The Valet sat relaxed and supple as his arm draped over his chair, and his eyes, no longer sharp, seemed to glow like blue topaz in the daylight. The youth caught Antonio looking at him as he drank water from his cup. Hermes felt himself burn again with hunger. Once he had resumed eating solid food, it became less strange as it nourished his human body. In silence, Hermes made a pact, there and then, at the table that he would live his life in every essence of himself.

'Come along' the Earl declared after a while, 'it's time we got going.' The food lay eaten, its remnants stuck to plates and cutlery, before being cleared from the table. The group gathered itself together. The Valet had belongings retrieved from rooms, outstanding bills paid, and warm farewells made. The Earl took his time to thank the portly Innkeeper for his hospitality and friendly staff, and then Antonio for his excellent taste. The maid seemed sorry to see the Earl leave when he passed her, as she lingered in the entrance hall polishing tableware - his smile and brief wave goodbye were a treasure to her. Details seemed to pass in a haze: before Hermes knew it, the rested horses were saddled, the coach driver and footman were in place, and they were all back in the Earl's carriage not more than two hours from Florence.

The ebullient conversation within the carriage rattled along, almost as fast as the horses could pull it. Hermes tossed in a comment when he felt engaged enough to speak, but otherwise occupied himself with the view outside. The Tuscan countryside impressed him with a majestic canvas of autumnal colours, even with some smudges of grey cloud in the sky, yet he began to feel the day had not been as spectacular as when he and Illawara arrived, as his jubilant feelings ebbed. As the carriage sped along the reality of human life seeped back into him. Again, he caught Antonio staring as he turned his head from the window: piqued by a particularly girlish laugh from Illawara, as she tapped the knee of the Earl in response to a joke that he made. The Earl smiled but moved his knee away from her.

'You seem far away', Antonio said to Hermes as he observed him,

'Do I?' he replied, shaking himself to attention.

'Do you find these parts so strange?'

'No, not here in particular' said Hermes with a shrug, 'It's just that life itself can be strange - don't you think?' his sentence paused the other conversation within the carriage.

'It's becoming the fashion for artists abroad to come here and paint the hillsides' said the Earl, trying to maintain the cheerful mood, 'I'm told they come for the light'. Hermes remained blank.

'Are you OK Hermes?' Illawara enquired, leaning forward,

'Yes, I'm fine' came his response, 'I'm just having a think - that's all.' The carriage lurched after hitting a stone on the road, making Illawara tumble into the Earl's lap. They all laughed with embarrassment, the Earl returning Illawara to her seat, but Hermes struggled to ignore the tingle that ran from his leg to his stomach when his knee clashed with Antonio's. He took a deep breath, fixed his eyes on the view, and waited patiently for them to all arrive in Florence.

After what seemed like an age for Hermes, the carriage, at last, began to trundle into the centre of the city. The clamour of farm animals, people, and oxen or horse drawn carts, carriages, and waggons grew ever louder as they came closer to the centre: 'Florence' Illawara exclaimed as the coach travelled past the imposing walls of the Fortezza da Basso. 'We're here already' she said excited and leant over to Hermes' side of the carriage, arm outstretched, to improve her view. Hermes took in the grim and imposing walls of the fortress pimpled with stone: so useful for deflecting artillery fire. He mused that the fort could defend itself with ugliness alone.

'It looks like the skin of an alligator' he said thinking out loud, Illawara's eyes widened a somewhat.

'What's an Alligator?' asked Antonio,

'It's a type of big swimming lizard', the Earl interjected to Illawara's surprise before Hermes could answer the question. She paused intrigued that the Earl had ever heard of one. Antonio twitched with confusion, but Hermes carried on:

'You can find them in Florida.' Antonio seemed intrigued.

'I think we should go sight-seeing before the party' Illawara interrupted, before bulging her eyes at Hermes 'we have a few hours yet' she said and gave another stare at the youth for referring to America. Antonio's eyes flashed:

'Oh, do you mean crocodile?' He said to Hermes, 'yes I have heard of those. Is it true they live in the Nile?'

'That's correct; they do live in the Nile as well as other places' Illawara continued. Antonio's brows tensed.

'I'm sure Hermes can speak for himself' said the Valet, 'but it seems that you're familiar with North Africa and the Americas?' said the Valet, Illawara swallowed, 'it's a very long voyage for anyone, let alone such a young woman - few come back.'

'Indeed, so I've heard' she replied, 'but I don't see how being a woman makes that voyage more difficult' Illawara sniped back, while she read a look of creeping embarrassment on Hermes' face.

'I'm doubtless you could cross the Atlantic on a boat of your own' Antonio added with arched eyebrows, 'you strike me as familiar with the natural sciences and *many* other things. I'm just surprised a language tutor could teach you so much.' Illawara gave an uncomfortable laugh, her head still in the grip of a hangover:

'Well, you forget the professor I mentioned. But Master Salvatore allowed me to read a bit, here and there, from the books he had collected. But I don't remember much; another time perhaps? Besides' she added, 'I want to explore this beautiful city.' Illawara then snapped open her fan to end any further enquiry.

The Valet puckered his lips and exchanged a glance with the Earl: Illawara may as well have slapped him across the face.

'I agree' said the Earl, conjuring a smile, while Illawara fanned herself. Hermes remained mute, and consensus fell upon the carriage. Illawara was relieved to have changed the subject but annoyed that Antonio had questioned her again, and that Hermes was the cause. She remained keen to play for time, for she had not yet figured out how to gain access to the Duke's party. After parking the carriage, and mooring the horses next to a trough Antonio, acting as the guide, suggested they all walk from the Basilica Santa Maria Novella, and through the marketplace to the Duomo before returning later to make their way to the Uffizi. The streets teemed with crowds: far busier than the later times in which Illawara and Hermes visited: when he first saw Florence - while peeping out of Illawara's bag. All of humanity clattered and jangled in front of them, as they paused next to a wall to take in the view of the Basilica. The pair did not have to act as if they had never seen the like before, as both were surprised at the sheer variety of life that surrounded them.

Children of all ages ran about streets screaming and yelling at the tops of their voices, while playing with iron rings that they rolled in front of them, throwing missiles, or grabbing at farmer's chickens before hurling them into the air. The ferret-like packs of children cackled, as the startled birds fluttered to the ground screeching, and the urchins scattered like mosquitos when furious market sellers scolded and swung at them with sticks. As the group walked to the Santa Maria Novella's piazza, women with bales of apples, and other produce called out in rough voices as they mingled through the crowds selling their wares: at night, when well away from the Basilica walls, other conveniences of theirs were sold.

Oxen pulled heavy goods-carts through the streets, laden and precarious, with cut stone for new buildings, held in place with ropes as their cargo creaked along. Shouts of animated greeting or swearing seemed to ring out from every orifice of the surrounding buildings, to be caught with a gesture, assessed, and then voiced back by the people of the streets below. The very populous seemed alive with raucous music, as citizens added their notes to the cacophony of sound.

As they all progressed into the market area, they spied small stalls that sold sweet foods and savouries. The Earl, from one seller, bought everyone a flavoured pie of their choice, still warm from the oven, and each declared their pie the best after trying one another's in turn. Spice merchants stood with pride in their rented shops, wearing expensive clothes, and displayed a bounty of exotic ingredients. Cloves, ginger, chillies and pepper from the new world sat resplendent in their shop windows, next to glass jars of ochre coloured Iranian saffron, Mexican vanilla pods, and the sweet dark bark of cinnamon. The air clung thick with the fragrant spices and burning incense that helped to overpower the humming sweat of workers, and the dung of their animals. The group as they walked became infused with the energy of the streets of Florence: each thrilled in their own way. When the opportunity presented itself, Illawara took the chance to speak to Hermes, as The Earl and Antonio engaged a merchant about his wares: 'Hermes, what was going on with you in the carriage earlier on? So moody' she whispered, taking him to one side,

'What mood?'

'C'mon, you know what I mean, you were distant, you hardly said anything the whole journey, and then when you did speak why did you talk about Florida?'

'I don't know? The fortress made me think about Alligators skin, and that made me think about Florida, and then about home.' Illawara's face flinched with anguish, but she fixed Hermes with a look before the pair avoided a man walking past with his goats.

'OK, I know we're far from home, but you need to keep quiet about America. It's too risky. We need to stay on the ball with this, and you have to back me up' she whispered, 'and you were warning me about slip ups - but I can't always cover for you.' She studied him, 'why are you acting all weird?' She said. Hermes stared at the floor before looking up: 'I'm sorry' he said, 'I don't know what's come over me. I feel very different than I did before.'

'Hmmm?' said Illawara with knitted brows. She squinted. 'Maybe it's a side effect of the change? Being human again?' She watched as Hermes tipped his head up to the sky with his eyes closed and let out a long breath. Illawara watched him and then scratched an itch at the back of her neck between her hair and Ruff: 'I may have to proposition the Earl'

'With what?' said Hermes, after paused reflection.

'I'm not sure, it's just I've no real idea how we're going to get into the party - and we don't have long.' Illawara wrung her hands and checked to see that the Earl and Antonio were still talking.

'I thought so: it's been on my mind too' said Hermes, 'and I don't think flaunting a pineapple is enough to do it.' Illawara gave a nervous laugh but nodded.

'Agreed... I've been thinking - do you think I should go as the Earl's consort?' Hermes frowned.

'I thought that we were each other's consort?' He said. Illawara grimaced.

'Yes we are, *sort of*, but I think it's more convincing if I'm on the arm of the Earl, so to speak.' Hermes folded his arms and scowled. 'Well, it's either that or trying to kick down a door or climb through a window... and to be honest, I don't think I can do either in this dress.' Illawara then made a demure sweeping motion with her skirts, adding a beaming smile as she fluttered her eyelashes. Hermes smirked, seeing, in his mind's eye, Illawara trying to clamber through a small unguarded window, him pushing from behind, with her clothed in her high collar, bodice, and farthingale.

'Ah, Illy' sighed Hermes, 'makes sense, I suppose. When will you ask him?' Hermes glanced over Illawara's shoulder to be sure the other pair were still talking to the merchant.

'I think I'll ask him in the Duomo; Antonio said we're going there next. I think I heard him say something about going to the top. I'm hoping Edward will be so impressed by the view that he'll just say yes.' Her eyes shone. 'Besides, it's not like he's got another woman with him.' The smile slid from Hermes' face.

'Do you like him Illy?' he enquired. Illawara avoided Hermes' gaze and tried to stifle a blush as the pair stepped aside to let a cabbage waggon pass. 'I wouldn't blame you' he added, 'he's very... "Dashing" - like a hero from some of those films you like to watch.' Illawara's expression changed as she absorbed his words.

'Well, I suppose I could ask you the same about Antonio?' She said. Hermes stood still and stared at her before he looked away, and his shoulders slumped. He then looked back at his friend before rubbing at his face and letting his hands drop to his sides: as if exhausted. A silent understanding passed between them, as Florentine life jangled by. They gazed each other, contemplated, and with nothing more to be said on the subject, they both returned to the sides of their companions.

Antonio proved to be an excellent guide. He gestured at every turn to some feature of the Florentine surroundings, or some old guild's mascot, upon a high wall, rendered impotent or half forgotten. He pointed here and there to buildings and palazzos, mentioning the architect that made it, or the noble family that commissioned it. Antonio gestured to new constructions of elaborate facades cleaved onto old buildings: straight classical lines contorted into bending ones as craftsmen hammered away above on their scaffolding.

Antonio, gaining momentum, spoke of the artisan's passion for 'the new style' as they made way through the crowds. He turned his palm in the direction of an open door of a palazzo, where gilded adornments glowed within, as a procession of workers marched goods through the doors. The group moved on, but Illawara paused, when a shrunken woman with a swaddle, limped to the side of the open door, sat, made a weak motion with her bundle, and muttered repetitive words at all who passed her. She sat there ignored by the workmen as they busied themselves, and invisible to another as he crossed off his goods list. After a while, the woman struggled to her feet, and almost forgot her baby wrapped in old fabric, making no protest, as it was laid on the dusty ground as she got up. Illawara looked on and saw the woman, wearing a tangle of rags, limping off with her swaddle on one arm, and the other hand, slack-wristed, waving at passers-by to no avail. Illawara stood, transfixed, to watch the woman before Hermes returned to tug her arm and pull her away.

It soon became evident to Illawara and Hermes that the Medici's crest could be seen everywhere: with its famous balls. There seemed almost nothing that Antonio did not know about the family: as they moved along Illawara and Hermes grew nervous. The Duomo with its high domed roof seemed the very beating heart of Florence. The streets, although still busy, were calmer around the immense Basilica. The breadth of the cobbles between the Basilica and Baptistery provided relief from the stifling clamour of the narrow walkways and oxygenated the citizens as they ambled along. Antonio became excited: The Basilica had always been his favourite landmark to show off to new guests in the city. Illawara and Hermes both looked shocked when they first spied the Duomo: both stood open-mouthed. Without its iconic and elaborate façade – that they had known from their later visits - to them, the building looked grand but naked.

'I see that you're both impressed' declared Antonio with pride. The pair manufactured nods before glancing to each other. 'I suggest we go inside so I can show you the ceiling, and then we go to the top of the Duomo itself. The view is spectacular.'

'So we're allowed up in there?' said Hermes almost recovered,

'I have a friend' said Antonio, beaming a smile. The Earl walked on ahead with Antonio, while Illawara studied his body language: he seemed bored. Neither she nor Hermes had been inside the Duomo before. The queues to get inside were far too long, in their time, when they visited with the Professor, and he had become impatient with the aimless chatter of tourists, as they all baked together in the sunshine. Priests and lay people mingled around outside the Basilica, as the group climbed the steps that lead to the Duomo's huge imposing doors: but these doors stood carved from wood and were not the ornate bronze narratives that they had expected. The pair disguised their mutual disappointment - reminded that splendours take time. Antonio began talking with a young priest to one side, with animated gestures as they exchanged banter. The Earl kicked at the ground and threw crumbs from his pie crust to the pigeons as they fluttered about the place. Illawara watched him carefully, as Hermes observed Antonio, and pondered how best to suggest her idea to the Earl. Antonio beckoned the three of them over and introduced his friend.

'Everyone, this is my friend Brother Marco da Perugia.' The young priest could not have been more than twenty-five. He wore his dark brown hair short, had olive skin and large brown eyes. His smiled exposed his neat square teeth, and he nodded as he clasped his hands as if in prayer. Antonio introduced everyone in turn, and Hermes and Illawara introduced themselves back in flawless Italian. The Earl spoke his Italian too, but with an awkward English accent. Niceties aside the group were granted access to the Duomo. Inside various elements of the clergy floated about in their pressed robes. Some held books and others lit candles or incense burners in preparation for evening mass. Antonio hurried the group along, as Marco left them. Illawara and Hermes stood awestruck as they looked up into the Duomo's painted ceiling: 'started by Giorgio Vasari, and finished by Federico Zuccari thirty-two years ago' said

Antonio. Illawara looked up in that instant and wished for her camera. The depictions of The Last Judgement glowed and seemed to reach down to pull up the viewers. Each person stood with their heads thrown back in wonder as if being lifted, in the ribcage, by the paintings.

'Stunning, absolutely stunning' said Hermes,

'This is what genius is. It's one of my favourites' declared the Earl, quite animated. Everyone's ears pricked.

'Have you seen this before?' Asked Antonio. The Earl stalled.

'No… well not in person, of course, it's just its fame reaches even England; Italian friends have spoken of it often, and I've heard it described so much it's as if I knew the piece already.' Hermes and Illawara exchanged glances with one another.

'I'm impressed' said Antonio satisfied, and then gave more detail about the various artworks around, before Marco returned and made a sign to usher them over to a corner of the space.

'Here, this is the staircase' said Marco opening a narrow door, 'you can take your friends up here.' Antonio thanked him and offered the priest a small bag of coins. Marco gave effusive praise and then waved the group off: 'thank you… and Ciao Bella Donna' he called after Illawara, she, surprised, then turned to smile and gave a curtsy. Hermes rolled his eyes and emitted a grunt:

'As if she needs encouraging' he muttered to himself.

Their ascent became laborious after fifty steps as the rest of the four hundred and thirty-seven footfalls lead the group upward. Illawara hung back a somewhat, although fit, as her dress swallowed up the narrow confines of the stairways: just wide enough for two slim people to pass. She pressed down on her farthingale to reduce her dress brushing against the walls and rubbing into ribbons against the bricks. Hermes' breath started to become ragged. As a little bird, he could have flown up the steps with ease, but human limitations brought heaviness and mixed feelings for him.

In leading the pack Antonio remained cheerful but focused, a glow of sweat clung to his brow. The Earl, however, seemed untouched by the experience, and exerted less effort in his ascent than of one shelling prawns or peeling an onion. In time the whole expanse opened out as the group emerged into the upper balcony of the painted dome. The painting shimmered with life and dazed the onlookers with its intensity. Christ sat majestic in the heavens surrounded by angels, beyond the reach of the demonic forms lower down, looking as if they had leapt from the pages of Dante's Inferno.

Illawara wobbled at the height and clung white-knuckled to the iron rail, as she peered down. The clergymen looked like tiny scraps of coloured paper in a breeze, as they milled about below. Hermes then lunged upward, as if to catch the air, overwhelmed by an urge to launch himself into flight above the floor many meters below and inspect the face of Christ for himself. Illawara almost screamed, but human reason netted Hermes before instinct could take over, as he lurched forward violently, only just managing to grasp the rail - the ambush of near death above the void made him swoon.

The whole group cried out as Antonio snatched Hermes back before he fell over the railings. 'HERMES' Illawara exclaimed before covering her mouth: her voice echoed around the dome as he fell backwards. The priests paused for a moment to look upward at the sound as Illawara gripped the Earl's arm for comfort. Hermes lay limp for several seconds, panting before he shook himself back to awareness.

'I'm alright, I'm *alright*' he said coming to, looking up into concerned faces as the group leant over,

'You tried to jump' said the Earl, glaring down at him.

'I just got dizzy, that's all', Hermes said, as he elbowed his way upwards before thanking Antonio for his athletic catch. But Hermes stood shaking from head to toe as his body burned all over.

'Well, this great work never fails to make an impact' Antonio declared, gripping Hermes by the shoulders, his face riven with concern, as he tried to make light of the situation. Antonio then moved forward, supporting Hermes, to resume leading the group. Illawara's hands trembled as she gave out a nervous laugh. She paused for a moment, seeing Hermes in flight no more than a day ago: a bird form that he had inhabited for so many years. The animal still compelled him. Illawara shivered. 'You're not the first to have fainted' Antonio whispered in Hermes' ear as he took the youth's arm over his shoulder to better hold him up. Illawara tried to calm herself and looked to the walls to avoid the view below. She stopped before reaching up to touch the grey tail of a demon painted on the wall: 'I wouldn't touch that' said Antonio, looking back, before entering yet another stairway, 'it's bad luck.' The Earl craned his neck round to look, but she had drawn back her hand from the painting,

'I'd keep your hands to yourself if I were you' he said. Illawara retreated.

'I just wanted to touch… a masterpiece, it's so rare to get the chance' she said. The Earl tilted his head to look at her before they moved on.

More toil awaited the group as they climbed to even more steep and narrow confines, while Antonio navigated the wooden construct on the inside of the dome's shell. As the group approached the pinnacle, they almost crawled on all fours, sandwiched as they were between the inner and outer domes. Then it was over. The group emerged onto the viewing platform and into the embrace of the sky. The city of Florence lay below in all its beauty. The recent overcast pallor of the clouds had cracked here and there, pierced by blades of the sunshine that fell upon hills and houses. Antonio left the silence of the group unchallenged as they drank in their surroundings.

'It's magnificent' gushed Illawara, before filling her lungs, 'truly stunning. I'll never forget this.' Even the Earl looked impressed, shaking his head at the wonder of it all. Hermes took in a deep breath, accepting a sky he could no longer fly in, and felt the vow he had made to himself at breakfast reaffirmed. Antonio strutted about, a man in his element, his chest puffed out like a pigeon:

'There's the river Arno and the Ponte Vecchio' he said, pointing this way and that, 'over there is the Palazzo Pitti, and the Uffizi'

At the mention of the Uffizi Illawara jolted out of her reverie. She set her sights on the Earl and waited for her chance to talk with him. The opportunity came while Hermes stood, rapt, as Antonio chatted away, commanding his attention as he gestured to the landscape and the outlying towns on the hills. Illawara walked to the side of the Earl as he stared with intensity in the direction of the Uffizi. She touched his arm. The Earl flinched: 'Oh' he said taken aback, 'I was miles away.' She searched his pale green eyes; they were vivid but joyless. Illawara hesitated before speaking:

'What a view…' she said, 'yet you seem troubled?' the Earl took a step back from her,

'Do I?' He said. Illawara stepped forward.

'Yes,' She replied, trying to read his expressions.

'It's nothing really; I was just thinking about the events this evening, and about whom I hope to meet.' Illawara's blood then rushed with adrenalin.

'Anyone important or special?' Illawara said, trying to sound carefree. The Earl walked away to take in more of the view, his hands braced behind his back.

'Yes, someone vital and very special.' Illawara's heart quickened.

'I see...' She said, clutching her hands together, before following him. 'Edward, I've something to ask you, but I find it a little awkward' she whispered, as the Earl's expression began to change. Illawara swallowed, 'well, there's no point in hiding I may as well come out with it.' Illawara missed the look of dread on the Earl's face as she turned to the view for inspiration, 'you see, I have a problem...' Illawara gripped the railings, 'I don't quite have the invitation... what I mean, is that I lost the formal dinner invitation for Hermes and myself.' She turned to him, his face looked relieved, 'I've been a fool, I must have lost it on the way here.' Illawara fiddled with her fingers, 'Hermes doesn't know' she whispered again, 'I couldn't bear to tell him, and I'm worried that without it, we won't be allowed in. So, I wanted to ask you a favour.'

'I'm listening' said the Earl, Illawara chewed at her lip.

'May I attend as your consort?' The Earl let out a peal of laughter, that paused Antonio for a moment in his animated teaching, as Illawara shrank back. Her stomach tangled in knots, but she allowed the Earl's laughter to subside,

'I don't see why not...' He said, 'but what about Hermes?' Illawara almost clapped her hands together.

'Oh, that's wonderful I hoped you would say yes. Maybe Hermes can be introduced as my cousin and chaperone as before? It's just that I will be with you.'

'Seems reasonable' said the Earl in a relaxed manner, 'if needed I'm sure Antonio could pull a few strings; that man has more connections than an octopus.' Illawara then clapped her hands with glee: relieved that she and Hermes would gain access to the banquet. But Illawara accepted that even if the Earl had a special lady waiting for him at the event, she would at least get to see her competition. Illawara paused as pang of guilt slunk through her: for forgetting about her father's welfare at that moment. But she overcame the mood as she stood next to the Earl, letting her worries melt into the Tuscan sunset.

Chapter 8

The Dance

The Uffizi

Illawara entered the Uffizi arm in arm with the Earl of Oxford in triumph. After the Duomo, they had all arrived in the Earl's carriage. Her heart trembled with palpitations as an official of the guard inspected invitations. He stood: stout, broad, and ruddy-faced as he eyeballed the guests. The elegant sword that hung at his side complemented his distinguished robes; the Medici clothed their staff well. The guests paused as the Official checked their names against scrolls, and the tufted eyebrows of the guest-list keepers twitched here and there while inspecting the newcomers. Some chancers, not quite up to scratch, were removed with discretion, and entreating looks sprang from others gathered there, only slightly better dressed, not wishing to befall the same fate.

As the group moved closer to the table of scrolls, the polished armour of the guards, bracing the hallway doors, caught the light. A pair faced each other, polearms crossed, disciplined and implacable. A couple further ahead took their turn to swoop up to the table. The man, lavishly dressed but ugly, made a sweeping gesture to the Official before embracing him, and kissing each cheek of the reserved man with his pockmarked face, and introduced his woman. She stepped forward, half stumbling on her velvet green dress, but gave a delicate bow, dipping her chin into her cleavage, which seemed to make more of an impact than the man who arrived with her. The Official gave an appreciative nod, the crowd wriggled, and the guards parted polearms to let them in.

The Earl shifted from foot to foot, Hermes stared at a painting, and Antonio positioned himself to catch the eye of the Official.

Illawara arched her back, tried to ignore the rising tension, and visualised herself already inside the party. She shone as she stood there, and the guards fought hard not to look at her but snatched their glances where they could. With a combination of the silver-tongued Antonio, whispering as he spoke, and the sheer number of guests, the Official used his discretion and waved the group on before they passed under the parting polearms of the armoured guards. It was not the first time that dubious nobles of doubtful origin had entered a Medici party. The Official, an old hand, fond of Antonio, had the experience to tell between the benign and the dangerous.

The group after passing security glided up the broad stone steps of the Uffizi on a wave of optimism, while bathed in the glow of torchlight. Guests, nobles, and dignitaries had begun to accumulate everywhere on the upper floor in the long hall. The babble of laughter and conversation trickled down the walls as they ascended the staircase. As the group entered the room the full volume of conversation and the heat of bodies caressed them - the scent of perfume mingled with those of fine wine, and food, as people meandered along the gallery of paintings and sculptures. The art and the candlelight rendered even the ordinary - be it object or person - to become transfigured into the sensuous and inviting.

That is when Cardinal Orsini saw her. Illawara seemed not to touch the ground when she walked. The diamond at her slender throat blazed like a comet, as it scattered the candlelight in thread-like shards across her amber skin. The mundane world fell away. She looked more like a star than a woman. Orsini failed to suppress a quiet thrill within him upon seeing her. Startled by her beauty every object and person within the extravagant hall became dull.

Cardinal Pietro Orsini, a man not as lithe and sinuous as he was in his youth, still had an imposing physique. Middle age had broadened a willowed waist, and time had robbed him of a full head of hair. But his Roman skin shone tan, and his eyes, still handsome, glowed bright and fierce. The deepening creases on his face did nothing to dampen the amber-green intensity of his dark-lashed eyes that had inclusions of brown spots: like little creatures caught in amber. But what time had stolen from youth she gave back in cunning, and the Cardinal had never been more powerful - had never been more feared. Like a caged Leopard Orsini prowled the edge of the room as Illawara and her entourage entered a gallery space to the left of the main hall. He crept past the mass of guests, as if in a hunt, as they sauntered about, deaf in his focus, ignoring the playful music that skipped through the air.

He kept Illawara in his sight, watching every turn of her body as she floated through the rooms, oblivious to the heads that craned after her. He listened to her laughter that fluttered, like a golden butterfly, and danced to his ears. He followed on, electrified, almost desperate as he caught her eye: not really seeing she gave him an unfocused smile and swept away, before her fairy-like laughter bounced from an arch and braced him from afar, to then tear into his heart and lay arson to a cold and barren place. Orsini paused to put his hand on a wall and to feel the heat in his chest: as if rubied-light were pulsing through his ribcage. The Cardinal caught his breath, and beckoned to a thin man that loitered at the fringes of the party: 'don't let her out of your sight' Orsini whispered in his ear while his hands shuddered. The man gave a weak nod as he focused his pale and watery eyes in Illawara's previous direction. 'I want to know everything about her. Who she is and where she's from. You know what I've come to expect. Stay back, for now; I'll give further instruction if I need to.' The thin man bowed. Orsini, recovered, swept forward with a lithe power as he mingled himself again with the party - only the blood red of his Cardinals cap defined him in the crowd.

Orsini went ahead to take a place on one of the long dining tables that were set up for the banquet. His fingers made a galloping sound as he tapped them on the starched white tablecloth, eyeing the expanses from length to length, and listened. He then withdrew as the other guests arrived, while admiring a painting that he knew too well, and waited for her. Illawara sat in a place nearer the end of the furthest table next to Hermes, the Earl and his valet Antonio. Orsini made excuses to guests he knew and stood up to change his place - ignoring their surprise. Orsini ducked. He snatched up his named parchment, swapped tables, and moved five chairs down the row and whispered to a man sitting there, who then vacated to let Orsini sit down. From his new vantage point, he could observe and listen - with slight effort - to Illawara and her entourage. All the remaining guests took their seats, as their glasses were filled with water and then wine before a silence fell upon the gathering.

A dignitary then walked into the dining room, before ringing a tiny brass bell, to formally announce and give thanks to the second

Grand Duke and his wife, the Archduchess Maria Maddalena - as the room stood the resplendent hosts walked in arm in arm. The young Duke, elegant and tall, reminded all of his great father Cosimo the first, and the Archduchess, swathed in pale taffeta and pearls, with her chin lifted and her smooth shoulders back, looked as if she owned all of Italy as she acknowledged the room. Illawara and the other guests admired the Archduchess, but Illawara outshone Maria without conscious effort. The dignitary then went on to announce Galileo as the guest of honour. A little man then followed the Duke and Duchess. Praise and glasses rose upward for Galileo, as the little eyes of the physicist twinkled in his ruddy face. He gave a brief bow, before he ambled to his place next to the young Duke, and the stalled conversations erupted back into life.

One by one elaborate dishes of food from the first service were piled upon the tables until they groaned. First, the efficient Trinciante kitchen staff laid down the starters: figs came with little pies of cooked eels, and small pastries filled with farro, then fish tarts of Pike tail were put next to those of sea bream, and little bowls of broth floated with stuffed veal in the Lombardy style. Quince pies shared space with pork loins, and colourful sauces came spiced or plain. Some of the guests were beside themselves with excitement, as they sampled the banquet. Others were more controlled in their reactions to better disguise the putting of food into purses and pockets: especially the poor nobles of grand names, crumbling estates, barren marriages, and even emptier cupboards. The bona fide wealthy picked at their food with casual indifference.

More dishes arrived after the previous course got cleared, but Orsini paid scant heed as the table heaved with the second service of roasted chickens, pheasants, partridges and songbirds. He observed the delicate movements of Illawara and studied her to see what pleased her most as her face glowed in the candle light.

The feast grew ever grander: three bronzed roast suckling pigs, with apples in jaws and crowned with rosemary, were eased onto the tables, accompanied by three fully dressed peacock pies, skin and feathers intact. The Trinciante held up and spread out the peacock's tails in unison which dazzled the room, and the theatrical gesture gained a spontaneous round of applause from all guests. The meat was carved and forked, as the servers then struggled to find space for biscuits, sweets, and cakes. A sailing ship made of marzipan bearing the Medici coat of arms was laid on the head table. Orsini observed the faces around the tables pink with pleasure, except for the Moorish youth's that sat next to Illawara. Orsini raised his empty glass in the direction of a server who, once beckoned, stood close as he filled the glass with red wine: 'any news on the fine woman?' said Orsini in an aside to the server. Conversations bubbled around them.

'No one seems to know much about her, your Eminence' he whispered, 'some say she's Venetian or Padovan perhaps, but she's called "Illawara"'. Orsini gave an intrigued expression, 'she came with Antonio and two other interlopers' the server gave a flicking gesture of his head, 'that one is English.'

Orsini did a quick study of the Earl's face before responding: 'huh, another "m'Lord" in Italy - more arrive every year.' Orsini then scrutinised the Earl's valet, 'that Antonio: yet another bastard son of an errant nobleman, and all of them trying to scratch out a place in this court.' The server shifted position and looked down to the floor as the heat rose in his face: Orsini noticed but did not care. 'Illawara...' he mused, 'a strange but pretty name, for a beautiful and enchanting woman.' Orsini then fixed the server with a look: 'when this banquet is over, I want her followed.' The server nodded and stumbled back somewhat, before visiting the glasses of other guests with an unsteady hand.

Orsini allowed himself to look down the table to Illawara as Antonio introduced her to his rival Cardinal Barberini. Her smile blazed as she laughed again and threw her head back, the Cardinal seemed taunted, as Barberini said something charming, and Orsini wished himself swapped with him in that instant. Illawara's head turned at that moment and her eyes locked with Orsini's, a current ran between them as a scorched thrill ran up his spine. Her smile faltered, and her eyes became downcast, as Orsini raised his glass to her. She turned away to regain herself before she laughed again at the joke that had past. Orsini chatted to his neighbour as Hermes and Antonio exchanged glances with one another.

The guests had eaten their fill from the delicious bounty in front of them. One by one they began to drift away from the table to either rest on chairs near the fireplace or partake of the tour to view the Medici's ever expanding art collection. Orsini sat back from the dining table, to recline on a chair sat next to a clerical official from the Vatican. Orsini nodded at the words of the cleric as he prattled on, and breathed deep, while he kept a sharpened eye on Illawara and her entourage, as they moved position and were then on Orsini's side of the table. To his eyes, Illawara seemed to be asking the Earl to accompany her on the tour of the collection. Orsini observed the Earl fidget, give a stiff smile, but then clench his hand into a fist under the table, unwilling to break off his intense conversation with Galileo and Cardinal Barberini.

Orsini saw the youth by her side coax her away in the direction of the gallery space. Illawara had resisted his tugs before she gave way. Antonio hung back and continued to listen to the conversation, rapt, before making a slow walk in the direction of the gallery and his friends.

'You see, your Eminence' the cleric said to interrupt the Cardinal's silence, 'the Protestants cannot be allowed to strangle the Church and her ways. Our traditions must be maintained. We need to become strong to be worthy of her. Every day we learn that Venezia still gives protection to infidels and our enemies.' Orsini nodded in vague agreements to the cleric:

'The Church will survive, Niccolo. Every day we do our best to strengthen her. God be praised' said Orsini, before he stood up, broke off the conversation, and followed Antonio out of the room. The Cardinal then made powerful strides toward the blond man ahead: 'I see that you're fond of this place' said Orsini, in catching up on the side of Antonio, but the young man leapt back as if stabbed.

'Uh, pardon me, your Eminence, I didn't see you.' Antonio's skin began to prickle, and a bead of sweat began to form at his back under the pincered gaze of the Cardinal, as the older man paused to size him up.

'It takes either a brave or foolish man to test his fate here with the nature of your disgrace', said Orsini. The colour washed out of Antonio's face before the Cardinal continued, 'yet I'm told you're rarely far from Court here' he purred. Antonio gritted his teeth and clenched his fists till his knuckles bleached, but tried to measure his words.

'If that's so' he swallowed, 'then I'm in good company.' Antonio glared back at the Cardinal before the older man snarled,

'There are too many of your sort cluttering up these noble houses.'

'I have every right to be here, or any other noble house: it's my birth right' said Antonio. Orsini huffed, but Antonio raised his chin, 'my mother loved as much as any woman and bore myself and her shame till it broke her. Are her exile and demise not sacrifice enough? Or do hypocritical jackals still wish to chew on her reputation?'. Antonio's face glowed red. The Cardinal narrowed his eyes and ran his tongue across his teeth:

'My, oh, my, it seems you've inherited a healthy dose of your mother's haughtiness, and your father's pride' said the Cardinal.

'Do you know my father?' said the younger man, looking frantic, and Orsini gestured with his hand to calm Antonio down and then turned the other to move them both on. As the pair walked, they grew nearer to the back of a large group attending the tour, and Orsini maintained a vigil to keep Illawara in his sights.

Orsini lowered his voice before he spoke again: 'there are few who *didn't* know your father my child.' Antonio's eyes widened. The Cardinal stopped walking to fix the young man, and then Antonio, for the first time, noticed the trapped brown flecks in the Cardinals glistening eyes and felt himself to be in the nest of an eagle. 'Your father long survived the scandal and still lives.' Antonio rested his palm on a wall to gather his breath, Orsini stood, unflinching, and gazed on, 'I have a proposition for you' he said. Orsini then placed a firm hand on Antonio's shoulder and squeezed, 'a truth for a truth' added the Cardinal in his deep baritone, his eyes not leaving Antonio's face for a moment, 'it moves me so to see you suffer my child.' Antonio doubted the sentiment and looked up to the ceiling at a new baroque fresco of a stag being chased by hounds, and wondered what Orsini wished to extract from him. 'Speak to me and do not lie' Orsini continued, 'who is the Englishman, and what brings him here?' Antonio hesitated,

'That's a difficult question to answer, your Eminence, as I truly don't know', Orsini's expression flattened.

'Insufficient my child, you can do better than that: you who share travel with all sorts, and welcome all comers, must know more than a little of your travel companions?' The pair began to walk again with a prompt from Orsini - eager to stay in sight of Illawara as the tour group moved on:

'Truly, your Eminence, I know little of him, as he doesn't reveal much, but what I do know is that he has a great admiration for the discoveries of Galileo...'

'A *heretic*' the Cardinal hissed, 'I might have guessed that a gullible Protestant would believe the cattle dung of that blasphemer!' This time Orsini had to correct himself for raising his voice, although unheard by the tour, due to the animated and flowery speech of the tour giver that washed over his attentive audience. Antonio scowled as he looked at the Cardinal.

'I'm told that Galileo is a man of faith, your Eminence, and by all accounts a good Catholic.' Orsini then waved his finger in the air,

'A good Catholic you say. I was in Rome for his visit in the spring, and not once did I see him at Mass either before or after meeting his Holiness. I'm told he never goes. *Philosopher*, they call him. He's little more than a concubine to fortune, an opportunist, a *hack* improving on the ideas of another for that spy-glass of his; with not one but three illegitimates to have crawled from the womb of his Venetian whore - Gamba.' Orsini's fist clenched, and his expression darkened as his venom spilt forth, 'a lifetime of shame couldn't kill that man.' Antonio looked on as Orsini frothed, spitting out his words, and waited for the Cardinal's anger to pass. The Cardinal then recovered, wiped his brow, fussed with his collar, and focused again: 'forgive me, child, I digress, tell me the name of this *common* Englishman.' A look of surprise and mockery gripped Antonio's face,

'Have your spies at last drawn a blank, your Eminence?' said Antonio defiant. The Cardinal's expression twisted into a scowl,

'Impertinent wretch' hissed Orsini, stepping forward and drawing close enough for Antonio to feel the Cardinal's breath on his neck, 'don't toy with me - *boy*' he growled. Antonio caught a whiff of the scented orange water on Orsini's skin and stepped back.

'He's not an everyday man, your Eminence, but an Earl in his land' Orsini rolled his eyes before replying,

'They all say that. He has poise, but he is not a high-born' the Cardinal drew close again, 'I can smell it in a man: there's better blood in you than in that *vagabond*.' Antonio pulled his shoulders back and raised his chin at the comment, Orsini observed the effect of his words before he continued, 'he's an Earl of what my child?' Antonio squirmed as if Orsini's eyes penetrated his flesh to the guts.

'He says that he's the Earl of Oxford.' Orsini raised his thick eyebrows into high arches,

'Oh does he now - which one?'

'I beg your pardon, your Eminence.'

'Gather your brains boy, and don't fidget. Which one?'

Antonio could not see the significance.

'He said he's the Seventeenth Earl of Oxford, your Eminence.' With those words, a profound and dark laughter began to rumble out of the Cardinal like a landslide. After composing himself, a look of triumph flashed in the Cardinal's eyes. Orsini then pursed his lips before he brushed some fluff off his velvet robes:

'And the youth, what of him?' He said. Antonio looked confused,

'But what of the Earl, and what do you know about him?' Antonio replied,

'That, my child, is none of your business' said the Cardinal, 'but I know what he is *not*, and I'm sure you'll find out soon enough. Again, I said, what of the youth?'

'He's called Hermes, your Eminence.'

'A Greek? Is he Orthodox?' Antonio shrugged.

'I didn't ask, but he's the chaperone of Illawara. I'm sure you've learnt of her already?' Orsini squinted, but almost smiled.

'Don't trifle with me' he breathed, 'the youth I said.'

Antonio looked down to the floor and coughed,

'He's her cousin' Antonio whispered, but Orsini belched laughter in his face,

'And I'm the Pope's *mother*' he scoffed, 'a likely story.' Antonio didn't know where to look. Orsini then shifted his head to peer down the hall at the brown-skinned youth next to Illawara, as the tour moved on again to the next artwork.

'He's a handsome Moor, and finely dressed - I'll give him that. I'm sure he'll be well looked after, especially knowing your reputation for care.' Antonio didn't speak, a deep blush of pink his only response. Orsini smirked but then gave Antonio a vacant expression, 'you may go now, my child before the group moves too far ahead.' Antonio looked startled, before he grabbed the Cardinal by the arms:

'But you said a truth for a truth, what of mine? What of my father?' The Cardinal yanked himself free of Antonio, stepping back, hissing like a panther, before raising his hand,

'How dare you *touch* me' Orsini declared with a sneer, 'I've a mind to clout you from here to Rome.' Antonio shrank back in shame, 'and for that truth you ask, my child, you needn't look further than the bawdy taverns of Venezia.' Orsini then brushed himself down as if attacked by fleas. Antonio bit his lip as his eyes welled up, Orsini then looked at him with a flat expression: 'I think we've spoken enough, let us part for now. Go, join the group, my child.'

With that statement Orsini waved Antonio off, but the young man glared back and made another step toward the Cardinal. The Cardinal swept his finger in front of Antonio to halt his advance. Antonio stopped, his eyes imploring before he turned and muttered something under his breath that Orsini could not catch and hurried ahead, wiping at his eyes, before he reached the group at the far end of the pictured hall.

The thin, pale man with watery eyes again joined Orsini, his presence cooled the air, as he seemed to hover between life and death. The Cardinal repressed a shudder when he smelled the man's body odour. The Cardinal spoke without turning his head: 'well?' said Orsini, the henchman mumbled but gave no clear answers. Orsini gave out a grunt, 'don't speak to me of news' he said with eyes like splinters, 'I've learnt in detail what you've struggled to define: the Earl's a cunning fraud.' The pale man looked over his shoulder as if the Earl were there.

'And what makes you so sure my lord and master?' said the henchman who had found and organised his words,

'I'm certain because I knew the Seventeenth Earl of Oxford, that talented rogue, in my youth as a student in Verona' Orsini smirked, 'the fun we had - too much, too much...' Orsini looked off into the distance, smiling with his square teeth, and shook his head at the memory before he regained himself enough to continue, 'so that English Protestant, that fraudster, that wigged peddler, that scrag-end couldn't possibly be him.'

'How so master?'

'Because the Seventeenth Earl is dead: and that brilliant man could never be impersonated - not in a thousand years.' The henchman gave a solemn nod.

'I understand, your Eminence' he said, and awaited instruction.

'When I've revealed the fraud, who seems to so enrapture that graceful woman...'

'Do you speak of Illawara, your Eminence?' Orsini nodded somewhat surprised,

'So you worked that one out' the Cardinal said. The thin man gave a weak smile of jumbled yellow teeth,

'That was easy, your Eminence: the guests speak of no one else, all wish to know who she is, and the men hatch plots in how to attract her attention - even the old ones.'

'Enough' said Orsini, with a sweep of his hand, 'when I've exposed the fraud, have him taken away and detained. A night on the wrack should reveal his intentions.' The pale man gave a bow, 'leave me now' Orsini continued, 'but remember to have the woman followed. I want to know where she'll stay when she's without her companion.' With that, the pale man walked into the distance before slithering off down a corridor.

■ ■ ■

Later, after the tours had ended, everyone gathered to hear the scientist Galileo debate with a professor from Pisa University. Even Orsini had to admit to himself that Galileo's demonstrations and arguments on flotation were triumphant. The scientist with his twinkling little eyes had proved himself a master of wit and commanded his subject and his audience with immense skill. He allowed himself to be swayed and even tangled, in the arguments of the hapless philosopher from Pisa, at stages even appearing to endorse his counterpart's arguments. But then the scientist would erupt and cut through the assumptions of the other professor, with a tongue like a rapier, leaving his opponent's logic bloodied and tattered.

Galileo proved to all, beyond doubt, that ice floated because of its mass and not its shape and felled a great tree of Aristotle's wisdom with one mighty blow. Even Cardinal Barberini, much to Orsini's annoyance, was asked to join in the debate and offered an opinion, but could only sing his praise for the Physicist.

Galileo's triumph, only matched by his opponent's disgrace, left the assembled audience and the Grand Duke thrilled with the performance of his chief mathematician. Galileo, a short and stout man, moved back from his demonstration table seeming ten feet tall, his opponent, thoroughly beaten, looked withered and bitter from the ordeal. Some members of the clergy took the defeated man off to one side and offered assurances. The group whispered as they eyeballed Galileo, who stood oblivious to their stares, as he spoke to his admirers - bold and blithe - that had gathered around him. More guests accumulated in dispersed clumps around the room eager to talk about what they had seen and fonder still to gossip. The mêlée of people splintered off further during the interlude before the dancing.

Orsini looked on, and observed the movements of the Earl who had regained a position next to the scientist, and seemed to be delighting him with some insight. He watched Illawara hover near the Earl, like a bee wanting a flower behind a bell glass: 'you're beautiful, but blind' Orsini muttered to himself, as he manoeuvred through the room to get a better look at the Englishman. Hermes assisted again with distraction, and moved Illawara off to a gallery of her new admirers, as Antonio engineered an introduction to the Grand Duke. The men jostled for position, as some female guests, outshone and overlooked, scrutinised Illawara to see how she would conduct herself.

Orsini placed himself near the vacated table where the scientist had given his demonstration, the floating ice had half melted into the water bath, and to better eavesdrop on Galileo's conversation with the Earl. Orsini tried to look interested in the scientific instruments that lay about: 'look at this rubbish' he whispered to himself as he gazed over the assorted equipment of the scientist, 'he's little better than a travelling Quack with his snake oil.' Orsini then turned his body toward a group that chatted of what they had seen, but twitched his ears to the Earl and Galileo to listen to them:

'You seem well versed in my work and theories' said the scientist, 'it's most refreshing',

'Indeed I'm an admirer, and I've travelled a great distance at much time and expense to be here this evening' said the Earl. The scientist seemed to twinkle.

'I'm glad to have it confirmed that my work is read, and admired, as far away as England. I guess you read the Venetian publications?' the Earl nodded, and Galileo sighed, 'the world seems to move faster every day.' Orsini gritted his teeth.

'It does indeed Professor, more than we know' said the Earl.

'Alas there are few men of broad mind as yours in Italy, my critics grow ever fiercer, ever more resolute to discredit me.' Galileo then glanced in the direction of his defeated opponent and his clerical supporters that plotted under their breath together in a corner.

'And disgrace is all you deserve' Orsini almost hissed aloud, before arching forward over the table and cringing as he ran his finger over a thermometer.

'I can assure you that your genius will not be forgotten, already you have your place among your Medici stars' said the Earl. Galileo laughed, and his little eyes shone,

'They teach great flattery in your land, and I'm encouraged by your confidence, but only the Lord in his great power can know the legacy of such things.'

The pair continued to talk, and Galileo gushed and wove tapestries of wonder in describing his discoveries of the craters, mountains, and canyons of the moon. Orsini listened, as if the scientist were a dangerous fool, but became more struck by the sheer fluency of the Englishman's Italian. When he looked away, he struggled to tell the difference between the Earl and the native man: there was no difference. The Cardinal moved around the room, between turns here and there, Orsini scrutinised the face and physique of the Englishman. 'Yes he's tall, athletic and vigorous' he whispered to himself, 'but I bettered him in my youth - look at that nose: like the beak of a vulture.' Orsini skimmed his eyes over the Earl again, shaking his head, 'why do young women so love a man of fine clothes and flattery?' The Earl then looked up from his conversation with Galileo as if prodded, and Orsini locked eyes with his rival. Something in the way the candlelight shone up from the small table, that the Earl and the scientist sat at, made his heart stop.

Orsini broke off his glance and walked to another part of the room with his heart racing.

'A mask, he wears a mask' he said to himself. Adrenalin coursed through the Cardinal's veins. He had seen disguises before, the Inquisition couldn't operate without them, but he knew his rival must be a master. As Orsini pondered what to do with such a cunning intruder the bell rang to announce the dancing.

Merry guests began to gather at varying speeds, and some were a touch lopsided after much wine. What remained of the food, that couldn't be stuffed into swags or pockets, littered the tables as the serving staff tidied up, before they laid out fruits and cheese. The Duke's musicians struck up a traditional folk tune, and some people began to dance. The music rattled out through the great hall as the musicians, also half filled with wine, played with gusto. Some men of the assembled court felt free to drop conventions as the music rang on, and took the hands of women that had caught their eye and spun them into an embrace. Then some of the chosen women, in turn, were happy to oblige, and glad to be free, if for a moment, from a possessive man or an annoying husband. Those same men, feigning protest, when relieved of their companions either feasted their eyes on other beauties: if they were married, or scanned the rooms for an upgrade if single.

Illawara shone even brighter than before, while she moved across the floor, as the queue of her admirers elbowed each other in waiting their turn to dance with her - for she ignited imaginations as she improvised on tradition and added inspired flourishes of her own. Orsini swept into the room and a corner, when he heard the music playing, and concealed himself among the seated veterans of the court, who had seen and survived the battlefields of love before. The wizened group shared a feeling of collective anticipation and exchanged sage words, and quips, before shuffling for position to see the night unfold. The tune became wilder than before, and the dance sucked in more guests like a whirlwind.

Illawara blazed across the room flashing from one corner to another, in turn, her blue dress swirling, as the men competed to dance with her. Illawara surrendered herself to the music as her spirit soared. To improve his chances, each man timed his steps to catch Illawara from his rival. Orsini had never desired a woman so much, and took a deep gulp of wine from his topped-up glass, and beckoned a servant of the house for yet another refill. Antonio and Hermes entered the room, followed close by the Duke and Archduchess. Antonio need not have pointed out Illawara to her new acquaintances, as she was visible everywhere: drawing gasps of admiration for her daring improvisations as she swooped, circled and pirouetted about the room. The young Duke, seeing her dance, became inspired, and snatched the modest Archduchess into his arms to join the others.

Orsini, with a foggy head, then saw Galileo enter the room followed by the Earl. Orsini's knuckles tensed to whiteness around the stem of his glass, as he took another gulp of wine. He saw the Earl pause and gaze upon Illawara and her dancing. The Earl's expression confused Orsini. His look conveyed not desire, but pride. Then the swift Earl moved into the dance with effortless grace, to clutch Illawara into his arms, and rescue her from a clumsy admirer as the music played on.

She looked elated as she glanced up into the Earl's eyes. Orsini writhed where he stood, emptied his glass, and almost broke it with his grip before he plonked it down and strode across the room to anticipate where the couple would pass. The couple spun closer to Orsini, and before the Earl could protest the Cardinal swept Illawara into his arms, prompting astonished cheers from the guests, and a crowd began to encircle them clapping. Orsini enthralled his onlookers by them seeing a Cardinal dance with a beautiful woman. The Cardinal's heart tried to leap out of his chest, as he gazed into Illawara's face who smiled at him and blushed deeper with every powerful sweep and motion of the Cardinal, and every cheer of the crowd. The Cardinal tried hard to stop his arms from shaking.

Orsini moved like the young man he was before he joined the Church, matching Illawara for pace, and danced as he once did at the infamous masked balls of Venice where reputations were won and lost. Illawara dazzled, her diamond glittering at her throat, as the heat rose to her brow, but she struggled to hold the intense gaze of the man that had watched her all evening. Orsini was powerful but smooth as his hand hugged her waist. The pressure of his hand moved through her bodice and warmed the small of her back. She danced on with him as he impressed the crowd with his skill and agility for a mature man, who far outstripped his younger rivals - even the Earl.

Orsini danced on as the years' fell away from him like tissue paper as he turned with Illawara, lost in the dark blue of her eyes, and re-lived an almost forgotten life - his memories of Venice - the dreams of his youth before he gripped her waist to lift her off the ground. She gasped. The crowd applauded, and then Illawara swept herself back, curving her spine, throat exposed and her arms arched, to accentuate Orsini's graceful lift which touched all those that saw it with emotion – a wild swan spinning in the arms of a prince. But in a moment it ended.

Orsini's pleasure then became a painful wrench from within, as the Earl snatched Illawara back from his embrace - the crowd oohed at the theft. Orsini stood still for a moment as if still holding Illawara, with his mouth ajar, his eyes dead, and his face barren: at that moment he looked lost, bereft, and old as Illawara spun off. The crowd then cheered his efforts, and the roar brought him back to himself. He gave a modest bow, a strained smile and turned away before his lips trembled.

Antonio observed the Cardinal with intensity, as the dance continued without him because he had never seen the Cardinal so softened, so enchanted, and then so wretched: blood had come from the stone. Orsini then clutched at his back that gave a spasm of protest. He moved with haste to the side of the room from where he glared at the Earl, who had brought Illawara to rest next to himself on a chair, much to the disappointment of the crowd. Many guests started to leave but paused to heap Illawara with praise before they moved on. With a tug from his Archduchess, Duke Cosimo the second took his wife's hint and retired to other rooms, although the musicians played on for the few not exhausted.

Four women gossiped with one another about Illawara as they made way to their carriages: 'she must be a Venetian: only a Venetian courtesan could dance like that' said one woman with a high collar, attractive face, plunged neckline and a green figure hugging dress.

'And I suppose you would know... What have you done with your old man, Constanza?' said one of the women to the tipsy laughter of the other two. Constanza paused to eye her friend up and down:

'Indeed I do know, and so would you, Clara - if you were *pretty* enough' came the retort. Clara was scorched into silence, her face like a brick, while her companions made eyes with hands over their mouths to stifle their giggles, as the group then moved down the hall to leave the building. Orsini's eyes burrowed into the Earl's head as he chatted with Illawara, and the Cardinal watched the man, who dabbed at his brow with a napkin. The Cardinal moved closer, and snatched up an abandoned wine glass to his mouth, and drank his fill. His heart pounded, and his head swam. In his glaring Orsini noticed that sweat had loosened what looked like peeling skin by the Earl's ear. The Earl continued to dab at his face, drinking his wine - forgetting himself.

As if possessed Cardinal Orsini then sprinted across the room. The Earl had scant time to react while he drank his red wine as Orsini approached from the side: *'scoundrel'* Orsini exclaimed as he tore off the Earl's wig and caught hold of the loosened flap by the Earl's ear and yanked at the mask with all his might. Illawara let out a scream as the Earl's red wine splashed up on his face. Orsini wrenched the mask half off, and the Earl looked bloody and torn. Such was the force of his tearing attack that Orsini knocked out one of the Earl's coloured contact lenses, revealing a distinctive grey iris, but also an elegant nose, and a shock of red-blond hair hidden under the discarded wig. Illawara then recognised the man in an instant:

'DADDY' she exclaimed. In confusion, Orsini staggered back with horror and lost his balance to crash on the floor as he took in the macabre wine stained face with most of its skin hanging off. The mask half peeled back revealed the face of a man who looked too young to be Illawara's father. With his disguise exposed, Professor Sloane bolted upright and made a dash for a door, as Hermes and Antonio rushed across the room followed by a guard who heard the commotion. The music stopped, and several shocked guests froze mid-dance to stare, while the quartet looked on dumbfounded.

The sages glanced to one another, nodded, and muttered amongst themselves - waiting to see what happened next: *'SEIZE him'* Orsini screeched, as he threw his arm in the direction of the fleeing Professor as he tried to struggle to his feet. Sloane flashed past the guard, including Hermes and Antonio, before they could grab him.

'Daddy, *no*, where are you going?' Illawara cried as she gave chase. Hermes gawped, shell shocked for a moment when he realised who he had seen, and Antonio also stood stunned by the revelation, as the flapping face had shot by before they gave chase as the Professor hurtled down a passageway. Orsini's pale henchman passed through the room like a ghoul as Orsini shouted orders:

'Get him. Don't rest till he's caught.'

More guards were alerted as the Professor ran on, and he snatched up objects to hurl behind him, in his desperation to escape his pursuers. Illawara hampered by her skirts had yanked them up to one side to keep pace, and Hermes pulled her along with him, light as a bird in his sprint. The Professor flew down stairs toward the back quarters of the Uffizi, and lobbed a torchlight behind him, as Antonio, sprinting, gained ground. The torch missed Antonio and the others by a fraction, but had the desired effect as two men of the guard were forced to stop and stamp out the flames that then erupted on one of the luxurious carpets, after Illawara and Hermes bundled past.

The Professor, dashing, reached the kitchens where he knew the courtyard and stables were nearby. Emerging from a darkened corner like a vampire, the pale henchman lunged at the Professor with a knife. The Professor managed to block the full force of the blow with his arm, but the sharp blade still sliced the skin as it cut through his wide-sleeved shirt, and stained it with a streak of scarlet blood. The Professor grabbed up a rolling pin left on a table in the vacated kitchen and used his new weapon like a sword to defend himself. The pair struggled: the henchman slashed at the air as the Professor avoided the blade, but the Professor connected with a strike of his own across the brow of his assailant. The ghoulish man stumbled back and clutched at his face as if punch-drunk, as dark blood began to flow from the bridge of his eye between his pale and twig-like fingers. The Professor scrambled to a door, and flayed with his hands at the bolts like a wild animal; the door streaked with his blood. Illawara, half falling down the stairs, had overtaken Antonio and emerged first into the kitchen. She screamed once more as the henchman; part recovered, had begun to lunge again in the direction of the Professor as he struggled with the last door bolt.

Within a blink, she scanned the kitchen, before she leapt to the side to yank a heavy copper pan from a hook, and ran forward to swing it, like a cricket bat, and slam the pan into the side of the henchman's head. The man crumpled to the floor, as the tattered face of the Professor looked back at the sound. Wide eyed he glanced at her before he flung open the door and ran towards the stables. Illawara stood, unable to move, and wept before she dropped the blood-stained pan with a clang,

'Please... *Please* don't leave me again. I'm sorry' she wailed as she watched her father sprint away, and a sob heaved out of her.

'We have to get out of here' Antonio said, his fear palpable, as he heard the clamour of guards making their way down the stairs. 'Quick, he's running to the stables, if we can get to our carriage, maybe we can catch him.' Antonio shoved Illawara and Hermes forward, and slammed the door behind them, as both men then ran across the courtyard and pulled Illawara along with them, limp and crying, to where their coach awaited.

Few carriages were left as most guests had departed for home, or for the brothels, or for the taverns of Florence. Up ahead the group caught sight of the Professor as he vaulted a stable gate, and in moments had untethered, and leapt onto the back of a black stallion, and jumped the gate again on horseback: as he clung to the horse's mane like a crazed man while the startled horse whinnied. The group reached the coach as Hermes flung open the door to push Illawara in, before Antonio leapt up into the vacated driver's seat, and whipped the horses into action. The original coach driver, and footman, then emerged from a side stable with flapping breaches, followed by a confused woman who stuffed her breasts back into her corset.

The coach lurched around to the left, as Antonio did his best to turn around and cut off the Professor before he could exit the courtyard. Several guards had assembled themselves to prevent escape by blocking the main gaits. The Professor reached into his blood-stained jerkin to pull out a small pouch before he charged at the men. The guards held their ground with their polearms outstretched to spook the horse, but the Professor dug his heels into the sides of the stallion to urge him on. The men scattered has the animal launched into the air to clear the blades, as the Professor threw the pouch at the ground with all his might. The pouch exploded with a flash and billowed with smoke obscuring all, and almost caused Antonio's coach to crash as his horses lurched away from the discharge. Antonio gave up the chase of the Professor, as a guard leapt forward through the smoke to intercept the carriage, but miss timed his lunge and became caught by a hoof of the sprinting horses.

The animals swerved to avoid the man, but the coach wheel then glanced off the courtyard gate, which knocked Illawara's head against the carriage interior, and crushed the body of the hapless guard: his anguished screams almost lost to the night in the din and squeal of horses. The guard's blood shot out his mouth as the iron-clod carriage wheel ran over his rib cage and burst his lungs, with a dull pop, and crushed his spine. Some other guards lay injured after trying to leap onto the carriage, and Illawara screamed as the guard's bodies thudded against the side of the vehicle, but the lucky ones clambered on.

Antonio, with one hand on the reigns, turned this way and that to whip at them all in the eyes, ruthless and accurate, before the guards yelled, and fell back clutching their faces, while their dead colleague's flesh lay mangled by hoof and wheel. In the maelstrom and confusion, Antonio thought of the safety of his passengers, as well as his own life, and twisted the coach down a side street. Illawara wept, inconsolable, as Hermes rubbed her banged head. Behind him, Antonio left the groans of the fallen, the stunned or the injured, to take a crossing at a quiet part of the river Arno and make their getaway.

The Professor, free of a carriage, continued his escape, at high speed, on the stolen black stallion by crossing the languid river Arno at the Ponte Vecchio. The city had begun to sleep, few people mingled about, but the hooves of the steed clattered like broken China across the cobbled bridge, and along past the shuttered jewellery shops, as the impostor headed for the hills and shadows. The Professor, bloodied but determined, his wig lost and shirt torn, rode on with grim focus, as his face flapped like a flag in the moonlight.

Chapter 9

The Fugitives

Outer Florence, before Dawn, Monday October 3rd, 1611

'I had a very strange dream last night' said Illawara, from where she lay, to Hermes as he rubbed the sleep out of his eyes, and got up from the chair where he had slept. He yawned and stretched himself like an amber coloured cat.

'What was it about?' he replied, before sniffing at himself.

'I'm not sure' she said, 'but you were in it as you are now. You were running, and you were holding a baby. Then there was a bright flash, and then I woke up.' Hermes looked as if a cold chill had caught him by surprise, and he gave an involuntary shudder.

'Do you remember anything else?'

'No' she said. Hermes nodded, before his shoulders relaxed.

'Where are we?' said Hermes, yawning again, as he took in the unfamiliar surroundings of the living room where they had spent the night. Near to the wooden chair where Hermes had slept stood a large stone hearth that still gave out some warmth from the firewood burned in it the night before. In another corner stood a cabinet-come-bookshelf laden with ecclesiastical books in fanciful bindings. Nearby a small round table lay strewn with hardened bread, and food scraps from the hasty meal eaten the night before. In the feeble twilight that struggled to enter the dim room, between the gaps in the shutters, Hermes figured that they were in a basement dwelling.

Antonio lay asleep on the floor beside the fire swaddled in a green blanket, except for a tuft of his blond hair that had escaped from the wrapping he had made for himself: looking like an ear of corn. Hermes observed the blanketed figure on the floor, smiled, and recalled that Antonio had insisted that he take the chair, before offering a makeshift bed to Illawara. Antonio had then laid himself down by the fire as if he were a street urchin - ignoring any discomfort he may have felt.

Illawara lay draped across a wooden bench, softened with a scrap of an old mattress, and clung to her blanket, decorated with flowers, with a listless expression. She looked like Ophelia in her river as she gazed up empty headed to the ceiling as if waiting for the ceiling to speak back to her. Hermes turned to look back at her - her face pale - but thought it best to leave Illawara alone.

Instead, the youth turned away and crept across the room to open a door, before halting to ponder the playing cards and dice that lay strewn upon the lower shelf of the book cabinet. The door creaked behind Hermes as he walked into the passageway, and smelled the scent of cooking. Hermes crossed the stone floor, almost in darkness, and followed his nose. The smells of frying pork lead him into the kitchen via a side door. Inside he found a man standing over a frying pan, and wood-burning stove, pushing sizzling cubes of pancetta around with a spoon and looking out through a window into an enclosed courtyard.

When Hermes entered the man then turned, and Hermes recognised him as the young priest Marco they all had met the day before. 'Buongiorno signore, are you hungry?' he said with a smile, Hermes nodded. 'Take a seat. I'm making an omelette before everyone wakes up.' The priest then threw some chopped leeks and onions into the pan with some seasoning and continued to stir with confidence. 'Quite a night you've all had, so I hear' said Marco.

'Yes, I guess it was' replied Hermes, looking for somewhere to sit down.

'A man is dead I'm told.' Hermes covered his mouth as he gasped.

'What? That's horrible' he said. Hermes then cast his mind back to when Illawara struck Orsini's henchman with a copper pan and dreaded she had killed him.

Marco was the type of man who struggled to hold back when something juicy was to be said. He had savoured Hermes' reaction before he continued: 'Antonio thinks he may have run over a guard with the carriage.'

'Oh?' said Hermes, as his expression darkened. 'I believe we did hit something, but I thought it might have been a cornerstone...' his voice trailed off, but Marco gave a look that urged him back to speech. Hermes rubbed at his forehead, 'well, things were desperate at that moment, there was so much confusion, we didn't know what was going on. The guards seemed to be everywhere. So much shouting and yelling...' Hermes shook his head as if trying to eradicate the memory.

'Oh, don't worry yourself' said the priest with a dismissive waft of his spoon through the air, 'I say he deserved it; a lot of the Duke's guards are bastards. A bunch of lying, cheating bastards - all of them.' Hermes' eyes bulged.

'What? But you're a priest aren't you supposed to cross yourself and pray for their souls or something?' The priest rolled his eyes.

'Do I look like a nun?' Marco then mused for a moment and rubbed his chin. 'Maybe you're right, and I should say something.' Marco then made exaggerated signs of the cross in the air before raising his hands in mock prayer: 'dear Lord bless the bastard' said the priest before thumbing his chin, and dashing a bowl of beaten eggs into the sizzling frying pan. Hermes closed his mouth but shook his head before he sat himself down as the priest continued talking. 'You're all in a sticky situation: Antonio tells me that Cardinal Orsini is after you, and he's not a man to cross.' Hermes rubbed again at his brow,

'I knew this was a bad idea' he thought to himself. Hermes clutched at his stomach, before releasing the wind out of his mouth. 'Well, he does have something about him' Hermes then said aloud, 'He's unsettling, he has some kind of power, some kind of...' Hermes trailed off,

'Intensity?' said Marco, Hermes nodded, 'oh yes, that dragon is well known for it - he gets what he wants.' Marco then wriggled his brow with a tilt of his head. Hermes cradled his chin in his hands and looked on at Marco's preparations with blank emptiness. Antonio and Illawara entered the kitchen. Antonio looked younger to Hermes with his hair ruffled and his face still soft from sleep. Illawara came into the kitchen behind Antonio as if in a trance, her usual spark much dimmed. She had taken off her diamond choker, chopines, and high ruff collar: she looked bleached. 'I think you need to sit down and eat some food' said Marco to Illawara, after just one look at her. Hermes pulled out a seat for her at the table, and she fell onto it like a tattered rag without speaking. All three looked on with concern at the unfamiliar, docile, creature before Antonio spoke to break the silence:

'Oh God, I'm a dead man' he exclaimed, 'what a night.' Marco seemed almost amused at the declaration, 'kind brother' Antonio continued, 'I've not been able to tell you the half of it.' The Priest smirked,

'Well, what you said last night was feast enough for any man, are there yet more dishes to be added to the table?' said Marco. He enjoyed his visual pun, as he portioned out the steaming omelette onto four plates, before raking a gnarled stump of Parmesan over a grater and dusting the pieces with the cheese.

'Oh brother. Where to begin and where to end?' said Antonio, dragging his fingers through his hair, and tensing his jaw, before he blew air out of his mouth. 'I'm saddened, but running over that guard is not the worst of it: I fear I've caused a scandal for the Duke. All of Firenze will ring with the news. I'll never be allowed back at court again, and we'll be hunted by that crocodile Orsini.' At the mention of the Cardinal's name, Illawara roused a somewhat from her wakeful sleep and seemed to take more interest in the conversation.

'Well, you've given him good reason to chase' said Marco, with a side look to Illawara that Hermes did not miss.

'Indeed I have' said Antonio, throwing his arms aloft as if pleading to God, before clamping his hands on the crown of his head and walking to the kitchen window. 'The Cardinal is relentless - we've all heard the stories, but I *know* him. I know what he's like - what they say about him is true' Antonio continued, 'this is going to be tough, very tough indeed.'

'Ah, so it is' said Marco with a philosophical sigh, 'Orsini stops at nothing to get what he wants, but for now, you can't run on empty stomachs. Eat, my friends, before the food gets cold.'

Antonio obeyed and made his way to sit with the others, and all began to eat their food. Illawara ate with slow mouthfuls, but the meal started to give her some colour, although she looked like a tepid thing - still eclipsed by her former self in the glory of the night before. After half finishing her meal, Illawara paused in thought before she spoke up: 'can he be so bad?' she said, the three young men turned to look at her, 'he's an excellent dancer…'

'Are you talking about Orsini?' said Marco, frowning.

'Yes,' she said, 'is that so wrong? How old is he? Because he dances like a young man.' All three men widened their eyes at her. Antonio cast an aside look at Hermes, and then flicked his head in Illawara's direction, but the youth could only shrug his shoulders.

'You don't know him, Illawara' said Antonio. Marco coughed as if he were an actor on a stage:

'He's is older than Judas and twice as cunning' boomed Marco, shaking his cooking spoon in the air. 'I'm surprised that jackal can dance at all - what a charm you must have had on him - most of the Cardinals I know are too gouty to dance on feathers without soiling themselves.' Antonio reached out to grasp Illawara's clammy hand:

'Don't be taken in Illawara, Orsini is powerful, but he's a dangerous man. Dancing or not, we'll have to be careful with our movements from now on.' Illawara snatched her hand away from Antonio's grasp.

'Fine, but Orsini doesn't frighten me?' Illawara raised her chin. The three men exchanged glances and looked at Illawara again, 'ok, he frightens me a bit' she said, 'yes, especially the way he looked into me...' Antonio gave a shudder of recognition. Illawara's eyes glazed over as she spoke, 'it was like he knew me, really knew me. It's *impossible*, of course, but I felt like he saw every part of me. I couldn't hide from him. I felt...' Illawara turned away, 'I felt - naked.' Illawara clutched at herself as if reliving her dance with the Cardinal - remembering his eyes, face, and embrace. She sat staring into the distance as if still listening to the music.

'Illy, what are you talking about?' said Hermes, shaking her shoulder. Illawara had shivered before she seemed to rouse from her reverie. Illawara considered the faces of the men around her.

'But someone who moves like that can't be *all* bad' she continued, 'he has poetry in him - I can tell.' A silence fell between the men as they pondered Illawara who seemed to occupy another realm.

'I can tell' said Marco, pointing to the bruise on Illawara's forehead, 'that you must have walloped your head on the carriage door when Nino ran over that guard?' Antonio winced, 'I've never heard such talk about Orsini - you speak as if that reptile were a prince' added Marco tutting while shaking his head. Marco then used his finger to mop up the last remnants of his omelette into his mouth, before releasing the digit with a petulant pop.

'But he *is* a Prince' she said, 'he's a Prince of The Church, no?' added Illawara before she scratched her fork around her plate like a pauper in response to Marco's chastisement. Marco pouted, shook his head, and sniffed at the air.

'You're confused' said Marco, 'a lot of Cardinals ACT and are treated like Princes, but it doesn't mean they are ones...' huffed Marco, 'only a matter of time though – there's much talk of it in The Church – I'm against the idea.' Hermes studied Illawara's face before she looked out to the window and sighed.

'Where do you think we'll be safe for now, Marco?' whispered Antonio to Marco as if Orsini could burst in at any moment.

'It's difficult to say, Nino, as there are few places where the eyes of Orsini do not see, but I know a friend who has a safe-house in another part of town. It's not too far from here. It's further up the hill toward Arcetri.' Antonio beamed a smile.

'Good, we'll go there. What's your friend's name?' said Antonio,

'Riccolo, he's a spice merchant, but you'll have to find him first' said Marco, 'the house belongs to his relative, but you can find him in the taverns - or the brothels.' Hermes raised an eyebrow,

'What kind of priest is this?' Hermes thought to himself, before focusing his attention on Antonio.

'Which one?' Asked the Valet, 'there are so many places - does he have a favourite?'

'Try Da Francesco Taverna first, he likes to eat there, or then there's Il L'azzurro Madonna' Marco paused to smirk, 'he likes to eat there too.' Hermes frowned at Marco's words, but Illawara seemed oblivious.

'The Blue Madonna? That's quite a name to give to a whore-house' scoffed Hermes.

'But what of it?' said Antonio. The smirk died on Hermes' face, 'a man must have his pleasure.'

'But what about my Dad?' said Illawara, released back into reality.

'You have a father in Florence?' said Marco, stepping forward, like he wished to give up his vows. Illawara's face faltered.

'Well yes, and no... I don't know if he's still in the city: it's complicated.'

'That's not even the half of it' Hermes sniped, crossing his arms, 'her father is the reason we even came here in the first place - but we couldn't be sure where he was. Then we were offered a ride in the Earl's carriage - that's how we met Antonio - but he turned out to be her father.' Marco's mouth dropped open, 'Yes' said Hermes, shaking his head, 'we thought her father would be at the banquet, but he was with us all along.' Marco looked incredulous. He addressed Illawara.

'So you were travelling with your own father, and you didn't recognise him?' He shook his head as if scolding a toddler, 'you're not a bright girl' added Marco. Illawara shrank with shame, 'but don't worry, pretty one, I'll be your *father.*' Antonio pushed his friend back.

'He wore a disguise' said Antonio in Illawara's defence, 'none of us knew until Orsini tore off his mask - he had us ALL fooled.' Marco arched his brows – quite tickled.

'It just gets better' said Marco, wallowing in the revelations, before he crossed at himself, 'oh Madonna, you really are in a *lot* of trouble.'

'We know that' spat Hermes.

'Oh shut up - all of you' shrieked Illawara, 'Let's just *find* him, and get him home' she said, before clamping her hands to her head. Illawara grasped at her hair and began to sob like an abandoned child. More concerned looks passed around the table.

'I think he may come back, Illawara.' said Antonio. Illawara shook her head, and tried to regain control of herself, her head pounding.

'Why would he?' she whispered, 'He clearly doesn't care about me.'

'But I think he must come back' offered Antonio, 'because he's left his case in the carriage. I don't know what's in it, I asked, but he wouldn't let me handle it.' Hermes and Illawara looked at each other, 'so I guess it's important to him, if so, he may come to you instead.' Illawara blinked several times, and her expression freshened.

'Yes, I hope so. Dad must have forgotten it in the rush...' said Illawara, as she pondered the potential contents of the case.

'Did he say anything to you, Antonio?' asked Hermes, as he rubbed Illawara's back.

'Not much' said Antonio 'I travelled with him down from Torino before Pisa, and we talked about several things. I arranged accommodation, I know the inns, but I can't imagine I know more than about him than his daughter does.'

'You could know more' said Hermes, 'It's been a while.'

Illawara began to compose herself as Marco looked on - much entertained by his guest's plight. 'After last night I don't know what to believe' said Antonio, 'but he's a man of reason and culture. We spoke of many things, and especially of Galileo - he knew a lot about him.'

'The *heretic*' said Marco, who waved his hands in mock horror, enjoying himself. 'I've nothing personal against him' added Marco, 'but all in The Church call him so: Orsini despises him, and encourages everyone he knows to discredit the man.' Antonio bristled.

'Stop your teasing, Marco' said Antonio; 'I'm told that you have illegal books bound in Bible covers. What do you think the Inquisition would say about that?' Marco shrugged,

'I don't care - we all need something interesting to read. They always ban the best books' he huffed, 'I'm sure Galileo's will be next.'

'He's an enlightened man of our age' Antonio continued, in earnest, 'The Starry Messenger and Galileo are far ahead of their time, they will change the minds of men. I'm sure of it. I can understand why the Earl, I mean your father, was eager to speak with him.'

'I had you down for a social climber, not a philosopher' sneered Marco.

'*Hush*, let him speak' said Hermes, 'you were saying...' Antonio cleared his throat and commanded himself.

'He mentioned wanting to see someone at the convent of San Matteo, soon after we arrived in Pisa' said Antonio.

'But it's just a bunch of old nuns that live up there' said Marco, shaking his head, 'and the young ones are all ugly - well, except for one. She's...'

'Can you lead us to him, Antonio?' said Illawara, 'I must speak with my father.' Antonio flapped his arms.

'But who *is* he? And what is he doing here?' he said. Illawara and Hermes looked at each other again, before their eyes rested on Marco.

'I can't explain now' she said, 'I promise I'll tell you later, but we must hurry. My Dad could be in danger.' Marco looked on half surprised, and half amused by the revelations that poured out from his fugitives. The lay priest could not remember when he was last so entertained, apart from the lewd banter of the inns and brothels he frequented.

'Marco' said Antonio, 'we must begin to make our move before it's too late. Tell me where your friend's house is, and we shall call on it before we try to find him in the taverns.' After shaking his head with a half-smile at the group, Marco wrote directions to the safe house and the names of Inns, brothels and taverns on a scrap of Chinese paper while his fugitives made ready.

Antonio and Hermes, though irritated, thanked Marco for his food and hospitality. Illawara told herself to calm down, drying her eyes, before giving her own thanks, although she had been insulted. In the gathering morning, yet to break, the group made their way to the carriage. Antonio located the Professor's case for Illawara and gave it to her.

'Travel safely, bellissima' Marco called after Illawara - restored to her finery. She ignored him as she got in. Hermes then paused with his foot upon the carriage step, before he turned to Marco:

'Why did you become a priest?' He asked. Marco shrugged,

'It's not my calling, but I'm the youngest son - what choice do I have?' he said, grinning, before Hermes slammed the door shut, and Marco saw them all off. Antonio glanced back at his friend, a waving shadow, before the sun would rise and banish the last of twilight, and the first church bells would ring before the morning bustle returned to the streets of Florence.

Antonio folded the scrap of paper handed to him bearing the notes and scrawled map of their new destination and shoved it into his breast pocket. Illawara had handled Professor Sloane's dark leather-bound case before she clutched it to her chest. Antonio cracked his whips to rouse the sleepy horses into action and became comforted by the sound of wheels on cobbles leaping in his ears, as they progressed toward upper Florence and Arcetri.

Chapter 10

The Convent of San Matteo

The outskirts of Florence, before dawn

Professor Sloane had slept rough that night just off the roadside that leads up to Arcetri.

He had found an alcove that faced inward to a narrow carriage yard with a dead end. Winston thought it best to avoid the taverns that night, as that would be the first place Orsini and the authorities would look for him. He needed to keep a low profile and wait for the danger to pass. It had not taken long for the stallion to abandon him once he got off the beast, he understood the animal had no loyalty to him and wished that he could have stolen a car instead.

Still lying in the alcove, before daybreak, he shivered and brushed off the dew that had crept upon him in the night. He sniffed at the air: cool, mossy, and fresh in contrast to the bitter taste in his mouth. More leaves had fallen during the night, and they littered the carriage yard like coloured pencil shavings. He tried to get up, failed, tried again, failed, and then decided to roll forward. He used his momentum to stand at the third attempt: uncurling himself like a fern frond.

His body ached all over: his skin covered in bruises, his joints clicked, and his right arm sore where the knife had slashed his skin. But his linen shirt had done a good job of staunching his blood, and a thick scab had formed underneath the stained shirtsleeve, where the fabric had mingled with it. He winced somewhat as he freed shirt fibres from the clotted blood. The Professor did not look good. His clothes were still grand, but grubby and stained, his hair a gerbil's nest.

He shook his head and body to reject the cold and the previous night, stumbling forward, before his mind turned to food and water. He looked back to the ground where he had slept and saw that toadstools had grown around him during the night. The spotted red caps stood arranged in the outline of a man's body as if to mark the scene of a crime.

'I hope she can feed me' he said to himself. A dark grey sky hung overhead, and the blush of dawn began to peep in the east. One or two birds sang, but the rest didn't bother. The Professor then tottered back to the street and looked around. No one, just pastel coloured houses, and a thick mist up the hill. He would have gone further toward the convent of San Matteo, but the stallion's gallop was too loud. Professor Sloane guessed at a fifteen-minute walk and made his way up the Via San Leonardo. On the way, a cat crossed his path, looked at him, hissed and then ran away. The Professor shrugged, walked on, and then caught sight of his reflection in a cow trough: a phantom stared back. He peeled off the remainder of his disguise, took out a contact lens, and regained another silver-grey eye. The cat had done him a favour. The Professor scooped up some water, closed his eyes, and splashed his palms on his face to revive himself, and then moved at speed up the hill to reach the convent before anyone could see him.

The road to Arcetri lead up steep and narrow. Professor Sloan had surprised himself by how often he had to stop for breath: his body unwilling in the effort. The silent and narrow road, flanked by houses, had gathered the mist like a funnel, and it eddied as his tired body walked through. After longer than expected he emerged at the top of the hill of Arcetri. The sudden opening of the environment left him exposed, so he scurried to the side of a low stone wall, only to be engulfed by the sight of a vast valley cradled by undulating hills.

The Professor forgot his situation, stood still, and became possessed by the view. The silvery mist of the valley hid the trunks of the olive trees that clung like creatures to the hills in the steeper parts. The intensifying blush of dawn began to colour the mist, and Winston saw himself as a boy again - holding his mother's hand at the Oxford County Fair - as if looking into a valley filled with candy floss. His eyes began to water, and he gripped the wall while ambushed by emotion. His vision blurred, and his nose ran as something below moved in the valley. The Professor had missed the figure of the woman at first, but his eyes began to focus when she sang. A sweet, but deep, voice rang resonant across the valley. The birds stopped singing - as if to listen.

He spied the curves of her as she swept herself in circles, and stirred the pink mist. In one hand she held herbs, in the other a thin rod of iron and a silver mezzaluna. Oblivious to him the woman continued to hum and sing in the mist, and to make graceful swoops down, here and there, to another herb before chanting something to the plant, drawing a circle around it with the iron rod, and then cutting a part of it off with thanks and blessings. The Professor stood transfixed.

With one hand full of herbs and the other with her tools she stood again, then swayed, and swung into another spin when a frond of sunlight broke the horizon and illuminated her body. She then stopped her motion, and turned to face the sun with eyes closed and arms outstretched in a gesture of welcome: her body glowed naked save for a thin mesh of organza, studded with crystals, that she had entwined about her arms and shoulders - she glistened in the light. Then the woman stopped her singing, unfurled her cloak of crystal in the sun and uttered: 'I am a Goddess' and then swept the shining garment about herself, before vanishing into the air with laughter. The Professor then rubbed at his eyes dumbfounded and confused, unsure of what he had just seen yet convinced to his core that the vision had been real. He then considered the toadstools that had grown around him in the night as if they had somehow affected him.

■ ■ ■

Professor Sloane had taken some time before he reached the door of the convent of the Poor Clares of San Matteo. He had walked in a daze after witnessing the vision of the enchanting woman dancing. He shook his head as if to dismiss the woman from his mind. He looked up to the large wooden gates that stood between hefty stone posts that abutted the high walls of the convent. The Professor looked around for a bell or knocker with which to attract attention but was apprehensive to do so. He then spied what looked like a small rectangular hatch lower down to one side of the wooden gates, and considered knocking on it, while the light of day grew brighter around him. His eyes darted about the place - he did not have long before someone would see him. The Professor had hesitated before he reached across to tap his fist on the hatch - when it flew open to reveal the wrinkled face of an old woman. He leapt back and clapped his hand to his mouth to stop a howl escaping,

'Am I so ugly?' said the withered face cracking into a smile of very few teeth.

'No' came the breathless reply, 'you just shocked me. I was looking for something to ring or knock.'

'Did our Mother Superior not give proper instruction?' said the face with a voice like dry bark shuffled in a timber yard.

'I followed her instructions' said the Professor, 'but as to getting in she wrote nothing.'

'Is it not the sunrise of the third day, on the tenth month on the day of our Lord?' said the face.

'Yes, it is' he added,

'Then that is enough, what is the safe-word?'

'Safe-word?' he replied, confused.

'Yes, what is it?' The Professor looked baffled; there had been no mention of a safe-word in his letter from the Abbess. He looked at the old woman, guessed her deranged, and so he made something up. His mind cast back to the words of the vanishing woman: 'Aphrodite' he said. The little eyes in the face lit up, and the lines around them crinkled like filo pastry:

'Not *quite,* but good enough. You're wise' said the face, 'you may enter.' The Professor seemed relieved as the door hatch closed and he heard bolts moving. A door within the large wooden gates then opened. The nun looked minuscule, and the slight stoop of her neck put her well under five feet tall. The little nun in her black habit and white shawl stood back to let the Professor in and gave another gappy smile. The Professor had to stoop low, almost to crouching to enter before standing again.

'You're tall and broad, young man' she said, admiring him, as she bolted the door closed behind him and fetched up under her arm the stool on which she stood to open the hatch. The nun fixed him with a look: 'I was beautiful once you know' she said, and cackled with a sound like dry wood crackling in a fireplace. The Professor struggled for a word of reply, 'yes, I know' she sighed, 'hard to believe now, but follow me' she whispered. 'We'll have something to help that heal' she added, gesturing at his blood-stained arm, before she moved at some speed, with a pronounced limp, across an enclosed courtyard of stone and arches.

In the Chapel, the Poor Clares had begun to sing in morning prayer as the man followed behind the nun, and her little feet patted out a rhythm in counterpoint to the sweet high notes of the nuns in Chapel. 'This way' the little nun said, pausing her hippity-hop as she lead Winston across the courtyard, under an arch and into a passageway and antechamber. 'Wait here' she said, glancing about, halting him with a gesture before clasping his hands in hers, and looking up into his face. Her hands felt like warm tobacco leaves: 'listen to me. What I say to you now is vital. When you enter the Abbess' chamber, do not touch anything unless she allows you too. To do otherwise, young man, is dangerous indeed' she eyed him again, as she felt up his forearms, 'but you're healthy and wise' she muttered as she massaged his flesh.

'How do you know I'm wise?' said the Professor, trying to wriggle his arms free,

'By your safe-word' said the little nun, enjoying her grip on him,

'But I made it up' said the Professor,

'I know' she replied, 'but t'was a good one, it will please her, you have already made a good start.'

The little nun released the Professor to open a door, off the antechamber, to a hallway lined with stained glass depicting scenes from the Bible: which illuminated the way to a tall black door at the end of the passage in a kaleidoscope of colours.

'Kneel down' said the little nun, after checking they were still alone. She clasped the Professor's hands again, but he resisted her before he obeyed. She then took his face in her hands and kissed his forehead; she smelled of urine and lavender. The Professor coughed. But her little dark eyes twinkled: 'think before you speak, and all will be well, speak before you think, and things could end badly' she said, 'now kiss me' she added. The Professor's eyes almost leapt from their sockets.

He tried to move his face, but the little nun had strength. She puckered her shrivelled lips, as she held him fast, and the Professor squinted before closing his eyes. The wrinkled wet kiss was over in an instant, and when he opened his eyes for a moment, he saw a pretty young face looking back at him. He blinked several times, in disbelief, but the face of the nun, which looked like a brown paper bag, had returned: 'as I said, I was beautiful once.' The little nun let go of him with another crackling chuckle, wished him luck, groped his buttocks while he stood up, and then pushed him down the hallway before scampering off.

The Professor shook his head in disbelief, and tried to rub sleep out of his eyes. 'Never in my life... groped by... No, I'm *hallucinating*. It must be the toadstools?' he muttered to himself, 'I must have touched them in the night; it will wear off.' He then ran his hands through his hair to tidy it, before he checked behind him to see that he remained alone. The Professor then approached the ebony door at the end of the colourful passage, which seemed to loom ever larger as he walked toward it. When he reached the door, he studied some of the detailed woodwork that was far from Christian. There were satyrs, animals, centaurs, flowers, and dancing women rendered in exquisite detail around the edges of the pointed arch door. He gave the wood a light touch and the door opened, ajar, and a smell of incense and perfume oozed out of the gap.

The Professor took in a heady breath, readied himself, and entered the warm darkness before the door closed behind him.

■ ■ ■

Antonio followed Marco's map, but it had taken time before they were in the intertwining streets that surrounded the Palazzo Pitti. Activity had begun to increase in the walkways. Market sellers had loaded their produce onto wooden carts: one man's cart loaded with cabbages and onions, another piled his with squash and courgettes, yet another loaded his cart with bottles of olive oil wrapped in straw and stuffed into boxes.

Antonio rode on and looked for a place where he could tether the horses on a side street without drawing too much attention, while a robust woman, with a ruddy face, crossed the road holding a large wicker basket filled with mushrooms she had picked before dawn - her fingernails still dark with soil. The noise and jabber of the public increased as people started their day, and made their way about amongst the jangle of goat bells, donkey brays, and the smell, muck, and fuss of everyday life.

Antonio's fear began to increase as more people mingled in the streets. He looked from his vantage point, above the increasing populous, trying to detect looks of suspicion, and he listened to the banter of people as they passed by to hear if anyone spoke of last night's events. Lawyers walked with their apprentices before serving the needs of their clients; prosperous wives walked with their retinue of relatives, maids, and children on the way to buy produce in the Mercato Centrale. The farmers moved their livestock along the streets which added sounds of honking geese and grunting pigs to the increasing noise of the alleyways as the day progressed. No one seemed to have much interest in Antonio, or the carriage, as he turned off the Borgo Tegolaio into the side street of Via D. Petti.

Antonio, once satisfied they had not attracted attention, brought the horses to a stop, climbed down, and then tethered them to a wooden railing next to a trough. The animals drank as Antonio made a short walk to a man selling hay bags at the alleyway, and bought one each for the horses. Antonio could see the looks of Illawara and Hermes, turning their heads this way and that, scanning the crowds, as they watched him attach the nag bags to the muzzles of the hungry horses. Antonio then entered the carriage and closed the door behind him: 'the horses were hungry, they needed feeding' he said to the pair who shifted themselves in their seats, 'I could be wrong, but for now at least it seems no one is looking for us.'

'I doubt that' said Hermes, as he looked out of the window again and inspected people as they passed by the carriage.

'Yes, you're probably right' said Antonio, 'but it seems the alarm may not have been raised fully for fear of a scandal. Orsini could embarrass the church and compromise his position if the Pope finds out.'

'The Pope?' said Illawara: wide eyed,

'Well, yes' Antonio continued, 'you told my friend, that Orsini's a Prince of The Church, even if he was he still has to answer to his master: The *Pope*.' Antonio gave Illawara a look as if she were an imbecile.

'Oh, of course, how silly of me...' she added before she looked out of the carriage window and saw the beggar woman with her listless baby again as they swayed through the streets. Illawara cringed and bit her lip, as she clasped her hands on the Professor's dark leather-bound suitcase. Antonio studied her face with a look of questioning before continuing.

'Alright, the day is getting on' said Antonio as if to rouse Illawara and Hermes from their mood, 'once we find Riccolo we'll be safe for a while. We'll try his safe-house first on foot, though I can guess where he may be. Then we'll try the other places. But maybe, with time, your father will come to us for that case you're holding.' Antonio made a gesture in Illawara's direction, but she shrank back and tightened her grip. Antonio then paused before he turned his attention to the youth: 'Hermes I need you to come with me to find Riccolo in the taverns - or the other place – if he's not at the safe-house.' The youth hesitated and looked at Illawara, 'naturally, Illawara will not be able to attend: it's not proper for a woman of Illawara's rank to be seen entering such places' Hermes blinked a few times, before remembering what Marco had mentioned at breakfast. Illawara shrugged somewhat.

'Will you be ok to stay here, Illy?' said Hermes,

'I suppose so' said Illawara who continued to study the beggar woman, and the other paupers that made a return procession down the street asking for alms.

'It's not ideal, but it should do for now' Antonio continued, 'we won't be gone for long as there are only a few taverns to check in this area, and Il L'azzuro Madonna is the only brothel this side of the Arno.' Hermes felt a stir of excitement rise in the pit of his stomach - which surprised him,

'Are you sure you'll be ok, Illy?'

'Yes, I'll be fine' came her reply, somewhat distracted. Illawara then ignored the young men and seemed keen for them to leave. Antonio and Hermes then looked at each other before they stepped out of the carriage.

'Try not to speak to anyone who tries to get your attention, and don't leave the carriage' Antonio warned, 'we won't be long.' Illawara nodded and gave a weak smile before they closed the carriage door. After Hermes and Antonio had walked a few steps, the Valet spoke to the youth: 'what's in that suitcase that Illawara's holding?' Hermes tried to avoid Antonio's curious gaze, and ignore how his blue eyes caught the light,

'I'm not sure?' he said, but Antonio seemed unconvinced. 'Neither of you is Italian, are you?' said Antonio, as Hermes avoided his gaze and struggled to find words as they walked on. Illawara watched Hermes and Antonio walk off down the street, as they talked, and sat confident that she would be alone for a while. She then turned her attention to the Professor's dark suitcase, slid back two brass panels near the handle to reveal the little combination locks hidden underneath. She turned the numbered dials to the correct master combination and sprung the locks open with the press of her thumbs.

The case lay full of bottled tinctures and potions the most of which she recognised, but there were a few more she did not: she looked on, absorbed, as she inspected the different bottles in the light - and they glowed with their various mixtures. Illawara became so absorbed in her study that she did not notice the figure of a hooded brown robed man, with a pale, drawn, face and a bruised raw cut above his eye, as he peered into the carriage.

Chapter 11

The Bedchamber

Inside the Convent of San Matteo, Arcetri

It took time for Professor Sloane's eyes to adjust to the dim light in the Abbess' chamber, as the door had closed behind him without being touched. He smelled more than he saw as a rich, intoxicating aroma of cinnamon bark: cloves, vanilla, frankincense, and clary sage filled his nostrils, which made him feel blissful and light headed.

A beeswax candle burned in a far corner within an amber glass, which produced a dim orange light. He walked forward careful not to make a noise as he began to see some of the room's many adornments. A rich tapestry hung along one side of the wall, which depicted Diana, Goddess of the hunt, bathing with her nymphs in a lake, and Actaeon being transformed into a stag as she splashed him with water. Along another wall of the large chamber hung with celestial maps of the zodiac, and diagrams of those signs in relation to the body, a wide selection of Grimoires sat shelved. It struck Winston as odd that an Abbess should own so many magical books, but then he reflected on what he had already seen, and corrected himself.

One of the magical books lay open on a table under the bookshelves. The Professor paused and held his breath in the dim light. He tiptoed forward, inspecting the book closer with his eyes, and confirmed his suspicions: it was an original binding of a Grimoire long thought lost almost four hundred years into the future. He drew closer still, and the hairs stood up on his arms as he saw some of the rare Hebrew symbols depicted on the open pages. He had only known them from referring to other books - books that had taken him years to discover.

His pulse quickened, verifying the find, as he reached out to seize the book and flee. His hands prickled above the book, the sensations running up his arms before he remembered the little nun's warning and then drew back.

The Professor then heard a woman's voice, deep and smooth, coming from what sounded like a room next-door. The Professor then turned back on himself, almost tripping over some gold figurines of Buddha and Durga, to follow the voice and noticed that he had passed a door, draped with dark purple velvet: the fabric had obscured a door to a small chamber before his eyes had adjusted to the darkness. He drew closer to the door that stood ajar and peered inside.

The Abbess stood facing away from him draped in a dark blue robe, fringed with pearls and cloth of gold. She stood, absorbed in prayer and meditation, as she made symbolic gestures in front of a crystal ball that sat cradled within a pair of upturned eagle's claws. The crystal orb began to swirl and glow within as she continued her incantations, and images began to form inside the ball. Unable to help himself the Professor stepped closer to get a better look at the crystal. The utterances of the Abbess intensified as murky images became clearer, and the Professor almost shrieked when he recognised what looked like his rented carriage, and then the contents of his dark leather-bound suitcase. He had almost forgotten the case in his haste to evade capture the night before, and seeing it, as well as Illawara's hands inspect the bottles in the light, reminded him of why he came to Italy in the first place. The Professor stood slack-jawed, covered in Goosebumps, as the Abbess continued her magic, and watched with horror as Illawara took out one of the bottles, then closed the case before hiding it under her seat, and stepped out of the carriage. The Professor clamped his hand over his mouth to stop a howl of incredulity and foreboding, as he saw Illawara cross a street to approach a beggar woman holding a baby. He could see via her image within the ball, although clouded at times with mist, that Illawara had begun to walk with the woman into a side street as the wavering eye of the crystal blinked, and hesitated at times before following on. Professor Sloane tried to shake his head, but could not move as the scene played out, and the Abbess continued to chant, and gesticulate.

The vision continued, and the Professor could see that Illawara had begun talking to the woman, and seemed to be offering her comfort. The beggar woman gestured to her limp baby, before clutching at her breasts with defeat.

Illawara nodded, appeared to say something, and wiped away the beggar woman's tears and then her own, before she scratched around on the street, in her grand dress, like the chickens for stray grains of corn. The Professor almost shouted when he realised what she planned to do, but bit hard on his thumb to stop himself exclaiming. The Abbess continued with her chanting and gestures, and the Professor could see, to his horror, that Illawara had opened a phial of Transformation Tincture and sprinkled some of the liquid onto the grains of corn. The Professor witnessed Illawara crouch, to try and hide her efforts in the side street, but he also saw the obvious elation of the beggar woman as she screamed, almost dropping her baby, as the corn turned into golden coins.

'She's a witch, she's a witch!' the Abbess began to cry, and pointed her finger at the ball, and a bony finger of a man within the orb did the same - marking Illawara out. The Professor saw the beggar woman rush forward to fill her pockets, as the image then began to fill with people:

'No, Illawara' whispered the exasperated Professor through gritted teeth - unable to hold back any longer. The Abbess stopped her craft immediately, and the crystal grew dark before she turned faster than a spindle to scan the room with her glowing green eyes.

'Who goes there? Have you come? Are you the soul I seek?'

The Professor's heart raced, and he pondered fleeing the scene, as the Abbess stood with her eyes glowing like Medusa, but yet unseeing: 'you have witnessed my craft' came her voice, dark and intense, as the glow faded from her eyes, and the Professor struggled to speak. Not since he had been a little boy had he felt so scared: 'speak up, or I shall cut out your tongue when my mundane sight returns.' The Abbess gestured to a dagger that lay on a table nearby. The Professor wanted to run, but he held fast.

'Yes, I am he' came the Professor's voice which, to his irritation, trembled.

'You're wise to be afraid' said the Abbess, still blind, as she reached for a square of black velvet that hung on a hook to one side, and then walked forward with the fabric outstretched to cover the crystal ball: 'do you know the story of Actaeon?' she said,

'Yes' said the Professor, regaining his usual command,

'Then you know what will happen to you if you cross a Goddess. Remove yourself from my door for you have already seen too much, and retreat into my chamber where I shall visit you.'

The Professor dared not disobey and waited with patience as the Abbess made ready. When he saw her again, she wore a nun's habit. Even in the dim light, the turquoise eyes of the Abbess shimmered, before she then concealed her long flaxen hair beneath the jet-black veil of her habit. Her face shone young, in the dim light, but every move of her portrayed experience as she strode to where he stood next to the open Grimoire. The Abbess addressed him, as he studied her, without looking at him but moved instead to a small mirror she then uncovered to check her veil and clothing.

'What did you see within my orb as I made my craft?' she said. The Professor readied himself, as the blood pumped in his ears,

'Not much: a street, a few people' he said. The Abbess turned to face him, and he felt struck by her beauty,

'Lie to me again' she said, 'and you will not live to see another sunrise' he swallowed hard, with all doubt removed, in the full knowledge that his vision on the hill had been her.

'You saw me then?' he added,

'I see many things' she replied, 'now answer my question.' The Professor tried to calm his breathing before he spoke again,

'I saw my carriage and a young woman opening my carry case before she stepped into the street.' The Abbess nodded.

'Who is she, what is her name, and what are the objects in the carry case?' she said, before she swept past him, leaving a waft of her perfume, and took up a candle from a sideboard to light it with the flame of the other, and put it into a lantern of red coloured glass.

'Her name is Illawara' he said,

'She's as pretty as her name.'

'Yes, and...' he hesitated, 'she's my daughter.' The Abbess swept herself round,

'*Daughter*, you say?' The Abbess then walked forward to inspected him by raising the red lantern and casting its pink light upon his face. She scrutinised him: 'you tell the truth - but you look like a man who's not seen thirty years, and yet you have a fully-grown daughter. How so?' The Professor took in the Abbess' gaze and flawless complexion as she looked at him.

'You may already know the answer to that,' Abbess' said the Professor. She raised her eyebrow, 'for you look no more than twenty-five years, yet you're head of this institution.' A wry smile crept across the Abbess' face,

'You're no fool, and you're no boy...' she added in a sage tone, 'and you have a tongue as silver as your eyes.' The Abbess then moved the lantern around to cast more light upon him. 'She is dark, and you are fair: how so?' The Professor took a deep breath and pondered how he could answer without lying. The Abbess observed him struggle: 'was her mother, a Saracen?' she said,

'Possibly, but I don't know her mother' the Professor confessed, the Abbess raised both her brows into high arches.

'*I see*. So you're her father in name but not in deed?' She said. The Professor nodded, closed his eyes, and blew out a breath that lasted some seconds. The Abbess paused to look at the Professor - her eyes glittering in the dark. 'A weight has come off you' she said, sweeping closer, 'unburden yourself yet more, and tell me of the contents of the carry case.'

'But what of Illawara? You've used that person, you've possessed, to denounce her in public.' The Abbess gestured to the plush surroundings,

'If you were so worried about her you'd be by her side, not here in my bed-chamber' she said. The Professor looked away, paused, and saw no point in holding back in front of a master - it seemed she could read his mind.

'The contents of those phials represent over twenty years of research. There are few Grimoires that I've not read, and few countries that I've not travelled to in my quest for knowledge.' The Abbess narrowed her eyes and tilted her head back as she pondered him.

'Impressive, so you're a philosopher and a sorcerer... though I suspect that you've not read the book that rests over there - and so fixes your attention' the Professor's eyes darted to the book then back again.

'That's true' he said, 'but I don't consider myself a sorcerer.'

'Then what are you?'

'I'm a physicist, a chemist and a botanist.'

'You're what?' She said, the Professor raised his chin and pulled his shoulders back,

'I'm a man of *Science*' he declared. The Abbess turned from him and tutted,

'So you're a disciple of Galileo - you admire him, and yet seem to be an acolyte of some other things I've not quite heard of before. Yet, I know you've become much more than that' she purred.

The Professor swallowed, as if in great thirst, before she raised the lantern over the open book. 'You see this book here' she said. The Professor nodded, 'if you were not a sorcerer the book would be invisible to you. If you were not worthy of its knowledge, the book would have closed itself. If you were to touch it without respect, the book would harm you. So don't say you're just a man of "Science", for there are things you understand that not even I know.' The Abbess began to encircle the Professor, holding her lantern aloft before she continued. 'What I do know for certain is that you've come here for that book, and I'll teach you of its contents, but first, you'll teach me everything you know, and if you do, you'll leave with yet more knowledge - and your life and body intact.'

The Professor had never met such a woman in his life, and dropped all pretence of holding back information, for now: she, above all others, could be told and understand what he had learned up to that point, and he could only anticipate, with reverence, all that she could teach him in return. The Professor spoke again:

'My Illawara, you called her a witch, and used your finger to point her out - and others ran to her - you've put her in danger.'

The Abbess tutted,

'She put herself in danger by practising magic openly in the streets: she's *foolish* - but every false witch spares three real ones - she'll have to get herself out of it. I didn't know you were her father: why didn't you teach her better?' Shame silenced the Professor and a look of knowing passed over the Abbess' face, 'I see' she said but spoke no more of her thoughts. The Abbess bid the Professor to sit on a cushion and rest. She took up a bowl, covered with cloth, from a dark place on a shelf and wrung out the sponge that floated in the liquid before exposing his slashed arm with a gentle touch, and daubed the wound. The Professor flinched and tried to draw his arm back, but she held him firm and cooed in low tones to sooth him. The Abbess then rubbed some balm over the scab before wrapping his arm in fresh linen and secured the wrapping with a pin.

The Professor sat still as the Abbess turned again and walked over to a wooden chest with iron trappings, opened it, and took out a small bejewelled box. She took the box over to the Professor and then kneeled to place the box in her lap before she opened it. 'You're hungry' she said. The Professor recognised the contents immediately and allowed the Abbess to feed him the syrupy pieces of pistachio baklava. The Abbess then uncovered a low bed in another corner of the room, and bid the Professor to lie down, he did. The Abbess then whispered something in the Professor's ear before she touched her slender fingers to his temple whereupon he fell to sleep. She stopped to look at the Professor as he slumbered before she pulled the covers back over him and left the room.

Chapter 12

Bedlam and The Blue Madonna

Florence, near the river Arno

Antonio and Hermes checked the safe-house but no one answered their call. The Pair then walked from tavern to tavern on the north side of the Arno and asked the landlords if they knew where Riccolo had rested. It had become clear by the time they had reached the fourth tavern, from the various descriptions of the landlords, and those people that had overheard and chimed in saucy details, that Riccolo had spent the night at the brothel. The pair of men walked at a pace in the direction shown to them by those that knew and tried to ignore their innuendo, giggles, and laughter. However, the pair soon paused their advance, and Hermes clapped his hands to his forehead when they rounded a corner and saw the Blue Madonna.

The establishment looked much like a tavern or wine house save for the wooden sign that swung in the wind, embellished with an ironic copy of the Mona Lisa, wearing a blue shawl - and her knowing smile.

'I don't want to go in there' said Hermes, as men of various classes stumbled out of the establishment, and blinked in the daylight, before making off for a church confession or the taverns to eat. Hermes face contorted as he watched the men shamble out, 'I'm surprised the Inquisition doesn't close the place down: it's obvious what this place is for' Hermes added.

'Everyone goes to the whore house' said Antonio with a shrug, 'and the clergy are no exception, except those that prefer other entertainment' he said tilting his head. Hermes pondered what Antonio could have meant, 'and besides' he continued, 'it's one of the best ways to get information. If you want to know anything interesting: ask a whore.' Hermes looked surprised, 'they won't close these places down. There's little a man won't confess when in the arms of his lover' added Antonio, with a suggestive whisper, before he gave Hermes' shoulder a squeeze. Hermes felt the blood rush to his face, but could not stop himself smirking, 'the Inquisition like the whores, really' Antonio continued in a breezy manner, 'they make the best spies and some of their finest mistresses. They couldn't do half their work without them - so we'll have to be very careful of what we say when we get in there.' Hermes seemed unconvinced by the statement but felt himself in no position to argue.

The two young men walked up to the dark wooden doors of Il L'azzuro Madonna and then took two steps back as a male client almost tumbled out the doors after tripping on the step. A young girl, no more than seventeen, gave out a shrill giggle at the sight before she tugged a strap of her dress back onto her shoulder. The middle-aged man turned, after his stumble, to take off his hat and give a sweeping bow to the girl as if to say goodbye to a Gentlewoman. The gesture delighted her into even more laughter, as she waved off her client who then wobbled down the street and into a trattoria. The girl almost closed the door before she noticed the pair: 'Nino' she exclaimed, when she saw Antonio, before flinging her arms around the young man. Hermes face clouded,

'You know this girl?' he said, as he eyed her up and down,

'Yes, she's like a little sister to me' said Antonio as he swept the girl into a twirl, which made her giggle all the more.

'I'm Chiara' she said, looking at Hermes with a face full of joy and freckles. Hermes' face did not move. Chiara, like a court dancer, then gave a curtsy with the swish of her hand, and a coquettish flutter of her lashes framing her brown eyes. Hermes lips then twitched into a smirk, before he remembered his manners and introduced himself.

'Chi Chi' said Antonio, 'we need your help. We've come here to find a friend, and some people said that he might be here.'

'What's his name?' said the girl as she ushered in her guests off the street, and closed the brothel doors behind them. Hermes scanned the room. Inside it looked as if few people were around. On the floor laid a worn Persian carpet, with colours long faded, covered in scuffs and scrapes that added to its intricate pattern:

'He's called Riccolo' said Antonio. Then the girl erupted into more giggles,

'O Dio. We know him. He's always here' she said and shook her head.

'Do you know him personally?' said Antonio,

'Not *personally*, Nino: he says I'm too skinny for him' she whispered, 'he prefers the bigger ones like Georgiarella.' Chiara then flicked her hair, took on a haughty manner, before pouting an impression of a woman much larger than herself: she wobbled imaginary breasts some distance in front of her own and Antonio, and Hermes laughed at her antics.

'Chi Chi' said Antonio, once recovered, 'it's important that you don't tell anyone we were here.'

'Why Nino, are you in trouble?' said the girl, frowning. Antonio nodded,

'We need a place to hide for a while, and Riccolo will have somewhere for us safe to stay. Would you be able to find him for us? There're so many rooms here.' Chiara gave an eager nod,

'I'll find him for you. Wait here' she said, and then Chiara turned to dash along the hallway, and up a flight of wooden steps with almost no sound. Hermes followed the girl with his eyes.

'She's so young to be working here' said Hermes, 'she's just a girl.' Antonio shrugged at the observation.

'Her family couldn't afford to give her a dowry, so they sent her to a convent - it's cheaper than marriage.' Hermes scratched his head.

'Then why is she here?'

'Because the nuns threw her out when she had her baby, and wouldn't give it up.' Hermes' face dropped.

'She's a mother already? And she got pregnant in a nunnery?' said Hermes,

'It happens... there's more than just prayers behind some convent walls' said Antonio, holding Hermes gaze.

'Where's her baby?' said Hermes, turning away to scan the space. Antonio looked down and shook his head,

'It's tough to feed a baby when you're on the streets. When it died, she came here' Hermes balked, 'what else could she do?'

'Oh?' said Hermes, hanging his head. He stood perplexed for a while and looked into the distance, 'does she not have any family?' he said.

Antonio shook his head again, 'they disowned her once they found out she was here, so she stayed. But I've taught her how to read, sing, and play the Lute: she can earn more if she has virtues... she'll earn her freedom one day.' Antonio smiled, proud of his efforts. But Hermes stood for a while suspended in thought, emotion passing over his face. Hermes reflected on what he learned about Chiara when she returned in a glowing rush:

'He's upstairs Nino, the last room on the left' she breathed, 'but he's still asleep in bed. I daren't wake him.'

'Thank you, Chi Chi - my little bell' said Antonio, 'I have to talk to him before too many people see us.' Chiara told them the room number in which Riccolo stayed before Antonio bid Hermes to follow him up the creaking stairs.

'Go softly, Nino' said Chiara, 'but watch out for Georgiarella - you know what she's like' she added in a stage whisper after them. The pair arrived on the wooden landing at the top of the stairs and walked down to the last door on the left while trying to make as little sound as possible. Various garments lay strewn about: shirt collars, hose, and cuffs mingled with bustiers and breeches in equal measure. Some of the items lay stained with bodily fluids: spittle, dried semen, and some with blood. Hermes tried to turn his nose away from the musky sticky smell in the air of the humid hallway but could find no relief. Antonio navigated the space unfazed.

Hermes could hear, from some of the rooms they passed, that even by the late morning a few clients had yet to finish with their molls - as sounds of pleasure and gratification seeped into the hallway: a sensual vision of Antonio flashed into Hermes' mind.

Startled, Hermes turned to glance at the Valet, ashamed, as if Antonio could see his thoughts. Antonio smiled, paid scant interest to his surroundings, and squeezed Hermes shoulder again,

'Your first time in a place like this?' Hermes nodded, 'bless you' he said, as they reached the last door on the left.

Antonio ushered Hermes forward to knock the door, and then made a shake of his knuckle. Hermes' eyes widened into saucers, but Antonio insisted - so the youth gave the door a delicate tap. No response came, so Antonio gestured and bid Hermes to open the door instead. The youth shrivelled, but again Antonio insisted, so Hermes bared his teeth before he gave the door a push. The door gave out a tortured creek as he peered inside, to find a fair skinned redhead woman looking at him. She wore half a bed sheet and a scowl.

The woman raised a plump finger to her lips as Hermes got pushed into the room, but her expression changed when she caught sight of Antonio. She then rolled her eyes, smirked, and pulled back the rest of her bed sheet to reveal a robust, bearded, and pot-bellied man sleeping on his back while giving out a convoluted snore. The woman raised herself up from resting on her elbow, and the motion swung one of her pendulous breasts to the side, clashing with the other, and dislodged the bed sheet that had draped her other bosom. The woman then made a sweeping gesture above the sleeping man with her hand, as if presenting a ribbon at a cattle fair. Antonio gave a wink and nodded. Hermes did not know where to look. The woman made no attempt to cover herself:

'So who's this brown virgin you've brought into my bedchamber, Nino?' the woman whispered. Hermes felt the heat rise to his neck under the seasoned inspection of the prostitute.

'Gi Gi, this is my friend Hermes' said Antonio,

'A special friend?' said Georgiarella,

'NO' said Antonio, before Hermes gave a wounded look, 'well not special in that kind of way' he said as if to comfort the youth whose brown skin had turned a shade of pink.

'It's a shame' she said, 'half of the clock with me and I could teach him the world.' She cooed, eyeing the youth up while coiling a finger through her auburn hair. Hermes could think of nothing worse and hoped for a trapdoor to drop open and consume him.

'Gi Gi' Antonio whispered, 'I need to talk with your friend here. I've a favour to ask of him.'

'Would you like me to wake him?' asked Georgiarella, as she stretched her soft white arms above her head and yawned, which displayed the flame like tufts of her armpits before she flounced at her long thick hair and tussled it over her breasts like Lady Godiva.

'We need to speak in private' Antonio continued,

'It will cost you' said Georgiarella, and she rubbed her fingertips together in a gesture of anticipation. Antonio reached into a chest pocket and pulled out a coin. The woman gave him a dirty look, and Antonio reached in for two more coins which drew approval from her. Georgiarella took the coins in her palm and then put her hand under the bed sheet, which still covered her lower body, and Hermes turned away before he could see where she hid the money, 'I don't want Madam to tax that' she said to Antonio, before she shook the snoring body of her companion, and rubbed at the dark glossy hair of the man's head and chest. He began to stir. 'Buongiorno, my little cupid' she said to the man as he half awoke, and he reached up to give a squeeze of the woman's breast like a nursing child. The woman kissed the man's hand and forehead, before she rolled off the bed to face away from the men, and tugged her clothing over her voluptuous body. Riccolo almost fell out of the bed when he came to - finding two male strangers in his bedroom. Georgiarella gave a playful wave to her companion and blew him a kiss before she sauntered out of the room:

'She's a piece of work' said Riccolo in a cheerful way, and rubbed his head, when he had got his full bearings. Riccolo looked on with increasing concern after Antonio introduced himself and then wasted no time to inform Riccolo of the situation.

■ ■ ■

By the time Riccolo had dressed, and the three men had returned to Illawara's carriage several people were rocking it from side to side: 'oh, Gods' exclaimed Hermes, as all three men then ran towards the vehicle. Illawara looked terrified and struggled to keep her balance within the carriage, as people of all descriptions clamoured and ranted at her:

'I saw her do it' shouted one man, 'she turned corn into *gold*.'

'She's a *witch*' shouted one beggar woman, 'it's the Devil's power that she commands.'

'Shut up table wench' declared a stooped man with white hair and a walking stick, 'you accuse her because she refused you. I care not what she is, let me speak with her: she could cure all of my ills.' Then a well-dressed man who looked like a lawyer shouted:

'Get out of the way, withered old man, not even the almighty could cure you of your foolishness - but I'll make her my wife, and be *rich*.'

Illawara listened to the comments with alarm. More and more people became attracted to the commotion, and a palpable sense of excitement and anticipation passed like lightning among the growing throng. Illawara's head twisted this way and that as if to look for an escape, but had little hope as more people joined the crowd.

'I've never seen such a clamour before: *what* has she done?' said Antonio, turning to Hermes, his face expressing a jumble of questions,

'We have to help her' said Hermes with a look of panic on his face as the men neared the carriage.

'*Wait* a moment' said Riccolo, before bringing the young men to a halt, 'is that not the Cardinal Orsini I see there?' He said as he pointed to the powerful from of a man that strode forward in a scarlet cap and dark robes. Antonio's blood froze.

'You know him?' Asked Antonio. Riccolo nodded.

'Who doesn't? A Cardinal in town is always an occasion.' The Cardinal began to shove aside some of the crowd while accompanied by his pale, thin henchman, that hovered near him with a cut above his eye. Antonio blanched:

'Yes, no doubt it's him. He's dangerous; he could have more of his men nearby.'

'But what about Illy?' said Hermes, his voice shaking, 'we have to make them stop: they're all crazy - they're attacking her.' Illawara gave out a scream as the people jeered and shook the carriage yet harder, almost turning the whole thing over, while two strong blacksmiths held onto the bridles of the horses as they whinnied in distress.

'We'll have to create a distraction' said Riccolo; it could give us time to get her out of there. I have my own carriage close to Il L'azzuro Madonna. If we could get her to it, you could well make your escape.'

'What shall we do? We must hurry, or they'll *kill* her' exclaimed Hermes in desperation. The mob shook at the carriage with increasing ferocity.

'I've thought of something' said Riccolo, turning to Antonio, but the man did not get the chance to continue before the deep baritone of Orsini's voice clapped like thunder across the noisy crowd. The Mob fell into silence as he spoke:

'*GOOD PEOPLE OF FIRENZE*' the Cardinal declared as people crossed themselves and made pious gestures, 'stop your wild clamouring and be calmed. There is little to fear from a witch when the presence of *God* is at my command' said Orsini, as he raised a golden crucifix aloft, and thrust it above the crowd as if to ward off evil.

Seeing that they were pacified Orsini walked forward toward the side of the carriage as the people, then five people deep parted like water in front of a ship. He gave a brief look into the carriage to see Illawara: frightened and trembling as her tear-streaked eyes looked back at him as if to beg for freedom. Orsini's heart gave a pang before he turned to address the crowd with a dramatic sweep of his arms and crucifix held aloft. He relived then how he spoke before, when he gave sermons to the faithful with passion like he once had, when young from the pulpit: 'this may indeed be a witch' he said, Antonio frowned and glanced at Hermes again, 'but she has no power in my presence' Orsini declared, as he fixed the rapt crowd with one of his looks. He maintained their full attention, all except for another beggar woman whom Illawara had refused. The woman, dressed in rags, raised her voice in defiance to the Cardinal:

'But she does have power, your Eminence. I saw her turn grain into gold with my own eyes. But the black-hearted wench wouldn't give me a coin, and gave all instead to another woman with a babe; does she not know that I suffer too - that I hunger and thirst?' With her statement, the crowd began to rouse itself again with some saying that Illawara should be burned, and others that she should give them some money too, as Hermes, Antonio, and Riccolo made their way to the side of the carriage with stealth.

'*Shame* on you, woman' Orsini declared, before glancing at Illawara, while his henchman and the rest of the crowd looked on, 'so she helped another in greater need, yet you only think of yourself, just like some others I've heard here.' The Florentine crowd then huddled and muttered to itself, portioning blame, as if to agree with the Cardinal, as he turned his own mind over in how to get Illawara out alive and out of the mess. 'Does the church not warn of the vice of avarice and *envy*' he chastised, 'who's not to say that the girl is not falsely accused?' The crowd guffawed, 'look at you' Orsini boomed, before pointing at the beggar woman, 'with your lank hair, sallow complexion, and a dress made of dirty tattered rags. Who's to say that you didn't cook up the story out of jealousy and spite - pricked by her generosity and beauty; you're a wretched STREET-HAG.' The crowd collectively drew its breath at the comments of the Cardinal, and some began to point and titter at the astonished beggar woman. But within a blink the woman - who had turned purple with rage - with nothing to lose, challenged the Cardinal:

'It was not *I*, but the misty-eyed creep that stands next to you that called her witch first. I lie not. Unlike the men of your cloth that double deal, whore about, fill their pockets, and offer thin *gruel* as alms for the poor.' The crowd gasped, many scolded her, and some cheered at the woman's boldness, but she had not finished. 'If I lie then let the Lord strike me down with a thunderbolt, for I and we know what we saw: that thing, as pretty as she is, took up grain and turned it to *GOLD* with the sprinkling of juices.' Some in the crowd nodded as she spoke, but some muttered in disbelief at the boldness of the beggar woman, 'she's a witch if I ever saw it. And if you have power as you say, bid her repeat it, and you'll see for yourself - that's if your Roman eyes are not clouded by her charms. I TELL THE TRUTH.' She shouted, before tossing a handful of corn at the Cardinal's feet.

A silence fell over the crowd after the woman's voice had rung out. They had never seen or heard such defiance in front of a Cardinal. Orsini, like everyone else, stood taken aback, some looked to the sky for thunder and lightning, before he regained his wits: 'beggarly *whore*' he roared, arms outstretched and crucifix aloft, 'ye who grubs about the streets like a warthog, selling yourself for bread or cheese, dare say such things to *me*.' Orsini glared at the woman as if wanting to combust her into flames. 'If you were not already desperate and miserable I would have you flogged for the insolence you have shown for a Cardinal of the Church: but your sorry state and iniquitous life is punishment enough for a street crawler like yourself.'

The crowd gasped at such volume it was as if a gust of wind had whipped between them: they had never heard a Cardinal speak in such a manner. If the beggar woman could have done so, and lived, she would have struck Orsini dead, but she had to endure the insult and curse him under her breath. 'However' Orsini declared, confident his blistering critique had restored his authority, 'I will demonstrate that the *witch*, as you call her, has no power over me' he said before he turned to the carriage and bid Illawara to come out. Illawara thought carefully. Shivering, she peered out from her carriage and looked at the crowd that had grown ten deep. She realised she could not defy the Cardinal in such a public place although her friends were powerless to help her.

She hesitated before she retrieved the Professor's carry case from its hiding place, held it by the handle, and stood up. Orsini encouraged her with a compassionate look, before Illawara dried her tears, composed herself, put her leather bag on one shoulder, held the case forward, and stepped out of the carriage like a Duchess. Illawara's skin and hair glowed in the October sunlight as the diamond at her throat splintered the autumn sunshine across her dress and people below. The crowd, which had gained more people yet, shrank back in fear and awe as they ogled her. Orsini could not tear his eyes away from her as she stood on the steps of the carriage with the case held aloft.

Orsini's mind raced while Hermes, Antonio, and Riccolo whispered, unnoticed, as the crowd looked on. Riccolo began to reach into his side pocket as the Cardinal spoke: 'I am a man of God' said Orsini in a mighty voice, swinging his crucifix aloft with one hand and extending the other in Illawara's direction, 'with the power of the Holy Spirit, I can touch thee and remain unharmed.' Chattering broke out among the crowd that fidgeted like Gerbils, as the Cardinal, with much tenderness, reached with his arm outstretched and took Illawara's cold hand. The crowd gasped. Orsini looked at her and she at him as the corner of her mouth began to tremble. Orsini swallowed but resisted the urge to sweep her into his arms again, like when they had danced the night before, but he had to rip his eyes away from her to work the crowd over. 'You see' the Cardinal said, with a voice a somewhat shaken, 'she has no power over me.'

All assembled stood motionless, looked on, and then drew their own conclusions. Orsini clung to Illawara's hand, refusing to let go, before he gestured with his crucifix at the ground where the grains of corn lay and said: 'if you are indeed a witch as they say, then change this grain into gold.' Illawara hesitated, and Orsini who had not seen the cause of the commotion hoped with all his heart, that even if she were a witch, she would not be so foolish to repeat the trick and condemn herself to a burning.

Illawara looked around in silence at those gathered, as all activity had stopped in the street, and at the people that stood twenty deep: rapt with the spectacle. Illawara made a move to speak before Riccolo flung his arm up to the sky and tossed the contents if his moneybag into the air, to scatter Orsini and the crowd with every gold Florin he had on his person. In an instant, the crowd rushed forward, in a gale of noise, and fought with each other to grab a coin, the most of which few had handled but once in their lives. The beggar woman, so swift, with a screech of victory, managed to snatch up two gold Florins before the desperate Mob fell on the rest. Hermes, Antonio, and Riccolo trampled forward to yank Illawara from Orsini's grasp as he became overwhelmed by the crowd, and howled, 'NO', in anguish at being separated from Illawara again. The Mob of one mind, in a frenzy for the coins, forgot Illawara at that moment and set about increasing its wealth in the knowledge that they, collectively, and their families could be fed and clothed for months ahead with just one coin.

The horses bolted, spooked by the sudden onrush, and the blacksmiths abandoned their reigns to snatch up what they could, as Orsini and his henchman then leapt aside to avoid being run over. The horses and carriage then barrelled down the street and caused mayhem as people and goods were flung aside as the wild-eyed horses, and runaway carriage tore through the streets. The fugitives elbowed their way out of the throng, as more people ran towards the mêlée to grab at a coin within the mass of churning people: that rose, fell, turned, and flapped like guillemots feeding upon sardines in the swell of the sea. 'We have to get out of Firenze immediately' said Antonio almost breathless, 'it's too dangerous to risk staying here.'

The fugitives fled and carried Illawara along, who then snatched glances back here and there to see what had become of Orsini, as she clung to the carry case with all her strength. 'Take my carriage, it's the black one' said Riccolo as they all ran forward, 'but we must get your friend into different clothes, or she'll be recognised. She's dressed much too fine as she is.'

The men carried Illawara along at a pace as Riccolo explained his idea to the others in hurried gasps, as they reached to the side of the Il L'azzuro Madonna. Riccolo dragged open the door as the fugitives hurried inside. Chiara stood with a broom of birch twigs as she swept at the threadbare carpet, which made a scant impression on the grime, and Georgiarella seemed to be having a heated discussion with a stern looking middle-aged woman. All three women stopped what they were doing when the fugitives burst in: 'Chi Chi, come here' said Antonio, almost out of breath, 'take off your dress', Chiara looked at Illawara, and understood what he meant in an instant before the Madam spoke.

'Hold your horses' said the mature woman in a bold tone, and held out her hand to halt the group, 'no one commands one of my girls without my permission in this house. We discuss a *price* before the clothes come off' said the Madam, hands on hips with reproach, 'are you so *hot*, that you'd rut here like a stag with a doe on my carpets?'

'Mama' said Riccolo, coming in last of the bunch, as the woman's face lit up with surprise at recognising her son within the unfamiliar company, 'I can't explain now' he said, as he pointed to Illawara, 'but this woman needs to change her dress very quickly.' The mature Madam swaggered over to give Illawara a closer look, as Chiara loosened her own stays.

'Very fine, very fine, boy. Where did you get her?'

'She's not for *sale*, she's not a prostitute' spat Hermes with narrowed eyes blazing, the Madam knotted her brows as she glared back at the youth:

'Shut up swarthy Moor - no one asked you' she hissed back, 'let me look at her' she said as she pushed Hermes aside. The Madam studied Illawara as if inspecting Murano glass. 'Dark glossy hair, shining blue eyes, and golden skin: you're as lovely as an icon, my child' said the Madam, as Georgiarella shifted from one full hip to another, crossing her arms, with her face set like a stone. Illawara held the Madam's gaze and said nothing, 'why not let her stay here?' The Madam said to her son, 'she'll fetch a high price',

'There's not enough space for her here' Georgiarella interrupted,

'Don't be jealous, dear' said Madam, 'You'll still be my best girl.'

'That cannot happen, *Madam*' said Antonio with conviction; 'we're leaving for Padova immediately.' The group turned their faces to Antonio at his revelation. The Madam then gave out a deep cackle,

'So, you seek the protection of the Venetian Republic. Do you think The Church and its spies can't reach you there?'

'What makes you think we flee The Church, Madam?' said Antonio. The Madam adjusted her jewels,

'My girls are everywhere and tell me everything: including what happened at the Uffizi last night.' Antonio froze, 'dare say there's quite a price on your head should someone come knocking'

'Mama, not now' said Riccolo, before pressing his finger to his mother's mouth, the woman looked intrigued, 'I'll explain later. They need our help' he said, and removed his finger, before turning to Illawara. 'Please swap your dress with Chiara's before we run out of time.' Illawara did not want to part with her dress, which she had sourced and assembled at great expense. She had collected its different parts with such care when back home - the dress represented months of toil and effort. Illawara looked down at her billowing skirts, and her embellishments as her dress glinted in the light: it was magnificent.

The situation was desperate. Illawara cringed, took a deep breath, and closed her eyes for a moment before she loosened her stays. 'Can someone help me undress?' she said. The group reached forward and made light work of the garments, helping Illawara disrobe, but kept back her accoutrements, satchel and the Professor's carry case. Once her dress and ruff were off Illawara then stepped out of her farthingale as Chiara had done with hers, standing in her underclothes and bodice. Hermes then handed Illawara her dress and ruff to give to Chiara. Illawara's eyes welled up, but she choked them back and reached forward to give the garments to Chiara. The girl looked exhilarated, and to Illawara she seemed like Cinderella being given a dress for the ball.

'I can wear the dress' said Georgiarella, who then stepped forward to intercept the exchange,

'In your dreams' snapped Hermes, 'you couldn't get a leg in there.' Georgiarella stepped back as if stung, as the company around exchanged glances at the feisty put-down. It had been the first time that Madam or Riccolo had seen Georgiarella put in her place, and a part of Illawara glowed inside as she swapped dresses with Chiara. Illawara, naturally, did not part with her diamond choker, putting it in her bag, and could not be expected to do so. She pulled on the cream coloured, plain, and simple dress of

Chiara's, still warm from her body, which, despite the girl's cloying perfume, smelled less than feminine, and bore stains in places.

But there was no choice as madam laced Chiara into her new clothes. Illawara stood back to observe the effect the dress had on Chiara. The girl spun with her new skirts out wide, cried tears of joy and danced about, before she declared herself beautiful, curtsied to Illawara, and sprang, glittering, to the shoulder of Madam who then clasped the girl to her breast and agreed.

'We must hurry' said a grim-faced Antonio, before the group left for Riccolo's carriage, and Georgiarella stomped off upstairs. They located the carriage: not as grand as the Professor's, but still good, within the side street where Riccolo had left it the night before.

'My mother would have fed and watered the horses. Make haste' said Riccolo, as Illawara and Hermes jumped in, and Antonio took up perch in the driver's seat. With haste, the fugitives thanked Riccolo for his help, and he, in turn, bid them well - not asking for payment or explanation.

'Your kindness and carriage shall be returned' declared Antonio, before he drove the carriage the short distance to the river, and over the Ponte Vecchio before the raving Mob had dispersed.

Orsini, in his attempts to control the situation, threatened hell fire and damnation to the violent crowd, which fought each other for every scrap: by pulling hair, scratching, punching, gouging, and biting one another to get at the last of the gold Florins. The beggar woman with her babe had long since left the scene, but the second - who had given Orsini a piece of her mind – had wrestled, with commendable vigour, two different men to the ground, and twisted at their loins until each man howled with pain and let go of his catch. She would never have to beg again, and gossiped aloud, not without insight to Orsini's great shame, that the Roman Cardinal had no intention of having the mysterious girl arrested.

Orsini gave up and made way with his henchman, defeated by numbers and frustration. In time the roughed-up crowds dispersed, bruised but much entertained and could speak of little else in the taverns and inns besides their new Florins, the spectacle, and the sheer scandal of it all.

Chapter 13

After a Deep Sleep

The Convent of San Matteo, Tuesday 4th October 1611

Out of the blackness hissed ancient voices:

We see all,
We don't sleep,
We'll have all,
This world we'll keep.

The Professor awoke with a start, sweat clung to his brow, and his heart raced. For a moment he had forgotten where he was, and looked again, almost with fresh eyes at his curious surroundings. He lay splayed on the bed; the covers tossed aside. The words of his dream floated in his mind and chilled his spine. His body twitched all over, yet his limbs were leaden, and he struggled to move. He lay still until his feeling of dread had passed, and his breath had become regular.

Professor Sloane then heard the voices of three women approaching, and he covered himself again with the sheets as if asleep, and listened to the women as they walked into the Abbess' chamber via a door at the opposite end of the room. He recognised the voice of the little nun as she spoke:

'Do you think he still sleeps, Lucia? He's a fine figure of a man' said the little nun in hushed tones,

'Do you know from whence he has come?' said another female voice the Professor did not recognise,

'Of that, I'm not sure' replied the Abbess, 'but I know there is much to commend him, he's shown great courage in getting here.'

One of the nuns moved her head like an owl to inspect the sleeping Professor.

'He doesn't stir' came the unfamiliar voice again, lighter in tone than the Abbess, but from a woman that sounded mature. The Professor kept still and listened: 'have you drugged him Lucia' came the voice again, 'he looks strong, and his feet hang over the bed.' The Abbess smirked,

'You know as well as I, Suor Celeste, that I can handle any man I wish, drugged or not.'

'So can I' said the little nun, the Abbess chortled.

'Can you think of nothing else, Suor Arcangela?' said the Abbess,

'No, I don't think she can' said Suor Celeste, with a nasal tone.

'And what would *you* know of men?' Cut back the little nun as she twisted around and looked up into the sunken face of Suor Celeste. 'You don't know what you've missed' she hissed, her face scrunched like a paper bag, 'you arrived here as a dull, dry, and unwanted virgin - and you still are - you've never known a pleasure in your life.' The Professor raised his brows under his sheets at the salty put down by Suor Arcangela.

The Abbess scoffed, accustomed to their bickering, as Celeste glared back at the diminutive Arcangela, gathered a thought and sharpened her reply: 'well, at least I wasn't a tired streetwalker, with a drooping womb when I got here' said the taller Celeste with venom. Suor Celeste then looked down her long thin nose before she continued her attack, 'how many babes did you bare and abandon, or worse, before you arrived here to the kindness of our Abbess? Ten, eleven, twelve?' The Professor's eyes bulged under his blankets as he listened to the candid rebukes between the nuns.

Little Arcangela then screeched and made a gesture like a tarantula, before she snatched off her built-up shoe and attempted to hurl it at her taller companion's head. The Abbess raised her hand and halted further action: 'Sisters - *Sisters* - calm yourselves, don't fight' she said in smooth tones. Arcangela huffed, then put her hefty shoe down with a plonk and began to strap her foot back into the wooden block that would have cracked Celeste's head open. Celeste glared at Arcangela as she crouched as if she were a beetle she would like to crush underfoot. The Abbess glanced at both women, and shook her head: 'the Lord sees and forgives all that come and confess in him' she said turning to each woman and tutting, 'let's not remind each other of our past wrongs - or shortcomings.' Celeste looked troubled,

'But he doesn't forgive everything - does he, Lucia?' said the taller nun as she turned to look at the Abbess. The half-smile dropped from Lucia's face.

'And what do you mean by that, Suor Celeste?' said Lucia with narrowed eyes. Celeste blanched and drew back. She began to tremble,

'Mother Superior - Lucia - I want to say' she whispered, 'at times... at times, I feel guilt for our craft. At times I feel sorry for what we've done.' Celeste wobbled, as the Abbess stared at her, but she then steadied herself to continue, 'at times I think what we do is against...' Lucia pressed forward,

'Against what, Suor Celeste?' The Professor tried not to wriggle as he listened to the exchanges.

'Against... against, *God's* will' Celeste mumbled. She held Lucia's gaze, but the Abbess fixed the plain woman with a look and hissed:

'And what do you think we women should do when the odds are so stacked against us?' said Lucia, before encircling Celeste like a she-wolf about to strike its prey. The Professor tried to keep himself still as he listened to the women speak, 'in these times, a woman has to help herself, or help her own. Do we not help our precious sisters in distress? Do we not help to right wrongs? Do we not advise, give herbs, give alms, and give council when our sisters that are harmed or ravished by strangers or, God forbid, their relatives?' Celeste shrank into herself as Lucia continued to walk around her, 'where would they turn or go without us? How would they get justice? How would they gain their revenge?' Celeste began to shake, under Lucia's glare, while spittle clung to the Abbess' chin before she swept it off: her eyes, wide open, seemed to vibrate in their sockets.

A silence fell among them as Celeste looked to the ground and chewed at her thin lips to stop them trembling. Arcangela stamped her built up shoe on the floor. The Professor flinched at the sound but tried to not move a muscle and lay instead like a plank of wood in his bed as he listened. After some moments Lucia's mood seemed to pass, and she changed the conversation, but she still eyeballed Celeste. The taller nun avoided her stare while Lucia spoke: 'is the Abbess conducting the prayers well to the others?' she said,

'Yes' replied both nuns who also bowed in unison. The Professor squinted, scrunching his brows, and held his breath to listen better while he pondered what other Abbess that Lucia could be referring to - apart from herself.

'Good' said Lucia, 'while she conducts prayer we have some time to focus on the accounts.' Both the nuns nodded and swept forward to the wooden chest with iron trappings, smooth and quick, like two hunting dogs in the pursuit of fallen a bird. The two nuns whispered with each other while collecting the books and lists of accounts from the chest. The Abbess Lucia glided to the side of the Professor's bed to check if he still slept. His pulse quickened as her perfume crept over him and he turned away, as if in sleep, from the Abbess to the wall with his eyes closed as she studied him. 'He'll sleep a while longer yet' she whispered to the nuns who had gathered the necessary paperwork from the chest and were laying it out on a desk next to several lit candles. Lucia turned back around and walked to the nuns as they prepared to brief the Abbess. The Professor began to breathe again and listened.

'Donna Serena Marta Ravolio still owes one Giulio for the herb preparation we made for her' said Celeste, before reading out a list of other women, and some men, that still had accounts outstanding. Lucia shook her head at the length of the list, and grumbled for a moment about interrupted cashflow.

'That Donna Ravolio is always buying, but she always owes' mused Lucia, 'I may have to speak with her again: but first a letter. What else?'

'Donna Maria Barolo still owes half of what she paid us for that tincture we made for her impotent mule: one lira' said Celeste,

'She buys a lot from us. Why doesn't she just get herself another mule: a younger one?' said Arcangela with a shake of her head.

'Did the tincture work?' asked Lucia,

'Yes' replied Celeste, 'even better than the last, and she'll pay us when her husband returns from Genoa on business.' The Abbess rolled her eyes,

'That tired story' she said, 'what a miserly tramp - she's never without new lace for confession, they say, but comes short for our goods.' Lucia glanced at the Professor to make sure that he still slept, 'I'll make sure she pays after Mass this Sunday - but if I see her she'll hear harsh words from me at the Sabbat tonight.'

Celeste then snapped to attention, and the Professor felt his skin chill - his eyes widening again under his covers.

'You will attend the Sabbat again?' said the plain nun. Lucia paused,

'Yes, I shall attend again' she said with her smooth chin raised. Arcangela clapped her little hands with glee,

'But today is the Feast of St Francis' said Celeste,

'And what of it, Celeste? He's the patron saint of Animals, not privation'

'But the nuns will want some extra words from you on this day, is it wise to be away?' said Celeste. Lucia wafted her hand.

'The nuns will have extra food and wine tonight, Arcangela has seen to that. You have instructed my counterpart: have you not?' Celeste nodded, 'then there is little to worry about. The Sabbat will be particularly busy tonight: there's much opportunity – it cannot be wasted'

'I'm so glad, mistress. I wasn't sure if we'd ever go again. *Ooh*, I can't wait' Arcangela exclaimed, spreading out her habit as if it were a ballgown. 'We shall feast and dance with handsome men in the moonlight, and I shall be like my young self again' said Arcangela, pausing work with the overdue accounts to sweep herself into a dance with an imaginary man. Celeste looked on but did not say a word: her face as blank as a sheet of paper.

'I didn't say you were invited, Suor Arcangela' said Lucia with her brow raised. Arcangela stopped her dancing as if struck by a heart attack, 'especially after the way you behaved last time. I thought I would die of shame and at the Sabbat of all places: where shame is impossible.' The little nun clutched her hands together and mewed at the Abbess like a kitten left in the rain.

'Oh please let me go, Lucia. I promise to have some restraint this time.' Celeste's face churned into an unpleasant expression, but the Abbess' mouth slipped into a smile. She considered the wrinkled face, and shiny dark eyes of the little nun who, despite her great age, had the spirit and appetite for adventure of a young woman. Suor Arcangela had a vitality that eclipsed even the young girls in the convent that were waiting, impatient, for a husband to bring them escape via marriage.

'What appetites you have, Arcangela - insatiable, but you may attend with me' said Lucia, who then shook her head with chastisement and admiration.

'Thank you mistress' said Arcangela before she sprang into the air, and skipped into fleeting dance about the table. Suor Celeste stood unamused.

'Abbess Lucia, I worry for you' she said, 'do you think it wise to visit the Sabbat again when HE could be there?' The Abbess shot some air out of her nostrils with an abrupt snort,

'Don't lecture me, Celeste, not everyone is as timid as you are when it comes to living life. As you have seen, many times, I can handle myself in any situation, with any man: be he Dark Prince or not.' A pulse of dread passed through the Professor as he listened. He chewed at his lips before the plain nun gave out a deep sigh, shook her head, and wrinkled her brow: 'with respect mistress - he's not a man - and witches like us must watch our step.'

'Ha!' declared Lucia, 'I'm no ordinary witch that's out of her depth.'

'But...' said Celeste as she paused to look at an animated Arcangela who had written out a letter to deliver to Donna Ravolio. She then folded it after drying the ink with powder, sealing the edges with hot red wax, before stamping it with Lucia's insignia of a flying owl clutching a wand.

'Done' said Arcangela, dusting off her hands, 'the work is done. I'm ready.'

Celeste drooped, looking at Arcangela, shaking her head as she spoke, 'Lucia, my mistress, please *heed* me.' Celeste reached out to touch Lucia's arm, but the Abbess pulled herself away, 'please Lucia, even a sorceress as powerful as yourself has to answer to someone. Gifts such as yours don't go unnoticed' Celeste warned, but the Abbess ignored her. The Professor gripped the bedsheets as he listened to the witch's conversations: at times amused, but more often concerned at the situation he found himself in and pondered how he could get himself out of it without his carry case.

Lucia spoke again, blithe and free to address Celeste: 'I gather then that you don't wish to join us at the Sabbat tonight.' Celeste shook her head, while Arcangela gave out a crackling hum of playful tune, paying no heed to Celeste's concerns, and busied herself by tying a piece of red ribbon around the cream coloured letter she had written. When she finished, she dropped the letter into a large wicker basket filled with many others. 'Suit yourself Celeste, but you disappoint me, I shall attend again with Arcangela - which reminds me' said Lucia, scanning the room, 'do we have enough unguent for the both of us to travel?' Arcangela nodded in unison with Celeste, and hopped back over to the wooden chest with her usual clip clop, and dug out two glass jars that contained a buttery mixture flecked with herbs,

'She made some more for us, just in case' said the little nun flicking her head in Celeste's direction.

'Thank you, Celeste' smiled Lucia, her white teeth illuminating her face, 'but I'm still cross with you, however, before I dismiss you both be sure to deliver my letters to our patrons so that we may keep them in line.'

'And our guest?' added Celeste, keen to make amends, for she could not bear to be at odds with her mistress.

'Please bring some lamb stew for the man: he'll be hungry when he awakes.' The two witches, disguised in their nun's habits, attempted to make off, but Lucia raised a hand to pause the women and turned her ear to the far door. She paused, 'the nuns have stopped their singing, so my Abbess will be here soon. I shall put her to rest. I dismiss you both.'

The witches nodded again, and bowed with respect, before Celeste took up the wicker basket filled with letters, and opened the door at the far end of the room. When the witches turned their backs, the Professor craned his neck to peep at them from under his covers when daylight flooded through the door. Suor Celeste and Suor Arcangela bowed once more when, as if in a trance, a woman walked in who looked like the perfect twin of the Abbess Lucia. The two witches hurried out with the black cloth of their habits lifted by the breeze, as Lucia ushered in her double.

The Professor's eyes almost popped out of their sockets at the spectacle. He twitched his head, and he clutched his pillow as the Abbess Lucia closed the door, and put her hand on the other Abbess' shoulder to turn her around. The Professor turned in bed once more. Lucia clicked her fingers three times across the glittering stare of the woman in front of her:

'I am your maker, I gave you life, I gave you voice, and now I give you rest' she said, as her twin's eyes glazed over. She obeyed her mistress like a human robot and allowed herself to be lead to a chair where Lucia sat her down close to the Professor's bed. The Professor did his best to remain motionless and tried to control his ragged breathing, resisting the urge to leap from his bed and sprint for the door. He watched Lucia use her fingers to close the glassy eyes of her double and lay her palms in her lap. 'I know you're awake' said Lucia, the Professor flinched, 'I don't care what you've seen or heard: it's better that way I feel' she added, not turning to him, as she smoothed the fair hair of her double after taking off her wimple. 'It's better still that my companions think you asleep. You've heard some of our secrets, and, like for like, you shall reveal yours.' Lucia dusted down the clothes of her double that seemed then to be devoid of life, sat like a waxwork in a chair: a perfect copy of Lucia herself.

'What is it?' said the Professor who had begun to shake. The Abbess turned to look at him,

'I think you know what it is, don't you recognise a Golem when you see one?' Recognition then bolted to his mind before he answered,

'Yes, I've read about them, but I never thought... in my life, that I would ever see a real one.' The Professor then clung to his pillow like a boy after nightmares and hoped the Abbess could not detect his shaking. Lucia's eyes shone - a complete authority in her power.

'What is your name?' said the Abbess. The Professor recalled that he had not said so,

'I'm Professor Winston Jeremy Sloane, Lucia' he said, forcing his words out.

'Sounds Protestant' she cooed, 'but I didn't say that you could use my true name, *Winston*' she added, satisfied that her body double looked immaculate, 'but given the circumstances, I'll allow it.' The Abbess' voice took on a creamy tone, 'tell me - Winston - how did you get here?'

'You know how I got here' he said as he sat up in bed, and itched at his bandage that fell open. He noticed with shock that the scab on his slashed arm had already begun to crumble away to leave the skin as if it had been unharmed. The Abbess smiled and moved closer to where the Professor sat:

'The balm is good isn't it' she said, the Professor nodded, 'I can teach you how to make it. Now tell me how you got here.' The Professor stretched himself and yawned.

'Well, before I walked up here I arrived in Florence two days ago, and I came via Pisa and Turin before that...' Lucia seemed unsatisfied.

'You say the name of those cities in an English way, and you're also missing my point' the Abbess interrupted, her tone changing,

'how did you get here in this *time?* My dreams, my visions, my cards told me of your coming, for your needs of my knowledge, which made me scribe for you in the first place, but all said you'd not be of this time: how is that possible?'

'Does it matter?' he said,

'Of course it matters' the Abbess raised her voice, 'you didn't come here looking for Easter eggs. Where are you from, and how did you *get* here?' The Professor palmed the stubble on his chin.

'I don't think I can tell you that' he said, looking sideways, but Lucia hissed like a viper before she snatched his neck in a vice-like grip without touching him: her outstretched hand enough.

The Professor writhed like an eel as he struggled for breath, thinking he would pass out, as Lucia with a sweeping gesture lifted him into the air, by his neck, till his hair brushed the high arched ceiling of the room. 'Do you want to die?' she spat as the Professor clawed at his throat. He managed, just, to shake his head, before she hurled him down from the ceiling, and onto the bed that gave out a loud crack as his body slammed into the covers. The Professor lay gasping for air. 'Don't *trifle* with me' Lucia said, in a low voice as the Professor sprawled over the bed and spluttered: his breath coming in gulps and heaves as he tried to recover. Her voice chilled the air as she spoke, 'this is your last chance; how did you get here?'

The Professor had no choice when he, at last, spoke, realising that, for all her power, she could not know everything. 'You're a violent woman' he spluttered, between coughs and wheezes, checking himself for sprains and breaks. 'I... I used a Hermeporta to get here' he said, trying to recover. The Professor sat back and rubbed at his neck that looked red and swollen. Lucia's eyes widened in stark contrast to her static Golem, which had not twitched during the commotion.

The Abbess paused to squint: 'a Hermeporta?' she mused, 'does that mean Hermes' Gate?' she said, turning her head. The Professor nodded, 'what is it?' The Professor coughed up some spittle but swallowed it again to soothe his throat. He coughed as he patted at his tender neck. His breathing and heartbeat were out of kilter.

'It's a portal - a portal to other times and dimensions.' The Professor resigned himself to his fate - accepting the defeat of full disclosure, 'I first discovered a Hermeporta in Turkey: what you would call Anatolia'

'Yes' the Abbess nodded, her face a picture of intrigue, 'I like the East. I know some Ottoman merchants there' said Lucia, 'they sell me rare herbs I cannot grow here, and saffron via the Venetians I know in the Republic. Decent men: but they prefer not to deal with women directly in trade.' The Professor gave a listless nod before continuing,

'It seems you're a woman of enterprise' he said, allowing himself to look around the large room in more detail. He could see from his bed through to the side room with its covered crystal ball, many instruments a chemist would recognise for making distillations and manipulating compounds. A lot of glass jars of various sizes, brimmed with an assortment of contents, lined the walls from the floor almost to the ceiling. A wooden railed ladder allowed access to the shelves at the top. He thought he recognised things, but the details escaped him. There was much in the place that represented early versions of some of the equipment he had used in his own lab. 'It seems you have quite a business on going here.'

'I have help' she said,

'From the other two?' the Professor said with a limp gesture to the far door. She nodded,

'Yes, but it's only the three of us.'

'I guess no one knows, huh?' The Professor tried to laugh but coughed instead, his neck burned and his back strained.

'I doubt many know of your *Hermeporta*' said Lucia. The Professor shook his head, 'such a thing is beyond value. Imagine what one could do with such a thing. That is a great, *great* power' she said, lifting her shoulders upward and taking in a deep breath of air as if savouring a treasured victory. 'One could manipulate the very workings of time: history itself.' Lucia raised her arms in the air to announce her thoughts; the Professor flinched, 'how does it work?' she declared. The Professor closed his eyes, and pulled his hand down his face, grinding his teeth. Lying would be pointless. She could kill him. The Abbess looked on and waited to suckle every word that would fall from his lips - he gave out a deep sigh: 'the Hermeporta uses human sacrifice - that's how it works, how it gains its power.'

'*What?*' said Lucia, before she peered at him with one eye closed and thrust her ear toward him,

'That's how it transports people. It needs a human soul.'

Lucia gasped and clutched a hand to her breast before she sat in the lap of her Golem to steady herself. The Professor pondered the bizarre scene of the Golem sat as if carved from wood, eyes closed, while its identical twin fidgeted with life in her lap. Lucia's eyes seemed to flash with light.

'You've come at even greater cost than I thought to be here: far higher than I suspected. You've taken human life; you've used the souls of the living to get here. You say I'm violent, but you… You're a *murderer*.'

The Professor grimaced with the comment that cut him to the quick. 'It's not murder – it's… it's research.' Lucia scoffed. The notion had not once occurred to him as murder; the Hermeporta took the life, not he.

'Why?' Asked Lucia, 'why do you do such things to be here? Oh!' she gasped again, almost covering her mouth with shock, 'that means that your daughter is a murderer too, for I suspect she came on her own.' Another blow: not once in his life did he feel he needed to defend Illawara, convinced she could look after herself. At that moment, he saw himself wringing Lucia's slender neck to try killing with his own bare hands for once. But he dared not risk another beating: he would not survive another attack from Lucia. The Professor swallowed again, puckered his lips, and gritted his teeth till the sinews of his jaw protruded.

'It's the *Hermeporta* that takes the life; one doesn't have to do much' he said, 'all one need do is lead or throw the victim to the snakes.'

'The *snakes*' she exclaimed, the Abbess looked from corner to corner as if vipers were let loose in the room, 'I think you're worse than the Devil' she added with nervous excitement.

'Yes, the snakes...' added the Professor, as if he were telling a campfire story, 'the marble snakes that writhe and come to life when it's time feed on a human soul. The finest living sculpture that your eyes will ever see' he said, beginning to relish the effect of his words on the powerful sorceress - impressing her. Lucia could not sit still as she listened, rapt, to his story unable to tear her mind away. The Professor started to perform: 'the snakes surround a huge marble dish of Quicksilver, I'm sure you know what that is' she acknowledged the comment, 'it reflects reality like a mirror, but it's a doorway to the beyond. The victim rises in the air hypnotised or still fighting depending on the viper's mood before they attack to break the bones and wring the body dry of life until it's a withered husk.' Lucia attempted to cover her ears, but the Professor raised his voice to be sure she heard every word, 'most scream as they die, a dreadful howl until their hair and eyes turn white, and their soul is devoured. The Vipers then toss the consumed body aside, a wafer of crust - just like a digested rat coughed up by an owl.'

Lucia sat with her hand clasped over her mouth, at times aghast at the list of the grizzled details. The Professor suppressed a smirk when he read the reactions of the Abbess, before adding: 'I doubt Illawara is a murderer by the way. She has a noble spirit - that I know. Only ritual sacrifice is needed between feedings. I suspect no one lost their life when she came here.' But the Professor did not seem convinced by his hypothesis.

'I think you underestimate your daughter' said Lucia, sensing his unease and reckoned that Illawara might have done otherwise. The Professor wrestled with the concept in his mind before speaking.

'But that didn't stop you putting her in danger, did it? I heard your lecture to Celeste about protecting women, about defending them, but you've put Illawara in harm's way. Why did you do that?' Lucia paused, a flash of conscience on her face for a moment, before her face became unreadable again.

'You wouldn't understand' growled Lucia, 'besides, if you care so much why were you not with her to guide and protect her? You're not without guilt.' The Professor glared at Lucia for some time. He swallowed, before raising his chin:

'You wouldn't understand' he said.

A consensus of silence fell between them. She turned away from him. The Professor then sat back on his bed after divulging his secrets and watched the effect his story had on Lucia through half closed eyes. The sorceress turned this way and that in her habit - her mind a nest of ants. She let the Professor keep his secret as she had kept hers. She got up, she sat down and got up again to pace about the room. Her mind fidgeted with other matters - the Hermeporta. Lucia had heard of such Hermetic devices as myth and legend: old Rabbis and elders had hinted at things, as she travelled through the world. The oldest of witches she knew had made veiled comments, her book of Hekate suggested yet more, but never could she have guessed that such a thing existed. Lucia's mind reeled at the possibilities, and her heart set aflame with a desire to see and use the Hermeporta for her own bidding.

The door at the far end of the room opened. The Abbess had stopped her pacing to turn to the door. The Professor didn't bother to look to see who would come in, and just listened to the clip-clop of a built-up shoe, and the shuffle of another pair of feet behind. The Abbess made a gesture and a nod to the two witches that paused to do something before they advanced. Arcangela then approached, slow and measured, with a tray laden with an earthenware bowl filled to the brim with steaming lamb stew with white beans. On a wooden plate sat warm bread with salted butter to the side. The Professor's mouth watered. He had not eaten a hot meal since the Medici banquet.

Lucia and Celeste looked on as Arcangela went to the side of the ragged Professor: 'a healthy man like you must have an appetite' said Arcangela with a gentle voice, as she looked up into the Professor's young face. She flinched when she saw his neck. Arcangela gave the faintest shake of her head. Celeste's eyes flicked from Arcangela to Lucia, but the Abbess seemed distracted. The Professor gave a feeble smile as the delicious smell of the hot food wafted up to him: 'eat this' said Arcangela, as she put the tray in the Professor's lap, 'it will restore you, and complete your healing.'

Winston glanced at the bowl with suspicion but eased when he looked into the wrinkled face of the little witch and saw the contrite look of her wan-faced companion. The Professor assumed the two, in their silence, felt solidarity with him, imagining that they understood his predicament. Celeste took the opportunity to step forward, and to place clean folded clothes next to him on the bed.

'Eat' said Lucia, 'you'll need your strength. We'll also bring you hot water to bathe in before you change into those clothes.' The Professor obeyed her command. The lamb stew comforted him with its depth and flavour - tasting just like his mother's cooking. He saw his mother again, telling a joke at her kitchen table, as he ate, hearing her voice, and wondered what she would make of his situation. To the witches, he devoured his meal with obvious hunger. He used his last crust of bread to wipe the bowl clean, as the witches looked on. When he finished eating Arcangela took the tray back. Lucia turned to Celeste and spoke: 'has the water steeped?' the woman nodded, 'fetch it please, it's time he bathed.' Celeste gave a bow and hurried back to the door to open it and bring in a wheelbarrow that contained a large vessel of steaming soapy water scattered with herbs.

Celeste rested the wheelbarrow near the Abbess before she scuttled back to the door to close it. When she returned, the Abbess said some words over the steaming water in a language the Professor found familiar but hard to understand. When Lucia had finished her Yiddish prayer, she bid Celeste to take the wheelbarrow into the side room. The plain witch obeyed but turned the wheelbarrow with some difficulty into the chamber, her thin arms wobbling before she returned. The Abbess addressed the Professor as the other two witches looked on:

'Take off your clothes, Winston, and use the water and sponge to clean yourself. Please keep your feet on the white muslin provided to catch the drips.'

The Professor paused, almost refusing before he looked either side of him, then nodded and stood before he began to take off his clothes. Celeste turned away, but Arcangela waited for more garments to come off. The Professor took pride in his body, even after many years, and many lovers, it had served him well: through his own innovation and discipline, he enjoyed having the physique of a much younger man. Once bare-chested he tossed his slashed shirt aside, revealing the sculpted shadows of his torso in the light, and made a start on his stockings that clung to his muscular thighs - he began to peel them down: 'you may step into the room now' said Lucia. Celeste still faced away, but Arcangela swore under breath.

The Professor gave a wry nod and strode into the doorway of the side room, before half yanking down his stockings to moon his onlookers. Lucia tilted her head: the suggestion of a smile on her lips for a moment. He then strode forward to continue to undress. Arcangela craned her short neck after him: her eyes drinking in the powerful grace of his body. The Abbess looked at the little witch and wagged her finger, 'not yet' she whispered.

After the Professor had dragged off his stockings in the side room he luxuriated for a while as he washed his hands and forearms. The Professor then wobbled for a moment, somewhat light-headed, but regained his balance to dip the sponge into the hot soapy water, the colour of milk, which gave off a heady scent of herbs. He stood on the square of white muslin that Celeste had placed on the floor of the side room and soaped himself to lather suds all over his body. He didn't care that anyone watched: and delighted in the clean and perfumed feeling as he scrubbed away at his armpits, groin and backside, and felt the blood, grime, and sweat of the previous day get washed away. The Professor wobbled again, as he scrubbed his feet, but continued to sponge himself with the soapy liquid, covering him in frothing suds, until he finished. Winston, standing warm, wet, and naked, raised his palm to his flushed face: 'it's hot in here' he muttered to himself. He yawned, clutching at his forehead, and struggled to stand. His vision began to blur as he clung to the side of a table. He reached down for the muslin to dry himself, but almost toppled over. Maps and recipes stuck to the walls began to go out of focus. He dropped the sponge. He tried to shout out in protest: 'you... you've...' he mumbled, but could not formulate more words as the room spun. The Professor then staggered and weaved closing his eyes as he fell, down into darkness, and into the braced arms of Lucia and Arcangela that caught him before he hit the floor.

'Well done little one' smiled the Abbess, 'help me put him on the bed.'

■ ■ ■

Antonio steered the carriage as best he could over the rough roads that lead to Bologna on their way to Padua, as they sped for his mother's house, for her exile, and the refuge of the Venetian Republic.

'We'll have to stop soon' he whispered to himself, as the sun started to set with a coppery glow that stained the clouds to the colour of honey. The burnished light mingled with the autumnal display of the trees - except the Cypress pines, evergreen and unchanging, standing like sombre spears in a cauldron of fire coloured leaves. The carriage rattled on as the wind blew, at times cool and others cold, as winter began to breathe and rouse herself from sleep. Winter would awake before long to kiss the leaves with frost, turn puddles into glass, and spider's webs to necklaces - exchanging her sister's coloured pallet for whites, silvers, and greys.

Hermes and Illawara looked out of their windows and watched the leaves blow, and the countryside roll away. They said almost nothing and sat like strangers to one another, and strangers yet to themselves. In a short time, so much had changed.

■ ■ ■

The Cardinal had gone to the Roman Embassy in Florence, that evening, with his head hung low. News of the debacle had reached every inn, tavern, trattoria, and brothel by the time he had returned. He had sent off his henchman to find Illawara and the others soon after their escape. The Cardinal rubbed at his brow and heaved up a deep sigh that made the Embassy spaniel, Lupo, cover his long ears with his paws, and look up from the floor with eyes like boiled eggs. Orsini croaked out the odd word to his attendants that fussed around him.

'Your Eminence, where were you last night? Your hosts had feared the worst for you. They refuse to believe the rumours – but they heard there was a great tumult and disturbance near the river – and feared the worst' said the chief of security. Orsini gave no reply to the question. Orsini's Chef hurried to his side when he heard that his master had returned. But Orsini only asked for chicken broth to eat, much to the surprise of his Roman chef - accustomed to providing hearty evening meals to the robust

Cardinal. He knew better than to question his patron. The Cardinal refused the company of his hosts, requested his bedroom shutters be closed with curtains drawn, and asked to be left alone. He heaved his body up a broad stairway embellished with a tangle of Baroque paintings - on which the paint had yet to dry. The Cardinal looked on unmoved. When he had entered his lavish private apartments, the Cardinal kicked off his shoes, not caring where they landed, skipped his evening prayer, and eased into his bed like a snail.

Orsini then lay on his back, after adjusting his pillow, and groaned as he looked up to the dim painted ceiling. The Cardinal grimaced as he tried to wriggle himself to comfort. Orsini struggled with the heaviness of his body, and his shoulders deflated as the sounds of whispering, gossip, and muffled laughter played in his ears. He looked up to the fresco painted above and replaced the faces of the feasting scene with those of his rivals, that looked down and sneered at him. Orsini, with effort, turned himself in bed to rest on his side, and hide his face from the imagined critics above.

He would have to answer to the Pontiff when he returned to Rome. He groped for the pillow next to him and held it close until Illawara was in his arms, smiling, warm, dazzling, and beautiful. He clutched at his pillow until he danced with her again, breathing her into his heart, while the years and his cares fell from him like coins into a fountain. Orsini sneezed and shook his head, but she had vanished, and the full weight of his life returned. 'You've lost her, old fool, you've lost her' he mumbled to himself before he coughed again and fell into a weary sleep. A while later the snoring Cardinal did not hear the nervous tap of an usher to bring him his chicken broth.

■ ■ ■

The Professor awoke to find himself tied naked to the bed. He fought and struggled, but to no avail. His mind began to clear its fog. He looked around to find many candles burning, a dozen at least, which illuminated the room. The colours of the tapestry of Diana had become clear and vibrant, and the Professor then saw even more of the curious assortments that filled the rooms. Small orreries that showed Copernicus' view of the heavens, others Kepler's, many vellum scrolls of spells written in different languages, books on Natural Philosophy, and almost fifty carved figurines from the known world. He turned his head around to look for the Golem, which sat there lifeless as before but wearing a different habit. Celeste sat next to it, on another chair. Celeste stared through the Professor, looking half dead herself.

'Who's tied me to the bed?' he asked her,

'They did' said Celeste, in a faint whisper.

'Can you untie me please?' he said, but Celeste shook her head like a little girl and looked to the far door,

'I can't touch you' she said, 'not until they finish the ceremony.'

'What ceremony?' said the Professor as he again struggled at his bonds.

'You'll see' said the deadpan witch. The Professor wriggled and shook, but his bonds would not yield.

'You have to help me' he said, but the witch just sat and watched the far door.

'You'll have to be quiet' said Celeste, 'they'll be here soon.'

'I don't want to be QUIET' shouted the Professor, giving a wild struggle. The bed creaked, but the leather bonds at his wrists and ankles kept him spread-eagled on his back.

'No one can hear you' she said, 'the walls are thick, and the nuns are asleep, it's not long till Matins.' The Professor then thrashed his head about and wailed. The pallid witch sat and watched the door until He had finished.

'I'm dreaming. This must be a nightmare?' he said. Celeste looked at the man with concern and seemed to him more nun than witch, but she made no move to help as the door at the far end of the room creaked open.

The Professor shook himself to convulsion when two nightmarish figures walked in and closed the door behind them. The pair stood covered head to toe in wolf skins with the canine jaws hanging over their brows, fierce eyes staring, ram's horns at either temple and long black robes like ragged burkas that covered their faces and bodies. Both figures held long clubs in each hand

and held them aloft, and glided like two monstrous apparitions to the side of the Professor's bed.

They then began to tap on the ground with their heavy clubs, thud, thud, thud and started to chant. The mass of wolf skins flopped about in bedraggled motion and seemed to take on the life of a hunt in the candlelight - chasing, leaping and ready to tear flesh. The figures began to howl, wild and animalistic. The pair gained more intensity, babbling and chanting and continued to hit the ground, harder and faster than before: crack, crack, CRACK. The Professor looked on, helpless, tied, naked, and exposed - the whites of his eyes like shattered porcelain - he then let rip with a guttural howl that would have moved any living wolf to compassion: the bellow coming from the very depths of his being. The wolf skinned pair carried on their motions, the horns on their heads threatened to gouge, their fangs threatened to rip, and their wolf eyes glinted with the flash of death. Celeste rocked backwards and forwards in her chair and joined in with the incoherent mumblings.

The Professor writhed and flayed at the bed, his wrists and ankles rubbed raw with his efforts. The Professor, his eyes wild and head thrashing from side to side began to jabber to himself as his body slicked with sweat: 'they want to kill me' he mumbled. Then the chanting intensified, and the three figures spoke in one tongue, with one voice. The ghoulish figures then raised their clubs high above his body. An extended shriek escaped through the Winston's gritted teeth - he tensed his muscles to resist a bludgeoning. The horned pair joined their clubs above him in the sign of the cross, in a fever of incantation, before they tossed their clubs aside with a clatter. The two figures then tore off their wolf skins and attire.

Lucia and the little Arcangela stood in front of him nude.

'Oh *God*' said the Physics Professor for the first time in his professional life and would have prayed if he had known what to say. He stared up defenceless at the sorceress and witch that stood above him unrobed and free. Lucia's figure could not be faulted and would have attracted him if the circumstances had been different. As for Arcangela, he looked upon her figure with horror staring at the lopsided, wrinkled, heap of her body: with her two uneven breasts that dangled, between her chest hairs, like dried oranges in stockings. He saw her untamed grey pubic hair, that almost hid a fleshy protrusion that peeped out from her crotch, and ran up from her groin, along the sides of her layered torso, ravaged by time, to join with the tangled wig of her armpits. The Professor had never seen the like before - the wolf skin showed more mercy to his eyes. 'I'm in *HELL*' exclaimed the Professor, his eyes searching and frantic for escape spied the faint bald patch through Arcangela's thinning grey hair, which fell lank and brittle upon her stooped shoulders. Without her clothes, he could see her built up shoe and saw how much that one leg was shorter than the other.

The little witch stood legs akimbo, relishing Winston's fear, and tossed her hair about as if it were a mane of gold - she did not care a crumb for the Professor's thoughts. She bent to loosen her shoe-strap, her torso a concertina of flesh, and then kicked off her shoe to take a lopsided stance. Arcangela stood there, holding herself with pride as if she were a prize-winning squash at the village fair: bold, vulgar, and alive. The Professor resisted weeping but had no choice but to accept whatever came his way.

'Fetch our headdresses and unguent' Lucia said to Celeste, who then got up and went to the wooden case with iron trappings to retrieve one of the glass jars filled with a buttery mixture, a crescent moon headdress made of silver and diamonds, and a bandanna made of woven gold. Celeste stood to one side with the glass jar and opened it. A sweet, waxy, and pungent aroma filled the glowing room. Lucia put on her crescent moon headdress and said: 'I am Diana' before scooping a handful of the ointment from the open jar Celeste held and used her hands to rub it over her face, her hair and her body. The Professor struggled to believe his eyes as Lucia's figure became even more alluring when her skin, almost in an instant, took on a silvery glow of its own. The sorceress shimmered like a shaft of moonlight where she stood and gave extra illumination to the walls and furnishings. Lucia then untied the lower braid of her blond hair until it fell loose about her shoulders – her hair alternating in colour from gold to silver and back again. The stunned Professor struggled to move his eyes from her. Arcangela took up the bandanna of woven gold, tied it around her head and said:

'I am *Circe*.' The little witch then reached up to Celeste to take a scoop of the ointment, and like Lucia rubbed it into her face, scalp, hair, and body. Lucia handed back the jar to Celeste. The Professor looked on to see what effect the unguent would have on such a dilapidated figure. Nothing happened, at first, although Arcangela stood erect with her eyes closed and arms held aloft. Then the witch began to change.

First, her shorter leg grew to the correct length to match the other, and then her stoop straightened out to take the diminutive witch to just over five feet tall. Arcangela then began to swing herself into a dance. As she moved her body changed, and every sweep of her arms turned back the years and bestowed grace upon her jaunty frame. Lucia and Celeste began to clap out a Spanish style rhythm as Arcangela continued to weave and move in circles - her speed increasing with the clapped rhythm. Her once drooping flesh grew taut and smooth, her shrunken breasts became bountiful, every hair on her body grew dark and supple, and her face then changed from prune to peach. The little witch then stopped her spinning and declared with arms flung wide:

'I'm magnificent, I have power, I am *beautiful*.' The Professor observed, slack-jawed, the plump impish prettiness of the little witch, even with her overgrowth of hair. Celeste looked on, unmoved it seemed, but Lucia smiled and wiped away moisture from the corner of her eye.

'It's time we made ready' coughed Lucia, 'the Sabbat will begin soon, we must hurry before the nuns wake for Matins.' Lucia then focused her attention on the Professor. Her eyes then searched his nakedness before they settled on his loins. 'Fetch the shears' Lucia said to Celeste. The Professor's face turned white. The sullen witch shuffled back to the wooden box with iron trappings, and pulled out a pair of silver sheep-shears studded with opals and amethysts: the edges of the razor-sharp blades caught the light. Lucia walked forward.

The Professor's teeth chattered, and he fought with all his might at his bonds, as Lucia spun the shears in her hands, before slicing the blades in the air and pointing to his loins. 'No, *no*. You're *crazy*. You can't do this to me' he screeched as Lucia drew closer. The Professor wailed and twisted himself away from her, before half freezing when Lucia drew the open shears across his taut stomach to his groin. 'No...NO, you *evil*, depraved *bitch*' he squealed, 'please don't do this I beg you!' But Lucia gave out a shrill laugh, her smile and skin flashing in the light, and she twitched the blades together to make a slicing sound, before putting her warm palm on his groin to grip his manhood. The Professor gave out a deafening cry and writhed and wrung his body away from her touch to try and free himself.

The Professor felt his flesh tug under her grip. The shears sliced and the Professor felt part of himself become removed. He screamed – a blood chilling scream. Lucia laughed, before she shook her prize aloft above her head. She brandished a tuft of his red-blond pubic hair. The Professor looked up at her prize before he lost any self-composure he had left and sobbed. Hot tears streamed down his face, while his ribs convulsed and his nose began to drip.

'Fetch my locket' said Lucia to Celeste, who obeyed and reached again into the wooden chest to pull out a bejewelled silver locket that dangled from a silver chain. Lucia opened the locket, once handed to her, and put the Professor's pubic hair into it, and then closed it again with a click, before she wore the item next to her glowing skin. The Professor turned to hide his face away, that burned pink, and to shun the white salt lines of his tears and the gaze of the witches. Lucia looked at him where he lay, as his body still spasmed with emotion.

Lucia then turned her attention to Arcangela and took up her shears again: 'bless the Madonna' she said in mock surprise, 'you have sprouted like an unruly hedge - let me prune you, my dear.' The little witch offered herself up to the shears without fear and allowed Lucia to trim down her armpits and pubic hair to more tidy proportions. When Lucia had finished her work, Celeste gathered up the pile of Arcangela's shorn hair and stuffed it into a velvet bag before putting it back into the chest. 'More unguent please' said Lucia, and Celeste fetched up the jar again. Lucia scooped a modest quantity into her palm and then climbed onto the Professor's bed. His heart pounded as he looked at the witch with her crescent moon cradled in her hair, with her skin glowing like moonlight upon water, and wondered how a thing as glorious as she could be so wicked. She rubbed some of the ointment into his genitals and the rest into the cleft of her bottom. To the Professor's disgust and humiliation, his manhood responded, drawing admiration from Arcangela:

'He's blessed' she gasped.

'Indeed he is' purred Lucia, before she eased herself down to squat on him.

The Professor could only feel heat and pressure on his loins, from the numbing ointment, as Lucia began to pleasure herself. She rode him, against his will, as if he were a wild horse tethered to her saddle. Winston lay still, and watched Lucia take her pleasure of him with a surreal detachment, as if he were separated from his body. He saw her sensuality increase to free abandon as she commanded his body and stimulated herself. With time Lucia's skin grew brighter and brighter, as her pleasure increased, grinding on him in a frenzy before she cried out in convulsions as light beams shot out from every pore of her body – shining like a mirror ball - scattering the walls with light. The Professor floated above himself but slid back into his body when the sweating figure of Lucia took his face in her hands, letting an orb of light appear in her mouth before she tongued his lips open with a kiss.

In that instant, his body crashed into a tidal wave of pleasure that overwhelmed him till his very soul groaned with ecstasy. Winston gave out a ragged cry as he erupted inside Lucia, rocking the bed, his body tingling with electrified sensations, and convulsing as if an earthquake had shattered his body. Lucia held on and gave a glittering laugh as she looked down at him in conquest. Lucia waited for all his convulsions to pass before she pulled herself off the spent man who laid limp and dazed. 'Now I'm ready for the ball' she breathed to Celeste, while Arcangela pranced about as a dog does when waiting to be fed. Lucia smiled at her: 'you may clean him, my dear' said Lucia to the little witch, who sprang to the loins of the Professor, eager and ravenous, and used her mouth and tongue to clean every intimate part of him. When she had finished, Arcangela used her hair, which had become thick and luscious again, to mop him dry. The Professor lay in a stupor, neither willing or able to move. He groaned again, bleary eyed, as another pulse of pleasure ran through his limp and exhausted body. Celeste looked at him with despair.

'Time to leave' said Lucia, patting herself dry with a fresh sheet of muslin. 'Fetch the rods' she said to Celeste, who then turned, zombie-like, to hand Lucia and Arcangela back their clubs, but this time with some sorghum grass bound to the ends with ribbon - having added the dry grass as Lucia toyed with the Professor. 'Good craft' said the sorceress, as she inspected Celeste's swift handiwork. Celeste bowed before Lucia, and Arcangela scooped up more of the ointment and rubbed it into the brooms before laying them on the floor. Then Lucia and Arcangela spoke over the brooms with a short German spell, and the broomsticks then levitated before they glanced at each other and winked. The Professor looked on at his abusers, his eyes still dim and half closed, and tried to hurl abuse as the pair mounted their brooms that bore their weight. He failed, his body incapable of speech. The couple turned his way when they noticed his efforts and whispered something incoherent, flicking their fingers at him, before he sighed and passed out again. Lucia chuckled to herself while she looked at the Professor as she floated above him. 'He's a fine figure of a man - and very spirited' she said, before she rubbed off some unguent from the greasy stick, and reached down to massage it into his temples. Lucia spun her locket over his head, whispering another spell, as she floated next to the bed. 'I want him to see everything' she said to Celeste, who then nodded and gave a bow. 'Give me my shawl' said Lucia. Celeste obeyed but struggled to look at Lucia as she hovered, diaphanous, like an elemental being before she wrapped Lucia's crystal covered shawl around her arms as she hung suspended in the air. 'Thank you' she said. Celeste nodded,

'It's an honour, my mistress, Diana.' Arcangela wore nothing but her nakedness and bandana,

'Diana, it's time to go' she said, and the sorceress agreed,

'True, it is, Circe' Lucia replied, before turning to Celeste, 'make haste and open the hatch before the nuns start praying.' The plain witch obeyed and looked even more pale and ghostlike in the tremulous light given off by Lucia before she went into the side room and wound a crank on the wall to draw back a hatch on the ceiling. The two women hovered on their brooms as the trap pulled open, and the light from a full moon swept down into the room. Lucia and Arcangela looked at each other and cackled like Hyenas, clapped hands with one another and declared: 'to the ball!' The pair then glided into the side room, levitated up to the hatch, and sped out as fast as hawk moths into the cool air and silver moonlight.

Chapter 14

The Witch's Ball

Midnight: a clearing in the Tuscan countryside

The Professor slept and dreamed: and found himself in the air behind the two witches in flight, high above the houses of Florence moving at great speed. Diana shone with her silver skin and the crescent moon in her hair, and Circe focused her attention on the view ahead, with her bandanna of woven gold the only thing to tame her brunette locks that billowed out behind her. The clouds raced past as the women flew on, high above, and over the river Arno. Within minutes the witches, who steered their brooms with grace, had cleared the boundaries of Florence and passed the Fortezza da Basso and headed for the fields beyond.

As they glided further into the countryside, the pair waved at a flock of geese that flew towards them in formation: 'where do you fly to?' Diana shouted out to the approaching birds,

'We fly to The Great Swamps of Babylon to rest, and feed our young' honked the leader,

'One of them is tired' shouted Circe, who then stretched out her arm toward a young goose that trailed behind its family.

'We cannot look back' honked the leader, so the little witch turned her wrist to lift the air under the struggling bird, which helped it catch up with its siblings and parents; a honk of thanks came back as the formation flew on.

'Tell me what herbs you find there when you return to us in the spring' Diana shouted after the flock, 'I know some traders in Baghdad.' The leading geese gave distant honks back that they would. Diana smiled to herself and looked forward to the return of all the migrating birds - for they had some of the most interesting stories to tell - they brought her news of the world.

'Lake Surreale is near, Diana' said the smaller witch, 'everyone will arrive soon',

'Yes, I think I can see the lake now' Diana said, as she gestured to a bright reflective spot on the horizon that looked like a shard of mirror surrounded by trees. The Professor floated behind, in spirit without his body, while the witches descended as they approached the lake. As the women slowed their flight and lowered altitude, the Professor observed a multitude of torches lit below: some burned with a green flame, others with orange, blue, or pink. They lit up the trunks of the birch, oak and willow trees that flanked the edges of the small lake and made them glow with colour. The witches slowed their approach yet more as they drew closer to the enclosed field, with grass kept short by the day grazing of goats and sheep. As Diana and Circe descended the air grew warmer below them, heated by the torches, and mushrooms sprouted upon damp wooden stumps in the longer grass nearer the trees of the isolated woodland. The Professor could see from his vantage point, as the witches drew closer, that many guests were arriving in the clearing.

Men and women of different ages and some much younger guests had arrived using varied means of transport.

The Professor could see a middle-aged woman wearing a splendid diadem studded with jewels, and a long white silk cape, arrive saddled on the back of a huge rooster with a bit and bridle in its beak. A teenaged boy, wearing a blue silk bandanna and a black body stocking, held onto the woman's bare waist. The pair exchanged glances, as they lowered behind the trees: 'I'll have words with *her*' said Diana, as the pair jockeyed off their brooms, and wedged them into the lower branches of an olive tree. In unison, they said: 'bleib gelegt' (stay put) in German, before they prodded at the brooms to be sure they were fixed and well behaved.

Once satisfied their transport was secure the pair walked past several other brooms like theirs but with different coloured ribbons or fabric to tie the sorghum grass: each witch or warlock expressing their preference or style. Some chose to ride metal pokers, or bits of broken furniture, most of which were wedged into tree branches and hung at jaunty angles. Diana and Circe stopped a short while to point and titter at a greasy leg of salted mutton, and a black hoofed Spanish ham, used for transport, wedged into the branches of an oak tree. They joked that there would be some good cooks among their number that night. More guests could be seen arriving as the witches walked through the trees and toward the clearing.

Many couples, opposite and same sex, walked hand in hand as they emerged from the trees at the opposite side of the grassy expanse. The murmurs of conversations and a sense of anticipation rippled through the night. A gang of six women and three men arrived at the gathering each upon the backs of gigantic cats, almost the size of horses, which came up the clearing to the south of the lake in great leaps and bounds over bushes and grass, as their glamorous masters clung to their fur. The riders brought the cats to a halt, and the felines then stooped to allow them to dismount, before the animals quenched their thirst at the lakeside with whiskers as long as oars, which dipped into the water as their vast tongues lapped at the lake's edge.

The new arrivals drew some admiration from the other guests, for their bold entrance, as the Sabbat assembled, more than a hundred strong, around a large fire lit within a stone circle in the middle of the clearing. A man and woman began to beat out a rhythm on their leather drums, and a group of satyrs began to play on their wooden pipes, which drew spontaneous cheers from the crowds as they mingled and spoke with one another. Several smaller fires, of different colours, were lit around the larger one, as meats roasted above the flames and cauldrons were put to boil as guests tossed various ingredients into the vats - to give enchantment or add flavour.

The crowd grew to almost two hundred as the witches and warlocks chatted, flirted and laughed with one another, some began to dance, while their familiars occupied themselves or took rest near the trees. The sound of voices and music thronged in the air spiced with the scents of cooking and the mingling of bodies. Diana and Circe picked up some drinks, poured into fine glass or gold goblets, which had appeared on tree stumps used as low tables. The liquids shone in the moonlight as the witches sampled the beverages.

'The drinks are flowing tonight' said Circe, with throaty pleasure, before slurping at her drink.

'Indeed they are' said Diana, taking a sniff of the liquid before she sipped, 'what are you drinking?'

'I've no idea' replied Circe, 'but it tastes good.' The two witches crossed the clearing as guests milled about, and they made their way toward the witch that had arrived on her rooster. They had to pause their advance as a large centaur, at least seven feet at the shoulder, crossed their path and eyed the pair up. Circe gave a coquettish glance over her goblet in the centaur's direction as he passed, fury chested and broad shouldered. The ground trembled as he walked past, snorting his appreciation of what he saw. Circe followed the centaur with her eyes, holding his gaze while he strode on - as he left a scent trail of sweating horse and man. Diana tutted under her breath,

'Be careful, Circe' said Diana, 'centaurs can be aggressive.'

'I know' said Circe, craning her neck, 'I've never tried one before: but that one... that one looks like a *stud*.' Diana raised an eyebrow and sighed,

'You'd be sore in the morning my dear, sore in the morning.' Circe scoffed and took a deep swig from her goblet, tossing the cup aside, before she stooped down to pick up another drink. More guests arrived using branches, rods, or whatever came to hand: one court musician had greased his violin to get there, and then used his bow on the instrument to accompany the tune of the satyrs. More rode on the backs of hares with long ears and bright amber eyes or bridled toads and foxes. Every arrival was adding to the atmosphere. One, obese man, whom many suspected to be a clergyman, had chosen to arrive on a hairy pig and got the first big laugh of the evening. The hefty pair had flown through the air like a furry pork ball, and landed on the ground with such a thud that both man and pig broke wind with a reeking gust - much to the amusement of those that saw and heard them. Diana and Circe threw their heads back in laughter, before continuing their advance towards the side of the woman who arrived by rooster. A few of the guests took pains to present themselves to the witch wearing the diadem and white cape.

The pair were just about to tap the talking witch on her shoulder when a very mature man, not to be upstaged, with an immense silver beard grown to his knees, then arrived on the back of a unicorn with two shapely women - young enough to be his granddaughters. The Sabbat turned to applaud the warlock and two women who sat perched on the magnificent beast. When all eyes were looking the beast reared up, hoofed at the moon, and uttered an ethereal whinny that echoed around the clearing above the music. Its passengers slid off its well-groomed back to rounds of applause. The dazzling unicorn then cantered to the lakeside for a drink next to the cats, before joining a group of centaurs that greeted the beast with joyful slaps on its back.

'Good evening to you, sisters' said the caped witch turning, before Diana could touch her, 'that was quite some entrance' she added, with grandeur, tilting her head towards the most recent arrival - the complement not intended for the pair. The diamonds of her diadem and white cape caught the light - she looked like an empress. All three witches then looked at the bald and bearded man as he walked off arm in arm, towards the roasting food, with his comely, and organza wrapped companions.

'Indeed that was, Hera' said Diana, looking on before the witches exchanged dry kisses with each other: Hera acted as if the pair had perfumed themselves with manure. Diana paused to study Hera: 'and that's quite a pair he's found for himself' she added. A silence fell between the three witches. Their bodies did no move. Diana took another sip from her glass and followed the new arrivals with her eyes. She then turned her shoulders away from Hera. Circe tapped the rim of her half empty glass before she looked at the ground. No one spoke.

Hera looked Diana up and down, as she waited, and smirked before she made her reply. 'Two village twins from Prato, so I'm told' said Hera, with a waft in the direction of the two women that arrived with the old man,

'I see, thank you' said Diana,

'I'm sure your famous tinctures help him keep "up" with those two beauties.' Diana had narrowed her eyes before she chewed back her smile.

'I'm sure you'd know' she said, 'you've bought enough of it for your needs.' Circe took a long slurp from her cup, as her eyes shifted between them. Hera pouted and sucked at her teeth,

'We all have our needs... I hear you're no different - though I give my men a *choice*' she said and glared at Diana as her silver skin glowed in the moonlight. Diana took in a deep breath of air as a sinew rose in her neck. She pulled her crystal studded shawl over her shoulders before she crossed her arms. Diana's face then set like a papier mache mask.

'While we're on the topic of needs, Donna Maria Barolo, there is something I need from you: may I remind you that your account is outstanding.' Hera scowled,

'Don't bore me with your money talk here, and how dare you use my Christian *and* mule's name while at the *Sabbat* - people could be listening.' Hera's eyes shifted as she scanned the crowds, 'most of us come here to forget our husbands - or enjoy another's.' Circe raised her glass in salute at Hera's statement, before Diana cut her a look. The glowing sorceress shifted her stance. 'You have no respect, have you not eyes in your head?' the witch continued, 'I'm Hera tonight' she said, sweeping at her cloak to reveal Peacock eyes painted onto the underside of the white silk. 'I wouldn't be calling you Lucia "Borghese", in front of others, "Diana", even if you owed me a fortune.'

Circe listened with intent, not used to hearing her mistress criticised - or her last name. Diana pouted, her fingers digging into her arms, but spoke again:

'Fair enough, suit yourself' she said with blank expression, 'but your account is long overdue, and you know it. I want you to pay me after Mass, the Sunday after next: that's almost two weeks from now. If you don't pay, I'll have to stop my dealings with you.' Hera scoffed, but Diana carried on, wagging her finger 'it's a long, *long*, boat ride to the Far East on your own to get what I have to offer, Hera. Your rooster can neither swim in nor run on water. Bear that in mind the next time your lovers are lying exhausted next to you.'

Hera grimaced at the threat, but nodded. Circe dried her cup with her tongue before she took up another drink, and a bite to eat, that passed on a tray held by a handsome youth wearing a toga. The smaller witch ogled his buttocks as he passed, before she scanned the wider area, while she drank and ate, and made mental notes of males she liked in the jostling crowds. Diana also surveyed the area, between stilted small talk with her client, as she sipped at her drink. Diana looked about but made mental notes of who owed her money, and the fresh business she could drum up from the eclectic gathering.

Hera then made a gesture to catch the eye of the youth with the blue bandanna. He left his friends, and before long he stood next to her: 'meet my son, Giacomo' said Hera. The silver skinned sorceress tilted her head in welcome, and the youth bowed. 'Giacomo, this is Diana, the famous woman I told you about.' Diana's expression softened, 'it's his first Sabbat.' The fifteen-year-old smiled, and complemented Diana on her beauty before he used his charm to engage her in pleasant conversation.

Circe tuned out of the conversation, scratched at her armpits, and sniffed her fingers before she downed her fresh cup and made her excuses. She swaggered towards three well-dressed men near the lake edge. 'Time to get back on the horse and try again' she said to herself as she made unsteady progress towards the men. Silent as a ghost the Professor, who had seen and heard all, followed her in spirit as his vision unfolded.

'What do you see?' said the voice of Celeste next to the Professor as he lay on the bed with his eyelids closed but his eyeballs twitching beneath. It took a while for him to respond:

'I see all sorts of people and beasts at a clearing near a lake, there are fires everywhere, people are mingling, and Circe is approaching three men who are standing by the lakeside.' Celeste scoffed and shook her head.

'Typical, she's as stubborn as a rash' Celeste snorted, 'it's the Guapano brothers: they'll turn her down again. What else do you see? Is there a man there that's much taller than the others?' The Professor twisted his head as if to look about,

'The Centaurs are tallest' he said, 'but the music is getting louder and more people are starting to dance.' Celeste moved closer to the Professor,

'Tell me more, tell me everything you see, has anyone new arrived?'

The Professor mumbled and frowned at the question as his head turned from side to side, sweat clinging to his brow: 'no, no one new has arrived; I think all are here' the Professor said, and then grew still for a moment. Celeste wrung her hands, stood, and then paced up and down. She looked at the Professor where he lay feverish and restless, as he struggled again at his bonds, and turned his head this way and that as is if searching the whole area of his vision. He then froze and spoke again: *wait*, I think I see something' he moved his head as if scanning his eyes over the tops of trees, 'yes, I see three birds in the sky.' Celeste's expression changed, her brows knotted,

'What three birds? Describe them to me.' The Professor moved his head as if looking for a better view before he spoke again:

'Large water birds, they could be geese, no, no, I'm wrong they're swans, yes, the birds are swans - two white and one black.' The Professor stretched his neck forward as if peering to get a better look, 'they're flying down now, and they're landing on the water. They're huge.' Celeste fidgeted.

'What are they doing?' She said, her breath catching short in her throat. The Professor craned his head yet again, eyes still closed, scrutinising.

'They're swimming towards the shore, and they're almost here... oh, but they've just dived under the water' the Professor's head bobbed and weaved, 'I don't see anything, just ripples on the surface.' Celeste pulled a face, and the Professor paused for a long time as if looking.

'Keep talking' she said, 'you must tell me all that you see' the Professor struggled as he slept and his trance unfolded,

'Something's happening. Heads are rising out of the water, a man with a dark beard and two women with white skin...' The Professor became agitated, 'but his clothes are dry, the water doesn't touch him, and he's tall, very tall indeed.' Celeste clutched at herself as if stripped bare in an Arctic wind.

'It's Him, it's HIM' she shouted, and clapped her hands to her head, 'he's come' she said, her voice loud and strained, 'it's the dark one, the Dark Prince' the witch shook all over. 'Tell me what you see Winston, spare no detail.' The Professor's words then came at speed,

'The white skinned women have horns, and their eyes glow. They're the colour of ivory, but they have long black nails. People are moving out of their way, and the music has stopped. The man is even taller than the centaurs, maybe eight feet, he follows them, and he wears a long black robe with red slashed sleeves: he looks like a priest.'

'It's Him; I know it. I've no doubt' Celeste exclaimed, 'he's come to talk with her. I've warned her of this. I warned her, *warned* her, but she wouldn't listen.' Celeste then clutched her hands to her face, turned herself back around to run to her chair, and rock herself backwards and forwards. 'Heaven help me, I can't bear it... what's happening? Please, you're too silent' she said, as her feet tapped on the ground and she wrung her knees with her hands. The Professor lay rigid as if unable to move,

'He's walking towards Diana, and all have moved aside. She stands alone. Everyone's watching.' Celeste reached under her wimple and started to pull at her hair as the strands fell,

'Oh Lucia, why don't you listen to me, when it's I that can keep you safe?'

Celeste turned pink and started to cry, but the Professor carried on his reporting: 'he's reached out his hand to her, I think he's inviting her to dance, but no one's moving, everyone's quiet... silent as death. Diana hasn't spoken...' The Professor paused, unbreathing before he drew in a sharp breath, 'she's refused him... everyone is shocked, she's walking away.' Celeste leapt out of her chair as if jabbed with a pin:

'I can't hear any more' she exclaimed and lit a stick of incense before she said a short prayer and then passed the incense under the Professors nose.

The Professor awoke from his trance at that moment with a stifled shout, to find himself back in Lucia's room. Celeste untied his bonds and tossed him the clothes she had presented him earlier. The Professor shook his head and pawed at his face and eyes as he readjusted to his surroundings - his ankles and wrists burned as he rubbed them. Celeste then retreated into the lap of the Golem, the perfect replica of Lucia, and ran her hands over its body, before she clasped one of its breasts and wept on its shoulder. The Professor froze mid-motion, with his mouth ajar, to look at Celeste, with deep thought, and observed the witch as she sobbed and clutched at the rigid Golem here and there. The Professor sat still for a while to observe Celeste before he spoke: 'you're in love with her, aren't you?' he said, before he swung his feet off the bed, and began to put on his new clothes. Celeste wiped at her bloodshot eyes and left damp patches on the sleeve of her habit as she dabbed at her long, thin, and red nose that dripped like a twig after rain. Celeste gave a fractional nod.

'I'm cursed... with an affliction. I've known since I was a girl. God won't rid me of it no matter how much I pray to be delivered.' The Professor nodded his head.

'So you came to a nunnery... to escape temptation?' said Winston,

'It's not like that' said Celeste, wiping at her eyes, 'I came here to escape marriage, to escape childbirth... to escape *death*. Do you think I'm alone?' Celeste fixed the Professor with a look, and he regretted his previous remark. She wiped at her nose again, 'Lucia's never touched me, yet it's all I crave, but not once, not even to use The Grip if I displeased her.' The Professor rubbed at his bruised neck in memory,

'Is that what it's called? You don't want to be touched like that, trust me' he said.

'It's better than nothing' said Celeste between heaved sobs, her speech interrupted, 'she's used The Grip sometimes on Arcangela, and I used to envy her, can you believe it? I envied her: even when Lucia threw her across the room. She deserved it though; Arcangela's stubborn and mouthy, and she can't keep her hands to herself. I'm sure you've learned that already... but she knows better now - not to touch what Lucia considers hers.' The Professor heard bitterness creep into Celeste's voice. 'But I do as I'm told, I prepare everything, and get no reward for it.' Celeste looked up to the ceiling and then heaved up more tears, and abandoned herself to sorrow as her shoulders shook. The Professor shook his head, sighed, and looked again at the forlorn witch as he spoke:

'Is that why you cling to that thing then?' he said, pointing to the Golem, 'is that the closest you can get?'

'She's not a thing, she's a WOMAN' said Celeste as she wiped at her tears, and slug-like nose that gurgled and bubbled with the effort of breathing. 'I read to her, and talk to her when Lucia's away, and when Arcangela sneaks out of the convent at night to go gambling.' The Professor smiled to himself when he thought of the little witch and tutted, 'when they're gone I comb her hair, and tell her stories.' Celeste ran her fingers through the Golem's blond hair before she neatened it back on her shoulders. 'We cuddle sometimes, don't we?' she whispered into the Golem's ear, 'and we speak a little' the Professor looked on but shook his head.

'You shouldn't do that. You're not supposed to read to, or touch a Golem: it develops their mind, and it develops their feelings' he said before he stood to tuck his new shirt into his stockings, 'she'll want to live, you know, and it could be dangerous.'

'I don't care... and who are you to lecture me? You're just a plaything' said Celeste with another wipe of her nose, 'but she already reads prayer to the nuns, very well, when we let her... I'm her teacher... the nuns can't even tell the difference: they're stupid - just like you' replied Celeste. The Professor tensed his jaw:

'You're jealous...' He said. The Professor made a move to add more, but held back, 'why are you telling me this?'

'Who else can I tell?' She said, throwing her palms in the air, 'I have no one: nothing. Do you suppose I can unburden my heart of this at confession - and avoid being beaten, tortured, or burned?' Celeste almost laughed, 'what does it matter? You won't be here for long. She'll discard you when she's bored, just like the others.' The Professor pondered her words but didn't argue.

Celeste sat still for a while, and looked at the floor, before she wiped at her tears again, and took some deep but unsteady breaths before she stood up and entered the side room to turn the crank and reopen the sky hatch. The moon had moved, and the starry sky had lightened from black to dark blue, to look like velvet scattered with glitter. The Professor stood up from his bed and took the chance to consider the side room in more detail. Celeste didn't protest when he walked in as she continued to turn the crank. 'Time is passing' she said, looking up through the hatch that framed a patch of sky as it grew lighter, 'they'll have to return soon' she added as the Professor walked past a large mirror draped with fabric, and toward a bookshelf, he had not seen before. 'They must return before cock's crow.'

'What's this?' said the Professor reaching out for a small rectangular box wrapped in purple silk decorated with gold stars. Celeste screamed,

'Don't touch that' before the Professor drew back as if slapped, 'if she sees you touch that box she'll kill you, I mean it, she would.'

'What's in it?' said the Professor, taken aback.

'I don't know' came the reply, 'but once Arcangela tried to find out, and managed to touch the box before Lucia used The Grip on her. I've never seen Lucia so angry; she threw Arcangela like a stone.' Celeste stood transfixed as she spoke as if reliving the experience, 'Sour Maddalena had to nurse Arcangela for two weeks, we all thought she would die, and of course, I could say nothing. When the nuns asked questions, I said she fell down the chapel steps after prayer: I hated lying, and I'm not sure they believed me, but what else could I say?' The Professor nodded. Celeste stood still with a blank stare going beyond the room, with her hands suspended in the air as if pleading for mercy as she told the story, she then made a sign of the cross before she recovered herself to finish turning the crank on the wall. Celeste spoke again: 'please get some sleep; they'll be here soon.' The Professor nodded, his mind then filled with questions before he turned to the witch,

'How do I get out here?' he said, Celeste shrugged,

'I don't know... why don't you go back the way you came.'

'But you want to be rid of me, tell me how to escape with...' The Professor trailed off.

'You want her Grimoire, don't you? I can't tell you how to take that and stay alive. But maybe she likes you? She told us you've come to learn from her, and her books.' the Professor nodded, 'you're fortunate that she wishes to teach you. You must know something that she wants, or she wouldn't bother. Most men she discards after one use: they don't interest her for long.' The Professor raised his arms:

'Well perhaps if she didn't tie them down she'd get to know them better...' he said before he rubbed at his wrists and his voice trailed off. He then made his way to his bed and got under the covers. Celeste followed him.

'Most times she doesn't have to' she continued, 'but you're different, it seems' said Celeste, before she blew out all the candles, accept one, and retired.

The Professor turned to the wall in the gloom but struggled to sleep, his mind going over what he saw, what he heard and what Lucia did to him. Two shadows appeared above the hatch. The Professor tried to ignore the witches as they floated down, through the twilight, into the side room to return from the ball. Lucia then turned the crank herself to close the hatch. Arcangela giggled to herself and shuffled around in the shadows, to then pick up her things and bump and wobble her way out of the room.

The Professor heard a cock crow as the hatch wound shut. Arcangela's limp and years crept back upon her at the sound, as she walked to her bed, and she lost more of her enchanted youth with every step she took. She held up her hands in the twilight of the courtyard and watched her young flesh wither back to reality with every exclamation of the farm bird. Arcangela's wrinkled lips trembled, as she felt her body contort again with age. She shook her head and dried her eyes on her mottled hands before she slipped back into the darkness of her nun's cell. The Professor, through squinted eyes, could still detect the faint glow of Lucia, and her sweet perfume, before she blew out the last candle and made way to her bed: in passing, she drew close to him and stroked his shoulder in the warmth of the dark.

■ ■ ■

The Convent of San Matteo, morning, October 5th, 1611

The Professor awoke with a start, bolting upright, as if from a nightmare: the sound of ancient snakes hissing, and taunting, still whispering in his ears. Cold sweat soaked half of his pillow. He flipped it over before he turned onto his back and looked up at the ceiling. Winston shook his head as images ran across his mind of the night before. 'What's happening to me?' he said, soft and quiet before he covered his face with his hands. Much had changed, everything was real, and he could not be the same man again. He sat back up and looked around the room at Lucia's figurines, books, and tapestries that had become familiar. He heard the nuns of San Matteo singing in their chapel, high and sweet, in the mid-morning. 'It's Terce' the Professor whispered to himself.

Winston turned his head from side to side to scan the room - no one present - before he threw back the covers to stand in silence, peering, and listening for movement: nothing. He then turned, on tip-toes, and then walked over to Lucia's Grimoire. The Professor admired the book and ran his finger over its elaborate leather-bound cover. His fingers tingled with sensations as he caressed the book and opened some of its pages: a book he had travelled through time to find. The Professor peered around for a bag large enough to fit the Grimoire into, but could not see anything. Winston then headed for the door that he had entered from the passageway, and tested the handle. He gave the handle a twist to the left and then right before he shook at the door with force - but the door did not yield. Winston then shook the door handle much harder till it rattled: 'it's locked' came Lucia's voice from behind him.

The Professor stood frozen before he let his hand fall from the door handle, and turned to her with a blank expression. Lucia stood in her black Habit, her luminous face framed by the dark fabric, and looked every inch a pious Abbess - an innocent incapable of ruse - in stark contrast to her Goddess like presence mere hours ago. Images of Lucia, gleaming naked, from the night before, flashed into the Professor's mind. He narrowed his lips at the memory that rendered her woollen Habit see through for moments before he dismissed the images from his imagination.

'You must be hungry' said Lucia, suppressing a smile as the Professor looked at her, 'I'm getting Arcangela to bring you food' she said in a soft tone, before avoiding the Professor's glare.

'Where's the Golem, I don't see her' he said, as he looked over at the empty chair where the Golem had sat the night before.

'She's with Celeste' she replied, but the Professor frowned,

'You shouldn't let her spend too much time with it, it will learn more and want to live' he added, Lucia shrugged,

'The more it learns, the more freedom for me.' The Professor squinted as he looked at Lucia.

'You know she loves you - don't you?'

'Who? The Golem?' Lucia scoffed,

'No, Celeste - she's in love with *you*.' Lucia's mouth then twitched before she looked away,

'All the nuns love me, I'm their Abbess, it's natural' said Lucia advancing to her mirror, projecting her voice as she went. She continued to speak to him as she smoothed her appearance reflected in the mirror: 'we live here in seclusion; our bonds are strong. Who else can they love but me - and each other?' The Professor looked Lucia up and down, but she avoided his eyes.

'For Celeste, that Golem's a substitute for you, do you know that?' Lucia swept away from the mirror, 'she's in love with you Lucia, and her love for you is going into that Golem, and that could be dangerous.' The Abbess blushed,

'Don't lecture me. You exaggerate, I know the risks. We made the Golem together, but I can destroy it too, alone, if I wish, one wipe of the seal on her forehead from me and she returns to clay and dust.' Lucia fussed with a figurine that she had snatched up from a shelf and wiped away imaginary fluff from its glazed porcelain surface.

'I need to leave' said the Professor,

'You'll leave when I allow you to' said Lucia, and fixed the Professor with a look as if to remind him of her power - but the Professor did not flinch and glared back at her. Lucia softened her expression, tilted her head, and smiled before she spoke again with a lush, creamy tone: 'let's not argue about things as they are, these are the circumstances you find yourself in, and that's how it is for now.' Lucia walked towards the Professor, 'we have much to share and learn - now that I've initiated you...' The Professor took a step back,

'Is that what you call it?' He said, almost shouting. Lucia frowned at his tone and pointed to the open Grimoire.

'Your initiation was essential. Without initiation, you couldn't turn one page of that book without your hand blistering, stinging or burning - without the book resenting it.' Lucia folded her arms and stroked her elbows before she continued, 'that book was made by women, *for* women: it contains thousands of years of OUR secret and SACRED knowledge. No uninitiated man can touch it - you should be grateful I even bothered with you.' The Professor chortled and shook his head:

'Spoken like a true misogynist.'

'Like a what?' said Lucia frowning, as the Professor continued to shake his head at her,

'I get it now; this is what women talk about - *this*' he said gesturing at her. Lucia had glowered before she scoffed.

'You're talking gibberish' she said with scorn, 'as if a man would know what a woman feels, what she must endure. Anyone of my nuns could tell you stories that would break your heart, snap it in two.' Lucia swept herself to one side, as she side looked the Professor: 'and you dare to complain of my Initiation, something few men have ever had, and those that know of its value beg for.' Lucia then shook her finger at the Professor as her eyes blazed, 'what I did to you was a privilege, and didn't I give you an ecstasy beyond all measure when I shared my light with you?' The Professor cast his eyes down, his mouth tense, as the heat rose to his face. Lucia's brow raised, *'aha,* so you remember that part now' she chortled with defiance, 'when I "lit" you, you were writhing like a maggot on a hook.'

The Professor stood still, red-faced, and saw himself snatching up a figurine and cracking it across Lucia's forehead. He coughed back the idea, fearing The Grip: an agonised death would be his reward for daring. The pair stood glaring at each other when Arcangela hobbled in with food, which softened their deadlock. Bleary-eyed she paused and turned her face, left and right, from the Professor to Lucia, tutted, and seemed even more of a heap of wan skin than the day before: swaddled in her nun's habit she looked like a withered baby. Arcangela saw the pair with their arms crossed, and said:

'Ehgh!', with a shrug, before she then limped over to a table to place down a spoon and a bowl of warm porridge scattered with soft fruits, and nuts, streaked with Honey. Lucia addressed Arcangela in a bold voice,

'This is all that he's to have today.' Arcangela clutched at her head and wobbled at the sound, and had to hold onto the table to steady herself. Lucia looked at Arcangela, shook her head and muttered under her breath, 'we're to fast before his first teaching' Lucia said, in an even louder voice as if Arcangela were deaf, and the little witch swooned and clasped at her forehead, but gave a weak nod of acknowledgement. As the Professor pondered Lucia's words, he noticed a familiar smell drift up from Arcangela; the boozy waft conjured up an image of his late father: transported, Winston saw his father slump, into the Golem's chair, as if he just had yet another argument with his witless second wife, Maud.

He saw the seat morph into his father's favourite leather chair, that time and use had moulded to the heft of his body: Gerald sipped his cognac, spinning his ice cube through the bronze liquid with a turn of his hand. Winston saw his father reach into his tweed top pocket and take out a framed photograph of his mother and sister. The man then caressed the edges of the frame before he pressed the picture to his lips. Gerald and his leather chair vanished when Arcangela shuffled over to Lucia.

The Professor turned away when Arcangela moved, the warm taint of alcohol mingled with the spiced scent of unguent, which still clung to her skin, smelled just like his father's cologne. The memory of his father, immediate, unexpected and intense made the Professor tremble; for the first time, in a long time, he missed his father and ached to hear his voice, listen to his advice, or have him tell one of his funny and outrageous stories.

The Professor coughed to clear his throat - eager to avoid the sting of tears. The two women observed him - lost in himself. Arcangela turned to Lucia with a concerned look, but the Abbess bulged her eyes and shrugged back in return. As the Professor coughed, wiping at his eyes, he stayed turned away from the pair before the little witch spoke up. 'Did you enjoy the ball?' She said leaning toward him, but to no response came. The Professor then snorted, furious at himself, and made an exaggerated point of rubbing at his face as if waking from sleep before he turned to look at her - his eyes were pink.

'I'm not sure if "enjoy" is the right word' he said with a sniff, his voice sounding gummy.

'Somewhat strange, I know, for the Initiate' said Arcangela, as she searched his face, 'but glorious too, no? Do you remember me in all of my beauty?' Arcangela turned herself like a little girl, 'just as I was when I could afford to be foolish - when I was young.'

'I don't think I'll ever, ever forget it' he said, Arcangela then gave one of her cackles that sounded like the stirring of dry leaves,

'I'm told, that in the taverns I'm still remembered' she declared.

'I can believe it' said the Professor, wanting to distract himself, before she beamed with a gaping smile,

'And do you remember, Him?'

'Him?' said the Professor,

'Him' she added, 'the Prince, the dark one.' Lucia cast a sideways glance at the little witch but let her continue.

'Oh... Him' said the Professor in a quiet voice, 'I think I understand what I saw. But...' The Professor hesitated, 'I don't believe in the...' He frowned as his voice trailed off. The two women looked at each other, Arcangela spoke again to confirm her suspicions,

'Don't you believe in what you've seen? You've born witness, yet you doubt.' Silence came from the Professor, but Arcangela looked on and continued, 'you saw the black swan arrive with his maidens no?' The Professor took in a breath but nodded, thirsting for a strong drink, and Lucia glanced again at Arcangela, 'so you saw then what the swan became, what it turned into?' The Professor nodded again as the scene played out in his mind, 'then you saw that the Prince asked Lucia to dance and that she refused him: the THIRD time she has done so. Can you believe it?' Arcangela exclaimed, 'did you see what happened next?' The Professor shook his head, and Lucia coughed hard to interrupt,

'No' he said, 'I woke up'. Arcangela gave out an exasperated sigh and slapped her leg,

'I suppose that meddling goose broke the trance' Arcangela hissed, full of mischief before she glanced again at the concerned Abbess,

'Well' Lucia said, 'that's quite enough Arcangela - quite enough' she added with force, and a glare, to break Arcangela's words as she took a step forward. The little woman sulked like a toddler at the remark, and the twinkle went out of her eyes: 'please leave us now, we've much work to do.' Arcangela had no choice but to leave, so she turned back to the table to hand the Professor his porridge:

'Eat this. You'll need your strength' she said before she gave him a tender smile.

'Is it drugged?' said the Professor. Arcangela looked down, shook her head and then huffed, turned, and then gave a wobbly, but extravagant, bow to her Abbess. Lucia arched an eyebrow at the display and called after Arcangela just before she left the room:

'Be sure to talk with Celeste, and advise her to let our Golem teach Meister Monteverdi's new Vespers to our Sisters: I'll fulfil their request, as they speak of little else.' Arcangela nodded as she turned to face the door, 'music unfit for the Pope is fine enough for *us*' called over Lucia, smirking, in a haughty tone.

Arcangela, in a flash of inspiration, then clapped her hands before she turned back to banter: 'it tickles me when you spite your Uncle' giggled the little witch. The Professor blanched at the Arcangela's comment. 'Let's not let the composer's work be in vain for my dear libertine - the Duke of Mantua. You know I love him so.' Arcangela almost swooned with desire, 'how about we disguise ourselves, Lucia, as MAIDEN courtesans and dance at his court, blazing in like comets, and then tear off our clothes to entertain and outrage them all.' Arcangela flung her arms wide as if receiving a round of applause.

Lucia struggled to remain deadpan but shook her head, and a hopeful smile died on the little witch's face. Crestfallen, Arcangela bowed again, 'please return with Celeste before Compline' Lucia continued, 'as I'll need you both later to discuss a future calling.' Arcangela's eyes bulged somewhat at the request.

'The Pope's your *Uncle?*' said the Professor.

'She's not legitimate – his brother's love child' said Arcangela with a huff, candid after her night of heavy drinking and frustrated with Lucia for denying her a longed for visit to Mantua. Lucia turned to scowl at the little witch, and dismissed her by pointing to the door. Arcangela obeyed, bowing, before she then turned, walked, and glanced off the doorway before she left the room.

Chapter 15

A Return to Rome

Florence, Morning, Wednesday 5th of October 1611

Orsini resolved to go back to Rome, incognito, before leaving the embassy that morning, in the sureness that the news would be travelling before him via a man on a fast horse: 'good news walks, bad news runs, but gossip flies' Orsini muttered to himself as he got his coaches packed up in haste with what he needed for his return, and braced himself to face the choir. For once, in a long time, he paused his usual machinations of how to scupper the careers of his rivals and hoped the Florentine street brawl would not be too damaging for his own. Orsini resolved to travel without the pomp he had grown accustomed to: no heralds or announcements of his Eminence, and minimal staff, to arrive in Rome with as little fuss as possible. He accepted that news of the incident at the Medici residence, let alone the fight, would leak into the Pontiff's council. Orsini paused - looking off - while giving an instruction to an assistant, when he saw Cardinal Barberini sliding silver-tongued details into the Pontiff's ears: undermining, with relish, Orsini's chances of ever claiming the Papal Tiara for his own. Orsini cringed and shook his head until the image left his mind.

'Are you troubled, your Eminence?' asked the footman,

'Boy, just secure the case as I asked' hissed Orsini. The footman shrank back as if burned, Orsini then hesitated, looking at the footman's wounded expression, before he walked forward and helped him secure the luggage in place. The footman smiled and bowed with gratitude: 'off with thee... off with thee' said Orsini waving the youth away, before he shook his head at himself, and ran his palms down his face.

The Cardinal's behaviour had given a golden calf to every one of his rivals and enemies: he had even saved them the effort of constructing plausible lies - they just needed to relay the truth. Orsini cursed his times and the new strictness; he once enjoyed, that permeated The Counter-Reformation Church: years ago, he mused, he could have dismissed events as 'horseplay' during the third course of a banquet without serious challenge. Orsini shrugged, paced, and growled to himself next to his carriage, oblivious of his assistants who paused to look on. Due to the size of his retinue, it would take him at least ten days to arrive in Rome, enough time for the news to spread, but he intended that the Pope hear his version of events. Once in Rome, he could then try to nullify the lurid gossip of the laity, courtiers, diplomats, and his vengeful rivals.

∎ ∎ ∎

The Cardinal lamented his suffering on his journey to Rome: the inns along the way were bad, and the incognito Cardinal suspected the best rooms were not offered to him - an insult to a man accustomed to luxury. Many of the inns and taverns lacked a decent clean place to sleep, and the autumn wind had exploited draughty wooden shutters and gaps between floor boards. The best accommodation was booked up by wealthy pilgrims or merchants. The Cardinal, in anticipation of his ordeal, brought his own linen for each new bed and then ordered that it be burned after each night's stay: lest he carried back unwanted pests to his beloved, plump, four-poster.

In a moment of frustration, faced with a night at a dilapidated tavern, Orsini suggested to his assistant that he spend the night in his carriage, but the idea got vetoed on the grounds of security. The Cardinal, in troubled sleep, would turn, night after night, in his cold uncomfortable beds like a stone upon the shore, to then awake, bleary-eyed, to appalling breakfasts. Orsini's personal chef, exasperated, coloured the air with torrents of swearing and complaints to cooking staff on behalf of his master. At one lodging, in a fury, he barged his way into the kitchens to prepare better meals for Orsini, only to find the best food hidden from sight and essential equipment stowed away. That day, between reluctant sips of watered down wine, the Cardinal chewed at salt cod, and even drier bread, and speculated aloud, for all to hear, at how Jesus had found the strength to manage in his lifetime.

■ ■ ■

Padua, late morning, Sunday 9th of October 1611

Antonio, Hermes, and Illawara arrived in Padua in less time it would take for Orsini to reach Rome, but had also fared better. The inns of the north provided superior services, on their six-day journey, with innkeepers eager to satisfy the frequent visits from the affluent merchants that paused for rest and refreshment. The inns served the merchants of Genoa that moved north by carriage from the Thyrinnian sea; or the tradesmen of Modena, Bologna, and Milan on their way to do business with the entrepreneurs of the Venetian Republic - and all others in between.

Antonio breathed a sigh, and his shoulders eased when he saw the rust coloured bricks of the fortified walls of Padua. He drove the carriage north through the south city gate of Porta Santa Croche, accepting the welcome of the guards as he passed through the city walls, and along the Piazzale of the same name. He guided the carriage along the streets and looked for his mother's house nestled within the centre of the town.

Illawara and Hermes exchanged comments of admiration with one another as they peered out of the windows of their carriage, and looked at the domes and spires of St Anthony's Basilica: a harmonious blend of Gothic and Venetian-Byzantine styles. The bells of the Basilica rang out in intervals to summon the faithful to Sunday Mass. Illawara muttered and pointed out Padua University to Hermes, when Antonio turned off the Via Roma, into via San Canziano - telling him that the institution was already three hundred and eighty-nine years old. Hermes nodded along. Professors and academics strolled about everywhere.

Antonio turned the coach into the piazza of herbs, overlooked by the Palazzo Ragione - the palace of reason - while the students of

Padua University mingled with their professors, and other intellectuals, in the coffee houses flanking the market space, for conversation, beverages, and sweet treats. None of the market sellers were trading their goods, as the faithful made their way to church along the roads that lead to St Anthony's. But Antonio breathed in the scent of coffee, and spiced treats that were all blended together in air that pulsated with debate and daring conversations. To Antonio, it seemed the atmosphere of Padua itself stimulated his mind like a tonic - an antidote to the leaden dogma that subdued the spirits of those that lived further south.

Antonio smiled, waving at those he knew as he passed along the familiar streets of his childhood, and enjoyed seeing the diverse international visitors the university attracted from Europe, and beyond. He noted with pride how the domestic and international populace intermingled and exchanged ideas with one another - in a mood of collegiate friendliness - far from the ears of The Church, and the reach of the Pope. But he also liked how the faithful were not intimidated by such freedoms, and gave their blessings to free thoughts that enriched their own. Antonio's face clouded for a moment, atop the carriage, as he recalled his mother had not written back to him, for weeks, in the last half year, or so, of his absence – which was unusual for her. Antonio turned his carriage into his mother's narrow street, and its line of drab tenements, which constricted and confined those that passed along it.

Illawara looked out of her window at the washed-out surroundings, and then looked down at her dress and shrugged: 'I guess it can't all be glamorous', she said before she looked over to Hermes who gazed out his window with a concerned expression. Apart from their recent comments on the city, the pair had not spoken much during the trip.

After a while, Antonio brought the coach to a stop outside a dwelling with several floors, and many apartments. Some of the roof tiles were missing, the plastering of the outside wall had cracked and faded, and some bricks lay exposed beneath. The claustrophobic side street the building inhabited had not space enough for two carriages to pass. The daylight dimmed to grey in the narrow confines. Hermes looked at the tired looking clothes that hung from balcony windows and dangled pegged to washing lines. The lines were perched upon by sparrows that chirped, and left their droppings on garments whose owners were too slow to bring in their laundry - or just did not care anymore. Hermes rubbed at his face as if he had not slept in weeks, as he peered out his window before he looked across to Illawara, who could not meet his eye. Antonio parked the carriage and tethered the horses before he jumped down from his driving seat and opened the carriage door. His sunny expression changed when he read the faces of his passengers, but he smiled anyway - like a wedge of ivory carved into a doll's face.

'Welcome to my home' he said to Hermes and Illawara, before sweeping his arm toward the residence. The pair took their time to get out the carriage, while Illawara clutched onto to her satchel and the carry case. The pair stood still and looked up at the residence as if just marooned by a shipwreck upon a desolate island.

Antonio had bitten his lip before he closed the carriage door behind them while they both stood in the street. He then spoke to the pair in a lowered voice: 'look' he said, 'I know this is no Medici palace, but it's the best that I can do for now.' He moved closer to whisper to the pair, 'we may live here in exile, but at least here we're protected by the Republic... the Pope's power and his Cardinals are limited here - especially after the Interdict.' Antonio tried to sound upbeat as Illawara and Hermes nodded their acknowledgement, 'I know it's not much, yes, but I'm grateful' he added before he glanced at the dilapidated door of the residence. Antonio then clenched his fist and held it aloft as he spoke: 'one day I'll regain my birth right, and see my noble mother and family name restored to their rightful place.' The pair flinched but then nodded before Illawara cast her eyes about the street and its shadows.

Hermes took a keen interest in Antonio's words, but Illawara looked down at herself and then up at the walls of the residence and struggled to tell the difference between herself and the building. Antonio bid the pair to wait outside before they entered. He untethered the horses and then leapt up in two powerful strides to his driver's seat, and turned the carriage to drive the horses off to a nearby inn to rest. The pair looked on as he drove away.

'This wasn't in the plan, was it?' said Hermes, empty-faced.

'I know, I'm sorry' Illawara breathed, before looking down again at her stained dress, 'things have got out of hand. They'll be a solution to this. But let's just lay low for a while.' Illawara raised her luggage in the air, 'Dad will need to come to me for his case' she said, before she pressed the dark item back to her chest, 'I have to speak to him, and ask him why did what he did.' Hermes gave a listless smile but shrugged without answering. An argument between a couple in a tenement down the street began, and their baby started crying. Illawara shook her head.

Antonio returned, after a while, and tried to ignore the flat expressions of Hermes and Illawara: 'OK, let's go in' he said, and fetched a key from his pocket. They passed through the main door into a passageway that lead to flights of stairs, and beyond to a small square courtyard with light even dimmer than outside. Antonio gave the pair a brief tour of cracked plant pots that contained dead bushes, or things that had gone to seed amongst the debris and bird droppings. The half-dried corpse of a pigeon, with its withered entrails and ribs exposed, lay half eaten behind a plant pot amongst its plucked feathers which lay strewn, and undisturbed, around the courtyard. Stray bits of rubbish and other detritus mingled with dirt and moss in the corners. Some colour rose on Antonio's face, regretting giving his new guests a tour before he directed the pair up creaking wooden stairs, which reeked of damp that leeched out of the walls of the stairwell. Illawara ascended without touching the gnarled bannister, knifed with inscriptions, and Hermes walked on with his arms crossed behind his back. The troupe had arrived at the top floor before Antonio ushered them to a door of peeling red paint that had faded to pink in places. He stopped in front of the door to brief them in lowered tones:

'OK, we're here' he said, 'Mother isn't expecting us, there was no time to send word, as you both can imagine.' Antonio then stepped forward to take hold of each of his guest's hands, 'but she's a good woman, really... a very kind woman.' The pair had exchanged glances before they considered Antonio's eyes that moistened as he frowned. He squeezed their palms. Hermes and Illawara looked to each other once more, then back to Antonio and nodded: both softened in their way.

Antonio then turned to face the door, tidied himself and fussed at his hair before he gave three loud taps on the door. After a while, footsteps could be heard approaching, and Hermes and Illawara both took in breaths when the door creaked open. A mature woman with the same complexion and eyes as Antonio, creaked her door open and yelled with surprise. 'Nino, my darling' she exclaimed, 'my dearest son. What a surprise' she said as she flung her arms wide. Her hair was grey and unkempt, her forehead plucked high, and she wore a tired dress long faded from glory. Antonio stepped into her embrace. She hugged him before she held her son's face and covered it with kisses.

Hermes smiled and turned to Illawara who stood like marble - as if seeing something strange - and looked on with a lax mouth and wide eyes at the hugging pair. Antonio did not resist his mother's embrace and let her finish petting him before he prodded at her, and stroked her hair: 'you've lost weight, Mama' he said squeezing her arm with concern. She removed her arm from her son's hand, 'and why didn't you write back to me? I was worried - and you've had to answer the door yourself. Where's Dondo and Grizelda?' he asked. His mother ruffled at his comments as a bird does when it feels cold.

'Don't scold, Nino' she said wagging her finger, 'things are tough, you know how it is with me. Grizelda and Dondo are on leave – they'll be back next week'

'Both at the same time?' The woman looked past Antonio's shoulder, 'will you be wearing this to evening Mass?' added Antonio rubbing a piece of his mother's dress.

'Who's this?' She said first looking at Illawara and then at Hermes.

'They're my friends; Mama' said Antonio before gesturing to each of his guests in turn. 'I'll introduce you: this is my mother Bianca' the pair nodded, 'and, Mama, this is Hermes' the youth gave a small bow, 'and this is Illawara' who did the same.

Bianca gave a curious smile as she eyed up the pair: 'a foreign student and a town girl?' She said, 'who wears expensive blue shoes' Illawara blanched at the comment before looking down at her glittering chopines. Bianca looked again at her son, 'you're just like our cat my dear, vanishing for months, before returning with something unexpected to my door.' But Bianca then smiled and prodded her son aside to beckon the pair to her, and welcome her new guests each with a warm hug. When Bianca embraced Illawara she had to prize herself free: 'my, my, you're a *friendly* girl' she said, untangling herself from the hug that lasted much longer than expected. Illawara blushed, surprised at herself, ambushed by her rush of emotions, 'and what's that smell?' said Bianca sniffing the air around Illawara.

'I had to borrow this dress' she said, casting her eyes down.

'I figured that' said Bianca, scanning her eyes over the nineteen-year-old, 'but I can smell something sweet, like fruit.' A flash of recognition passed over Illawara's face before she took off her satchel and pulled out the fragrant item. 'A pineapple!' Bianca gushed, 'I've not tasted one of those for *YEARS.*'

'It's yours' said Illawara, 'please accept it as a gift from Hermes and myself.'

'Thank you. What a generous girl you are' Bianca said, before she clutched the fruit in her hands, closed her eyes for a moment, and took a deep sniff, '*mmmh, delicious*' she sighed, before plucking out a leaf at the core. 'It's very ripe. What a blessing. We'll eat it after evening Mass, before its past its best.' Grinning from ear to ear Bianca stepped aside to welcome in her new guests and son. As they all entered Bianca's home, Illawara realised, to the fullest, in her young life how much she had never felt the love of a mother.

■ ■ ■

<u>Rome, morning, Sunday 16th of October 1611</u>

After eleven days of undignified travel Orsini came down toward the Holy City from the north, smiling, on his southward progression from Florence, as if delivered from Purgatory. When the outskirts of Rome drew near the Cardinal's aching body eased somewhat, and it took most of his self-control not to yell for joy as Rome's hills and monuments came into view.

When his carriage and waggons reached the centre of town, he slid down the window of his door to let in the noise and clamour of the Holy City. Church bells rang out in jangling sounds for Mass – the Pontiff would be addressing the faithful St Peter's. The Cardinal sniffed at the familiar, but damp, south Auster wind that blew in his face. He closed his eyes and filled his lungs,

'Civilisation at last' he muttered to himself, as his coaches processed along the Via Del Corso toward the Capitoline Hill. The

Cardinal looked upon the ragged splendour of the littered ruins as his Roman blood surged with confidence. He glared at the carriage loads of tourists and pilgrims that came to admire the Holy City, hear the Pope, and receive the Sacraments. Their number seemed to increase year on year. The newcomers were greeted by vagrants on the streets with enough talent to dash out generic watercolours of the famous ruins, and peddle their wares to gullible visitors eager to take any memento of their travels home. His coaches made slow progress through the crowds.

A soup of people composed of clergy, artists, mystics, poets, tourists, gentry, laity, vagabonds, fraudsters, merchants, prostitutes and all those in between wandered the streets still immune from the chills that began to grip the northern cities. Some local people begged for alms, others gossiped, some came to preen. But some, with discretion, came to sell knickknacks, trinkets, paninis, fruit, or cheap rosaries: although the official markets were closed. Orsini almost smirked: he had arrived back to Rome, the squalid yet splendid Holy City - his capricious and beloved home.

The Cardinal's coaches passed along the Capitoline Hill, and Orsini then grinned when he saw, faced opposite, his noble family's most recent proof of aged esteem: the Palazzo Orsini. The Cardinal gave a sigh of relief as his coaches reached the side of the dramatic property: with its foundations attached to the remains of the ancient Marcellus Theatre, imagined by Caesar, realised by Augustine, and inspiration for the Coliseum. Orsini bloated with ironic pride when he thought of his family's imaginative use of the ruin, which predated the Vatican and Christianity itself. 'Home' said Orsini, taking in the arched columns of tuff and travertine that curved and buttressed the front of the palace the Orsini had built on top; like a loaf of bricks cradled by the stony spine of a fish.

He stepped out of his carriage when it came to a halt before his people could fuss, and cast his eyes upon the tiny island of Isola Tiberina which stood, proud, amid the polluted river Tiber, filled with all sorts, that flowed past the Vatican and the Castel Sant'Angelo. Standing in the sunshine, the Cardinal filled his nostrils with a deep breath of the fetid air, which no longer reeked, but smelled then like a perfume to him. The Cardinal strode ahead as he gave his instructions to his carriage staff, as they carried in his luggage, and looked forward to resting in his apartments, and perhaps the inner garden before he received a briefing from his advisor on what he could expect from his superior - Pope Paul V.

Orsini's greetings to his household received a muted response; several of his most trusted staff could not meet his eye when he addressed them: their uniformed bodies stiff, their smiles painted. The Cardinal did not ponder the reasons for long. Orsini eyeballed his staff from where he stood below: 'tell my advisor that we shall meet for luncheon in the dining room this afternoon after Midday Mass and when I've changed and freshened' he declared, tense jawed, to those that stood overhead and looked down on him from the staircase.

'We're informed that he's attended morning Mass already, your Eminence' said his head of staff, 'and has already had an audience with his Holiness.' Orsini swallowed.

'Very well, but luncheon is to happen as I've stated. I'll take evening Mass after I've rested. That is all' said Orsini. Orsini's Chef nodded, and the man beckoned down his deputy, with a snatch of his hand, from above so that they could both get to work. The Chef knew that Orsini could not face the Florence subject on an empty stomach. Within his sumptuous apartments Orsini took a nap. When he awoke Orsini freshened with soap and orange water, powdered, and changed himself into his newest resplendent red robes that he adorned with a Baroque gold crucifix that dangled from an ebony rosary. He then went downstairs, stealing a moment, to see his favourite pets. The two donkeys, twin brother and sister, were tethered in the garden and strained at their ropes to move toward him when he entered, 'did you miss me?' He said to the beasts that fussed over his hands and nuzzled him. He could not help smiling as he ruffled their manes and petted them, 'you're more loyal to me than my *staff* he whispered to the animals, that competed for his attention before he made his way to the dining room. The Cardinal sat at the dining table and plucked on the fabric at his waist, noting the extra space in his clothes, as he sniffed at the air ravenous, watching the door, with his spoon clutched aloft, before it opened. Orsini had heard a voice before he saw any food.

'He wants to see you in the chapel, your Eminence' said Orsini's chief adviser and secretary, Benfico, without greeting him. The short sighted but gifted man, with a bald scalp, thin lips, and even thinner sense of humour lead in the food platters, with his loose-hipped walk, to be sure Orsini paid attention to him. Benfico glided forward within the stuccoed walls, and frescoed ceilings, of the dining room. The expectant smile crashed from the Cardinal's face at the sight of the short man as he sauntered past before he inhaled and chewed his lip.

'I suspected he'd want to see me there... Will he have the choir?' said Orsini,

'Of *course*, he will, you know his style' said Benfico, who sat himself down with a prim swish of his clerical robes. The man then flashed his eyes over the Cardinal before breaking into a rare smile, 'you've lost *weight*' he said. Orsini fidgeted under the admiring gaze,

'The food was bad' he replied, rubbing at his brow, and making a sign of the cross on himself before saying a hurried prayer to bless the food laid in front of him. Benfico looked on with pursed lips but said nothing. The Cardinal, who had not had a good meal for almost two weeks, attacked his soup like a caveman. Benfico, poised like a debutante, used his silver utensil to cradle the broad bean and ham soup into his mouth. The Cardinal's spoon clattered through his dish, before he tore off a clump of dark bread from a basket, and used it as a shovel in the butter pad. Orsini then scuffed the bread around his soup bowl, to absorb the dregs, before shoving it into his mouth. Benfico side looked Orsini, as the Cardinal fed himself, before tilting his nose in the air. 'Aren't you going to ask me how my journey was?' said the Cardinal between mouthfuls of butter smothered bread, after a brief pause to burp and swallow. Benfico sat, stiff-backed, and sipped kitten like from his spoon, 'it was awful' Orsini continued, 'I swear the inns are getting worse, and the beds wriggle with pestilence. I'm sure they've not been this bad since the Sack of Rome' added the Cardinal, belching, aghast. Benfico raised an eyebrow before answering,

'I'm more interested in what happened in Firenze' he said in a sweet tone. The Cardinal stopped chewing,

'I'd rather discuss that with his Holiness' said Orsini, Benfico then leant forward - his head tilted back,

'I suggest that if I'm to advise you correctly, your Eminence, I think it better you share your version of events with me first.' The Cardinal's jaw clenched,

'What version have you heard? What have they said to you?'

'I suspect you'd rather not know, your Eminence' came Benfico's reply with a tilt of his head, as he focused his myopic eyes on the Cardinal, and gave a delicate dab at the side of his mouth with his napkin. Orsini undid a neck button and cleared his throat before he began.

'They, the crowd, were calling her a witch, but I had the situation under control.'

'Did you? I heard you were nearly run over by her carriage and almost trampled by a mob.' Orsini huffed and knotted his brows,

'Someone tossed fifty Florins into the air, what else could one expect? They're poor people; they fought with their lives for the coins, I've never seen such acts of desperation - there was less sin at the fall of Babylon.' Benfico arched his brow, 'what else could I do?' continued Orsini, raising his palms in the air, 'would you have me jump in to tear up the scrum and have my legs broken?' Benfico looked on dry faced and unmoved,

'I guess the witch is "the beauty in blue" they speak of?' said Benfico. Orsini grimaced at the word - witch - used to describe Illawara.

'I doubt she's a witch, and yes, she wore blue - but it's irrelevant - it became evident to me that she was in danger. It's natural that a man defends a woman's honour - especially a woman of high birth and rank.'

'But you're not a man; you're a Prince of the Church, in all but name, your Eminence – I'm doubles the next Pontiff will make it so...' said the adviser. The Cardinal wrung his napkin into a rope,

'What is this, Benfico? Do you wish to join his Holiness' Inquisition? I say it wasn't clear that she was a witch at all' Orsini motioned at the air with his hands, 'you should have seen them, they were shaking her carriage and causing her much distress. I had to calm the situation... I had to protect her honour.' Benfico gave a blank stare,

'How can you be sure she's a woman of rank, a woman of *honour?*' said Benfico. The Cardinal looked confused,

'Because I told you so. What else could she be? You think my eyes don't work in my head? You must mistake my eyesight for yours.' The adviser's face had narrowed before he scratched his fingernail at the table cloth. The Cardinal noted Benfico's response. He listened to the man scuff at the fabric and tried to suppress a smirk. 'Between you and me' said Orsini, pausing, and narrowing his eyes, 'I think she's the finest creature I've ever seen.' Orsini then licked his spoon clean, as if it was his lover before placing it back in the bowl. Benfico watched Orsini perform, and dabbed at his brow with his napkin as the colour rose to his face. Benfico paused, admiring the spoon for a while, his mind far off, before he coughed, giving a flick of his head as if to try to dismiss the Cardinal's actions. The Cardinal nodded as some house staff entered and made to clear the starter. The advisor waited for them to leave the room before he continued. He straightened his back yet more and decided to add firmness to his voice.

'It is said, your Eminence, that no one has heard of this "Beauty in Blue" before: no one can trace her family ties, no one knows of her dwelling or house, and most can only guess at what city she's from... it were as if she appeared by magic.' Benfico held the Cardinal's gaze without blinking. A vein rose in the Cardinal's neck before his adviser carried on, 'no one seems to know who on God's good Earth she is - even the Medici, after your little... *performance*' said Benfico with a twist of his wrist, 'they have drawn a blank: even with all of their connections.' Orsini turned almost as red as his gown and gripped his scrunched napkin in his right hand,

'That's quite enough, Benfico' growled Orsini. But the advisor ignored him.

'Many speculate' the blithe Benfico continued, taking pleasure in the Cardinal's discomfort, 'that she's likely a - COMMON - courtesan from Venice.' Orsini's eye's flashed, 'so, as a hinge of The Church, your Eminence, the question is...' Benfico hummed, before pausing for dramatic effect, 'who were you defending? A witch or a well-drilled whore?'

The Cardinal slammed his fist on the table making one of the house servants drop his vegetable platter on the floor - surprised by the boomed sound as he had walked in. The other servant just managed to hold onto his braised rabbit, when the Cardinal's fist had cracked the varnish under the table cloth. Benfico froze as the Cardinal bellowed: 'how dare you question me and my judgement. I only answer to his Holiness, and I'll not take insolent correction from a half blind mincing faggot!'

The attendant with the braised rabbit placed down his bowl on the table with haste, and then yanked up his colleague from the floor who had made a desperate attempt to scoop up the spilt vegetables. Orsini didn't care, and vented his rage, as the servants scrambled for the door: 'who in Dante's Hell do you think you are to question a Cardinal of the Church and an Orsini at that?' He shouted, standing up to point his finger at his advisor, 'I don't know what unholy favours YOU gave to get your position, and it's true that I've never liked you, but to suggest that I'd defend a witch or a WHORE is beyond *impertinence*.' Orsini then hurled his desert fork at Benfico, catching the man on his wrist before he continued. 'My family belongs to, and has fought for, our Mother Church, we've paid in blood to be here, and, in my own house, I'll no longer abide such questioning and insult from a fickle, ass-licking-rodent like yourself.'

The Cardinal's voice exploded like cannon fire, and Benfico's face became pale as his lips quivered. Orsini fixed his adviser with a look that seemed to stab the man in the face, and the consultant looked away before he attempted to reply. Benfico trembled, he had never seen Orsini so enraged let alone state his open dislike of him, and he took some time to respond as his eyes began to well up. Orsini, hot-faced, glared at the man till he shrivelled into his chair: 'I'm sorry, your Eminence' Benfico answered, clutching his injured wrist, his breath becoming shallow while his lips would not stop trembling, 'I see that I've greatly offended you. I was impertinent' coughed Benfico as he shook and garbled his words out, 'and I humbly seek your forgiveness.'

The short-sighted man spoke with his head bowed, but he chanced a look up at Orsini and wished he had not when he saw the face that had darkened with rage - Orsini seemed like a Gorgon: 'GET OUT' spat the Cardinal. With a gasp, Benfico bolted upright, and nodded with speed before he fled from the room, skidding on the cooked vegetables, as he sprinted for escape and closed the door behind him. Breathing like a wrestler, the Cardinal took up the braised rabbit platter and emptied the cooked meat onto his plate. He then flung the dish at the door, smashing it to pieces, where it fell near the other broken vessel. The house staff and courtiers, who had pressed themselves against the door from outside, leapt back and clutched at their ears in pain at the deafening smash of heavy porcelain. The other staff rallied round to comfort Benfico who quaked, inconsolable, as they took him down the stairs to the kitchen to give him fortified wine. The Cardinal grumbled his dissatisfaction, hearing the fuss and simpering outside, before hunching over his plate to devour his cooked rabbit like a beast from a dark forest.

When the Cardinal had finished, he wiped his hands and downed both glasses of wine that the staff had poured out for him before the start of the first and second courses. He stood, and then took a swig from Benfico's untouched wine, crossed the room, and pulled open the door to sweep the broken china and mess aside with a scrunch. Some of Orsini's staff cowered on the lower stairs, while offered strict council by the Chef, before Orsini brushed at his clothes and stepped out of his front door to make his way to the Vatican. The great house had taken on the atmosphere of a morgue by the time Orsini had slammed the door behind him and strode his way towards the riverside.

■ ■ ■

The Cardinal crossed the polluted Tiber river, leaving the Palazzo Orsini behind, at the Ponte Vittorio bridge after a long walk up the river embankment, and ignored some of the unpleasant things that floated by in it. Orsini then marched the short distance to the Vatican via some of the side streets that usually buzzed with market stalls, and the sounds of creaking waggons laden with late harvest grapes from the Alban hills in the south. He saw the remnants of stray grapes, from the previous day's harvest, that were crushed underfoot by the Sunday crowds. Orsini closed his eyes for a moment and saw a glass filling with sweet Frascati; his favourite Roman beverage. In the late afternoon sunshine Orsini emerged from the side streets in his scarlet robes, and sparkling gold crucifix, like a flame. He turned to face the Vatican's new façade that neared its completion. Hundreds of pilgrims and worshippers milled about everywhere in the recess before the Pope called evening Mass.

The scaffolding, which looked like clusters of matchsticks, on the front of the Vatican did little to diminish its grand impact. The Cardinal recalled the master craftsmen at their work amongst the clinks of chisels and clouds of dust. Orsini sneered: all of them were Maderno's men; the architect charged with completing the dead Michelangelo's vision in stone. Local people milled about, some stopped to look, point, and grumbled at how the façade obscured the dome - Orsini listened in silence but agreed within before he moved on. The Cardinal made his way to the far side of the Vatican and enjoyed the effect his rank had on the populous of Rome as he prowled through the promenade. The throngs of pilgrims, in various states of disrepair, either shifted out of his way or gave him a pious bow, or, more still, reached for his hand to kiss it before crossing themselves.

Upon seeing the Cardinal one scrawny man, in an acute fit of piety, threw himself down, prostrate, at the feet of Orsini and began to beseech and pray.

He shook and all over as if gripped by a trembling fever.

'Touch me, your Eminence' begged the pilgrim, before explaining to the Cardinal, that, per wise words said to him, his elderly father would become cured of an illness that made him too sick to journey from Tivoli. Orsini swooped himself down to pick up the ecstatic man that clung to the Cardinal's strong arms as if saved from drowning. He dusted off the angular frame of the Pilgrim, who then covered the Cardinal's scented hands with kisses. Other pilgrims looked on; goggle-eyed before they shuffled forward in hopes of a kind word to them.

'Your *faith* will bring your father's blessing' Orsini said to the Pilgrim with majesty, making a sign of the cross, before he swept off as the man gave praise and swooned in his sackcloth. Orsini began, at his leisure, his mood mellowed by deference and wine, to make signs of the cross here and there in the air, and relished the effect his presence had on the pilgrims that limped in from all parts of Christendom. Orsini approached the side of the Sistine Chapel after making a left past the main Basilica, and gave a nod of recognition to the Swiss Guards, in their bright pied livery, before the two men parted their polearms to let him pass. Orsini gave greetings to the guards he recognised but paused for breath when they whispered to him that His Holiness already awaited him inside.

Orsini hesitated before he crossed the threshold, closed his eyes, and then stepped into the chapel. When he opened them again, his eyes were struck afresh by the sheer magnificence of the place, and he crossed himself and thanked God for Michelangelo's genius. The figures on the ceiling depicting man before the arrival of Christ, and those of the last judgement on the far wall seemed to writhe with movement and expression upon the lapis painted walls. The Cardinal walked on and saw the figure of a man knelt in prayer, looking as if wrapped in gold leaf, on the ground at the base of the far altar on which a Papal Tiara rested.

The splendour of the Pontiff's exquisite robes outshone the grandiosity of the frescoed walls. As the footsteps of the Cardinal echoed through the chapel a hidden choir struck up with a paean of fragile, yet clear, voices, full of lament and sorrow as if forced, by hand, to drag Christ's limp, dead, and bleeding body off the cross.

Orsini shivered. The Pontiff never missed a chance to hammer home a point - Orsini's expression faded to greyness with the music as he approached, impotent and isolated, his stature diminishing as he drew closer to the Bishop of Rome. Orsini climbed the steps of the altar as the Pontiff spun around on his knees with surprising speed, and then used his great golden crozier to stand erect and majestic. The fifty-nine-year-old Pontiff extended a robust hand bedecked with rings in Orsini's direction and waited for his kiss. Orsini grazed his mouth as he pressed his lips to one of the Pontiff's hefty jewels as he kneeled before His Holiness.

The Pontiff then raised his arms, as the Cardinal sank, to stretch out his robes like the wings of an eagle. Orsini bowed down to the floor as the choir sang onto a higher pitch, that seemed to lift the ceiling and open a trap door to heaven. Orsini, humbled at the feet of the Bishop of Rome, shrank as if every eye of the painted frescoes were upon him. The Pontiff said nothing for a while, as he looked down, but then gave a gentle waft of his staff to halt the music. Together they resided in silence until the Pontiff spoke: 'my son' said the Pope in a rich tone, 'I hear that you're troubled, that you've made errors in judgement, and that PASSIONS afflict you. Is this so?' Orsini swallowed, his mouth dry, and kept his head bowed for some time before he answered:

'I sought... your Holiness, to try and save a soul from danger, an INNOCENT that needed guidance: a lamb to be protected from the wolves.' The Pontiff had listened before he made a deep inhalation and then spoke again so that his imposing voice undulated from the walls.

'They say that this innocent of which you speak of is not a lamb, a lost member of our flock, but a *witch* you had chosen to save in Firenze. A woman that turned grain into gold, no less' said the

Pontiff, with arms outstretched commanding the air. Some members of the choir had taken the liberty to peep through the grill and enjoyed witnessing the Pope take a strip off a powerful Cardinal who had once criticised their singing. The Cardinal felt their eyes upon him but did not dare turn around.

'This is what the crowd accused her of, your Holiness, but I didn't see the act with my own eyes as the others said they had.' Orsini then clasped his hands together as if in prayer, 'to turn grain into gold would be quite a feat indeed, and seems too far-fetched to be true, your Holiness: surely you cannot believe this?' Orsini cleared his throat and looked up at the Pope, his eyes full of longing, 'she's a delicate creature, your Holiness, and it seems she had given alms to the poor - a wretched fallen woman with a babe - is that not a Christian thing to do?' Orsini searched the Pontiff's ruddy face for mercy, but the Pontiff stood above him with his face unmoving.

'It's our Christian duty to give alms to the poor' echoed the Pope. Orsini seemed encouraged,

'Indeed, it's a noble virtue no less, and surely a sign that her heart is good? It was evident to me that those less needy, than the said woman, were ENVIOUS and vengeful that her generosity and alms had not extended to them.'

Pope Paul V stood, looked, and listened for a while before he spoke: 'do you believe what you say to be true my son?' Orsini nodded and looked up into the distinguished face of the Pontiff. The Pontiff stood resplendent as the Cardinal gazed up at him from the floor. 'I believe you, Pietro' said the Pope with his face raised up to the ceiling, 'a man of your rank and birth would find it impossible to lie in the house of God' the Pontiff paused, 'but there's a problem, my son.' Orsini frowned. The Pope looked down to the kneeling Cardinal and continued to speak, 'word has got out that you've embarrassed the Medici House - an *ally* - and word has also spread that an Eminent member of the Church has let a witch slip from his grasp: this can only help our enemies, *be the accusations true or not*, do you understand?'

The Pontiff looked down at the Cardinal, who had bowed before he continued in elevated tones, 'the Republic of Venezia: that plague riddled seething cesspit of iniquity, vice, and sin will seize upon any shortcomings, or weakness, of The Church for its own advantage.' The Pope then declared: 'let alone what that disgraceful Paulo Sarpi, our despised enemy, who's very life seems to be guarded by the Devil himself - what poisonous things would he say about this to the Republic and its Protestant sympathisers?' The Cardinal attempted to protest, but the Pontiff stubbed his crozier on the ground, splintering the air, before he carried on, 'this situation that we find ourselves in presents a real and grave danger for our Mother Church, my son, and it must be resolved in the clearest of terms.' The Cardinal looked bewildered.

'But, your Holiness, the matter has past and by all accounts the woman has fled. The matter will soon be forgotten and all will be well' But the Pope shook his head. Orsini frowned. 'Then what do you suggest?'

'Purification by FIRE' boomed the Pontiff who let his voice ricochet around the chapel. The Cardinal searched the Pope's face,

'Purification of what, your Holiness?'

'Of her, you *fool*' said the Pontiff to an audible gasp from the gallery. Orsini clutched at a sudden pain in his chest with a rush of adrenalin as he comprehended the Pontiff's words.

'But, your Holiness... this is not the Holy Roman Empire - we are not *Franks*' said Orsini blinking, 'we do not burn women by the dozen in these lands – this would be exceptional: she is not *Giordano Bruno*' But the Pontiff shook his head.

'Do I need to remind you, Pietro, that our Mother Church is under attack from all sides? We must defend her and her rights with every sinew of our bodies, and the might of our righteousness.' Orsini crouched struck dumb as the Pontiff continued, 'our enemies grow ever stronger, and we must show them that we're not weak, that we'll not spare them punishment.'

The Pontiff struck his crozier on the ground, just missing Orsini's fingers, again cracking the air with sound. 'We must strike the FEAR of God into the very heart of the Republic - that floating cesspool - that protector of witches, quacks, Protestants, God deniers, and Saracen infidels. We must let them know that we'll give no quarter, and leave no doubt of The Church's supremacy under God himself.' Orsini tried to protest again but the Pontiff had not finished, and he turned to snatch up his Tiara and Crown himself.

The Pontiff then raised his voice yet further to thunder the chapel from all sides: 'we *burn* her so that the reputation of our

Church remains immaculate, intact, and unstained. We burn her to rid ourselves of her sin, and we *burn* her to show that Republic, her *homeland*: a floating turd in that putrid lagoon, that the authority of my Pontificate will never be challenged again!' The Pontiff swung his arms aloft in rapture like God had spoken through him, while his voice rang out as if addressing to the amassed faithful from the Basilica window. Orsini rubbed at his stomach and turned his face away from the ecstatic Pontiff. 'Stand up my son, and embrace me' said the Pope, once calmed after his invective outpouring. The Cardinal stood and obeyed.

The Pontiff grabbed Orsini by the shoulders, after their brief embrace, with a firm grip and looked into his eyes, but Orsini tried to avoid them. 'This will happen, my son, so discard your feelings for the girl' he said, 'do you think yourself the only man of faith that loves what he cannot have?' Orsini struggled to control himself at the Pontiff's words. 'It is for the best my child - my Inquisition has already begun to prepare the case.' Orsini stood powerless to protest. 'When we find her, the purification will proceed, and your damaged reputation and rank will rise once more unsullied from her flames, restored and vigorous again.' The Pontiff lowered his voice as if to console a child. 'You're talented Orsini; it would be a shame to waste ALL your prospects when with such a good chance of gaining my Holy office.' Orsini nodded, and closed his burning eyes before he kissed the Pontiff's bejewelled hand,

'Thank you, Holy Father, your words are beyond wisdom' croaked Orsini. The Pontiff's face looked on with a warm smile, but cold eyes. He bade the Cardinal goodbye with a gesture of his bejewelled hand and another waft of his staff to the gallery. The Pope spun around, with the rustle of his robes, and walked through a door to the side of the alter only just wide enough for him, his tiara, and the expanse of his clothes.

When the Pontiff vanished, the choir struck up with a triumphant Hallelujah that rattled through the Cardinal's ears. Orsini made his way down the steps, in a daze, buffeted by sound, to the far door where he had come in. He drooped past the Swiss Guards in silence, who then looked at each other with concern when they saw his face. Orsini walked at a slow pace and clutched at his stomach. When Orsini passed from the sight of the guards he ran and vomited in the first vessel he found.

Chapter 16

A Steep Learning Curve

Padua, Sunday October 16th

Illawara wanted to do her best to make herself useful to Bianca, and she treasured any attention given to her by the former grand lady. Illawara helped as best she could, as did Hermes, while Grizelda and Dondo were away: accompanying Bianca to market and assisting with light chores. Bianca, in turn, fussed over Illawara and her appearance, vowing, over the coming days, to take out her old dresses (that no longer fitted her) from storage chests and updating them to source new appropriate clothes for the young woman.

Illawara could not believe her luck, and as they bonded, she could have listened, and often did, to Antonio's mother talk all day. Bianca was quick to throw formality aside, and confide in Illawara as a true ally. While sat at the living room table Illawara listened to the exiled noblewoman, fallen but still proud, talk without fatigue on all her favourite subjects. She discussed people of the town, her meagre stipend allowed to her - from profitable family lands - her difficulties in finding good servants to assist her, the price of food, and the price of the love that had ruined her. Illawara drank up every word from the exile like a baby on the breast, and Bianca, glad to have a female in the house that could not barter gossip with the neighbours, let her jaw run loose in telling her every observation of life to her. Bianca also let vent her and Antonio's frustrations at trying to restore themselves to fortune. Within a matter of days Bianca could not resist telling intimate family secrets to such willing ears.

'Daughter' Bianca proclaimed, much to Illawara's joy and astonishment, after returning from morning Mass with Antonio. The mistress of the house bustled into the living room where Illawara and Hermes sat at the table before she snatched up Illawara's hand: 'I've told *everyone* about you at church' Illawara wriggled and looked away, 'I know you and Hermes both had headaches this morning, but next Sunday I must *insist* you come – the community are dying to meet you...' Bianca turned to Hermes for a moment, 'and you too of course.' Illawara smiled, but pulled back and wrung her hands. Bianca paused, before then busying herself by tacking off her gloves and cloak and putting them to one side. Antonio stuck his head into the living room and beckoned Hermes to join him in the kitchen. Hermes got up to follow him. Bianca followed him with her eyes. 'Are you and your friend feeling better, my dear?' Illawara nodded, 'Good, I'm glad to hear it. Now that we're alone we can talk' Bianca scanned the room, filled with trinkets, as if someone lay in hiding. Bianca took up Illawara's hand again, as she was accustomed to do. 'Daughter, let me share some truth with you. I confide in you now what I dare not say to my confessor: they say we women are fickle, but men are worse.' Bianca massaged Illawara's palm, 'not a day goes by when I don't think of Antonio's father' she sighed, before crossing herself, and clutching at her throat with her free hand as she continued - Illawara sat attentive and wide-eyed. 'Daughter, let me tell you, with all that I've been through, with all that I've suffered, with all that I've *endured*, there are few things worse for a woman than a dull marriage...'

At times, in the previous week, Antonio would overhear his mother talking to Illawara, and interject to admonish Bianca for being too candid, but Illawara would protest, and defend Bianca as if she were her own mother, and beg for the woman to continue. Antonio grumbled to Hermes while in the kitchen, familiar with his mother's gossip tone, that he detected, and shook his head before continuing his conversation with him. 'Yes, yes, my dear' Bianca continued, 'a dull marriage can drive a woman to despair, or murder' she whispered, 'it is said that some women poison their husbands out of boredom alone.' She pulled Illawara closer as her eyes searched the corners of the room. 'I'd been married for almost two years to Tito, and still felt practically a virgin - so little I'd been explored by my husband' she confessed, rolling her eyes to glance at the ceiling as she cast her mind over her past. Illawara giggled.

'Bianca, really?' said Illawara, with one hand, rested on her chin, and the other in captivity as Bianca built momentum. The exile took a deep breath:

'Yes, tis the truth daughter, tis the truth. With age comes wisdom, and I see now looking back that I was dying, *dying* in that marriage. By the time Rodolfo - Antonio's father - wooed me' she said in a stage whisper, 'I'd almost lost the will to live.' Bianca took on a contrite expression, releasing Illawara's palm for a moment to wring her hands, before snatching it back before she continued. 'I resisted him of course, as any true lady should, but he was so handsome and relentless when he pursued me: gifts, flowers, perfume and jewellery were all showered upon me; as if I were a princess.' Illawara watched Bianca as her bosom heaved at the memory of her younger self, letting full vent to her feelings that she had bottled inside for so many years. 'I would argue with him, of course, I fought him back.' Bianca thrust her free arm outward as if defending herself from attack, 'he knew I was married, but he read me - *I know not how* - and if I were alone after church he would steal kisses from my hand.' Illawara exhaled. 'For months I'd ignore him and say "I don't want you" and take delight in seeing him crushed for days, but at night in bed next to Tito, while he snored, my husband may have slept, but my body burned.'

Bianca tilted her head, lifted her shoulders, and squeezed Illawara's hand again at her memories: 'one day he told me, and I believed him: "If I can't have you I'll die", and he said I'd never see him again.' Bianca dabbed at herself with a scrap of lace as he relived her past. 'I swooned, wept, and wrung my hands, quite overcome, and confessed that I adored him - that I'd loved him from the beginning.'

'How romantic', gushed Illawara delighting in the details of Bianca's life. Bianca delivered her life story with relish, re-illuminating her heart with passionate memories.

'So I let him love me' she continued, 'I let him worship me, foolish girl that I was, and thus invited my ruin: after six months it was impossible to hide the evidence of our unions... Then he left me' Bianca flicked her wrist, 'just like that, and...' Bianca's voice trailed off as she looked to the wall in the direction of her son, hearing him muttering with Hermes in the kitchen. Both women fell into silence.

Illawara breathed, and wandered off into her mind's eye before Orsini pressed her into his arms and swept her into their dance once more. She felt herself move as she looked into his intense eyes. Her pulse raced with danger and excitement. Then she saw

Orsini when he had held her hand with tenderness as she stood at the doors of the carriage and, for a moment, he commanded the mob to protect her. Illawara felt Bianca's grasp but relived Orsini's touch.

Then she saw the face of the Professor looking bloody and torn, his arm scarlet with blood as he flayed at the Medici door to escape.

'Are you still there, my girl?' said Bianca, shaking her hand, before Illawara recovered herself. Illawara puzzled at her feelings. Bianca unburdened and in great excitement, stood up from the living room table still clutching Illawara's hand and declared, so that all in the house could hear, that she and Illawara would take tea in her drawing-room - which she liked to keep reserved for rare visits from valued guests. Hermes and Antonio ignored Bianca's declaration and moved instead to the kitchen balcony that overlooked the main road that stretched to the centre of Padua. Antonio discussed points of local interest with Hermes, as Bianca moved Illawara to the drawing-room. Antonio then closed the kitchen door before he unburdened himself to Hermes about his struggles.

Bianca, enthused, gave orders to Grizelda, as soon as she had come back from the markets that day with cake, mutton, herbs, and potatoes. 'Oh, Grizelda', Bianca called out, when she heard the burdened woman cross the threshold, 'come in here please.' The maid dragged her feet to the drawing-room, 'what are we giving our guests for dinner?' she added as if she could not guess, before gesturing to Illawara and flicking a hand in the direction of the kitchen. Grizelda's shoulders slumped,

'Roast Mutton and potatoes, Bianca.' The mistress of the house made eyes at her maid, 'Donna Marconi', Grizelda added, with a brief curtsy. Bianca nodded,

'Please make sure there's enough for four, and yourself and Dondo, of course'

Illawara took her chance to study the maid as she stood in the doorway, from where she sat. She gazed upon a woman who seemed fashioned from resentment itself. Her lank brown hair, lined with grey, just reached her shoulders, and her dark-circled puffy eyes contrasted with her angular jaw and slab-stone forehead. Illawara mused that the one feature which redeemed

Grizelda were her full sultry lips that sulked at the edges but added much-needed softness to her hard face and wiry body. The maid and Illawara looked at each other in silence. Bianca chirped up:

'Grizelda, I know you've been busy with no time to talk...'

'I've not stopped all day', said the maid. Bianca turned to her guest.

'Illawara, as I've mentioned, this is my maid Grizelda and I hope you'll now get the chance to talk' continued Bianca, 'indeed, we spoke about you early this morning while you were asleep...' added Bianca to her protégé. The maid made no attempt to engage. Illawara glanced at Bianca before she gave the maid a stiff smile. Grizelda then flashed a look at her mistress before she took the measure of Illawara – her mind made up about her character.

'It will be a PLEASURE to serve you, Donna Illawara' Grizelda replied in a sweet tone with a hollow sound and made off in the direction of the kitchen. Bianca's face cringed before she called after Grizelda:

'Will Dondo be back soon?' she asked, 'you're good at knowing his whereabouts.'

'Yes he will, Donna Marconi - I chanced upon him earlier' came the flat reply from the hallway, 'he'll be here with firewood before long I expect.' Bianca relaxed,

'In that case, then' she added, 'with the last of the wood, please put some water on to boil, as we'll take tea with some of that delicious almond and orange cake you've brought, here in the drawing-room.' A long pause had come before Grizelda replied,

'Of course, Donna Marconi, as you wish' she said before she sloped off to the kitchen.

'I'm sorry' said Bianca, 'she's a good cook, but there's no grace to her' whispered Bianca. Illawara gave out a nervous laugh, and glanced in the direction of the kitchen,

'I guess it's a lot of effort for her?' she said, not knowing how else to answer. Holding back the cake, Grizelda barged into the kitchen and tossed down the rest of her produce onto the wooden kitchen table with a loud crash that startled Antonio and Hermes as they chatted. The pair spun round, as some of the potatoes tumbled to the floor, and saw the sullen expression of the maid as she stood there,

'Grizelda, when did you get back? How are you?' said Antonio. Hermes took in the stony face of the woman, with one hand holding a cake and the other hand on her hips. She scowled, and eyeballed the pair, Hermes stepped back, before she placed the cake down, and her expression then gave way to crack into a white smile as she walked forward with arms raised and outstretched.

'Nino, my dear, I returned first thing this morning, you were all asleep accept for your Mother. I'm baring up, how are you?' Antonio walked into her embrace, and the two rocked together for a while - Hermes looked on and felt a burn in the pit of his stomach. 'It's been so long' she said,

'How are things, Grizzy?' Antonio said when the maid released him.

'Oh you know, the usual... nothing changes, time passes...' she sighed, running a hand through the new greys in her hair. Antonio considered her face with a slight crook in his brow.

'Tell me the truth: how's my mother been?' He whispered. Grizelda rolled her eyes,

'Unbearable, I mean, charming as ever. When you're gone, she still laments your father like a young maid, saying he'll marry her and rescue her from strife.' Antonio flicked his eyes at Hermes, before he muttered something under his breath to Grizelda. The maid raised her brow before she made a gesture across her lips. Hermes eyes flicked between the pair.

'And Dondo, how is he? I've not seen him since I've been back.' The maid scoffed,

'Still a block head - we'll see more wit and spark in the firewood he brings back for the hearth, when he returns.' Antonio gave out a little grunt but raised a gesture in Dondo's defence, and Hermes suppressed a smile at the candid maid's words. Grizelda then shifted her head to the side to look at Hermes again, her hazel eyes acute and inquisitive. Antonio turned round: 'Grizelda, this is Hermes. Hermes, this is Grizelda, my mother's confidant and maid.' The youth gave a polite reply and shy nod as the maid eyed him up like a magpie.

'I've not seen you with a brown one before, Nino, this is new for you - but they do say travel broadens the mind.' Hermes flashed a look at his host before air seeped from Antonio's mouth.

'You grow *bolder* by the year, Grizzy, remember my mother is your keeper.' The maid slanted her eyes at Antonio, shrugged and toyed with several grey hairs on her head.

'Forgive me; I blame age. They say that every grey hair loosens the tongue.'

Antonio crossed his arms in a display of mock anger, 'I tell the truth' smirked the maid, 'your mother's grey - and her tongue runs like a river' mewed Grizelda.

'Then I suggest you keep your hair dyed and your tongue short because she is your mistress, and you can't afford to lose your place' said Antonio, wagging his finger with a wry smile. The maid clucked,

'But she can't afford to be without me, Nino: I'm her eyes, hands, and ears.' Antonio tutted as the maid then picked up the potatoes that had tumbled to the floor, and busied herself to boil water. She then sliced and plated the almond and orange cake she had brought, arranged a tea service, using Bianca's least cracked china, sliced bread and butter for Hermes and Antonio to graze, before she would later prepare the evening meal of herb-rubbed Spit Roast Mutton, and potatoes. Hermes eyed Antonio with suspicion: Grizelda's words still humming in his ears as he speculated how many males had passed through the house before himself. Hermes watched the maid carry out her tasks with confidence and efficiency, sweeping the hearth, as she chatted with Antonio - sure of her place.

As Hermes observed Grizelda at work his eyes glazed over and stared beyond the walls while his mind slipped into ancient memories: Hermes watched himself sweep the Temple floor of Serapis with a bundle of twigs. He took his usual care and attention, mindful of getting the incense dust and food crumbs from offerings out of the temple corners. Hermes saw himself stop his work before he stood up and turned as if called. He looked at the statue of Serapis, stood on the marble floor, the face framed by the yellow locks of his hair and beard, before he walked closer to the figure. He scanned around him before he leant forward to clasp the face of the God and press his ear to the lips of the statue and listened. Hermes had neglected his dust pile, with his ear pressed to the God's mouth, not hearing the steps that approached beyond the temple's marble pillars and along the steps that lead down to the Library of Alexandria.

'You're very devoted to the God, Hermes. Serapis is fond of you, but don't forget the God you're named after - he has even more to teach you' came the deep voice from the tall robed figure of the Temple priest stood behind him.

'You missed a bit' said Antonio to Grizelda as she swept the hearth before Hermes snapped out of his memory with a start - shaken by another fragment of himself that he had rediscovered. Hermes shook his head and rubbed his eyes as if waking from sleep as he watched the maid flick ashes Antonio's way before the two chuckled. Hermes saw then that the house had become Grizelda's temple and that she kept vigil over Bianca and Antonio. The maid used the last of the firewood to boil water in the copper pan over the stove, and Grizelda complained at Dondo's lateness, as she poured the hot water into a teapot, cut lemon, and arranged the sliced cake on small plates that were cradled by the battered tea service.

'You've forgotten the milk' said Hermes on impulse. Both Italians stared at him as if his skin wriggled with flies. His face grew hot, 'it's just that the Professor and Illawara always have milk with their tea...' More blank stares came his way after Antonio, and the maid exchanged glances,

'There's a cow tethered in the fields if you'd like to fetch some milk' Grizelda said,

'Excuse me' said Hermes, 'it's been a long day',

'It's neither None nor Vespers, m'Lord' added Grizelda with an English accent and a curtsy before she left the room with the tea tray.

'She doesn't like me' said Hermes to Antonio when she left,

'She doesn't like most people' he said, 'but when you get to know her...' Antonio paused, 'milk in tea?' Antonio grimaced, 'and I heard you say, Professor. Is that what the Earl, I mean what Illawara's father is?' Hermes looked away and rubbed at his neck, 'neither of you say anything about him, you promised to tell me more, but I realised he must be the other Professor you both mentioned in the carriage when I first met you. The one from Oxford. All that time he was questioning you both, he was really asking questions about *himself*' Antonio shook his head, almost laughing before he frowned. 'And what's in his case that Illawara has with her? Why won't she open it? Has she shown you? And why do neither of you talk about it and what really happened in Firenze?' Antonio pressed forward. Hermes turned away from him, his face strained. Hermes spun back round, his brows knotted.

'How many men were here before me, Antonio?' Hermes interjected as if thinking out loud. Antonio gawped, somewhat, his mind derailed, before he crossed his arms and tilted his head as he looked at the youth:

'That's a very big question, Hermes, and even less of your business.' Hermes coloured, after crashing Antonio's thoughts, the heat creeping up his neck. Antonio then turned away from him to walk back to the kitchen balcony and gaze down the street, as the afternoon progressed. Antonio beckoned to Hermes to join him. He put his arm over the youth when he reached his side.

'These are difficult times for us Hermes: exile isn't easy, but I want my mother kept as best as we can afford, but her pittance is not enough to maintain a woman of her birth and breeding.'

'Does your mother know what you do?'

'So you guess at what I *"do"* now, do you?' Hermes did not blink as he looked at the Valet. Antonio shrugged before lowering his voice, 'I *do* no more than others do, in my position, to make ends meet: but what she doesn't ask, I don't tell.'

'Did you do anything with the Professor?' Antonio turned to Hermes with vexed brows,

'*NO*, it wasn't like that. He didn't want *that* from me. I watched things, I catered for his tastes, but he did no more and no less than what most men do when away from home - are you judging me?' Hermes remained silent, 'but what else do you think people do if they don't have money? Magic up gold in the street?' he taunted, 'everyone knows it, even The Church: there's many I know who would starve without their patronage.'

'That's quite a thing to say of such men of your faith' added Hermes, but Antonio dismissed his words with a waft of his hand,

'It's common knowledge: but a man's choice of lover neither makes him good or unholy – but how he lives in his heart' murmured Antonio. Hermes scuffed at the floor with his foot. 'I've held back, much to my loss, but I know friends, with no family honour to protect, that have made a fortune, and gained grace and favour from their services.' Antonio's voice hardened as he finished. Hermes chided himself for letting his question blurt out as butterflies rippled through his stomach.

'I wish I were rich' said Hermes, longing to buy Antonio's freedom, buy whatever the man needed - buy him. Then Hermes turned to his host and held his gaze, as the Valet noticed his expression change, 'I'm sorry' said Hermes, with his voice shaking, 'I should have kept my mouth shut, but you're too good to have to live this way... *Too* good.'

'You don't know me' said Antonio. He saw Hermes did not know where to look. Antonio stroked Hermes' arm: 'but that's a kind thing to say, and you're right: I *am* too good for this' he said, looking around the kitchen. Hermes searched Antonio's face, so like Serapis', illuminated for a moment when the sun triumphed over the gloom, as if he was the most beautiful creation he had ever seen. The Valet, unburdened, pulled him into a hug, and Hermes held on tight and filled his lungs with Antonio's smell as the two stood for some time.

'What's this then! Midnight Mass?' came a loud voice from the kitchen doorway, the two flew apart, and Hermes with the blood rushing in his ears saw a short, stout, white-haired man in his late fifties holding a large bundle of firewood under each arm.

'*Dondo*' Antonio exclaimed, 'I nearly died - you mustn't sneak up like that.' The man gave out a dirty laugh so knowing and grubby it could have soiled a Holy Virgin's Chapel. The man threw up both arms in greeting, revealing two sweat patches that spread from his shirt to his jerkin, as the bundles of branches tumbled to the ground.

'Nino' Dondo cried as he strode across the room to embrace Antonio in a bear hug that lifted the younger man off the floor, 'what a surprise, what kept you away so long? Are you well? How are things? And who's this?' he said, while he still had Antonio suspended in the air, and trying to breathe. Hermes looked on with surprise at Dondo's antics as Antonio wriggled in the air as if the pair were wrestling: Antonio signalled to be put down.

'This is my friend Hermes, he's from...'

'Torino' added Hermes.

'*Really?*' said Dondo, with a quizzical look, 'you're a bit dark for that.' Hermes' smile faltered, 'I'd say the far south, maybe Sicily, yes, but the *North*, no' added Dondo, but the man laughed before he greeted Hermes with warmth.

'I'm pleased to meet you, Signore Dondo, it's a pleasure' said Hermes with genuine politeness – still liking the mature man in an instant. Dondo gave a look of surprise.

'Foreign looks with such good Italian?' Dondo exclaimed,

'I spent years on ships with Italians that couldn't speak half as well. Where are you *really* from?'

'Alexandria' said Hermes, much to his own shock, not so much in that he remembered, but that he could speak it without pain. Antonio looked at him with surprise, but the seasoned man carried on unfazed. 'So you're an *Egyptian*, that makes more sense. But your name is not Saracen – strange. But I saw many from your land in my trading days, and my God: the WOMEN - wild and beautiful.' Dondo gestured a curvaceous figure in the air with his hands.

'I didn't know you've been to Egypt, Dondo' said Antonio as he reassessed Hermes.

'Nino, there is little land with a sea or a shore that joins the Mediterranean or Aegean that I've not seen, young man. All of North Africa, The Holy Land, Assyria, Anatolia, Spain, and most of the Greek islands in between' said Dondo with evident pride, 'we Genoise will go anywhere, and trade with anyone, fifteen years at sea will teach you a few things', Dondo chortled.

'But modesty is not one of them' said Grizelda returning with an empty tea service, 'or timekeeping.' Dondo stood with his mouth open, 'get out the way you old fart' she added before she elbowed her way past the man to reach the broad kitchen table. Dondo turned to her with another filthy laugh, and slapped Grizelda across her thin bottom as she passed which made her cry out with surprise, and almost drop the tray, 'you galley ship thug' she scolded, 'I should crack this service over your head.'

'If you had the strength, skinny woman', Dondo replied, before making a face at her, putting his hands on his hips, and shimmied himself to mock her expressions. Antonio laughed, and Hermes could not hold back a titter, as he saw himself avenged via Dondo's prank.

'Ooh, you old fool' she said, putting down the service, before stamping her foot, 'what took you so long with the firewood? I'm to cook for all of us tonight, and that mutton won't roast itself.' But

Dondo paid no heed, and snatched Grizelda by the waist and hummed a popular tune as he spun her around in a mock dance, Grizelda struggled with him. 'You sweaty block head' she said as her slender frame got jigged around the kitchen by the perspiring man, until her resolve cracked and she laughed, head thrown back, at the absurdity of it all.

'What a COMMOTION' came the shrill voice of Bianca from the kitchen door, and Dondo almost dropped the laughing Grizelda, 'are you up to your old tricks again - naughty sailor?' said Bianca sweeping into the kitchen, 'why do men never grow up?'

'Excuse me, Donna Marconi' Dondo said with a dramatic bow, as Grizelda steadied herself, still giggling, by the kitchen fireplace. 'To be in leave of your service was torture. I've brought back the firewood, as promised' he said, gesturing to the two large bundles Bianca had sidestepped, 'but I was so overwhelmed with Grizelda's beauty, that I had to spin her into a dance.' The noble woman laughed:

'You vulpine silver tongue' she chaffed, 'you know just what lies to tell a woman.' Hermes noticed the smile crash from the maid's face, 'if Grizelda were younger, maybe I'd be worried.' The two giggled while the maid gave a peevish smile, pretending she enjoyed the jibe, before putting on her apron that hung near to the fireplace. Bianca clapped her hands together and made an announcement. 'Everyone listen' she said, 'I wish to make a *presentation*.' Silence fell in the room, as Bianca made a wafting gesture towards the kitchen door. 'Illawara, you may step forward now.' Somewhat bashful, Illawara walked into the kitchen wearing a dress of pale pink with puffed sleeves, a scooped neckline and little red garnets sewed onto the bodice like pomegranate seeds - she looked radiant.

'Madonna!' Dondo cried and then rushed forward to Illawara's wide pink skirts, bent himself on one knee, kissed her hand and started to sing a sweet serenade to her. Illawara giggled as she looked down at the man, and didn't mind some of the bum notes that came out of Dondo's mouth as his sentiment seemed genuine; no one had ever sung to her before. When Dondo finished his serenade, Illawara spun herself into deft pirouettes, standing on point, swinging her arms upward as her skirts spun wide. All the Italians gasped at the gesture, but Hermes just smiled and nodded, having seen Illawara turn thousands of times at her ballet barre back home. She finished her three turns with a deep bow and gave Dondo thanks for his song of appreciation.

'You can dance on one toe' said Bianca and Dondo in unison, as if thinking from one mind.

'On *point* – sort of' Illawara corrected, before she smiled and nodded, bowing again like a ballerina taking her applause upon the stage. Grizelda shrank back into the fireplace as she glared at the young woman who looked like a rose in full bloom. When Bianca had recovered, she continued her presentation.

'I wanted to leave it until tomorrow, before we looked through my old clothes, but she's such a sweet thing I couldn't wait any longer, and I had to dress her immediately.' Illawara who enjoyed her new role as surrogate daughter, and doll, then turned herself around to show off the dress. Hermes saw Grizelda's face wash out to a pale grey-green, 'alas, my favourite dresses don't fit me anymore' Bianca trilled, 'such is the cruelty of time... but this dress fits her like a glove, and I must say she's almost as pretty as I was all those years ago.' Illawara gave a beaming smile, but the room stayed quiet for a moment as Bianca's words hung in the air. Those that could cast their minds back in time understood that Bianca had short changed her surrogate.

'So who *is* this ravishing beauty?' said Dondo, as Antonio walked forward to greet Illawara as if she were a different person.

'She's called "Illawara", whatever that means?' said Grizelda in a dull tone. Before anyone could answer, she stood up from the hearth and pushed past Illawara to pick up the firewood and took it back to the fireplace to get the evening meal started.

'My name means Flame Tree' said Illawara, 'called so for its bright red flowers - when in bloom the trees can seem to set the sky alight' added Illawara through a tense smile.

'Never heard of it' said Dondo, with a gesture of defeat, 'but you're another foreigner with perfect Italian' Illawara looked away and scrunched her hands behind her back. 'If you tell me you're from the North I'll not believe you' chortled Dondo, elbowing Hermes, as he read Illawara's poise and features and cross referenced those with the foreign women he had met or observed on his years of travel.

'Don't be *rude* Dondo. A woman's mystique is half her power' said Bianca. Illawara gave an involuntary curtsy by way of thanks to the mistress of the house. Dondo bowed, but his mind and experience, like an abacus, had already computed the likely origins of Illawara. He kept his finding to himself. He did not mind at all where she was from, and it was the same for Hermes. Foreigners put him at ease: it reminded him of the sea – and all its adventures. Loud clanging and rustling came from the hearth. Everyone turned to watch Grizelda as she reached for a tin box of kindling with her ashen fingernails, and clashed at two flints, like a blacksmith forging a horseshoe, to ignite a rag with sparks. She stuffed the burning fabric between the twigs and stray lumps of firewood and blew hard on the wood to further ignite the flames.

'Good thinking, Grizzy' said Bianca piping up through a strained expression, as the fire crackled into life. 'I'm sure everyone is looking forward to a meal later', almost all nodded in agreement, as Bianca asked her son, Hermes, and Illawara to wait for her back in the Drawing-room. Dondo stayed to help Grizelda spit the leg of mutton. The cooking of dinner became a full team effort when Bianca gave a hand to grind anchovies, garlic, oil and herbs into a paste which she then smothered onto the mutton, with a spoon, to help in the preparations - as she usually did when Antonio was not at home. While Bianca helped, she looked at her maid at times with quiet consideration. Bianca turned to speak to Grizelda in a low voice as Dondo poked the fire.

'You could be nicer to her, Grizzy, my dear' Bianca whispered, 'I've no clue where she's from, but I think she could be *useful* to us?' But Grizelda just pursed her lips, acknowledged her mistress with a dry nod, and carried on prepping the vegetables. Dondo walked back to reach over and lift the mutton on its spit, and wedge it above the crackling fire.

■ ■ ■

As accustomed, when on the rare occasions that Bianca had guests, and when Antonio was at home, Dondo and Grizelda ate in the kitchen while the mistress of the house entertained, and maintained her image of the exiled noblewoman on the cusp of regaining her fortune. The meal was delicious: the roasted mutton, tender and full of flavour, had perfumed the house with its aroma -

much added to by the forest wood, potatoes and sautéed vegetables. Grizelda heard herself being toasted in the Drawing-room after Bianca had dug out a well-stashed bottle of wine, but Dondo noticed the thin woman only pushed at her food and didn't eat with her usual vigour. Dondo stuffed succulent lumps of Mutton into his mouth.

'You're not hungry?' Dondo enquired. The maid had taken a while before she spoke,

'Not once has Bianca showed me any of her old dresses, not *once*. I had no idea' she said as she shook her head.

'Don't be jealous Grizzy; she's a lovely thing. Bianca has no daughter: let her indulge the girl.'

'But who is she? When I saw her earlier, she wore an ugly stained dress... no finer than a shop sweeper's.' Dondo shook his head,

'I've my own ideas: there's something Persian about her but mixed with something else – Asia Minor for sure' Dondo rubbed his chin, 'but why do women care so much about what another woman is wearing? To a man, a beauty like that would be just as lovely in a sackcloth.' Grizelda gave out a hiss as she tossed down her fork,

'Men, all you care about is a woman's beauty. For some of us, a woman *is* her clothes'

'And that is better thinking? So, clothes above beauty? You're clever, Grizzy, but no poet. If that were true, then poor women would never bare children. In the bedchamber every woman stands a chance.'

'That's not what I meant' Grizelda huffed.

'This is not you, you're not yourself, and I doubt you believe that a woman's virtue is only in her wardrobe, Grizzy. If you do, then you dishonour your sex and short-change your life' said Dondo as he put a warm arm around Grizelda's shoulder. Grizelda shook her head,

'Life you say, what *life*? If I looked as she did do you think I'd be here? Men are hypocrites. They sing of *virtue*, but all they want is a lady for church, a mother in the kitchen, and a whore in the bedchamber?' She said, and pushed his arm away as emotion welled in her eyes, 'this is not a life, Dondo. I don't have a life' said Grizelda gesturing at the walls.

'What is this from you? All this lamenting' he said tutting, 'your life is better than most. It's not like you to feel sorry for yourself' added Dondo, 'it could be a lot worse, and you know that. Be loyal to your mistress. Antonio could make a good marriage, and Donna Marconi could then return to fortune, and much to your benefit.' The maid shook her head as she laughed with scorn.

'You're an old fool. Everyone knows that Antonio can't inherit: he's illegitimate, and do you think a rich wife is at the front of his mind?'

'Legitimacy can be changed' argued Dondo, 'Cardinals can legitimise - if he's merciful or the price is right. And as for Nino and marriage, who cares of his tastes if there are children?' Grizelda shook her head with force. Dondo folded his arms, 'there's many a wife in this land who'd like rest from her birthing chair. Besides, no woman on Earth has stopped a man if he is so inclined as he: life at sea, or a spell of confinement, teaches you that.' But Grizelda snorted, before returning to the prior topic,

'Everyone can be bought these days' she said, 'I suppose you would buy Illawara if you could?' Dondo threw his hands up in the air,

'She'd ruin my heart, if not from effort, then from worry', the man whistled, 'no, no, she's too young, too fresh, too pretty, let a fitter man have her. Besides, I'm busy' said Dondo drumming at his chest, 'seeing to our mistress' needs are demanding enough.'

The maid then laughed and shook her head as she wiped at the corners of her eyes,

'You old fool. She still loves, Rodolfo, you know?' Dondo nodded,

'And I still love the sea' he said with a smile, 'but I can't go back, and neither can she. What's done is done. We all have our needs. Besides, I think Antonio's suffered the most. A boy should know his father: whoring braggart or not.'

With that Dondo stood, rubbed Grizelda's shoulder, and left the kitchen for the drawing room, returning after a while to give Grizelda the dirty cleared plates. Dondo returned to the drawing room, and then she heard gaiety and jokes exchanged after Dondo topped up the drinks, having one himself. Grizelda sighed and looked off, as if far away, before she scrubbed the plates clean in her wooden wash bucket.

■ ■ ■

Arcetri, evening, Sunday 16th 1611

The Professor almost shouted as he walked into the slow-moving brook far down the hill from the nunnery of San Matteo. 'Immerse yourself' said Lucia, who began to dry her hair with old linen at the side of the brook after her dip in the water. 'Remember what I taught you. You must be fully cleansed before we start the ceremony.' The Professor glared back at her with his hands over his groin, but obeyed and moved deeper into the brook: 'crouch down and let the water wash over you' she said, as she began to chant something in Hebrew. The Professor shivered as he waded barefoot to the middle of the brook but did as she wished, and crouched with his back against the flow: he let out a whoop with the chill on his skin, but then felt himself relax as the water flowed around him. 'That's it' said Lucia, 'let the water cleanse you. Let it wash away your thoughts, your woes.'

The Professor obeyed, as he had grown accustomed to doing so in the passing weeks: his resistance eroded by her tutelage. He allowed himself to become at one with the river as Lucia sang her prayers, and he thought, as the sun began to lower to the horizon, that he could hear the water murmur to him, and the secluded wood whisper its secrets. Time seemed to disappear, and all there was for the Professor were the mutterings of a brook, the dappled orange light that played on its surface, and the breath and whispers of the wood as the animals nearby looked on as Lucia came toward the end of her invocations.

She lifted her thin gauze-like dress and tied part of it into a knot at her side, to walk into the brook to retrieve the Professor who had crouched, like a smooth boulder of marble, in the eddying waters. 'Stand up' she said, and he did so as if hypnotised, before she lifted him with ease, her arms outstretched like Mary holding the body of Jesus, as she lay the naked and sleepy man on the soft grass - he did not feel the cold.

Lucia spoke purifying words over him, broke rare twigs, and smothered his body with the sap and juices of herbs that grew near brooks like the one he had entered. When Lucia finished she stood the Professor up - his skin streaked with green and purple sap and clothed him in Chinese silk that glowed and shimmered with the colours of sunset. Lucia took up his folded, civilian, clothes and walked the entranced Professor, in seclusion, back up the hill to return to the nunnery.

Winston entered Lucia's room with a dim awareness of where she lead him. Lucia, the sorceress, watched and waited for the Professor's trance to take full effect. She whispered to him and his lowered head raised up from its slumped position, from where she sat him at the end of the bed. Lucia held the Professor's face in her hands, to stop his eyes from wandering, till his wavering eyes began to settle on her: 'now it's time for us to start' she said.

■ ■ ■

Rome, evening, Sunday 16th 1611

Cardinal Orsini meandered his way back home after leaving the Sistine Chapel, lost in thoughts of Illawara, drifting via teeming main roads and side streets, before gazing upon the preoccupied inhabitants of Rome as they begged, chatted, negotiated, and swindled their way about, and, for once, felt himself separate from them. Not so long ago he was just like them: focused, determined, and ambitious. Orsini sat down at a Trattoria, in need of refreshment, ignoring the fuss around him, and mused on the words of the Pontiff that shook him to his core. He puzzled at himself as he sipped a cool drink. 'Forget her, forget her' he mumbled to himself as he downed the contents of his glass before he paid for his service and walked off. The staff of the trattoria gossiped and chattered with excitement, with many pausing their work to step outside and whisper to one another as they watched the Cardinal slope away. When the Cardinal returned home from the Vatican, he stepped into a household atmosphere like that of a crypt. The Chef was selected among the palace staff to update the Cardinal. Orsini's Chef and confidant informed him that his adviser, Benfico, had resigned his position, and had told the other staff, in histrionics, that he could not work for an abusive tyrant any longer. Orsini's shoulders slumped at the news, 'He'll tell every secret he knows to a new master' said the Cardinal. Orsini stood still for a while, cursing his temper, and gazed into the distance as if looking at a ship dip below the horizon: a ship of his Pontificate sailing further away, and fading from view.

The Cardinal then grumbled in a low voice to Chef in a side room off the corridor of the Palazzo Orsini. A knock came at the door: 'enter' said Orsini. The footman hesitated by the door he opened before he stepped forward, and approached the Cardinal as if he feared being bitten by a leopard.

'A message for you, your Eminence' he stammered. The Cardinal's eyes flashed when he saw the seal on the letter, before he snatched it from the footman's hands,

'Leave us' said Orsini, before the footman scurried away. Orsini recognised its author in an instant, the creamy paper and red insignia of the Holy See were unmistakable. With his heart beating Orsini made excuses to his Chef, clutched the letter to his chest, and walked back into his dining room. The house staff had cleared the room after his outburst. The rug still damp and stained. Orsini had almost forgotten the mess he left behind, as he stood still, his eyes wide and his heart beating. He tore open the stamped wax seal and tried to keep his hands still as he read:

Sunday, October 16th, 1611

To his Eminence, Pietro Maria Card Orsini

His Holiness formally informs thee that a full investigation into the unfortunate matters in Firenze are underway, with righteous vigour and intent, by the right arm and hand of his Holiness: The Papal Inquisition.

Matters are at hand, and rest assured that appropriate resources will be dedicated, to achieve a swift and forthright resolution to matters that will leave no doubt in the minds of those devout, faithful, and loyal to our Mother Church.

> *You are henceforth relieved of your duties to your titular church to undertake a period of prayer, reflection and rest: The Deacon will be informed.*
>
> *May the Lord give us his blessing in this task to nullify and expunge those that seek to corrupt: and thus rid ourselves and the Earth of temptation, and obliterate sin.*
>
> *Paul P.P V*

The Decretal letter bore the Papal seal on the front and the seal of the Holy Inquisition on the reverse. Orsini sat himself down, as adrenalin coursed through his veins, and rubbed his hands over his face. The implications of the letter could not be more clear to the Cardinal: 'she's as good as dead' he said, and held his hand to his mouth as if to trap the words that had already escaped his lips. The Cardinal bolted upright: 'I can't *allow* this. She's innocent' his hands shook, 'but there's still time' he whispered to himself.

The Cardinal did not delay. In haste, he made his way to his rooms and packed a swag of essentials, including an extra bag of money, Orange water, and his favourite gold crucifix. He dug through his clothes chest, selecting and tossing garments aside, while the sun set and the cooling blue of twilight fell upon the Holy City. He found a simple dark grey woollen cloak with a broad hood: 'this will do', he said before he stripped off his finery to wear a simple shirt, jerkin, hose, and the cloak. The Cardinal snatched a glance of himself in his wide mirror, pulled the hood to the brim of his eyes, and stood satisfied that he looked like a pilgrim. The Cardinal took up his swag and went downstairs in his disguise. The effect was immediate: at first, his household staff took him for an intruder, and they snatched up whatever lay near to apprehend him, not recognising him till he spoke. Orsini raised his voice to call all his staff present to attention. Orsini made a show of his transformation and wrung his hands with much lament and anguish.

'I make my pilgrimage south to atone and reflect in prayer...' he said, and then inserted the details of the most obscure church he could think of in Naples. '...For I'm deeply stricken at the loss of my advisor' he continued, 'and the manner under which he has left this great house.' Orsini then made a humble gesture and cast his eyes down before he spoke again: 'I leave you now to pray for him, and the souls of the unfortunate, and seek the mercy of God, and pray that he grants me temperance.' The household staff present looked thunderstruck and struggled for words by his sudden display of remorse and piety, accepting his remarkable display of conscience as genuine. But his Chef, knowing the Cardinal so well, had his suspicions. Orsini then gathered his staff around and made his, dumbfounded, but obedient, household give oath upon punishment of the Lord, that his pilgrimage remained secret for three days should there be enquiries about him.

Orsini's staff nodded, and he left the most competent member of his household team in charge and warned that he and the Chef were not to argue. The Cardinal then made strides to the courtyard of the Palazzo Orsini, followed by his Chef and his valet. 'Pietro, your Eminence, you can't mean to go into the depths of Napoli on pilgrimage?' said the Chef when they entered the courtyard. The Cardinal gave his Chef a cautionary look but did not reply as he continued to ready himself. 'Then let me accompany you as I did before to Firenze: you've only just returned, and have not spent a night in your bed. You need to eat, you need to sleep, and the roads down south are dangerous.' The Cardinal shrugged,

'The Lord grants me his protection' said Orsini, while he saddled up his Donkey Gino, and began to clamber onto the animal's back. The valet followed Orsini's instructions and attached saddle bags of provisions onto Gino before the Cardinal bid him to open the gate. The Chef made a fuss, but the Orsini paid no heed to his protests, waving the man off, but promising to return soon, as Gino's twin sister, Gina, tugged at her brother's tail with her teeth. Gino pulled away from her grip with the swish of his tail. Gina brayed and filled the courtyard with her noise, seeing Gino and the Cardinal leave, until the Chef stroked the muzzle of Gina to comfort her. 'Look after her' Orsini called back over his shoulder.

The Cardinal passed through the rear gates of the Palazzo Orsini and made a conspicuous effort of riding around the side of the house to turn his donkey south along the road, as the craned heads of his household followed him with curious eyes. 'There's only one place that Antonio can hide her' Orsini said into Gino's ear, before he tapped at the side of the animal's neck to gee the donkey onward. When the Cardinal became confident of being out of sight, he changed his progression and turned the donkey northward to get to Padua as soon as he could.

Chapter 17

Hekate's Message

The Convent of San Matteo, evening, Sunday October 16th 1611

Lucia locked her eyes with the Professor's who looked back at her with an unfocused stare. Lucia then raised her index finger in the air and wafted it side to side, Winston's eyes followed, then she moved it up and down, and his eyes followed again. Lucia nodded her approval, sure of her work, before she began her questioning: keen to extract the truth from her stubborn captive.

'What is your *real* age?' she said, irritated that she had to resort to magical means to extract basic information from the Professor: his secrecy only exceeded by his appetite to learn.

'I'm fifty-two years old' Lucia gasped, and paused before her next question, 'from what exact time have you come?' The Professor hesitated and seemed confused, so Lucia rephrased her question, 'what is the year of your times?'

'The year I left home was nineteen-ninety-seven.' Lucia's eyes bulged, but her business mind did the math,

'So you're from three hundred and eighty-six years in the future.'

'Yes' came his distant reply,

'What is your *real* purpose for coming to me?' Lucia's Tarot cards had told her much already, but the fine details escaped her.

'I've come to learn from the true book of Hekate. I've come to learn how to capture souls' he said. Lucia's eyes widened and she tilted her head as the Professor's motives became more apparent to her,

'For that, we shall have to ask the Goddess herself, and you'll have to have courage.' Lucia gripped the Professor by his shoulders, 'why do you want to learn how to capture souls?' Once more the Professor hesitated, his face troubled by emotion, and Lucia worried the trance would break, but the Professor answered:

'To fulfil a promise, and to answer the most difficult of questions.' Lucia frowned before she let go of him,

'Who's promise must be fulfilled?' The Professor paused again, and his mouth opened and closed as he started to rock backwards and forwards, his voice faltered,

'A promise to my... to my' His words trailed off. Lucia changed tack:

'Who made the Hermeporta, and where does it come from?' The Professor struggled to answer her and knotted his brow with effort.

'I, I can't be sure... ancient people long, long ago - before these times - I think the book will know.' Winston looked distressed, and Lucia could see the trance would break if she continued,

'Shush, shush' she cooed, 'there, there' she said, as she stroked her hands down through the air. 'Stubborn Ox' she muttered under her breath, 'it's easier to draw rusted nails from a rock.' Lucia wiped her brow. The Professor stopped his rocking and calmed down, 'that's it, rest, rest' she said, shaking her head. The door to Lucia's chamber opened, as the twilight settled into darkness outside, and Celeste, Arcangela and the Golem entered the room: 'my sisters' said Lucia, 'have you brought what I need?' The three then nodded before Celeste handed Lucia a large bag of items; something squirmed inside. Arcangela looked awkward as she held a bundle of twigs and branches under one arm. Lucia's eyes then glanced to the Golem, her twin image, who seemed more human than ever. Lucia creased her brow. She then checked the contents of the squirming bag. 'Good, well done, I have everything I need.' Lucia then glanced in the direction of the Professor, 'he's ready for the ceremony now, he's under my power' she said to them, 'but I'll need you all nearby to be sure that things go well' two of the three nodded, 'tonight I'll invoke Hekate.' Celeste and Arcangela looked to each other; their faces strained.

'Are you sure you still want to do this, Lucia? The Goddess is immensely powerful' said Celeste,

'I've petitioned her times before and lived' said Lucia with a flick of her wrist, 'I'm her priestess, whatever happens, is meant to be, but my visions have yet to fail me.' Lucia gestured to the subdued Professor, 'this man is remarkable, the best pupil I've ever had. What he knows is important, and it's only the Goddess that can answer his questions - if she so chooses to reveal herself.' The two witches looked concerned, exchanging glances again, but the Golem stood unreadable, her face like a waxwork, but her eyes brimming with life. Celeste made a bow,

'As you wish, mistress' she said, but she did not meet Lucia's eye. Lucia's expression relaxed,

'Good, that's a comfort' she said and turned her attention to Arcangela, 'did you drug the food as I requested?'

'Yes' said Arcangela, 'the nuns will not stir tonight, not an earthquake could wake them - you'll be left in peace.' Lucia raised her chin to look down her nose,

'And you controlled the dose?' Arcangela nodded, 'good, we want to be sure they all wake up this time.' The little nun shrank into herself with her head bowed down, 'I don't want a repeat of the last time's events' Lucia continued, wagging her finger at Arcangela, 'remember that Sister Mary was very likeable – her death was hard to cover up.' Lucia gestured towards the door, 'we can't let the nuns know about us, but we don't want them lying dead at the dinner table either: they're *our* innocents after all, and it's their innocence that protects us - and all that we do.' Arcangela bowed as her wrinkled face managed to blush. Lucia stepped to one side to command Arcangela with the sweep of her arm: 'please lay the oak wood in the hearth.' The little witch nodded and scurried past Lucia, with her hippity-hop, and put the bundle of lichen-covered oak branches in the mouth of the fireplace. The Professor sat mute as the witches talked: 'thank you, sisters, for your work. I shall begin the ceremony. Please stand to one side and keep vigil over us, and only intervene in an emergency' said Lucia. Celeste stepped forward,

'Do you want me to hold Hekate's book?' she said, her eyes wide and full,

'No, HE will hold the book' said Lucia, pointing to the Professor. Celeste's face twisted with darkness for a moment as she snatched a look at the Professor,

'He's a *man* Lucia; he could defile the precious book. Is this wise?' she added,

'Step ASIDE, Celeste' said Lucia, her voice hard, 'he's a full initiate now.' But the thin-nosed witch stood her ground, and snatched another look at him, her voice vicious:

'He could die, you know? The experience could KILL him' she said as if anticipating the demise of a great enemy. Lucia then glared at Celeste before she squinted, and her brow furrowed like a ploughed field,

'You can wish him dead all you want Celeste, but I'll have more use of him than a tired old maid.' Celeste gasped and shrivelled: stung by the words, and she fought hard with herself not to cry. Arcangela looked up into Celeste's miserable face and for once felt sorry for her. The Golem stood still, but her wax-like skin took on a faint glow before her eyes turned in their sockets to look at Celeste whose lips trembled.

'As you wish, my mistress' said Celeste, her voice shaking as she curtsied, 'you are wise, and I should not try to correct you.' Lucia made a sweep of her arm, and Celeste then walked to the side of the room with the others, as a tear ran down her face. Lucia stood as rigid as a mountain when she then called out to the Professor.

'Stand up, Winston, your time has come', her voice filled the room. The Professor stood up. 'Go to the book of Hekate' Lucia commanded, before she walked to her table to place the bag down. The Professor walked, in slow steps, towards the large Grimoire sat upon its shelf as Lucia reached into the bag and took out several items. The first: a necklace made of black, red, and white beads which she then wore around her neck. She then took out a candle banded with the same colours in wax and lit it upon another that burned nearby. Then from the large bag, she pulled out two small bronze containers, and a broad scooped bronze plate.

She laid the items upon the table and opened the bronze containers: one contained fresh grain, and the other wild honey from the Tuscan hills. Lucia then poured the grain into the bronze plate that rattled as the kernels fell, while the witches and Golem looked on in silence as the Professor neared the bookshelf. Lucia then removed two small bronze cups, and a long slender bronze carafe with a cork stopper, and placed them on the table. She plucked out the stopper, and a strong alcoholic smell of fermented grain and honey entered the room. Lucia sniffed at the carafe before she poured some of the liquid into the small bronze cups and watched the little bits of mushroom that swirled and bobbed to the surface of the drink.

The Professor reached the side of the Grimoire and awaited instruction from Lucia as she continued to unpack the contents of the large bag. Lucia then took out a bundle of herbs tied with white string, a small silver snuff box, and a little iron plate and spoon, while something moved again within the bag. Lucia put these items on the table with the others, opened the snuff box and used the iron spoon to scoop one measure of opium into each cup of liquid from the carafe. She stirred in the opium with patience, as all, except the Professor, looked on, while she whispered soft incantations over the potent liquid. Lucia then lit the bundle of herbs over the striped candle, and placed them on the little iron plate, and allowed the oily scented smoke to fill the room. Silence prevailed as the Professor stood motionless and the others admired Lucia's work.

Lucia became absorbed with her tasks in hand, as the room filled with the haze of the smoke - the Golem coughed. A startled Arcangela looked sideways to Celeste who gazed forward impassive, ignoring the cough as she wiped away tears from her face. Lucia and the Professor stood as if in a shared dream, as the Golem cleared her throat. Lucia then took a sheet of paper down from a shelf, before finding a lump of chalk and a stick of charcoal and put those items on the floor. Lucia crouched down and called up to the Professor: 'take up the book of Hekate, and open it in the middle' she said as she flattened the edges of the paper with her hands.

The Professor nodded, as if asleep, while Celeste looked on in anticipation as he reached forward for the book. A look of surprise and disappointment surged across Celeste's face when the book lifted itself from the shelf and fell into his hands. Winston's fingers and arms began to tingle, taking the book's weight, and he heard the distant hissing of ancient snakes in his mind. Somewhere within a dark space in Italy, the garnet eyes of a forgotten Hermeporta blinked into life, to cast their scarlet light into the gloom.

'Hold the book forth' said Lucia, from the floor, as the Professor obeyed and opened the book near the centre before he stretched out his arms. The pages of the book then turned themselves and stopped upon on a page with an illustration of a circle with symbols within its edge. Lucia took note, stood to examine the book, crouched again to take up the chalk and began to draw a large, accurate, circle on the floor using her rigid arm like a compass and copied the symbols from the book with as much care and accuracy she could.

With her work done, Lucia had created a circle wide enough for two people to lay within. She then left the paper and charcoal within the circle, and walked back to the table before she spoke to the Professor: 'let go of the book, drink a cup of kykeon, and then sit within the circle.' The Professor obeyed her without question, and released the book which then hung suspended the air; the sound of hissing snakes in his ears lessened when he let go, and he took up the bronze cup offered to him by Lucia, and they both drank down the potent, sweet, and intoxicating cocktail. The pair both paused for a moment, as the liquid took almost immediate effect. Lucia took his cup and gestured to the circle, and the Professor seemed to hover as he walked, oblivious to Celeste's glares, into the chalk circle and sat down. Lucia then checked on him before she reached her hand into a section of the bag that moved to pull out a sleepy black puppy, with soft glossy fur.

She cradled and stroked the warm animal, drugged to docile, before looking into its cute sleepy face as it yawned, and blew its milky breath into her face. Lucia then kissed the puppy before she lay it upon the grain in the large bronze bowl. 'There, there' Lucia said, as she patted its warm tummy before she walked over to open the wooden chest with the iron trappings. Lucia took a silver dagger out of the box before she returned to the plate to hold the puppy down. The blade flashed in the candlelight, and the puppy let out a whelp before it fell into stillness as its life blood stained the grain on which it lay. Lucia stroked the puppy's ears as its flesh cooled before she anointed its body with the wild honey.

Lucia then lifted the bronze plate from the table, her vision starting to blur, and perceived the dish and the dead animal's body as a slit in a dragon's eye. Lucia swayed from side to side and saw a blinking iris studded with grains of gold. Lucia paused to concentrate and steady her mind. She closed her eyes and saw scarlet scales that rustled in the wind as a dragon flew through the air with her and the Professor on its back; while the dead puppy's blood swirled to marble the honey and the yellow grain. 'Tis done' muttered Lucia, 'we fly upon the dragon's back' she added before she shuffled over, unsteady with the bronze plate, to sit and join the Professor in the circle.

The Professor lay as if asleep as he saw himself with Lucia upon a huge red beast that flew through the air, beating its wings, engulfed in clouds. The Professor felt as if his soul were flying like a kite tethered to an empty body. The book tilted itself towards Lucia in the air, bringing itself closer to her unsteady gaze, as the pages of the floating Grimoire turned themselves again. Lucia read out the names of the symbols scribed onto the pages and her chalked lines illuminated in turn as she did so: streaking the floor with light. The two witches muttered to one another, and the Golem looked on as the ceremony proceeded. Lucia began to chant, and both she and the Professor started to rock and undulate their bodies in unison as she sang louder. Some dogs in farm houses, scattered about the hills, began to howl and bark as if in one pack, and one mind, much to the confusion and annoyance of their owners. Then the three witnesses stood rooted to the spot, as Lucia and the Professor appeared to be thrown back by a mighty force against the floor, and lay twitching and spread eagled as their eyeballs rolled backwards to white within their sockets.

'Mighty Dragon... *deliver us'* Lucia struggled to say.

The striped candle on the table, along with the others, dimmed and then extinguished as the circle and its symbols glowed brighter casting more light into the smoke-filled room. The dry bundle of oak twigs left in the hearth then combusted and burned into life with a purple fire.

'We'll wait until the ceremony is over' whispered Celeste, drying her tears, as she turned to Arcangela and the Golem, 'to act now would be dangerous and foolish, but Lucia will be weakened for a while after she communes with the Goddess: let us take our stance then.' Arcangela chewed her lip and looked down to the floor for a moment, but the Golem agreed with Celeste's words as they all looked on.

The Professor heard, and then felt, the immense roar of a lion that thundered through his head and body, and shook him from his waking sleep. The Professor, compelled, then struggled to stand within the glowing circle, and looked back with shock to find his physical body laid down on the floor. The Professor could no longer see Lucia's room with clarity everything seemed to spin and undulate. Lucia's hair blew from side to side, where she stood, but her own body lay on the floor next to his. The room swirled with incense, smoke, and mist as the distant lion roared again, but even louder than before. Lucia whisked her head in the Professor's direction. 'The Goddess approaches, Winston, only speak to her if she speaks to you. If she asks you a question answer with all the truth you have, if you do otherwise she'll sever your soul away, and your body will die: hide NOTHING from her', she said, her voice tense. The Professor agreed as the noise increased and the sound of a howling pack of dogs mingled with the roars. Lucia spoke again, but in haste, her voice shallow: 'if she allows you to ask her a question, then keep the issue firm in your mind and show no fear before you ask her. DON'T leave the circle.'

The Professor showed he understood. Another mighty roar emerged from the direction of the fireplace which the Professor could just make out through the swirling mists. Then the purple fire in the hearth grew and expanded with the mouth of the fireplace, which yawned higher and wider till it reached the height of the ceiling. The sounds of barking dogs intensified, and the purple flames parted to let a glowing limb move through as the paw of a huge lion stepped out of the fireplace, and entered the room still engulfed in swirling smoke. The purple flames died down, and there, behind the mane of the colossal lion sat the Goddess Hekate. Her eyes blazed with a chemical fluorescence like burning zinc oxide, and the Professor's eyes would have stung if he perceived them with his physical body.

The Goddess' hair lay woven with oak leaves entwined about her head, a ring of large keys hung from her belt, and two, thin, golden snakes writhed about her waist and dark robes. Hekate held aloft burning torches in each hand. The lion then gave out such a mighty roar that it sounded like claps of thunder, as a pack of black dogs, sixty at least, yapped, yelped and howled in the fireplace with their haunted eyes aglow. The Professor looked down to check that his feet were still within the circle and tried to stay still as his spirit electrified with fear and exhilaration. The lion crouched, and Hekate stepped off her feline steed to walk forward in her bronze sandals - her feet echoed about the space. She processed with her torches held aloft, nonchalant, around the edge of the circle, her eyes like lasers, and admired Lucia's work before she spoke.

'A well-made circle of *protection*, Lucia, are you worried my dogs and lion would harm him?' said Hekate, with a voice that echoed like a strong wind blowing through a deep ravine - unbridled and elemental.

Lucia had swallowed before she answered: 'no... no, oh mighty and Holy Goddess, it is to protect him from himself: he's a new initiate.'

'I see' said Hekate, with slight mockery in her voice, her eyes shone as she continued to process around the circle. 'This time I'll let it pass, but need I remind you that I'm a *liminal* Goddess? The overseer of all gateways, all pathways, all beginnings and all endings; I don't like barriers.' With her words, a question flashed into the Professor's mind, and the Goddess turned her face in his direction for a moment. Lucia kept her silence and waited to be addressed by the divine being. The Professor sensed the Goddess notice the dead puppy on the bronze plate that lay within the circle. Hekate stopped walking as her fearsome lion looked on: 'I see you have a sweet offering for me, Lucia'

'Yes, mighty Goddess' the sorceress replied,

'But you have kept it WITHIN your circle' said Hekate. Lucia remained silent, the Goddess' voice darkened, 'do you wish to keep me hungry, Lucia? Do you want to haggle and bargain with me as mortals do at the market?' Lucia shook her head like a child accused.

'No, no, Holy Goddess. I would not deny you sacred rites as others have done.' Hekate walked up close to the circle, stood next to Lucia, brought her burning torches closer and eyeballed her from head to toe. The Professor could then see two spots of light trace their way over Lucia's form. Lucia stood like a condemned woman before the gallows, looking forward, and did her best to keep still. The Goddess placed her torches down before she raised her hand, with nails like talons, in a delicate gesture, and plucked on the forcefield created by the circle like a harpist testing their strings: the sound of static clashed, and jangled in the air.

'You're a very cunning sorceress' said the Goddess, before she raised her voice to a gale force wind, 'but if you call me again, and withhold my offering as you have done: I'll rip out your heart and eat that instead.' The colour drained from Lucia's face, and she looked as if she would faint before the Goddess spoke again, *'WINSTON'* Hekate said to the Professor. He flinched but turned to look up into the strange yet beautiful light filled face of the Goddess with shining eyes. 'Does this sorceress keep you against your will?' Lucia flashed him a look, but he remembered her warning, and he composed himself before he answered,

'Yes, divine Goddess, she does.'

The light from Hekate's eyes and her torches then dimmed before she spoke, 'people of great mind should never be bound to another's will, for it is the light of the soul and the mind that can free us all - *shame* on you, Lucia' hissed the Goddess. Lucia dipped her head like a snowdrop, 'you have abused your strength, Hierophant of Hekate' said the Goddess, 'but soon, your power could be taken from you as you have taken it from others.' Lucia looked shocked as the Goddess continued, 'for there are those you hold close that wish to be free of you.'

Hekate picked up her torches and sauntered to the enlarged fireplace, that seemed to wobble and swirl within the misty smoke. The Professor could see Hekate's ribs move under her skin as she reached up and rested her lanterns upon it. Hekate then glided to the side of her mighty lion and stroked it like a tabby cat, before she addressed the Professor again: 'bring me my offering, and I will answer your questions' said the Goddess. The Professor saw a frantic expression race across Lucia's face: to give the Goddess her offering he would have to breach the circle. He paused to watch Hekate comb her talons through her lion's mane as she watched him. To disobey Hekate would be worse than death.

The Professor then nodded before he sidestepped Lucia, who stood trembling and stooped down to pick up the bronze plate with the dead puppy. He held the plate forward, looking at the Goddess as she stood poised on the side of her huge lion, and breached the membrane of the circle with a static crash. When he did so every hair on his physical body turned to bright silver, but his face remained young. The Professor walked towards the Goddess, her great height, and her vast lion, as her hounds hushed their noise, while she stood there: the embodiment of darkness and light. He kneeled before her and raised the bronze dish aloft.

Hekate rushed forward to snatch up the platter, and he felt a wave of magnetism bolt through him when the Goddess brushed his hand. Hekate lifted the plate to her face and slurped at the body of the puppy, drinking its blood that mixed with the honey, before chewing on the grains with near gluttonous satisfaction. When Hekate had finished she gave out a mighty roar, almost as loud her lion, as she blazed all over with light - Lucia shielded her eyes against the glare. 'You have honoured me', Hekate proclaimed, her voice echoing in booms, 'I have not had such offerings since the great destruction of the temples, and when men and women were burned for believing in me' she declared. Hekate bristled with power, 'I've had but crumbs left by the roadside to sustain me for near endless years' she said, 'few mortal men can face a Goddess like me and live, let alone stand upright in her presence. You have crossed a *great* threshold mortal man' the Goddess swept her hand through the air, 'Lucia has no more power over you – your mind is your own.'

The Professor heard Lucia cough back a protest, but he did not look at her - as he felt his soul ripple with magnetic sensations. The Professor stood and bowed to receive the Goddess' complements. Hekate took up the limp body of the dead puppy in her taloned hands, licked off any honey that remained on its fur, held the tiny face of the dead animal to her lips, and breathed a gentle breath into its muzzle. At that moment the puppy came back to life in her grasp and gave out some shrill cries. Hekate tossed the bronze plate aside. The Goddess then smiled a smile of pure light which illuminated the animal, 'you're immortal now little one' Hekate whispered, 'I name thee, *Winston*' she said, stroking its face before she put the puppy down and her dogs barked, as if in celebration.

Lucia looked on dumbfounded. The puppy then whined as if in need, dazed by its surroundings. A nursing bitch shambled forward towards the edge of the fireplace and barked. The puppy obeyed the call and ran to her dangling teats to suckle as she lay down in the hearth unscathed by the low purple flames. 'Ask me your questions?' said the Goddess, as she looked at the puppy suckling. The Professor composed himself once more before he spoke.

'How do I capture the souls of the dead?' The Goddess turned to him, and he felt the light of her gaze inspect his face as she stood up to her full height.

'That is an immensely powerful thing you wish to learn' she said, 'why do you want to capture souls?' The Professor did not hesitate.

'I wish to capture souls, to liberate the mind of Man. I want to collect together the greatest thinkers that have ever lived so that they may speak with one another. Their combined Genius will end ignorance - and end mental darkness forever.' The Professor spoke with all his passion running through his soul, and the Goddess saw and heard him.

'*Ambitious* mortal, what you ask is very grave, such knowledge would give you the power of a God' Hekate shifted her stance, 'but then there are few things, if any, that cannot be moved by Man's true will and desire. Those are one of the God's gifts to Man.' Hekate continued to comb the mane of her lion with her taloned fingers before she moved to walk around the Professor in circles. 'What you ask can be done, but I warn you that the Fates have laid their plans for every soul, past, present and future.'

'But what if a person were wronged in death? Taken against their will' he said, 'what if they were innocent? What if...' urged Winston. But Hekate pointed at the Professor with her claw extended,

'You're *forbidden* from intervening to cheat a man or woman's death – no matter how much you may love or admire them: even though you traverse the borders of time yourself.' Hekate gestured to Lucia and Professor in turn, 'however, there are those that truly shape their own destinies and the Fates are kinder to them, but to meddle in this divine order is a sacrilege to us all that will not go unpunished. Do you understand?' The Professor nodded. The Goddess gestured at the Professor, 'you can borrow a body or soul offered to you of its own free will if that person wishes so before they die, or when it has reached the physical death Fated to it. But I warn you, mortal, all souls must return to of what they are made – The Source, the God of Gods: The Source that is behind *all* creation, to withhold from Source is to court oblivion. Do you understand?'

The Professor nodded again before the reinvigorated Goddess raised her hands above her head (her ribs no longer protruding) and turned them, as if twisting the air, to produce a vision of an unusual lantern that shone with polished brass and panes of glass. 'Draw what you see' she said to the Professor, while Lucia looked on agog at the lesson he received from Hekate. The Professor studied the holographic image the Goddess created as it spun above her hands, 'I name it: "Soul-lantern - the lantern keeper for the soul"' she declared. The Professor could see his physical body stir on the floor near to where Lucia stood. With the whites of its eyes rolled back the Professor's physical body reached for the charcoal and paper, and began to draw an accurate depiction of what the Professor saw above the Goddess. 'You draw well' she said before she continued, her voice becoming thunderous again as her eyes flashed like lightning, 'mortal man listen to me well. Any common witch knows that a soul will choose the form best suited to it when it leaves its body - as the wise have always understood: for the timid a mouse, for the spirited a bird, for the intelligent a moth, or butterfly, and so forth.' Hekate continued to process around the Professor as she gave her lesson and her holographic image of the Soul-lantern continued to turn in the air, 'the image I show thee when made real is not enough, the soul must be captured just after the moment of death, and for this, as if to catch a fish, a net is needed.' The Professor nodded, and Lucia hung onto every word Hekate said. 'As the great Athena knows: no finer mesh is woven than those of spiders. Find some of Arachne's daughters that weave golden webs; only they are swift and skilled enough for such work - Lucia will know where such spiders can be found.'

The Professor turned to look at Lucia, who gave a faint nod to acknowledge the Goddess before she continued, 'put this spider into the Soul-lantern and utter the correct rites above her, and she shall spin to capture the form of the soul upon her gilded web. You will then have three days to find a willing host for the soul, a living male or female, an animal, or those at the end of their time who wish their bodies to live on.' The Goddess raised her taloned hand into the air in a gesture of warning, 'if you do *not* find a host, then the soul and its knowledge will be consumed by the spider and lost forever, but SHE will grow wiser, and more powerful: it's Arachne's *revenge* - remember this.' The Goddess looked at the Professor: 'have you understood?'

'Yes mighty Goddess, I understand' the Professor said before he looked over to his physical body and saw that it had completed the drawing. Hekate lowered her hand and studied the Professor.

'You have more to ask of me' Hekate said, 'but for your earlier boldness, I will grant you another question.'

'Thank you, Divine Goddess' said the Professor, 'please, can you guide me to where another Hermeporta is located in Italy?' Lucia's face took on a look of great curiosity, and the Goddess seemed humoured before she replied.

'There were many more of them, once, in the times when men and women knew my name, and made me generous offerings, listened to me, and sought my council' the Goddess sighed. Hekate then knelt next to the puppy and patted its stomach with care and tenderness as it continued to suckle from its new mother before she stood up. 'I can answer your question with ease, Winston, for it was the God Hermes and I that created the first Hermeporta.' Lucia gasped at the revelation, 'and we shared its creation with the enlightened parents of *your* Illawara - no two mortals were ever more worthy of Godhood than they.'

The Professor's mouth dropped open as he tried to comprehend what the Goddess had told him, but she waved her taloned hand to silence his inquiry before she continued. 'That which you seek is one of few that remain after the great destruction of our temples when most of civilised Man abandoned its belief in us to the thoughts of one God alone.' The Professor raised his hand like a school child wishing to ask a question of a teacher, but Hekate would not indulge him. 'We Gods, *all of us*' she said, 'are manifestations of one all mighty power; The Source, each a facet of creation or destruction that maintains the divine balance. We are one and yet we are many.'

Hekate swept her hand over her robes to lighten their dark grey colour to a purple that matched the glowing hearth flames. Lucia looked on with envy. 'Winston, you have earned the right to learn this truth that I have just shared with you, for not even *she* knew that' said Hekate, flicking a claw in Lucia's direction. 'Visit my graveyard in the northern lagoon, to the south of the city that floats, where men are free to think and trade, and you will find one of my vessels there. Perform the due rites to empower it, pay the asking price as you have done before, and know you should, and you shall travel with my blessing - for you have won my favour, as few mortals have ever done. Listen for me and I will *guide* you' said the Goddess.

The Professor sensed Hekate make ready to leave, but one more question flashed in his mind, and the Goddess paused to address him: 'your spirit is strong, mortal man.' Hekate smiled, which scattered her high cheek bones with light, 'I will indulge you again, you may ask one more question' she said as she searched his very soul.

'Where is Illawara?' he asked, as the Goddess stood resplendent, shining in purple garb, toying with her lion's hair. Hekate then looked deep into the Professor before she answered. 'Illawara resides north and not far from the lagoon - she is unaware of her connection to the Hermeportas, the few that are left, and yet is drawn to them... in time she will understand. They cannot harm her. She's in the place where men come to learn, in temples of their own knowledge, and under the protection of the state that honours the minds of men. You are not to tell her about her heritage - like all mortals she must *earn* her knowledge as you have done - but find her before she is discovered.' Hekate then pointed at Lucia, 'for she sent the hounds to chase the vixen – and the vixen must be cunning if she's to stay alive.' The Professor looked at Lucia, but she could not meet his eye. 'But Illawara is Fated to learn of her lineage' the Goddess continued, 'and will, in time, find herself - her parents wait for her.' The Professor blinked at what he heard.

The Goddess made to move after her statement, explaining no further, but the Professor understood what she said, and where to find another Hermeporta and Illawara. 'Venice and Padua' he whispered to himself before he bowed his head low in front of Hekate, she acknowledged him with a nod and gestured, before he returned to the circle with a crackle. He passed close to Lucia, struck dumb by what she had learnt and seen. The Professor then stood next to his body as the Goddess took up her torches, her Golden snakes hissing and coiling about her waist, and mounted her lion which then gave out a warm roar.

'Come along my little, Winston' Hekate called down to the suckling pup, 'you will ride with me.' With some effort, the nursing bitch stood, and the puppy ran gallant circles around her, its tail wagging before the lion crouched its hind legs and the puppy clambered up its haunches to then scramble up the legs of the Goddess. Hekate laughed as she looked down at the animal that tumbled into her lap. Hekate's lion stood, and the yapping of the hounds clamoured as the flames rose again. The pack moved ahead, as the suckling female hung back, to be near the puppy, and the howls began to ebb away before the mighty lion roared. The beast turned and then walked forward with the shimmering Goddess and little Winston on its back, the new mother following, and into the purple flames of the closing fireplace.

Chapter 18

Love's Revenge

The Convent of San Matteo, late evening, Sunday October 16th 1611

Celeste, Arcangela, and the Golem watched the Professor and Lucia within their circle of protection: Lucia lay rocking from side to side, eyes rolled back, and the Professor, silver-haired, squirmed on the floor. The bright light of the circle, and its powerful symbols, faded back to chalk lines and the candles reignited to give some light back to the smoke-filled room: 'the time is now' said Celeste, her voice shaking as the smoke cleared, 'the time to speak, we've all had enough. We won't let her dominate us anymore.' The Golem nodded, but Arcangela spoke up; her face riven with concern,

'Celeste, what will come of this? What do you want her to say? She'll never give you what you want.' Celeste stepped towards Lucia, but Arcangela blocked her path. 'Is life here so bad?' she whispered, 'it could be worse: here we have a lot of freedom, even if we're not completely free.' Celeste looked down at the little witch, her eyes like slits,

'How often have you said that you wanted to break away, and escape this place? For years I've heard no end to your complaining, saying that you feel stifled and controlled: that Lucia is too violent.' Celeste then pointed at Arcangela as she spoke, 'you leave, but then you come back, time after time, even after you've raided the alms box, and drank or gambled away every scudo of the nun's money.' Celeste crossed her arms, 'there's not a tavern within a mile's walk that doesn't know your name - but you always come back for more but then complain.' Arcangela's face then scrunched like wrapping paper,

'You're a fine one to talk' she hooted, putting both hands on her hips, 'look at you, loitering here for years waiting to be touched. At least I've lived.' The little witch then gestured to Lucia who began to stumble out of the circle, 'why should a bright creature like her care for a dull maid like you?' Celeste seemed to chew at Arcangela's words, as her face filled with emotion again,

'Why must you be so spiteful Arcangela? This is our chance to demand to be *free*, to be treated with respect, and yet all you do is taunt me. I can't help my feelings: she's cruel but magnificent - she's like... a Goddess.' The Golem's mouth turned down and she shook her head at Celeste's words as the distracted pair argued. 'You've had many loves in your lifetime' Celeste continued, 'can you blame me for wanting to know her... as her lovers do?' But Arcangela rolled her eyes as Lucia staggered to one side and the Professor, with time, started to regain his awareness.

'What a goose you are' scoffed the little witch, 'if it's a lover you need there's no short supply here: but you're as blind as a cabbage and as deaf as a post' said Arcangela with a waft of her hand. 'The nuns may pray, but few are *saints*.'

'Fetch me water' said Lucia, exhausted, before she stumbled into a wall. Arcangela moved towards Lucia, but Celeste blocked her path again - her face glowing red.

'So why complain then of domination and abuse if life here is so free?' She said, 'as if here were one your taverns where you sold yourself like flatbreads' The little witch then gulped a breath before her lips narrowed into a multitude of furrowed lines, looking for a moment like the shrivelled udder of a dead cow. The Professor rolled sideways on the floor and attempted to stand up. The Golem flicked its eyes to him before glancing back at the bickering pair.

'There's no sadder sound in the world than the frustrated cries of an angry, wan, and bitter virgin.' Arcangela spat out as she faced Celeste with her fist in the air. 'I'm here because I grew tired, I'm here because I couldn't do it anymore, I'm here because I'm *old*. Yes, she's dominating and sometimes violent, but she's also brave, brilliant and wise – even now you still admire her. I've too many regrets, but what would you know of those?' said Arcangela flicking her finger at Celeste, 'but I forget them all, along with my age, in the youth she grants me for the Sabbat.' Arcangela spread her arms wide, 'when I'm there with her; I can have almost any man I want: and live out my dreams and fantasies. She gives me that' Arcangela raised her finger, 'but if she didn't, I'd leave her.'

Celeste listened to Arcangela's confession stony-faced, while Lucia slid down the wall and groaned, and the Professor squatted on the floor: both people trying to emerge from their stupor. The Golem kept a keen eye on the pair, like a guard dog. A sinew twisted in Celeste's jaw as she looked at the little witch with disdain, folding her arms, 'that's all you can think of, isn't it? Your lovers at the Sabbat, or your oafs in the taverns: the countless grubby men that stained, used, and ruined you. Every day you dream how you will triumph over all of them with borrowed youth. Wishing that they'd come back to you as if you were some marquise, some high-born woman to be adored and treasured: it's *YOU* that is sad.'

Arcangela clenched her fists and knifed Celeste with her eyes, her face shrinking as if the air had escaped from a balloon. Within the chalk circle the Professor struggled to his feet and rubbed at his platinum hair, and Lucia wobbled to the broad wooden table that still bore the items used for the ceremony. The Golem flashed a look in the direction of the two arguing witches, before focusing again on Lucia. The Golem flexed her arms and massaged her hands as if to ready them for battle. Arcangela stared up into Celeste's face, gesticulating, not done with the fight. 'And what would you know of such things?' spat the little witch, making a rude gesture in Celeste's face, 'what would a dull frump like you know of passion, and *tasting* life: both good and bad?' Arcangela said, looking her up and down, 'a woman too plain to make a dowry, dumped here by her family: even at your best a farm-hand wouldn't lift your skirts in a haystack.'

'Ha!' Exclaimed Celeste at the saucy put-down, before she turned to Arcangela with a look of triumph. She then made a gesture towards the Golem who then stood over Arcangela like a totem. 'Yes, I *confess* it. I'm all those things you say' said Celeste, 'it's true I'm plain, and by almost all I'm unwanted. Lucia doesn't love me, and I see now that's also true.' But then Celeste turned to fondle the Golem's arm. 'But *SHE* cares about me' the Golem nodded, 'she cares a great deal' added Celeste with passion, her chest heaving with excitement, 'but I do know something of love, and that's what STELLA has begun to teach me: what we've learnt and discovered *together*.' But Arcangela ran her dry hands across her face, and shook her head at Celeste's words, before letting out a slow wheeze,

'You've gone too far, Celeste. Why have you named her - you desperate fool?' But before she could continue Lucia called out again,

'Please fetch me water; my mouth is so dry' she said. Arcangela made a move forward to get a pitcher from the side room, but Stella snatched her arm with vice-like strength. The little witch tried to free herself from Stella's painful grasp, but the Golem glared at her with ruthless eyes until she stopped her struggle. Stella shook her head and then waved her finger with slow menace, before pressing it to her lips. Celeste smirked. Arcangela got the message, and Lucia's requests remained ignored as she and the Professor regained full consciousness.

'Where are you all?' gasped Lucia as she clung to the table, 'I said I need water.'

'You will get your water when we see fit' said the Golem with a voice like Lucia's but hard and cold. Lucia froze,

'Who said that?' she said, and turned herself around in a slow progression,

'Stella did, Lucia' said Celeste with a creeping smile. Lucia tried to focus her eyes in the direction of the voices, her hearing off and her eyesight still blurred from the intoxicating effects of the kykeon.

'Do you mean the Golem? You've given it a name?' came Lucia's incredulous response,

'I'm not an IT anymore; I'm a woman. I have a life, and I will *live* it' said Stella,

'I must be dreaming?' said Lucia swooning, still getting her bearings, before Stella made rapid strides across the room and struck Lucia across the face as hard as she could. Arcangela covered her mouth. The sound of the clap rang around the space, and Lucia stood stunned into silence, unable to move, as the imprint of a red hand-shaped mark spread on one side of her face.

'Still dreaming now?' said Stella, deadpan, raising her hand again before she struck Lucia so hard that she fell to the floor. Lucia's face stung with dazzled lights behind her eyes. The Golem stood over Lucia, laughing, while the lethargic Professor, gathering his wits, groped the floor for his paper, folding up his Illustration before he struggled to his bed to get out of the way. Stella made another move to strike before Lucia, from the floor, kicked Stella in her stomach to wind her. The Golem wheezed like a bagpipe as Celeste gasped at the blow. Lucia scrambled to her feet and then crashed a back-handed swipe across Stella's face with all her might. Lucia's fist connected with Stella's cheek bone sending her crashing to one side. Celeste screamed when she saw her lover struck,

'You ungrateful *bitch*' Lucia screeched, still unsteady, as Stella sprawled to the ground. Lucia made a lunge for the Golem, yanking off her wimple, and attempted to rub off the Hebrew seal of life upon her forehead. But Stella then elbowed Lucia in her left breast, with vicious speed. Lucia howled with pain, falling back, and clutched at her wounded bosom before the Golem stood to grab handfuls of Lucia's flaxen hair, and began to drag her around the floor. Arcangela looked on with her liver-spotted hands clamped to the side of her head as the struggle continued. Lucia fought to free herself from Stella's grasp, before she used the Golem's grip on her locks, like a tug rope, to drag Stella closer and then throw the Golem over her shoulder. But Stella held on as she flew through the air, and Lucia cried out when a clump of her long hair got torn out from the roots.

The Professor, groggy from the effects of the drugged liquid, and with Hekate's words still throbbing in his mind, tried to comprehend the mighty struggle between the two women that looked like twin sisters. Lucia leapt onto Stella where she fell, with part of her scalp denuded, and began to rain blows on the Golem with her fists, but Stella in her short life had gained a strong will to live, and an instinct to fight, then used both her legs to kick Lucia off to one side. Lucia barrelled across the floor to the far wall, crashing under the tapestry, from the sheer force the Golem could muster. The Golem then leapt up and ran forward to stamp on Lucia with all her might. Lucia took a blow to the face and shoulder from the Golem's frenzied kicks that blackened her eye and split her lip.

Arcangela bit her knuckles, transfixed, as the struggle continued as the Golem stamped on Lucia as if trying to kill a bug. A desperate Lucia, trying to dodge the blows, flaying at her sides, managed to snatch up a large figurine of the Buddha and hurled it at Stella's face. With a dull crack, she caught the Golem on the brow above her eye. The Golem saw a bright flash of light upon the impact, and Celeste, screaming, ran into the side room, as the Golem staggered about: 'you pathetic wretch!' Lucia roared as she dragged herself up from the floor: scratched, bruised, and bloody.

Lucia focused her mind and raised her hand high before she slammed Stella's throat into The Grip. The Golem began to choke, Lucia pulling her up, as her feet rose above the floor. Stella clutched at her constricted throat and tried to prize off the invisible grasp, but to no avail. Lucia lifted the copy of herself as she had done with the Professor, but with no intention of leaving Stella alive. 'How dare you' Lucia blazed, her neck streaked with blood, as she lifted the Golem closer to the ceiling. Stella fought hard but could not free herself as her legs cycled in the air, 'how could you? How could you turn on the one that created you?' *I'M* the one who gave you life from the dull clay you're made of: and that's what you'll become again. If I made you, I can destroy you' she seethed, as she made ready to break Stella's body onto the stone floor. The Professor and Arcangela looked upwards, petrified, as the Golem continued to rise into the air while a dishevelled Lucia fixed her copy with a stare of pure hatred.

'It's time to stop!' Exclaimed Celeste, who, in the maelstrom had brought through the large mirror, with its velvet cover, to rest flat against a wall of the room before she tore the velvet away, 'this needs to come to an end. Enough Lucia, ENOUGH.'

'What are you doing?' said Lucia, with blood stained teeth, as she glanced at Celeste: her attention divided.

'I've summoned him' said Celeste shaking, 'I've done it... I've called the dark one' she whispered.

Arcangela's mouth dropped open, and clarity came to the Professors mind. Lucia dropped the Golem from the air, where she tumbled to the ground with a thud, to turn on Celeste, but too late; the temperature then plummeted in the room as the glass of the mirror grew dark. 'What have you done you *fool*?' spat Lucia, her hot breath clouding the air, as the Golem spluttered for breath on the ground.

'This has to stop, Lucia, all of this has to stop. I've had enough, we've *all* had enough' said Celeste, shaking from head to foot.

'You imbecile...' shouted Lucia, before she moved in Celeste's direction to hurl more abuse when the long leg of what looked like a man began to step through the mirror. A sound of crackling static filled the air, and everyone heard ringing in their ears. All present saw their breath rise in front of their eyes, and Arcangela shivered as the temperature dipped below minus. The Professor felt his blood become almost as cold as the air as the figure of a very tall man stepped through the mirror and into the vaulted room. His presence seemed to fill the place from wall to wall with foreboding. 'How could you invite him here? HERE of all places... you half-wit' hissed Lucia. The Professor turned to look behind him, and realised, beyond all doubt, that the towering Priest like figure that stood in the room, was the one he had seen at the Sabbat with his ivory skinned companions. He stood, his head almost reaching the ceiling, and straightened his long dark robes after stooping through the mirror frame.

'Diana-Lucia' he said in a weighty, smooth, and sensuous voice, 'that's no way to speak to an invited guest...' His voice vibrated through all their bodies.

'I didn't invoke you, Dark Prince, and you're not welcome here - you can *NEVER* be welcome here' said the wild-haired Lucia, so filled with adrenalin and rage that not a shred of fear inhabited her body. The Devil's cat's eyes took on a yellow glow. He then squinted before he spoke, his slashed pupils menacing.

'That's what most interests me about you Diana-Lucia: not a crumb of fear in front of me. However, your dominion in this place is over - it belongs to me now.'

'NEVER' blasted Lucia, but the Devil let out a rumbling laugh,

'Too late, too late, my dear' he said, 'the rites have been performed' he added before he pointed a long elegant white hand in the direction of Celeste, and the prostrate Golem. 'They, together, have seen to it, I cannot be removed from here: this is *MY* house now.' The Professor shivered in the cold, his silken robe no match for the chill, and his stomach wrenched as he took in the scene. The Devil's thick black hair fell in waves to his broad shoulders. The Professor studied his angular features, and would have called the bearded entity handsome were it not for his sinister probing eyes, and the unmistakable feeling of evil about him.

The Professor had not pondered God much after his mother died, and even less about the concept of the Devil, but he struggled to control the terror that had begun to rise inside him when he realised that every atom in his body told him what he saw. 'It's over' said Celeste stepping forward, 'pack your things and get out.' The Devil laughed.

'Not so fast, Celeste' said the entity, with a calm gesture that lifted his dark robes, 'I must ask her if she consents', Celeste nodded, and dipped her head,

'As you wish, my Lord and Master' she said. Lucia's face trembled with emotion, and Arcangela bit her lip while she looked at the ground unable to maintain eye contact with anyone. Bile rose in Lucia's throat, but she choked it down before she addressed Celeste.

'You *whore*' she said, 'damn you for what you've done. As long as I draw breath, I'll never forgive you - *never*.' Celeste raised her chin, tears rose in her eyes, but her face looked hard as Stella groaned on the floor.

'I'll never need your forgiveness, and I no longer need your love. I no longer need YOU anymore', said Celeste. A silence fell. Celeste stood firm and resolute.

'Well said' the Devil purred, and clapped his applause with his long white hands. 'Diana-Lucia' he said, and turned his attention to the bedraggled sorceress, 'do you accept me as your master?' The Professor risked a glance at Lucia, her bottom lip trembling as she scanned her room as if to absorb every detail. She closed her eyes for a moment, and threw her head back to take a deep breath,

'As I said to you, Dark Prince, at the Sabbat and I repeat: "I may have come here for business, but I don't do deals with the Devil."' Lucia then pointed to Celeste and Stella, 'so you can take those two bitches with you when you go back to *hell*.' The Devil's eyes flashed an amber gold at her defiant words. He crossed his long arms and inspected Lucia for a long time. Then he then lunged forward with his hands outstretched and sharp teeth bared, and the Professor caught his breath. But Lucia did not flinch, even when her matted hair lifted with the onrush in the chilled air, as the Devil towered over her like a dark phantom with his blue-white skin. His eyes burned brighter than the candles as he glared at her, arms out wide as if to strike.

Lucia, implacable, stared him down. The Devil paused, and then folded his arms like delicate wings before he laughed again, longer and deeper than before: the Professor felt the laughter ripple through his diaphragm. 'It's a great loss, we could have done much together, Diana-Lucia, but there's no place for you here - time to pack your things and go.'

'That's right' spat Celeste, 'get out, GET OUT!' Her voice rent the cold air, and Lucia stiffened, she had never once heard the plain witch raise her voice so loud. Celeste's eyes began to take on a yellow glow like the Devil's.

The Professor looked around the room to remind himself where the doors were before the Devil fixed him with a penetrating stare till the slit pupils of his eyes rounded to circles of empty black, his yellow iris' gave off a neon glow: 'and what of you, Atheist?' He said, and turned to Celeste with an aside, 'some of my favourites by the way: no faith, no protection, and so easily swayed. They don't even think I exist.' Celeste smiled and nodded, as her eyes glowed brighter than before. Lucia did not recognise the woman that stood some way from her. The Devil addressed the Professor again: '*Atheist*-Professor, do you wish to stay here with us?' Lucia spun to look at him. The Professor shook his head with violence,

'I've no wish to stay' he said the with all the courage he could muster.

'Then *LEAVE* us' bellowed the Devil in a mighty voice that shook the furnishings, 'and thank your stars for the silver touch given to you; without it, I would have had you: mind, body, and soul.'

The Professor stood, snatching glances at a forlorn Lucia, a Celeste in possession and a troubled Arcangela as the Golem struggled upward from the floor. With shallow breaths the Professor changed out of his silken robe with haste to pull on his civilian clothes that were left on the bed, not caring who saw his brief moment of nakedness. He was mindful to keep his illustration of the Soul-lantern and tucked the folded image into his pocket before he checked himself for money and essentials. He made to leave. Lucia turned her face to the Professor, her eyes welling up, as he neared the door before she mouthed: 'forgive me.' The Professor understood her words and gave a slow blink of acknowledgement. The Devil and Celeste laughed out loud as he pulled open the door. Winston paused before looking back, and turned to address the Devil.

'A man, or woman, may not believe in God, or Gods, but they can still do the right things - I've seen and believed more than I could ever imagine, but in my opinion, you're *overrated*' scoffed the Professor, before he walked out the door. The Devil and Celeste growled in unison. When Winston reached the quiet street outside, his heart pounded. After exiting the front gate, he walked up the hill as fast as he could.

'So your friend has left you Diana-Lucia, and it's time you went too' said the Devil with relish. Lucia looked to Arcangela, her face bereft,

'Come with me' she said. The little witch hesitated, as Celeste widened her glowing eyes at her. Arcangela looked up to the Devil, his lips curled into a half smile, and then over to Stella, who struggled to the shoulder of Celeste, and weighed her options as her expression clouded. 'Please' said Lucia stepping forward, *'please* Arcangela, I beg you.' The little witch's eyes welled with tears in her shrunken face, and she made a half step towards Lucia. But the Devil blocked her progress with his long arm and touched Arcangela's shoulder in the freezing air. In that instant, the wood in the hearth sprang back to life, and any unlit candles ignited in their holders. The Devil used his hand to guide the little witch to the mirror where she saw a reflection of her young self: bathed in candle light.

She caught her breath and walked closer to the large mirror to inspect her image. Looking at her reflection the old woman raised youthful hands to her pretty round face, that looked even better than when she was in the full flower of her youth. Arcangela drew off her wimple and ran her fingers through her tousled long hair, which bounced again around her shoulders. Arcangela, without hesitation, then tugged off her clothes. Lucia saw a withered crone, with grey balding hair, her flesh in a state of collapse, gazing, awestruck at the young reflection of herself - admiring her extra loveliness in the long mirror. Lucia's mouth trembled when Arcangela looked up to the Devil with questioning eyes. '*Youth* is not everything' yelled Lucia, 'we all grow old – there's no shame in it' gasped Lucia, desperate not to lose whom she considered her ally and friend. Arcangela glanced back to Lucia and then the Devil again.

'Forever' he said, with a graceful gesture and jaunty smile. Arcangela looked back at the ragged Lucia, and then looked back at

herself: the smoothest, and prettiest she had ever been in her long life. The little witch made a prodding gesture upwards with her finger. The Devil smirked, turned his wrist above Arcangela and her reflection grew four inches taller.

Arcangela turned away from her stunning reflection to give Lucia a long look. She cast her eyes down before she shook her head. Tears then tumbled down Lucia's face before Arcangela turned, and pressed forward to kiss her reflection. In that instant, the witch matched her image, and her eyes took on an amber glow as she stared at herself. Lucia tore the air with a howl of anguish: 'NO, how could you? How could you betray me like this? After all that I've done for you,' Lucia sobbed. 'The *nuns*' she added, 'what about the nuns?' But Arcangela said nothing, admiring her reflection, and ran her hands over her new flawless body: caressing and idolising herself. Then Arcangela, turning herself around, once satisfied in all that she saw, sauntered to the side of Celeste who grinned like someone who had lost their mind: her eyes glittering with gleeful spite and revenge.

Lucia sobbed as Stella then limped to the side of the Devil before addressing her: 'get out' she said in a hoarse voice, 'it's over: I'm the Abbess here now. Make a swag and take your leave.'

Lucia looked around herself in desperation, but the troupe presented a united front. Crestfallen, Lucia moved like a ghost through her own bedchamber. She, ignoring all present, then picked up the velvet that had fallen from the mirror and drifted into the side room as the Devil and the others looked on. She then changed into warmer clothes. Lucia went to the shelf in the corner and took up the wooden box there wrapped in starry fabric, and placed it, with care, in the centre of the velvet. She then picked up her crystal ball, wrapping it in its fabric, a deck of her favourite tarot cards, and a leather bag of money she kept on the side and put them all in the velvet too.

Lucia wafted back into the room with her possessions where all three demonesses: Stella, Celeste, and Arcangela glared at her. Lucia rejected them all as she laid her swag on the table and reached up for the book of Hekate, which leapt into her hands, and accepted the prophecy the Goddess had given her. Lucia took up a comb before she opened the chest with iron trappings to take out her witch's unguent: the others would have no need for it anymore.

She then packed her silver scythe, and dagger and tried to tie her ungainly swag with a knot.

'Just take it all' said Celeste conjuring wheels and a handle onto the box with iron trappings with a waft of her hand: delighting in her new powers. Lucia obeyed and placed all her belongings inside and wheeled the chest to the door. Celeste then let fly with a triumphant laugh, cackling at the top of her voice until she held her ribs with her efforts.

Lucia paused to look at the crazed demoness, 'you're a *fool*' she said, 'take your poor substitute for me but know that the Golem and I are the same in another aspect: she'll never love you, but you can both rot in hell together.'

Lucia ignored the laughter that erupted from the demonic foursome, cursing the stupidity of Arcangela and Celeste under her breath. Lucia left slamming the door behind her to silence the noise. She dreaded what would happen to the nuns now they were under the Devil's influence, but she didn't dwell long on the idea: a few would embrace it, some would not notice, but most of the pious would fight with all their faith. 'Let the angels keep them' he whispered under her breath. Lucia could rebuild and begin a new life - she had done so once before - and she would do so again. She would find the Professor and the others later: and she could find the Hermeporta for herself.

Lucia: battered, beaten, and defeated exited the convent that night, slipping out into the dark, with her body pained but her spirit defiant.

As she limped away, she formed her plan to begin her journey north - north to renewal, north to freedom, north to Venice.

END OF BOOK 1

THE HERMEPORTA BEYOND THE GATES OF HERMES

ABOUT THE AUTHOR

Hogarth is an artist as well as an author and still paints commissioned portraits when he has the time, and has had many art exhibitions in London. He studied Graphic Design at Camberwell College of Art after completing his Foundation course at the same art school. The author is particularly fond of illuminated manuscripts and has ambitions to develop his writing in this creative direction. Hogarth, before and during his years of writing his first book, has had a very close association with Kings Place, an arts and concert venue based in London's vibrant King's Cross area, which has provided significant inspiration for his creative work: where music and live performance has influenced his writing in particular.

Hogarth is based in London, and has begun the development of the third book in the Hermeporta series. The second book in the series is complete and will be available soon.

Printed in Great Britain
by Amazon